No Quarter Given

Also by Neil Broadfoot

No Man's Land
No Place to Die
The Point of No Return

No Quarter Given

Neil Broadfoot

CONSTABLE

CONSTABLE

First published in Great Britain in 2021 by Constable

1 3 5 7 9 10 8 6 4 2

A CIP catalogue record for this book is available from the British Library.

ISBN: 978-1-47213-495-0

Typeset in Minion Pro by Initial Typesetting Services, Edinburgh
Printed and bound in Great Britain by Clays Ltd, Elcograf S.p.A.

Papers used by Constable are from well-managed forests and other responsible sources.

Constable
An imprint of
Little, Brown Book Group
Carmelite House
50 Victoria Embankment
London EC4Y 0DZ

An Hachette UK Company
www.hachette.co.uk

www.littlebrown.co.uk

To Alice. It's not Shakespeare or beachside poetry,
but I hope you like it anyway.

Now, pick any three numbers, it's your round.

PROLOGUE

It was the day winter finally bared its teeth on Glasgow. The sky was the colour of damp concrete, a slab glowering over the city, leaching colour and vitality from the day. The piles of snow, stained grey-black by a combination of footfall, grit and exhaust fumes, made the streets look dirty, used up. Old. The air was sharp and cold enough to burn your nose and lungs if you took a deep breath. Not that anyone did as they bustled along the streets swathed in gloves and scarves, intent on getting where they needed to be, driven by the hope their destination would offer some respite from the almost Arctic chill. The sound from the nearby M8 echoed through the frozen streets, low and plaintive, as if the city itself was an old woman moaning as the cold bit into her bones.

No one really noticed the flowers left on the street corner, an incongruous splash of colour in the chilled anaemia of the day.

No one, that is, except Connor Fraser.

He stood for a moment, studying the makeshift shrine. It was no different to the countless others he had seen on roadsides, tied to benches, fences or lampposts. A tribute, a show of love and remembrance for someone whom casual passers-by would never know.

But Connor did know who this memorial was for. He had made it his business to find out.

And the price of this knowledge? Well, that was yet to be truly known.

CHAPTER 1

Three weeks earlier

His pain made the world into a weapon.

The mirror above the fireplace? Smash it, grab a shard, use it as a blade. The poker beside the fire? Perfect for caving in someone's skull. The hardback books on the shelves? Swung just the right way, they could dislocate a jaw, perhaps even break it. Then drive the book into the windpipe, crushing it, robbing your victim of the ability to breathe.

Victim.

He closed his eyes, took a deep breath. Tried not to hear the screams as they replayed in his mind, the clatter of feet on concrete, the squeal of tyres, the hard, dull thud of a car hitting a body. Tried not to feel his lips on hers, fingers pinched around her nose as he forced his breath into her lungs, willing her to live. Felt bile surge up his throat as he remembered the sound of her rib cracking under his weight as he pummelled her chest, working frantically to get her heart beating again. Felt tears burn at his eyes at the sound of her gargled cough, hot blood spraying across his face as she spluttered out a breath and clawed her way back to life. To him, it was as sweet as a newborn baby's first cry.

He stood suddenly, seized by the desire to move. Paced around the flat, felt the walls close in on him as he fought the urge to unleash the tsunami inside him. Weaponise the world. Destroy everything, drown out the memories with a discordant scream of destruction as bookshelves were toppled, mirrors smashed and furniture was thrown through the patio doors into the day that seemed to mock him with its silent indifference.

A step forward towards the TV. He was halted by the shrill ring of his phone in a pocket. Instinctively he reached for it, felt a stab of dread as he read the name on the caller ID. Hit answer with a thumb that was not steady, spoke before the caller could say anything. If bad news was coming, he wanted to be in control.

'How is she?'

Silence on the line, deeper somehow than the shadows that seemed to creep towards him, splinters of darkness eager to claim him.

'She's alive. In intensive care now. Doctors say it's too early to know anything more than that at the moment, but they're keeping me updated.'

Relief and terror surged through him, a poisonous cocktail that made it difficult to breathe or think.

The caller dragged him from his thoughts, the voice so diminished and defeated that it screamed in his ear, like a bad chord in a symphony.

'We need to talk,' Duncan MacKenzie said. 'There's some things you need to know about today. There's more to it.'

Confusion clamoured through Connor's brain. He felt his body twitch, as though some fuse had blown and he was starting to shut down. Understandable. Everyone had their limits and, after seeing Jen run over, tossed into the air by a car like a discarded toy, then crashing to the ground, where Connor had given her CPR, he thought maybe he had finally found his.

'What do you mean?' he said, his lips numb, the words odd, alien things in his mouth.

'Not on the phone,' Duncan MacKenzie replied, his voice hardening as he moved on to more familiar ground. 'Can you meet me?'

'At the hospital?' Connor asked. He had been there less than an hour ago, left only when MacKenzie had arrived, his face a rictus of terror and barely controlled hysteria. The hardman façade had been stripped away, leaving only the face of a father confronting the reality that his little girl had been badly hurt. It was only now that Connor vaguely wondered how MacKenzie had found out about the . . .

There's more to it . . .

. . . accident?

'Yeah, I can meet you downstairs. There's a coffee shop in the main atrium. Know it?'

'I'll find it,' Connor said, eyes drifting towards the hallway that led to his bedroom.

'Text me when you get here. If Jen's OK, I'll come down and meet you.'

'Copy that,' Connor said, his mind already shifting gears, becoming a cold, calculating thing of violence and split-second decisions.

There's more to it.

He ended the call, headed for his bedroom. Slid aside a panel under his bed, reached into the darkness and opened the safe that waited there, the sound of screaming and Jen's blood-choked cough churning through his mind as he retrieved his gun.

The hard, blunt clack of the slide as he checked the chamber and racked the magazine home was like a full stop to the thoughts in his mind. Jen had been hit by a car outside the gym she worked at in Stirling. She had been heading inside, Connor waiting there to meet her as arranged before she started her shift. It was part of their routine if he was on an assignment with odd hours: they would meet at the gym, he would get a work-out while Jen coached clients or led exercise classes, then they would grab a coffee together while she was on her break. He had seen the car swerve across the street, mounting the pavement, barrelling towards her. Felt as though he was swimming through treacle as he took off towards her, knowing he wasn't going to be fast enough to get there in time. Saw her thrown into the air, long blonde hair fanning out like a halo, then heard the dull, hard thud of Jen hitting the ground.

He'd got to her a moment later, her body a feverish lump of bloodied flesh bent at impossible angles. Felt a flash of self-loathing for the half-second he took to glance up, memorise the number plate of the car that had hit her even as it sped off.

A hit-and-run. Kids, probably. He would deal with it later.

There's more to it.

Connor felt his grip tighten on the gun even as he flicked off the safety. For some reason, he didn't think safety was going to be playing a big part in his immediate future.

CHAPTER 2

Leith Docks, Edinburgh

With his sallow skin, neatly parted salt-and-pepper hair and small half-moon spectacles that winked in the overhead lights every time he moved his head, Martin Christopher looked to DS Susie Drummond more like a TV casting agent's idea of a civil servant than a real one. But the facts were undeniable. Martin Christopher was indeed a civil servant who had spent the last thirty-four years of his life working for, first, the UK then the Scottish Government. His record, which she had skimmed on the way here, was peppered with glowing performance reviews and words like 'efficient', 'diligent' and 'committed'. But this morning, Christopher had added another word to his résumé. One that would be with him a lot, lot longer than the warm words of his superiors.

Because now Martin Christopher was traumatised.

He sat across from Susie, eyes on the cup he cradled between two pale, delicate hands, head darting left and right as though he was studying some exotic flower rather than a bland white mug containing an oversweet cup of tea.

They were sitting in a large canteen in Victoria Quay, next to one of the windows that looked out onto Leith Docks and the Ocean Terminal shopping centre beyond. At the corner of the centre, Susie could just make out the mast of the *Britannia* peeking over the roof of the building. The former royal yacht was permanently moored there now, another tourist attraction in Edinburgh's already formidable arsenal. The appeal in seeing how an over-pampered family lived in opulent luxury at taxpayers' expense eluded Susie.

She pulled herself from her thoughts, forced herself to focus on the job in hand. Cast a quick glance around the canteen. It was a massive room, and would normally be bustling with civil servants and visitors as they grabbed something to eat, had a meeting or topped up their caffeine levels. Not today. Today it was as quiet as a church just before a funeral procession arrived. 'Sorry, Mr Christopher, you were saying?'

He looked up, bloodshot green eyes blinking rapidly as though he had been startled from a daydream. 'Ah, sorry, what?' he asked in a faltering whisper which did nothing to mask the perfectly formed east-coast accent.

'You were telling us how you found the deceased,' she said, gently trying to coax him into conversation.

'Oh, yes, yes,' Christopher said, the tips of his ears reddening as he spoke. His eyes darted right, out of the canteen and across a cavernous atrium to a set of double doors now cordoned off with large white drapes erected by the SOCOs to preserve the crime scene. And what a scene it was. 'Well, ah . . .' he coughed, took a slug of his coffee '. . . I came in early, you see, to use, ah, well, to use the . . .'

'Swimming-pool?' Susie offered helpfully.

'Yes, the, ah . . .' he stuttered again, as though the phrase was somehow offensive to him. After what he had found, maybe it was. 'Anyway, I went into the changing rooms and the lights were off. They usually come on automatically, you see, so I thought maybe they were switched off or a fuse had blown.'

Susie nodded, made a note. Worth checking. 'And then?'

'Well, I fumbled around a bit, couldn't find anything. Thought I'd check if all the lights were out of order, so I went through to the, ah, the . . .'

'Pool,' Susie offered again.

Christopher nodded vigorously, his ears growing darker. He would, Susie thought, be shit at poker. 'Yes, so I went through and that's when I saw . . .' His voice trailed away, and Susie saw tears glitter at the corner of his eyes.

She held his gaze, softened her voice to a supportive whisper. 'You're doing fine, Martin, this really is helping. But, please, just tell me what you saw. And what you did.'

He spoke quickly, as though it was an unpleasant task he could rush through and finish. 'The lights came on and I didn't understand what I was seeing at first.' His eyes darted frantically as the memory played in his mind. A memory he would be revisiting for years. 'When it made sense to me I, ah, well, I was sick. I'm sorry.'

Susie nodded. The SOCOs had loved that, their crime scene being contaminated from the off. 'And then?'

'I ran,' he said bluntly, the shame in his voice as plain as his crimson ears. 'I ran to the security desk, got them to call you. Well, not you, but the police and then I . . . I . . .'

Susie nodded. She knew the rest, had seen the CCTV images of him braced against the building's front security desk, bent over like a man about to collapse, silently screaming at them for help. The call had come into the call-handling centre at Bilston Glen and, in what must have been a minor miracle, actually been allocated to a station within striking distance of the location. Being less than three miles away, near the top of Leith Walk, and with DC Eric Baine driving like an extra from *The Italian Job*, it had taken Susie only ten minutes to get there.

She nodded slightly to a uniform, who was hovering at a table nearby. 'Thank you, Martin, that's been a great help. My colleague here, PC Redmayne,' she gestured to the tall, lanky woman who was now looming over him, 'is going to get a formal statement from you and then get you home. Is there someone we can call, make sure they're there for you?'

'Gina,' Christopher said, his eyes filling with a desperate eagerness that made Susie both pity and detest him at the same time. 'She'll come.'

'Good,' Susie said. 'Well, I'll leave you to it. Thank you for your time. No doubt we'll speak again.'

She watched as Redmayne ushered Martin Christopher away, then looked back out to the Docks. Weak sunlight was playing on the granite grey of the water, flashing silver as the wind rippled its surface. Susie closed her eyes, imagined the chill of the wind on her face, her mind emptying of everything. Felt her leg muscles twitch, her body crying out for movement, action. She would go for a run later, try to sweat out the day. It was already shaping up to be a bad one.

She stood up, heading for the white drapes and the SOCOs' crime-scene cordon. Wrestled her way into one of their white-paper boiler suits, then slipped a pair of protective covers over her shoes. She took a deep breath, then stepped forward, opening the double doors and walking inside.

The pool was in a large patio-style wing that jutted out of the side of the building. Susie had no idea if it was an original feature or had been grafted on at a later date. Either way, she marvelled at the thinking that had concluded a swimming-pool was an essential component of a working office.

A SOCO's camera flash burst into life, flaring across the water. It was a pinkish-red colour – *Weak Ribena*, she thought suddenly – and left pink tide marks on the tiles surrounding the pool as it splashed over the sides.

No wonder Martin Christopher had run. Susie felt the momentary urge to do the same.

She thought back to the pictures she had already seen, the ones taken by the first SOCOs to arrive. In the centre of the pool, bobbing gently, there had been a body. Face down, dark hair splayed out like a halo around the head, the pale skin of the back looking like a slab of greying wax that seemed to glisten, like seal skin, in the harsh light of the camera flash.

The normal impulse would have been to pull the body out, make sure there was no sign of life. Luckily, one of the security guards Christopher had summoned was a former police officer who knew the script. He'd taken one look at the scene, known that whoever was in the pool was beyond any help.

On the wall to the left of Susie, scrawled in a red so dark and hypnotic it could only be blood, was a message. Seven words. Seven words that sent cold spider's legs skittering across Susie's spine. *This is not murder. This is justice.*

Susie shook herself, looking from the message and back to the pinkish-red water. Martin Christopher had found it impossible to say the word. She understood. It was a pool all right.

A pool of blood.

CHAPTER 3

Connor never made it as far as the café. MacKenzie was waiting for him as he pulled into the car park at Forth Valley Hospital. A moment of panic as Connor studied him: the reddened eyes, slumped shoulders, clothes that seemed suddenly too big for him. What reassured him was the walk: strong, sure, impatient. Direct, as he paced around the entrance to the car park. If something had happened to Jen, Connor doubted MacKenzie would be on his feet. No, he would be on his knees.

He honked his horn once. MacKenzie's head darted up with the air of an animal sensing prey nearby. Connor drove on, MacKenzie nodding understanding and following on foot. But even as he parked, Connor felt something niggle at his mind, something that was wrong with this picture.

Something . . .

He pushed the thought aside as he got out of the car and saw MacKenzie striding towards him, shoulders straight now, chin jutting forward. 'Fraser,' he said, thrusting his hand out.

Connor took it, felt desperation in the grip. 'Duncan. How is she?'

The muscles in MacKenzie's jaw twitched, as though the words had stung him. He sighed, jammed his hands into his pockets, glanced back over his shoulder at the hospital. 'Being monitored,' he said at last, his voice so empty Connor could tell he was repeating what the doctors and nurses had told him. 'Still under sedation after they brought her in. Some nurse told me to take a break while they worked, that nothing was going to happen immediately. I needed to get the smell of that place out of my nose anyway. Doctors say the next twenty-four hours will be critical. They're going to lower the drugs she's on, bring her round then assess her injuries. They're being cagey, but I heard one of them mention the spinal unit in Glasgow.'

The words scalded Connor. 'Spinal unit? You mean that . . .'

MacKenzie looked him straight in the eye, as though challenging Connor to say something about the tears that suddenly welled there. 'Yes, Connor,' he said, his voice as dead as an echo in a mausoleum. 'The impact could have damaged her spine. They can't tell how seriously yet, but . . .'

The words faded out, as Connor's mind filled with the memory of Jen flying through the air. The harsh, blunt thud as she hit the ground, the eternity it took to reach her, the moment spent looking up, catching the number of the car . . .

. . . the car.

'You said there was more to this.' Connor snapped back to the present, surprised by the effort it had taken to form the words and speak them.

MacKenzie nodded, jaw setting, eyes hardening. 'Yeah,' he said, as he slid an envelope from his pocket and handed it to Connor. 'This came last night. Was waiting for me when I got home.'

Connor took the envelope, inspected it. It was standard letter-sized, good-quality stock. He noticed it had been sliced neatly open with a very sharp letter-opener or knife. On the front, scrawled in ink so black it could only have come from a fountain pen, MacKenzie's name was underlined twice. No stamp. Hand delivered.

They know where he lives, Connor thought.

'Open it,' MacKenzie said.

Connor held MacKenzie's gaze for a moment, then did so. He pulled out a single sheet of paper. Good quality again, handwritten in the same ink used to address the envelope. He could see the ghostly outline of writing on the back of the note, decided to take it one step at a time.

Mr MacKenzie,

I'll be brief. I know. I know what you did. So kill Paulie King or I will take your daughter from you, just as mine was taken from me.

Connor looked up at MacKenzie, couldn't read what he saw in the man's eyes. Understood now what had been bothering him when he arrived. Paulie, MacKenzie's thug in chief, wasn't with him. He spoke before the thought was fully formed in his mind. 'Paulie,' he said. 'You didn't. . .'

A smile, cold and empty as the sky above them, flashed across MacKenzie's face. 'No, Connor, I didn't. I tried to call Paulie about this last night when I got that, couldn't raise him. I was going to speak to him today, but then . . .' His voice wavered, and he gestured back towards the hospital. 'I've had people out looking for him, all the usual haunts, but he's gone. Vanished.'

Connor forced back the memory that was threatening to overwhelm him. Jen flying through the air, the thud as she hit the ground. The feeling of her rib cracking under his weight as he fought to get her heart going again. The . . . He coughed. Focused. 'What does it mean, "I know what you did"? What did you and Paulie do that led to a woman dying?'

A flash of rage in MacKenzie's eyes, his body tensing as though he was going to lunge at Connor. Then, as though he was a balloon that had just been pricked, he deflated, the outrage giving way to bewilderment and fear. 'I don't know,' he said, with a shrug. 'Look, Connor, I'm not pissing about here. Paulie and I have done some nasty shit in our time, but I have no idea what this letter is referring to. All I know is someone hurt my little girl, and Paulie is missing.'

'So what do you want me to do?' Connor asked. It was a pointless question: he already knew the answer. But he wanted, no, *needed*, to hear MacKenzie ask. He knew the reason, wasn't proud of it. The request would legitimise what came next, maybe even absolve Connor of some of the blame.

Maybe.

'Paulie's the key to this,' MacKenzie said. 'Find him, get him to tell you what this means. Then find the bastard who hurt Jen. And end them. For me. For Jen.'

Connor held MacKenzie's gaze for a moment, an unspoken conversation passing between them. Then he looked back to the letter and flipped it over, read what was there, scrawled in an angrier hand than the first page he had read.

This is not murder. This is justice.

CHAPTER 4

Every news channel was the same. Lingering shots of the sprawling façade of Victoria Quay, a blunt, concrete monstrosity, the gated entrance to which had now been draped with police 'do not enter' tape as though in a lacklustre attempt to decorate the building. Reporters going through the thesaurus as they found different ways of saying 'a body was found in unusual circumstances in the building' and then trying to fill the rest of their report with vacuous background. They knew nothing and, if he was right, they wouldn't get to know anything for as long as the powers that be could possibly get away with it.

But he knew. He knew it all.

He watched the news for a few more moments. It had now switched to old stock footage of various ministers arriving at Victoria Quay on previous occasions in an attempt to paint it as the beating heart of the Scottish Government. He smiled. One less heart beating today.

The thought warmed him as he switched off the TV, then headed for the back door and the garage beyond. It was, he knew, stupid on his part. There was no reason not to bring his work into the house now. Before, she would have objected to the intrusion of his chaos into her domain. But now . . .

. . . now . . .

He stopped, good humour evaporating as he looked back into the emptiness of the open-plan kitchen-lounge. At the tasteful furniture, the neutral colours on the walls offset by family pictures and carefully selected paintings. She had thrown her heart and soul into decorating this place, into making their home, and now that heart and soul seemed to scream at him from the silence.

He nodded acknowledgement to a message only he had heard, gripped the door handle and headed for the garage. There was work to be done. Plans to make. Justice to seek.

Moira's silent scream demanded it.

CHAPTER 5

The rain was thin and begrudging, sharpened into stinging needles by a chill that promised worse to come from a sky that was darkening as rapidly as Donna Blake's mood.

She was sitting in the Sky outside-broadcast van parked near Victoria Quay, listening to the rain. She wrapped her hands around the cup of coffee her cameraman, Keith, had passed her as soon as she had finished her to-camera report on the discovery of a body at the Scottish Government office earlier that morning. As ever, she couldn't remember anything she had said during the report, but Keith had assured her it was fine, an opinion he was now backing up with contented grunts and murmurs as he sat in front of a mini production desk and edited footage for later reports. And that, Donna thought, was the problem. Later.

She had seen the police press release on the body that morning as she skimmed the wires for possible stories, known straight away that it would dominate her day. It was a big story, nationally big, and she knew it would keep her in Edinburgh all day. After her initial report, there would be the standard police press conference down at Fettes as they tried to control the narrative and keep the public calm. Which, for Donna, meant waiting outside Victoria Quay for the police to organise themselves. Normally, this wouldn't be a problem. With her son, Andrew, safely deposited with his grandparents, Donna had the day to herself to dig up background on the story, maybe catch up with old contacts.

The problem was that another story, little more than a statement on the wires, was competing for her attention, whispering to her that sitting in a satellite van drinking bad coffee and listening to Keith's guttural sighs and mutters wasn't what she should be doing.

It had been a standard police release, announcing a hit-and-run outside the gym at Craigs Roundabout on the way into Stirling. The copy boiled the horrific down to the mundane – a thirty-four-year-old female employee of the gym had been hit by a vehicle that had subsequently fled the scene. The woman, who had yet to be named, had been transported to Forth Valley Hospital, where her condition was described as critical. Donna wrote up the story for Sky's website, knowing a local traffic accident without a fatality would never make its way to television, then made the call she knew in her gut she didn't need to make. She called the gym, got a receptionist whose voice was ground flat by tears. Didn't take her long to ascertain that it was Jen MacKenzie who had been run down. Jen MacKenzie, daughter of Duncan MacKenzie, a local haulier, who was rumoured to move more than furniture and fittings for the right price. Jen MacKenzie, girlfriend of Connor Fraser.

Donna had first encountered Connor three years ago, when a decapitated body had been dumped in the shadow of Stirling Castle. She had used that story as a springboard from local radio in Stirling to a job at Sky. Since then, she had built a career, and on the big stories that had helped propel her forward, Connor was there. She kept him out of the stories as much as she could, driven by her gratitude to him for saving her life and a sense of professional obligation, but it was hard to argue that Connor Fraser wasn't a magnet for trouble.

And now that magnet had drawn disaster to Jen's door.

She called Connor's mobile, not surprised when the call rang out and went to voicemail. She left him a message, asking him to call her back and wishing Jen well. Then she met up with Keith and drove to Edinburgh to cover the Victoria Quay story. But still the thought of Jen gnawed at her, as if a bell only she could hear was being rung somewhere, demanding her attention.

Donna blinked, swallowed the last of her coffee, annoyed with herself. Here she was, musing over the fate of a contact's girlfriend, when there was real work to be done. A murder in a government building. It was a national story, and one Donna was determined to be the reporting face of. The press release issued by the police had been predictably vague: body found, suspicious circumstances, no identification made at this stage, updates to follow.

Donna fished her mobile phone out of her pocket and started scrolling through her contacts. Waiting had never been her style. Or following. Time to get her own updates.

CHAPTER 6

After his meeting with MacKenzie, Connor had headed back to the flat. What he really wanted to do was go to the gym – calm the frustration and confusion he felt by torturing his body with heavy weights, losing himself in the agony as his grandfather had taught him in Newtownards all those years ago. But the events of that morning had poisoned what had been his place of refuge and retreat, turned it into a stark, brutal reminder of Jen and the pain she had endured – and the pain to come.

What was it Duncan MacKenzie had said? *I heard them mention the spinal unit in Glasgow.*

That had sent Connor to Google, to find horror stories of spinal trauma and possible treatments. He scrolled through pages on rehabilitation, heard the hard, metallic thump of Jen's body being hit by a car as he read about the potential for paralysis, the loss of bowel and bladder control. His thoughts became sharp, fractured, like a kaleidoscope of broken glass tumbling through his mind. What if she was paralysed? They had never really spoken about their future, but suddenly here it was, staring Connor in the face, asking for decisions and demanding answers. He would stand by her, support her, make sure she got everything and anything she needed, but then what? Move her in with him? Convert the flat, install ramps? Get another place that was more easily accessible? And what would she do for work? Would she even want to be with him if she was disabled? And, the thought shamed him, would he want to be with her? How would they . . .

'Enough,' he said, into the silence of the room as he stood up from a breakfast bar stool he had no memory of sitting down on. Grabbed for his phone with an angry swipe, closed the pages on spinal injuries he had just been reading. Later.

Right now, he had a job to do.

He found the number he was looking for, hit dial. Wasn't surprised when the call was answered before a full ring had sounded in his ear.

'Boss? Boss, how you doing? We, ah, we heard about what happened. If there's anything I can do, anything you need . . .'

Connor smiled. Of course Robbie had heard about Jen. After his meeting with Duncan, Connor's first action had been to call Aaron Douglas, one of the senior partners at Sentinel Securities, and tell him he was taking some time off. Douglas had done his best to sound supportive and understanding, but Connor could hear the concern in his voice. Sentinel had just landed the contract to protect an MSP who had been getting hate mail due to their stance on immigration in a post-Brexit, Covid-cautious world. Police Scotland had been called in when bullets had started to turn up in envelopes outside the MSP's home, but it had been felt that a more proactive approach to security should be taken. So, Connor and Sentinel had been drafted in. It was a big contract, bringing media coverage with it, and Connor had a reputation for getting results. For him to walk away was less than ideal to Douglas's accountant brain. Which was where Robbie came in. A former call handler for Police Scotland, he was a talented investigator who understood how the police would deal with such a case. Connor had explained this to Douglas, told him to tap Robbie for the job he was stepping aside from. Which might explain some of the stress Connor had just heard in Robbie's voice.

'Thanks, Robbie,' he said, dragging his thoughts back to the present. 'Actually, that's why I called. I need a favour, a licence plate running down. Can you . . .'

'This about what happened to Jen,' Robbie said. A statement. Not a question. The boy was learning.

'Yeah, it is.' His eyes drifted to the letter MacKenzie had given him. 'This one is personal, Robbie. I want to look into it myself.'

'So I take it this licence plate was somehow missed from your official statement?'

Despite himself, Connor smiled again. Robbie really was learning. A year ago, he wouldn't have dared to ask such a question. 'What can I say, Robbie? I must have been in shock.'

'Go on, then,' Robbie said. 'Give me the number, I'll see what I can do. How quickly do you need this?'

MacKenzie's words now: *Find the bastard who hurt Jen. And end them.*

'As quickly as you can,' Connor replied, closing his eyes against the sudden memory of Jen being thrown into the air by the car as he gave Robbie the plate number.

'OK, boss, leave it with me,' Robbie said, and ended the call.

Connor took the phone from his ear. Noticed he had a voicemail message. Played it, listened as Donna Blake told him she'd heard about Jen and was there to help if Connor needed anything.

He deleted the message, made a mental note to call Donna later. She had proved useful in the past, might be so again. But for now, Connor needed something else, something Donna couldn't help him with. He flicked into his messages, thumbed in a text: *I'm waiting. Where's that information you promised me?*

A bubble formed on the screen almost as soon as Connor had hit send, the answer springing to his phone a second later: *Was in with Jen. Still no news. Paulie's last address was Sauchenford Steading, Sauchenhall, Sauchenhall Plains, FK11. It's a converted farmsteading just off Falkirk Road, past Bannockburn. But, like I said, sent boys to look. He's not there.*

Connor considered this for a moment, then texted his reply, his mind already mapping a route to the address. *Doesn't matter,* he typed. *Got to start somewhere. Besides, it's on the way to another stop I have to make. I'll be in touch. Let me know if you hear anything about Jen.*

Connor hit send, then pocketed the phone. If MacKenzie was going to send an answer, he didn't want to see it.

CHAPTER 7

After making her phone calls, Donna headed for Ocean Terminal, the massive, block-like shopping mall that sat close to Victoria Quay. She made her way to a coffee shop on the second floor, memories of other days there when she was covering the Edinburgh beat for the *Western Chronicle* flitting around her mind, like the crowds of people she now wove her way through.

She found her way to the counter of the shop, made her order mostly on autopilot then set up camp at a free table. Unpacked her laptop and mobile, sent a quick message to her editor back in Glasgow, agreeing she would write an update to the story for Sky's website until she could give them more video footage from the press conference that afternoon. Not for the first time, the thought occurred to her that covering a story for broadcast was a lot like having a child: the voracious appetite, the constant craving for attention. If only she could get her mum to see it that way, it might go some way to persuading her that Donna's career choice wasn't a complete waste of time.

She shook her head, banishing thoughts of her mother's disapproval. Time for that later. It was a problem that wasn't about to change any time soon, unlike this story. It had only taken a few calls to some old contacts to get the details that were missing from the initial Police Scotland statement. She doubted they would feature in any future statements either.

The body being found face down in the pool at a government

building was bad enough, but the message that had been scrawled on the wall took this to a whole new level. The email that a career civil servant, Ruth Mackie – who hid dead eyes behind heavy-rimmed glasses and a smile crammed with too many teeth behind a slash of scarlet lipstick – had told Donna about was the icing on the cake. Despite herself, Donna coughed out a laugh. The story was a guaranteed splash, no doubt about it.

She went through the copy she had put together for the website one more time, to satisfy herself that she had all the main details, was balancing just enough of what only she knew with what the police would be happy with seeing in the public domain. Not that she really cared about hurting the feelings of anyone in Police Scotland's comms department. She just didn't need them to freeze her out before the main press conference. She had been down that road before, didn't want or need a repeat performance.

Her phone buzzed on the table. She half expected it to be Connor, felt a prickle of disappointment that was only eased by the obvious frustration of the messenger: *What do you mean you know the name of the victim?! Where the hell are you?*

Donna tapped in a reply then sat back with her coffee, waiting for the show to begin.

She watched her walk into the coffee shop, eyes scanning the room in the way only police eyes can. Her gaze was like a stone skimming across the water, bouncing from person to person, assessing, questioning. And then her eyes fell on Donna, and the stone plunged below the surface. Donna saw the newcomer's body stiffen slightly, shoulders rolling and back straightening as she set her jaw, accentuating her high cheekbones. Her gaze grew cold for a moment, almost accusatory, but Donna could see a flicker of humour at the corners of her mouth and dancing in her green eyes. She tipped her coffee cup to the woman in greeting, took a long sip to hide the smile she felt threatening on her own lips.

Susie Drummond crossed to the table Donna was sitting at, wedged into the corner, looking out of the glass façade of the shop.

On the table sat a latte and a muffin that she knew would be blueberry. Typical Donna, Susie thought, trying to bribe her way out of trouble. Problem was, it usually worked.

'So,' she said, as she eased into the seat opposite and lifted the latte, 'how much trouble have you caused for me this time, Donna?'

Donna took the mug from her lips, no longer even attempting to hide her smile. She gave Susie a pantomimed pained look, hand rising to her chest. 'Who, me? Why, Detective Sergeant Drummond, I don't know what you could possibly mean.'

Susie sighed, her eyes settling on the woman she had met years earlier, when she was a freshly minted detective and Donna was working for one of the bigger broadsheets. They had lost touch over the last few years, the acquaintance only being renewed when Susie had spotted Donna on Sky, reporting on a series of bloody murders in Stirling. Looking at her now; the perfectly tailored suit, immaculate make-up and a handbag she knew was worth four figures, Susie was forced to admit that the change had done Donna Blake a lot of good.

'Cut the crap, Donna. You said you had a possible name for the victim – how the hell did you get that? If you've run a name in the story before . . .'

Donna held up her hand, genuine unease replacing the false offence of a moment ago. 'Come on, Susie, you know I wouldn't pull a stunt like that. Look.' She spun her laptop around on the table between them. 'Story's just been put online now. See for yourself.'

Susie leaned into the screen, holding Donna's gaze for another second before turning her attention to the story. She skimmed it quickly, the knot of unease in her chest loosening as she did so. But only slightly. It was typical of the Donna Blake she remembered. She had all the details the police statement had given but, like a magician pulling a card from thin air, had added more, to which no one else had access. Like the victim had been found by a former police officer who had known enough to protect the crime scene, the fact that 'an unspecified but highly unusual message' had been left at the scene and then . . .

. . . then . . .

Her head shot up. 'Jesus, Donna,' she hissed, as she tore her eyes from the laptop. 'How the hell did you get that?' She jabbed her finger at the screen, and the picture from inside Victoria Quay at the doors of the pool, the crime-scene tape and SOCOs' screens draped between two spiral staircases.

Donna gave a shrug. 'You know, contacts,' she said, something between pride and amusement in her voice.

'Ford will have a fit when he sees that,' she said, handing the laptop back to Donna.

Donna could just imagine DCI Malcolm Ford's reaction to the story when he saw it. The moment of quiet, his pale brow furrowing as his neck and cheeks began to darken. And then the explosion, the rant, the voice that seemed to echo off every corner of the CID suite. The demand for answers, the vows of vengeance.

Ford and Donna had a long-standing dislike of each other, but it had begun to cool after Ford had been given an expanded role overseeing all major investigations across Central Scotland. Donna wasn't sure of all the details, but she had heard Ford had tried to resign after the case involving his former partner's son had gone disastrously wrong. He had been offered a huge carrot to stay with the police. Which told Donna two things – either Ford was very, very good at his job, or he knew where Police Scotland's bodies were buried so the powers that be wanted to keep a very close eye on him.

But this? This would pour petrol on the glowing embers of the enmity between them. And it would be Susie who was closest to the fire.

'Ack, Ford will calm down soon enough,' Donna said. 'Especially when a certain detective sergeant reports back that she's stopped a certain reporter irresponsibly running a possible name for the victim.'

'And just how the hell did you get that anyway?' Susie asked, a warning tone in her voice. It was bad enough that Donna had got there before them. God help her if she'd broken any laws doing it.

Donna thought again of Ruth Mackie, her dead eyes and her too-toothy grin. She had met her just over seven years ago: Donna had traced her to a government department responsible for an IT contract that had been awarded to the nephew of a young parliamentary secretary, who had not only the ear of a cabinet secretary, but a spare key to his Edinburgh flat as well. A quick search had shown that Mackie was, beneath the typical civil-servant façade of neutrality, a true-blue Tory in the mould of old Maggie, and no fan of the 'separatists', who had, according to a blog she wrote under a pseudonym, 'seized power by appealing to the *Braveheart* sentiments of the woad-wearing unwashed'. It hadn't taken much to convince her to give Donna some background and extensive quotes, everything she needed to make sure she had a solid splash and that the cabinet secretary got his locks changed. From then on, Mackie had proved to be a very useful contact, much to the annoyance of Donna's colleagues who worked from the Garden Lobby at the Scottish Parliament and were often hacked off at how she had scooped them on more than one big political story.

'Well?' Susie asked, her voice growing impatient.

'Contacts,' Donna said simply. 'And, no, I didn't bend any rules to get them to talk to me, or take that picture. And I was careful, Susie, promise. I told you, I don't want this to cause us problems.'

Susie toyed with the muffin, making a show of tearing it apart. Then she looked at Donna, the playful mischief of earlier gone from her face, replaced by concern. She was worried she had gone too far.

'OK,' she said. 'I believe you. Ford will have a shit fit, so you'd better tell me what you know.'

Susie saw relief flit across Donna's eyes as she dug into her pocket again, this time producing a bright yellow Post-it note that had been carefully folded in half. She passed it to her, fingers brushing hers as she took it.

'Who the hell is Tim Montgomery?' Susie asked, as she read the note, keeping her voice low and leaning forward to her. 'You think this is the victim? Why? Who is he?'

Donna leaned in too, eyes flitting left and right as though she was reading from a page. She probably was, Susie thought. She would have written all this down and memorised it.

'He's a high-up official in the culture and external affairs department,' Donna said, her voice dropping. 'Runs the funding operation for major festivals, including Edinburgh and the Fringe.'

Internally, Susie groaned. The Edinburgh International Festival was the annual celebration of arts held during the summer, which, before the pandemic, had attracted thousands of visitors to the capital, thronging the streets from the castle to Causewayside and making residents feel like unwanted guests in their own city. It was a worsening nightmare for the police every year, and any link to a murder inquiry, no matter how tangential, would magnify that nightmare tenfold. Especially in the wake of the pandemic, when the desire to get large-scale events back to normal hit a fever pitch as the world tried to get over a collective outbreak of agoraphobia. Thankfully, the festival was months away, but the response to it was almost Pavlovian for any Edinburgh police officer.

'And why do you think he's the victim?'

'Description of the body matches pictures and descriptions of Montgomery,' Donna said, ignoring the hardening of Susie's expression as she mentioned seeing the victim. 'Plus he's the only member of staff who swiped past the entry gates at Victoria Quay last night but didn't swipe out again. Which is all you've got, since I know the security cameras at Victoria Quay don't cover the immediate locus where the body was found.'

Susie ignored that, didn't even want to know how Donna was aware of it. 'It's still circumstantial,' she said, hearing the doubt in her voice.

'But suggestive,' Donna replied. 'Especially added to the fact that he's not answering his home or mobile numbers. And don't worry. Before you ask, I used a burner. When he's confirmed as the victim, there won't be any phone records leading back to me.'

Susie felt the oily unease lurch in her gut again. Burner phones and untraceable records? OK, it wasn't illegal, strictly, but still, how close to the cliff edge were they dancing? She forced herself to focus. 'So what's your next move?' she asked. 'Wait for the press conference later on?'

Donna leaned back, gave Susie a you-know-better look.

'Yeah, OK,' she said. 'But do your digging quietly,' Susie said. 'At least until I can request the security records and get this to Ford. You run this before I do and he'll probably hunt you down himself.' She stood up, ready to leave. 'I'd better get going. Ford . . .' She trailed off.

'No problem, I've got to get back to my cameraman anyway,' Donna said, as she began packing away her laptop.

Susie doffed the Post-it towards Donna. 'Thanks for this, Donna. And keep in touch, OK?'

Donna nodded, watched Susie go. Burner phones and murdered civil servants? She was in uncharted territory, on dangerous ground, yet there was nothing she seemed able to do about it. Or, if she was being honest with herself, wanted to do about it.

She grabbed the coffee off the table, drained the mug, then picked up her phone. Resisted the urge for all of ten seconds, then flicked through the contacts and dialled Connor Fraser's number.

CHAPTER 8

The moment Connor saw his gran, he knew he had made a mistake in visiting her.

She opened the door to her flat, her smile of welcome fading, like a guttering flame, as her eyes scanned his face, reading everything he didn't want to tell her. He saw the concern etch itself into her features, forehead darkening with lines as she frowned, eyes pinching behind glasses.

'Connor? What's wrong, bonny lad?' she asked, as she reached for him – her touch cool and strangely brittle on his forearm. 'What's . . .?'

He patted her hand, aimed for reassuring and got desperate instead. Felt a stab of guilt as cold and dark as the day outside. Why had he come here? To burden an old woman with his troubles? Make himself feel better at the expense of her peace of mind?

Stupid, Connor. Fucking stupid. And selfish.

'It's fine, Gran,' he said. 'Honestly. Just been a bad day.'

Her face twitched into a smile that told him she saw the understatement in his words. 'Come on away in,' she said, in a tone Connor knew so well from his childhood. 'I'll make you a cup of tea and you can tell me all about it.'

She bustled him into the flat, folding him into a seat so smoothly he almost didn't register sitting down, then made her way to the kitchen. Taking in the surroundings, Connor was again struck by the contradiction of the place. The flat was a suite of rooms in a nursing home in Bannockburn that Connor had found for her as her health had deteriorated. It was crammed with furniture, pictures and other mementoes taken from her former home in Stirling, items Connor knew as well as his own name. But their familiarity was jarred by the grab rails and panic alarms, constant reminders of his gran's increasing frailty.

Most of the time, he was able to remind himself that he had found this place because of the care it would provide his gran. But today he could see the other side of the story, which told him she was an old woman now, frail and infirm, her mind slowly betraying her as yesterday became her present and any sense of the here and now was distorted by the dementia that was eating away her sense of self.

There was a soft, almost musical clatter of crockery and he looked up, saw her heading for the dining-room table, clutching a tray piled high with sandwiches, cakes and biscuits. It was Ida's golden rule, an impulse dementia could not diminish, confuse or deny. Her grandson was visiting. The boy needed to be fed.

'Come have a seat, son,' Ida said, as she busied herself pouring tea. 'Tell me what's happening.'

Connor crossed to the table, took a seat in a high-backed wooden chair that instantly transported him to her former home in Stirling. How many times had he sat at this table, his gran looking after him? And how many more times would he repeat that ritual?

Ida took the seat opposite him, glasses misting softly as she held her cup of tea just below her lips, content to wait. Connor piled sandwiches onto his plate, took a sip of tea. Strong. Just like the woman who had poured it. He cleared his throat, knew it was pointless to stall. He was here now: the least he owed his gran was the truth. Or most of it. So he told her. Slowly. Carefully. About Jen. About what the doctors had said about possible spinal damage and the future. The only thing he missed out was the rest of his conversation with MacKenzie, his suspicions about Paulie and that letter.

This is not murder. This is justice.

Ida listened quietly, face growing pinched with concentration. And, despite himself, Connor felt relief as he spoke. Not just at forming the nightmare of the last twelve hours into words, but in his gran's response to it. Her eyes were clear, focused. There was no confusion, no hint of unanswered questions as to who Connor was or why he was in her home. In that moment, she was Ida Fraser again, the woman who had been the third parent in Connor's childhood, the parent who had understood him.

'I'm sorry, bonny lad,' Ida said, after a moment, staring into her cup as though she was reading the tea leaves for answers. 'You've been through hell. But it sounds like you did everything you could, and Jennifer is getting the best care possible. I know what you're like, Connor. You'll be feeling guilty over this, that there's something more you could or should do. But what more is there?'

MacKenzie's words in his ears now. *Find the bastard who hurt Jen. And end them. For me. For Jen.*

Connor blinked away the memory, hoping Ida didn't see it in his eyes. 'I don't know, Gran,' he said, frustrated impotence making his scalp itch. 'I've taken some time off work, going to look into a few things. I guess the best thing I can do is just hope she's OK.'

A small smile tugged at Ida's face. 'Look into a few things? You're not going to get yourself into any trouble, are you, Connor?'

Find the bastard who hurt Jen. And end them. For me. For Jen.

Connor gave her his best *who, me?* smile. 'Not at all,' he said, the words sounding as fake as the colour of the French fancies piled on the table in front of him. 'Just going to do my bit, give the police my statement about what happened, make sure nothing is missed.'

'Hmm.' She sighed. 'Look, Connor, you are who you are. And I love you for that. But from what you've told me, this was an accident. Nothing more. So let the police do their jobs, stay out of it. You're not a policeman any more. That part of your life is over. The best thing you can do is be there for Jen and her family. They're going to need you now more than ever.'

The phrase jumped out at Connor, like a splinter in a smooth banister. He got up, walked around the table and kissed his gran's forehead, took a moment to inhale the warmth of her skull and the scent of her hair. 'You're a genius,' he said, pulling back and looking down at her. 'Thank you.'

She returned the smile, cheeks reddening slightly even as the questions formed in her eyes. '"Thank you,' she said. 'I'm not sure what I did, though.'

Connor smiled again, her words echoing in his mind as random snatches of conversation fell into place like pieces in a jigsaw puzzle.

That part of your life is over.

He nodded a brief apology to her, then pulled out his phone and thumbed in a message. Hit send, then looked up to see her watching him patiently. Smiled at her, felt the need to explain. 'You, Gran, just told me what I'm looking for next. And, more importantly, why.'

CHAPTER 9

DCI Malcolm Ford leaned back in his chair and took in his surroundings: different location, all-too-familiar landmarks. Like the industrially painted walls reflecting the cheap strip-lighting overhead, casting the office in a murky half-light. The almost dilapidated furniture, from the chair he was now trying to get comfortable in to the desk littered with files and Post-it notes. A mountain of paperwork threatened to overwhelm the computer, as though the analogue was staging a revolution against the digital.

He smirked at that, couldn't quite bring himself to laugh at the symmetry of the analogy with his own position. Yesterday's man trying to improve tomorrow's world. Felt the smirk curdle and collapse on his face, give way to a more familiar expression.

He told himself again that this was not part of the plan.

It had all seemed so simple, so clear-cut, a year ago. After the whole ugly business with his former guv, DCI Dennis Morgan, Ford had finally summoned the courage to put in his papers. He would cash in his pension, fill in his days with Mary and the mundane rather than murder and mayhem. He had been committed to the course of action he had chosen, even gone as far as writing his resignation at Morgan's bedside, and posting it in the internal mail, for the attention of Chief Constable Peter Guthrie.

He should have known then that he wasn't quitting. Standard procedure would have been to submit his resignation to the chief super, not the chief himself. Of course he had told himself it was the stress of the Morgan case, of seeing his old mentor reduced to a husk kept alive by machines, that had led to the oversight.

But he knew better. In the days that followed, in the silences that seemed too loud after yet another argument with Mary, the truth whispered to him. Sending his resignation directly to the chief had been a warning.

And a plea for help.

The reaction had been just slow enough to allow Mary to hope and Ford to secretly despair. They had a whole weekend together, plotting their future without Police Scotland looming over their lives. Every promise of holidays, long weekends and DIY projects magnified Ford's panic. But then, on the following Monday, Ford had been summoned to Police Scotland's headquarters in Tulliallan, Fife. It was a large, college-like campus close to the Forth and separated from the industrial scar of Grangemouth by the Kincardine Bridge, where police officers were trained for what felt like an increasingly quixotic lifetime of trying to bring order to chaos. Which was, Ford thought, why Peter Guthrie was the man leading the fight. Recruited for his political savvy and nose for a headline more than any copper's instinct, Guthrie was the man who understood how to sell the Police Scotland brand to the public. Which was why there was no way in hell he was going to let Ford quit.

'Look, Malcolm,' he had said, after Ford had been ushered into his office and presented with an array of cafetières, teapots and pastries, 'I received your letter and, I must say, it troubled me greatly. We simply cannot afford to lose a man of your experience, especially now.'

Ford nodded; no interpreter needed. What Guthrie meant was that they could not afford to lose him straight after a former senior officer who had taken on the west-coast crime families had been linked to the protection of a serial killer and complicity in the framing of another man for the crime. To see another highly respected officer leave under a cloud would cast a shadow over Police Scotland that would not be banished by any of Guthrie's PR wheezes about bobbies on the beat or community engagement.

Over the course of the next hour, Guthrie had pleaded, cajoled and, finally, blackmailed. Ford would stay on with the police, but with an expanded remit. He would be consultant senior investigating officer on any crime that the chief deemed to be of national importance. In return, he would observe the investigation, and report directly to Guthrie with any suggestions to streamline the investigative process.

In other words, he would remain inside the tent to piss, rather than stepping out, then turning back towards Police Scotland.

Which was why Ford now found himself in a cramped office in Gayfield Square police station in Edinburgh. The murder of a civil servant on government property was the definition of national news and a press conference had been called an hour from now. Ford had no intention of speaking to the press, but he wanted to know the lines that were going to be given to them beforehand. This case was enough of a headache without giving those headline-grabbing vultures the chance to twist it into something else.

He was reviewing the statement the head of media, Liz Atkins, had drafted when there was a knock at the door. He looked up as DS John Troughton bustled into the room, face pale, eyes wide. Ford knew the look all too well. 'What?' he said, knowing he didn't want to hear the answer.

'Background on the victim, guv,' Troughton said, voice as anaemic as the lighting in the room. 'Montgomery. Makes for interesting reading.'

Ford sighed, felt a headache snarl. 'Go on, then.'

Troughton opened his mouth, closed it. Hesitated, then handed Ford a folder. 'Maybe best you look at it for yourself, sir,' he said.

Ford opened the file, started reading, gazed up at Troughton. Blinked. The young police officer nodded in return, eyes steady.

'Shit,' Ford whispered.

CHAPTER 10

The answer to Connor's text came as he was driving away from his gran's care home, heading south towards the address MacKenzie had given him for Paulie. He smiled as the caller ID flashed up on the car's dashboard, felt that smile sour as he realised how the conversation was about to go.

'Simon, what about ye? Thanks for calling back so quickly.'

'No bother, Connor,' Simon McCartney said, his voice filling the car with memories of Belfast. 'Sorry, was just coming off shift. Text seemed fairly urgent. Whassup? What shite have you stepped in now?'

Connor took a deep breath, felt dull sparks of pain in his forearms as he tightened his grip on the steering wheel. Then he started talking, telling his old partner from his time as an officer in the Police Service of Northern Ireland everything that had happened to Jen, the letter to MacKenzie and the disappearance of Paulie. He heard a coldness in his voice as he spoke, one officer giving a report to another. Wondered what it said about him that the disconnection he heard comforted him.

There was a moment of silence when he finished talking, static hissing softly through the car. Then Simon spoke, his voice as grey as the sky Connor was driving towards. 'Fuck, Connor. I'm so sorry. Anything you need, it's yours. And I can be there tonight if it helps.'

Connor smiled. Typical Simon. His friend was in trouble. He would help. No hesitation, no doubt. Even if the last time he had made such an offer he had earned a broken jaw and a savage beating for his trouble. Made no difference. Simon McCartney operated on a simple code. Do what you want. But fuck with me or mine and I will not stop until justice is served. Connor approved. 'No, thanks, Si. At least, not yet. What I need now is some off-the-record research. Think you can handle that?'

'Just tell me what you need,' Simon replied.

Connor remembered his gran's words now, the words that had driven him to contact Simon in the first place. *That part of your life is over.* True, she'd been talking about himself and his time in Northern Ireland. But those words could also apply to Paulie. What was it MacKenzie had said? *Paulie and I have done some shit in our time . . .* But what did that mean? Connor knew some of MacKenzie's business operations were less than legal, knew the man had had at least one police officer in his pocket over the last thirty years. But, although he had confronted MacKenzie last year after the business involving Colin Sanderson and Dennis Morgan, Connor had backed off the man in deference to his relationship with Jen. Had that negligence caused this? Was his unwillingness to dig into the father of the woman he was sleeping with somehow responsible for what had happened to Jen?

He shook his head, forced himself to focus on the task at hand. Time enough for guilt later.

'Background,' he said. 'Simon, I need background checks. On Duncan MacKenzie and Paul "Paulie" King. Whatever is going on, someone targeted Jen about something they did that got a girl killed. So dig into them. Criminal records, company accounts, anything you can find. Do it quickly, but quietly.'

'No bother,' Simon replied, voice distant now. Connor could tell he was already planning how he was going to tackle the task. As a serving detective with the PSNI, Simon had access to databases and information Connor simply could not touch. But he also had less reputable sources. Those who would give up a lot to have the friendly ear of a police officer who was friends with the people who patrolled the border between Northern Ireland and the Republic. In a post-Brexit world, they were very useful friends to have.

'Thanks, Simon. You find anything, I'll be on this number. Heading to check a few leads of my own.'

'Oh?' Simon said. 'Anything interesting?'

Connor shrugged as he indicated to take the side road that led off the A9 to Sauchenhall. 'Too early to tell yet. I'll let you know. And thanks, Si, I owe you.'

'Let's find the fuckers who did this to Jen,' Simon replied. 'Then we can settle the bill.'

CHAPTER 11

According to the reports and witness statements Troughton had pulled together, Tim Montgomery was a solitary man who was dedicated to two things – his career and his local football team, Galashiels Star. His playing days behind him, Montgomery had become a coach and general odd-job man for the team, driving the kids who played around the villages and towns of the Borders and the east coast to play weekend fixtures. He was seen as a pillar of the community and the bedrock of the club – good old Tim, the coach with a heart of gold.

He had served the club for years, until his advancing years, and progression up the career ladder with the Scottish Government, curtailed his time with it. They held a dinner in his honour when he retired – Troughton had even found some cuttings from the local newspaper with images of Montgomery being presented with an engraved quaich while he was 'honoured by players past and present'.

And then, in 2001, a man named Cameron Donald threw himself from Drygrange Viaduct.

Ford remembered the story from the time, and the newspaper report Troughton had found and added to the file, a front page of the *Western Chronicle*, the aerial image they'd used making the viaduct look like a slender stone finger snaking its way across the River Tweed. Above the picture was the headline 'Borders Bridge Death Plunge'. The story, written by a reporter whose name Ford knew all too well, was as blunt and by-the-numbers as the headline. Police 'sources' revealed that a dog-walker had seen a figure crossing the then-disused viaduct at approximately eleven a.m. They had thought little about it, the spot being popular with walkers, photographers, and kids looking for a place to hang out. They had walked on. Then, glancing back, they noticed the figure had climbed over the railings and was standing on the edge of the bridge. Before they could move or cry out, he toppled forward, falling silently to the ground more than a hundred feet below.

The official police statement in the file revealed that the victim had been positively identified as Cameron Donald, a forty-three-year-old teacher from Melrose. Donald was known to have been recently divorced and estranged from his children. The story didn't quite go as far as to say that was the reason for his leap from the bridge, but it got close enough for Ford.

Especially with what he knew *hadn't* made it into the public domain. The statement Troughton had dug up from Donald's estranged wife, Victoria, claiming it was all Montgomery's fault, that he had driven Cameron over the edge of the viaduct as surely as if he had pushed him. She claimed Montgomery had been an abuser, had targeted Cameron when he had coached him at the football club, that the birth of their sons had dragged the memories into the cold light of day, twisting Donald from a loving father into something fragile and cruel.

'I saw it in his eyes,' Ford read, 'whenever we gave the boys a bath. Something haunted. And something more. Something cold.'

He shuddered, remembered the message daubed in blood. *This is not murder. This is justice.*

He flicked through the file, looked up at Troughton. The DS shrugged in response to the unspoken question. 'I looked, boss,' he said softly, eyes darting over Ford's shoulder. 'No record of any statement taken from Montgomery in response to the allegations, and no further police involvement with Mrs Donald. If there was an investigation into the allegations she made, it went nowhere.'

'Check again, will you?' Ford said. 'Reports might have got lost in the merger and transfer of headquarters. So do me a favour, have another look. Can't imagine something like this would just disappear.'

Troughton nodded, doing well to keep his lack of enthusiasm out of his expression. It was a stretch, they both knew it. The merger of Scotland's eight police forces could be blamed for a lot of things - bureaucracy, wasted man hours, calls being routed to the wrong police station - but the loss of documents related to a suicide and allegations of child abuse? Unlikely.

Ford watched the office door close as Troughton left, then flicked through the file once more, returning to the newspaper report of Donald's death. Felt his headache intensify as he read the byline on the story. 'Mark fucking Sneddon,' he said, his voice sounding tired, even to him.

Mark Sneddon. Former staff reporter at the *Western Chronicle.* Mark Sneddon, whom Ford had seen two years ago, hanging from a tree in the Stirling countryside, his stomach ripped open, intestines spilling from the wound, glistening coils of flesh in the harsh fire-engine emergency lights. Another memory now, this time of Connor Fraser, and the way he had wrapped a protective arm around Sneddon's former lover when she had learned of his death.

He would be seeing that former lover at the press conference in less than an hour's time. And if he knew Donna Blake, she would be asking all the awkward questions.

CHAPTER 12

The house was like the man who owned it – small and squat and isolated. It sat at the end of a short, rutted farm track off Falkland Road, a bungalow island adrift in a fenced-off paddock, that looked to be more comprised of weeds and naked earth than grass. It was a neat, one-floor bungalow, harled walls clean and freshly painted, the slate-grey roof doing its best to blend in with the darkening sky overhead. To the left of the main house, a long outhouse looked as though it had once been a stable for horses but had now been converted for other uses. The heavy metal sliding door that took up the gable end of the building hinted at more industrial pursuits than horse-shoeing or agriculture.

And, somehow, Connor couldn't see Paulie as the farming type.

He killed the engine of the Audi, sat in the silence for a moment, taking in the scene. No sign of Paulie's pride and joy, a gleaming black Mercedes saloon he kept almost pathologically well maintained. Not that he'd really expected to find Paulie at home, slippers on, feet up, or doing whatever the hell he did when he wasn't being MacKenzie's pet psychopath. Whatever was going on, Paulie King was hardly the type of man to sit on the sidelines.

The question was, what type of a man was he really? And why did someone want him dead badly enough to take out Jen to see it happen?

Connor got out of the car, the cold biting at his cheeks as he emerged from the cocooned bubble of warmth. He stepped towards the bungalow, eyes strafing across the building as he ticked off a mental checklist, found the front door had no bell. Rapped a couple of times, heard the knocks echo inside the house in a way that told him it was empty.

'Paulie,' he called, knowing there would be no answer. 'You there?'

No reply. No surprise.

Connor closed his eyes, took a deep breath. Decision time. Until this point, everything had been hypothetical. He had gone through the motions, but had done nothing that could not be undone. But now he was facing a crossroads. He could walk away, call Ford, tell him what MacKenzie had told him, let the police handle it. Or he could choose door number two, which made the police less an ally and more a competitor.

He let out his breath, watched it mist into the sky. Who was he kidding? He had had no choice since the moment Jen had been run over.

Find the bastard who hurt Jen. And end them.

He reached into his pocket, took out a small leather pouch. Considered the lock, then chose two thin metal needles. He hadn't seen an alarm on the outside of the house, hadn't noticed any contact strips or wiring on the windows as he'd approached the front door. And, besides, why would a man like Paulie need a burglar alarm, especially in a remote location like this? No, Paulie would want to keep things quiet, deal with matters personally.

It didn't take long to pick the lock – a simple matter of isolating the tumblers then turning. He pushed softly at the door and it swung in silently, the gloom seeming to beckon to Connor. He stepped into a long, surprisingly wide hallway, tastefully decorated with light cream walls and parquet flooring that seemed to glitter even in the half-light.

Connor moved forward slowly, felt his senses strain as they stretched out around him, trying to discern the slightest movement or noise. But there was nothing, apart from his own breathing, and the house had the cold, empty feeling of a church that had been boarded up and forgotten long ago.

The hallway led to a large, open-plan living area dominated by a huge log burner surrounded by roughly hewn chunks of stone, turning the chimney into an industrial sculpture. The parquet flooring seemed to glitter more brightly here, basking in the soft wall lights that gave the room a warm, intimate feel despite its size. Surprise, surprise, Connor thought. Not the type of home he was expecting for a man who looked permanently creased, no matter how expensive the suit he wore.

The fireplace was faced by a large leather sofa, a wide table running along the back of it. The centre of the table looked like a shrine to malt whisky – expensive bottles flanking a crystal decanter and delicate glasses that Connor couldn't imagine Paulie holding without them shattering in his bear-like paw. On either side of the drinks collection was a smattering of photographs, the silver frames obviously chosen to complement the décor in the rest of the room. Connor took a step forward, then froze as the sound of car tyres crunching gravel echoed around the room, as loud as a gunshot in the silence.

He moved quickly to the window to the left of the couch, flattened himself against the wall and peeked out. Saw a Range Rover parked beside his Audi, two men circling the car, exchanging curious glances. They were casually dressed, designer jeans, open-necked shirts, suit jackets, moving in a way that told him all he needed to know about them. He took out his phone, snapped a picture of them and their car, sent a message, then considered.

Glanced back towards the drinks collection. Smiled. Made a decision. Then got moving towards the front door.

The two men were halfway towards it when Connor swung it open. They stopped dead, the man at the rear's arm stuttering towards the inside of his pocket. Connor let his smile grow wider as he saw this. It confirmed what he had known the moment he saw them get out of the car.

''Bout ye?' Connor said as he leaned against the door jamb, keeping his back rounded and his shoulders loose.

'Who the fuck are you?' the first man growled. He was tall, sinewy, cheekbones as well defined as the tailoring of his jacket. His eyes were as cold as the day that turned his breath into a mist, gaze scanning Connor, evaluating. Connor saw the man's glance dance from his legs to his chest, checking posture and build, pause a moment as he registered the full crystal tumbler Connor held in his left hand. A thin, silvery scar trailed across the man's left cheek, accentuated by the hectic colour the cold had brought to his skin.

'Me?' Connor said, rolling forward slightly, taking a sip from the whisky. 'Ah'm Connor. Question is,' he smiled again, 'who are you?'

The man looked over his shoulder at his colleague, a shorter, younger version of himself, with a shock of flame-red hair and the freckles to match. 'None of your business, pal,' he said, his voice low, guttural, consonants flattened in the way only someone born and raised in north Edinburgh could. 'What are you doing here, and where's Paulie King?'

Bingo, Connor thought.

'Paulie?' he said. 'This is his place. Told me to look after it for him, help myself to a drink, relax. So that's what I'm doing.' Another smile.

'So you're a friend of Paulie's?' the older man asked, reflecting Connor's smile with a flash of perfectly white teeth. There was cruelty in that smile, Connor thought. And the promise of violence. 'So you know where he is?'

'Not got a bloody clue, pal,' Connor said. 'Got a message from him, asking me to look after the place. Told me where the spare key was, and to make myself at home. I was just . . .'

Connor's phone chirped in his pocket. He forced out a bark of laughter as he reached for it, watching as the red-headed man tensed and the older man in front of him became statue still. 'That's probably him now, hold on,' Connor said, as he pulled out his phone and read the message. It was a reply to the picture of the men he had sent to MacKenzie with a simple question – *Your guys?*

No. Mo Templeton and Ewan Masters. Work for Dessie Banks in Edinburgh. Bad bastards. What the fuck are they doing there? Be careful. They'll be armed.

Connor grunted, pocketed the phone. MacKenzie telling him what he already knew about these men from the cut of their jackets and the way Redhead had grabbed for his coat.

'So?' the older man in front said, impatience pinching his voice into a hiss. 'Was that Paulie? Where is he?'

'No.' Connor took one last sip of whisky. 'No, it wasn't. But it answered my question about who you are. You're Mo, right? You look like a Mo. So, hey, Mo, want to tell me why Dessie Banks is looking for Paulie King?'

Mo's eyes widened momentarily, shock overwhelming his natural poker face even as Ewan started forward.

'Enough shite,' he said, gun appearing from the folds of his jacket. 'I don't know who you are or what the fuck—'

Connor didn't let him finish the sentence. He lunged forward, throwing the last of the whisky into Mo's face, then following through, sending the glass in a glittering arc to smash on Ewan's temple. He staggered back, hands flying for the wound, gun clattering to the ground. Connor kept moving, drove an elbow straight into Mo's nose as he gagged and spluttered on the whisky, then stepped around him, targeting Ewan's knee with a stamping kick that snapped the bone as if it was dried kindling. He ignored the man's screams, scooped up the gun, swept it over both men, who were now lying on the ground, writhing. Connor felt a flash of shame. Two men down. One with a shattered knee, the other probably nursing a broken nose. Overkill? Frustration? Or justifiable force?

The hell with it. Questions for another day.

Satisfied that Mo and Ewan were no longer a threat, Connor ejected the magazine from Ewan's gun, popped the bullet in the chamber, then tossed the weapon into a row of bushes running parallel to the farm road.

'Now,' he said, as he hunkered down beside Mo, reached into his pocket and relieved him of the gun he was carrying, which he tucked into the back of his trousers. 'Let's try this again. I'm Connor. I know why I'm looking for Paulie. Question is, why are you? And what has it got to do with Edinburgh's favourite Tony Soprano wannabe?'

'Fuck you!' Mo hissed, teeth made even whiter by the slick of blood that surrounded his mouth like some perverse lipstick. 'The boss is going to fucking kill you for this! You're as dead as that rat Paulie is!'

Rat? Interesting.

Connor sighed, grabbed a handful of Mo's jacket, hauled him upright. 'Look, Mo, I didn't want this to play out this way. But you and Ewan didn't leave me many options. So let me try one last time. Tell me why Dessie Banks is looking for Paulie King and I might leave you with some teeth. Keep playing the stupid cunt and . . .' He tightened his hand around the man's neck, felt blood-slicked fingers scrabble around his own as Mo's eyes bulged and his skin darkened. A moment of resistance, then frantic nodding. Connor eased his grip.

'The cops!' Mo spat, as he heaved for breath. 'Boss says Paulie was doing a deal with the cops, all the shit he knows about what Mr Banks does in return for immunity, something like that. He got a call about it last night, checked it out, sent us to bring Paulie to him. That's all I know, man. I swear it!'

Connor held Mo for a moment, the only sounds his ragged breathing and Ewan's mewling as he cradled his ruined knee. He thought for a moment, then let go of Mo, steadying him so he didn't fall to the ground.

'Get your pal and get out of here,' Connor said, eyes not leaving Mo's. 'Get back to Edinburgh, tell your boss I'll be in touch with him shortly.'

Connor saw a question rise in Mo's eyes. He shook his head. 'Now, Mo. Get Ewan and leave. While I'm still feeling sociable.'

He watched as Mo staggered across to Ewan and helped the man to his feet. Saw the hatred in Ewan's eyes as he glared at Connor, knew he would be meeting him again at some point in the future, and that whatever happened at that meeting was all that he deserved.

The Range Rover snarled into life and Connor backed up into the house, not wanting to give Mo a target. Watched as the car disappeared up the farm track in a plume of dust and over-revving, even as he tried to make sense of what was going on.

Frustrated, he walked across to the outhouse and followed the perimeter, found a small window and peered inside. Froze as he saw what was there, his mind suddenly filling with the sound of feet clattering on concrete, the squeal of tyres, the dull, hard thud of metal hitting flesh.

He walked to the front of the outhouse, to the metal door that dominated the gable end like a drawbridge. Inspected the large, heavy lock that hung from it. Drew Mo's gun from his belt and fired, the lock exploding after two shots. Took a deep breath then pulled the door open, the hinges squealing, like his thoughts.

He took out his phone, dialled as he stepped into the gloom of the garage and tried to swallow the hard knot of panic that seemed to climb up his throat.

'Boss?' Robbie answered, on the third ring. 'You must be bloody psychic. That car you wanted me to chase down? I just found it. And you're not going to believe who it's registered to.'

Connor read the licence plate on the car in front of him. The car he had watched mow Jen down only hours before. 'Paulie King,' he said softly. 'The car is registered to Paulie King, right, Robbie?'

CHAPTER 13

Simon McCartney sat in his Belfast flat, television on, glass of red wine poured. He wasn't one for watching the news, preferring instead Sky Sports as background noise, but after the earlier call from Connor, and a check of the news websites covering Scotland, he didn't really have much choice.

And, besides, what he was watching was sport of a kind. A blood sport.

He knew the set-up all too well. The long table at which the investigating officers sat, faces set, hands clasped, lips thin and bloodless as though they were facing a firing squad rather than a room of reporters. The lectern at the right of the table, branded with the Police Scotland logo. Change the force insignia and the names of the officers, it could have been any police force holding a press conference as a major investigation ramped up.

Except this was anything but just another case.

Simon watched as Police Scotland's chief constable, Peter Guthrie, read out a statement. It was meant to sound calm, measured, authoritative. And if someone else was delivering the statement it might have. But Simon couldn't shake the feeling that he was watching a man who was out of his depth, the uniform he was wearing only highlighting the gulf between the role he was playing and the man he was.

It didn't help that what Guthrie was saying was all bad news for him and great news for the press. The body of a civil servant had been found in the swimming-pool of a government building in Leith. An investigation was under way, the cause of death yet to be determined. Several promising lines of enquiry had been identified. Yes, the police were in constant contact with the First Minister's office and other colleagues in government.

Simon smiled at this, raised a toast to the television screen. 'Constant contact.' He knew from his own dealings with Stormont and the devolved government there that what Guthrie really meant was that the politicians were crawling up the arses of the police, demanding answers. Given what he knew of the case, Simon couldn't blame them.

He was about to turn the TV down, get back to the files on the coffee table in front of him, when he spotted a familiar face. She was standing about halfway back in the room, dark hair framing her pale face and accentuating the glacial blue glare she was now training on Guthrie, who, Simon could see, was now clinging to the sides of the lectern for dear life. Simon smiled at the image of Donna Blake, even as he felt a vague ache begin to pulse in his jaw, like a glowing ember of memory, from the last time he had seen her: she had been standing in the living room of her flat, terrified, begging Simon and Connor for help. That night had led to a confrontation with a murderer, and a shattered jaw it had taken Simon two years to recover from.

'Sky News has learned that a message was left with the body of the victim this morning,' Donna said, voice all business. 'Could you give more details on this, and tell me if it relates to the identity of the victim, which you've yet to release?'

Simon smiled. Checkmate. If there was a message, the last thing the police would want to do was get it into the public domain. And he could tell from the question that Donna was letting the chief know she knew damn well who the victim was.

He rubbed his jaw, listened for a moment as Guthrie sputtered his way through a noncommittal answer, then turned the TV down and got back to work.

After the call from Connor, Simon had quietly dug into the police databases, requesting everything they had on Duncan MacKenzie. It was an easy request to justify: since the Troubles and the days of gun-smuggling, haulage firms operating between the UK and Northern Ireland had always been closely monitored. With the catastrofuck of Brexit setting cross-Border trade back about fifty years, it had become a relevant issue again, with small businesses and sole traders seeking ever more creative ways to circumvent the red tape and export charges that were threatening to choke them to death.

He knew bringing the files home was a breach of protocol, found he didn't care. This was personal. If, as Connor had said, Jen had been hurt as a way to get to her father or Paulie King, the answer might be in the files in front of him. And if that was the case, Simon wanted to find that answer alone.

He opened the first file, topped up his wine and started reading. Waded his way through a half-dozen pages, was about to give up, then froze, his eyes drawn to seven words at the bottom of an after-action report. Grabbed another file, skimmed it, found what he needed. Laid both on the table then stood up, as though height and distance would help him make sense of what he had just found.

'Ah, shite, Connor,' he whispered, as his jaw began to pulse again. Not a memory this time, but a warning. 'What the fuck have you got us into?'

CHAPTER 14

Connor stood at the patio doors of his flat, the cooling afternoon breeze prickling his shower-warmed skin. He took deep breaths, trying to calm his thoughts, find some focus to help him process everything he had learned. The problem was that none of his usual tricks were working.

A search of the car Connor had found in Paulie's outhouse had only confirmed what Robbie had told him: tucked in the glove compartment was the V5 ownership document that listed Paul Joseph King as the owner of the vehicle. Connor had found nothing else in the interior except some empty juice bottles and a forgotten McDonald's wrapper, while the outside of the vehicle was dominated by the ugly, sneer-like twist of the front bumper and bonnet where Jen had been hit and thrown into the air. Looking at the damage, Connor had drawn Mo's gun and aimed it at the car, as though it was a wounded animal he was about to put out of its misery. He had resisted the urge, knowing the anger was misplaced, opted instead to search the rest of Paulie's home. He found nothing of note, except the same unexpectedly tasteful décor in the bungalow's two bedrooms. Returning to the living room, he examined the pictures that flanked the whisky collection. They were mostly shots of Paulie with Duncan and some other men at MacKenzie Haulage, grinning into the camera, faces smeared with dirt and the smiles that only a hard day's labour could bring. But there were two other pictures that interested Connor. One was of Paulie as a younger man, standing in a boxing ring, arms held aloft. He was slimmer in the picture, his hair fuller, the gut he now wore like body armour yet to mature, but it was undoubtedly Paulie. Connor could see the man he knew in the smile and nose that had already been remoulded by knuckles and violence.

The second picture, Connor took with him – it was a portrait of Duncan MacKenzie and Paulie, beaming into the camera, resplendent in dinner suits. In the centre was a striking woman Connor knew was Jen's mother, Hannah. He could see Jen in the shape of her jaw and the way her smile dimpled her cheeks. She had died of cancer when Jen was just a child, the loss forging the close bond Jen now had with her father. The bond that had stopped Connor looking into Duncan MacKenzie properly.

Until now.

Satisfied there was nothing left to learn at the house, Connor had wiped down any surfaces he had touched, pocketed the lock he had shot open, then left. He had thought about heading for the hospital, decided against it. It was still family members only at Jen's bedside until the doctors woke her up, and the last thing Connor wanted at that moment was to encounter Jen's family.

He had headed home, the gym rising in his mind. Jen called his need to work out an addiction, and Connor found it hard to disagree. It was a compulsion bred into him by his grandfather, Jimmy. A former amateur bodybuilder, he had taught Connor how to train when he was a student in Northern Ireland. It had become a meditation for him, a way to calm his mind by torturing his body. But after what had happened to Jen, the thought of visiting the gym – *their* gym – felt perverse. Instead, at home, he put himself through a bodyweight circuit of upper- and lower-body exercises that left his muscles screaming. He stepped into the shower, then headed for the patio doors, as if the answer lay in the garden beyond.

What did he know? Someone had demanded Duncan MacKenzie kill Paulie King in retribution for some action in the past that had apparently led to a woman losing her life. When that didn't happen quickly enough for the ransomer's liking, Jen had been run over with a car Paulie owned. The implication was clear enough: Paulie had been the one to run over Jen. It was too neat for Connor. He knew Paulie, had seen the way he doted on Jen like an overprotective uncle – the psychopath redeeming himself by forming one true human connection. There was no way he would ever see Jen hurt. Any more than he would strike a deal with the police, even if it was to put away an animal like Dessie Banks.

Like anyone who had a passing association with law enforcement, Connor knew of Dessie Banks. He had started out as a drug-dealer in one of the tougher estates in the east of Edinburgh, a place of faceless high-rise tower blocks connected by swathes of unkempt grass where glass and discarded condoms competed with used needles for the attention of the kids that roamed the streets in packs. Dessie had worked slowly and methodically, a cancer slowly metastasising through Edinburgh's criminal classes until he owned a piece of every illicit business in town. From drugs to prostitution to real estate and tax evasion, Dessie Banks was involved.

Which begged the question: how was Paulie involved with Dessie, and what did he know that Banks was so scared of him revealing?

Connor's thoughts were disturbed by a rustling in the bushes at the far end of the garden. He looked up, smiled as he saw a small tortoiseshell cat emerge, moving with the grace of a ballerina. 'Afternoon, Tom,' he called. The cat had started visiting Connor's garden a while ago, keeping a discreet distance. Connor didn't know where it came from, if it was a stray or a local cat with a taste for exploration and an opportunist's eye for a soft touch and a treat. He hadn't even got close enough to know if it was male or female. But when the visits became regular, he had fallen into the habit of calling the cat Tom, thanks to a childhood filled with cartoons, and offering it a can of tuna and some water. He watched as Tom approached, picking a path slowly over the lawn as if it were mined, then retreated to the kitchen and opened a can of tuna into a small bowl. He returned to the patio, laid the bowl down close to the stairs that led to the garden, then stepped back, giving the cat its space.

He watched as Tom ate, wishing all his problems were so easily solved. Nothing about what he had found at Paulie's house made sense, and by not telling Ford or the police what he knew about Jen being hurt, he had made himself complicit in a crime. But, then, what would he say? Sorry, guys, made a wee bit of a mess. Had evidence of a conspiracy to incite murder and proof that Jen MacKenzie's hit-and-run was targeted. Oh, and I beat the shite out of two armed gangsters and stripped and dumped an illegal firearm as well. Want me to write that up in a statement for you?

Connor reached up and massaged his eyes until dull sparks skittered across his vision. 'Where the fuck are you, Paulie?' he whispered.

As if in reply, Connor's phone rang on the breakfast bar in the kitchen. He retrieved it, smiled as he hit answer. A friendly voice at least. 'Simon, how's it going? You get anything on King or MacKenzie?'

'Aye, bloody right I did,' Simon said, his voice taut, stressed.

'Go on,' Connor said, eyes drifting to the gun sitting on the breakfast bar beside his wallet.

Simon began talking. And as he did, Connor knew that the moment the call was finished, the next person he would be talking to was DCI Malcolm Ford.

CHAPTER 15

Susie Drummond felt a tremor in her leg that was nothing to do with the too-sour, too-strong cup of coffee she was just finishing. She was back in her flat in Broughton, an area of the city separated from the fashionable New Town enclave of Stockbridge by a fifteen-minute walk, a change in postcode and a rise in property prices sharp enough to leave you with a nosebleed. After the press conference, she had needed to get away from the bustle of the station and other officers. But, although her shift was over, the case refused to leave Susie.

The press conference had gone about as well as she had expected it to. Donna's question about the victim's identity had forced Guthrie and the press office to confirm that it was Tim Montgomery who had been found floating in the pool. They had also confirmed the death was being treated as unexplained at this stage.

Opening her notebook, Susie read back what she had written down from the briefing with the pathologist, some old, tank-built guy called Tennant, whom DCI Ford had insisted take the lead on this case. She pondered this for a moment, wondered exactly what type of pull Ford had with the chief that allowed him to request whatever pathologist he wanted. She shook her head, pushed the thought aside. She had enough questions to deal with as it was.

Tennant had confirmed that Montgomery had died from exsanguination – his blood pumping into the pool from a massive wound to his jugular vein. Death would have occurred rapidly, and he estimated that Montgomery had been dead for no more than an hour before he was found, which he couched with the usual caveats about accuracy and the fact that the body had been floating in a heated pool, which made taking core temperature readings more problematic than usual.

Which gave Susie another headache. Victoria Quay was a typical government building with typical government security. The only way to get in was by swiping a security pass at the turnstiles at the front door or to be signed in as a guest. Access to the pool area was similarly regulated: anyone going into the changing rooms that led to it had to swipe a security pass to get past the locked door. Of course, it would have been too much to hope that there were security cameras at the poolside, but the cameras trained on the atrium-like hallway leading to it showed only Montgomery swiping himself in. They were backed up by the card-swipe records from the building's security logs, which showed he was the only person to access the pool before Martin Christopher found him more than an hour later. From what Tennant had said about the speed of blood loss, it was impossible that Montgomery had been killed elsewhere then dumped in the pool – a fact reinforced by the lack of any footage of anyone dragging the body to the swimming-pool. Suicide had been briefly mooted, then rejected on two grounds: the lack of a weapon to cut his own throat and the message left on the wall by the pool. *This is not murder. This is justice.*

Susie drained her coffee. Grimaced. Another bad habit she had picked up from a certain journalist with a taste for fast cars and a nose for trouble. She could have used his help now but, in light of what he was currently dealing with, he was the last person she could ask.

Another time.

She flicked through her phone, found a picture she had taken of the message scrawled across the wall. What could Tim Montgomery have done that demanded retribution like this? She had suggested to Ford that she carry out a background check on Montgomery, only to be told that it was being handled by another of his imports from Stirling: a lanky DS called Troughton. Which left her with what? A locked-room mystery with no way for the killer to access the victim, a cryptic message and a nagging feeling that, whatever was going on, Montgomery's death was only the start of it.

She glanced up at the clock on the living-room wall. Calculated. It wouldn't take that long to get to Stirling and, since the end of lockdown, Susie had found that her desire to get out and see other places had reached an almost manic intensity. Thinking of the volume of cars she'd seen on the roads in the last couple of months, she guessed she wasn't alone in feeling that.

She nodded to herself, decision made. Found Donna's number in her contacts and hit dial. Time for a road trip.

CHAPTER 16

Ford settled into the couch that Connor had gestured he should take, felt the weight of the day seep into his shoulders as he sat down. His last visit to Connor Fraser's flat had not been the most relaxing experience and, comfortable sofas and offers of whisky aside, he had a feeling this visit was going to be the same.

The call shouldn't have surprised him. Connor Fraser had a habit of getting involved in Ford's work, especially, it seemed, when the case was sensitive. What was surprising was the flatness in Fraser's voice over the phone. Ford had noticed that Fraser, a former police officer, was usually the model of trained-in polite deference, back straight, speech always clear and succinct, throwing the occasional 'sir' into the conversation. But this call? It was like talking to a different man.

'Need your help,' Fraser had said. 'I'm working on how Jen got hurt, found something you need to know about. Can you look up Operation Calderwood, meet me at my place later on?'

Ford glanced at the clock on his office wall, watched a couple of seconds tick by as he tried to process Fraser's words. He had seen an incident report on the hit-and-run in Stirling, been so busy with the Montgomery murder that he hadn't put it together with Jen MacKenzie, Fraser's girlfriend. Getting old, he admonished himself, as he made a mental note to read that report more closely when he got a moment.

He agreed to meet Fraser at his flat in the King's Park area of

Stirling on his way home to Bridge of Allan, a small village close to the Stirling University campus to the west of the city. Mary wouldn't like the delay, but Ford thought an extra hour or so after a fifteen-hour day wasn't going to lead to imminent divorce.

Not today at least.

He arrived at Fraser's place just after 8 p.m., was ushered in by a man who looked as if he was riding the world's worst caffeine buzz. Fraser had always struck him as imposing, with his sheer physical size. His tendency to look straight into your eyes when he talked, though, needled Ford's police instincts and marked him out as a man to watch closely as a potential threat. He had seen Fraser take on a lunatic with a knife, knew he was capable of devastating, efficient acts of violence when needed. But there was something more to him when he ushered Ford into his flat – a rawness Ford didn't like. As though the scab that had formed over whatever violence Fraser held within him had been picked and was starting to bleed.

Ford took the glass Fraser offered him as he settled into the couch, the smell of old whisky biting into his nostrils. He nodded thanks, considered the glass. Got talking.

'Look, Fraser, I'm sorry about Jen. I looked at the report briefly, seems like a hit-and-run. We've got officers looking for the car. But you said you were looking into it? If you're thinking of trying to . . .'

Fraser waved aside his words, impatience sparking in green eyes that were cold and somehow empty. 'What were you able to find out about Operation Calderwood?'

Ford nodded, took a sip of the whisky. Down to business, then. 'Not much more than you probably already know,' he said. 'It was fairly high-profile about twenty-five years ago. It was the operation set up after three kids, young girls between the ages of eight and fifteen, were taken from three separate locations around Scotland. All found dead. Operation Calderwood was designed to look into the cases, make sure there wasn't a serial paedophile on the loose, given the similarities in the disappearances. But no arrests were ever made, and no other children disappeared in the same circumstances.'

Fraser nodded, giving Ford the impression none of this was news to him.

'What's this about, Connor? Why are you asking about a police investigation from a quarter of a century ago, and what the hell has it got to do with Jen MacKenzie getting run over?'

Fraser opened his mouth. Closed it. Then moved across to a small chest of drawers, opened it, and handed Ford the envelope Duncan MacKenzie had given him earlier that day. 'MacKenzie got that before Jen was hurt this morning,' he said, his voice as hard as the crystal tumbler he had offered Ford. 'I did a little digging, tried to see what the hell MacKenzie and Paulie might have been into that led to someone's daughter getting killed. Found out they were interviewed as part of Operation Calderwood, officers trying to rule out a link between the disappearances and long-distance drivers who were moving around the country a lot. Probably trying to make sure there wasn't another animal like Robert Black out there. But then . . .' His voice trailed off. 'Ford? What?'

Ford tried to raise his head to meet Connor's gaze, found he couldn't take his eyes from the note he had just been passed, the note that was both threat and promise. The note that bore the same simple message he had seen daubed across a swimming-pool wall in blood earlier that day.

This is not murder. This is justice.

'What I'm about to tell you is off the record, completely,' he said, his voice little more than a whisper. 'Understood?'

Fraser nodded his agreement, something like hunger giving the darkness in his eyes a deeper hue now, even as he stepped forward.

Ford studied him, made a decision, then started talking. Told him about the discovery of Tim Montgomery in Victoria Quay and the message that had been left there. And as he spoke he could see the other man's mind whirling, taking every new fact, holding it up, like a jewel, and inspecting it, even as the simple truth of their situation went unspoken.

Whatever was going on, he and Fraser were looking for the same killer.

CHAPTER 17

Susie agreed to meet Donna at her place, taking directions on how to get to the best Chinese takeaway in Stirling on the way. She had politely declined Donna's suggestion of adding a bottle of wine to the shopping list and staying over – with Ford and Troughton on the loose, she wanted to be back in Edinburgh and sharp for whatever the next day would bring.

She found Donna's flat without much effort. It was in a small, nondescript development of new builds on the outskirts of the town. The location surprised her: it seemed too middle class and suburban for the Donna Blake she had known. Susie had met Donna when she was a newly promoted detective constable who had been sent to 'gain experience' with other detectives in what had been the old Strathclyde Police CID unit. Susie knew it was more a case of filling in the gaps in the rota that retirements and reassignments had created, rather than developing her deductive skills, but she was happy enough to take the assignment. Having cut her teeth in rural policing in the Borders, she felt she was ready for something . . . bigger.

Susie had first encountered Donna when she was sent for media training – part of a campaign to sell the police as more of a service and less of a force. She later found out that Donna had been given the assignment via some work she had done for Stirling University, but it was clear to her from their first encounter that Donna Blake knew how to dig into the guts of a story – and didn't give a damn whom she had to trample over to get to that truth.

Post-lecture drinks had turned into dinners and arrangements to meet up, the professional façade that had thrown them together giving way to a more genuine friendship. Susie found Donna to be both forthright and funny – and not prone to take shit from the male officers who had a problem with being told what to do by a woman, or hide what she really thought behind inanities. They talked about their plans for the future, about what they wanted to achieve in their careers, their vows to keep in touch gradually eroded by Susie's promotion to detective sergeant and transfer to Edinburgh, and whatever had happened to Donna that had led her from Glasgow to local radio in Stirling to reporting for Sky TV.

When Donna opened the door to the flat, Susie quickly found one piece of the puzzle. The hallway was littered with pictures of a boy, charting his growth from a tiny pink bundle in his mother's arms to a child of about three years old, all blond hair, high cheekbones and gap-tooth smile.

'Andrew,' Donna said simply as she ushered Susie into the flat, relieving her of the bags of Chinese takeaway. 'Three and a half now. Just me and him.'

They exchanged small-talk as Donna plated the food and arranged it on a large coffee table in the living room, then fell into a comfortable silence as they ate.

'So,' Susie said, as she decided against another prawn cracker and started rethinking that glass of wine, 'a son. Got to say, Donna, I never saw you as the maternal type.'

Donna stopped, looked at her plate, fork stirring the food as though she was picking through entrails. 'Neither did I really,' she said. 'Just sort of happened. But when I found out I was pregnant, Mark shit a brick and I ended up here with Andrew.' She gestured around the flat.

'Mark? He's Andrew's dad? I take it he's not . . .?'

Susie saw pain flash in Donna's eyes as she looked up at her. 'Mark Sneddon,' she said after a moment, voice heavy with old, resigned grief. 'We worked together at the *Westie* in Glasgow. Don't think you ever met him. Didn't work out. He's . . .' She paused, sighed, eyes sliding from Susie's. 'He died a couple of years ago.'

Susie mumbled an apology, the awkwardness she felt at bringing up the subject counterbalanced by something nagging at the back of her mind. Something about that name. Sneddon. And the *Westie* – the *Western Chronicle*. Something . . .

'Susie?' Donna asked. 'You OK? Zoned out there for a wee minute.'

Susie shook her head as the answer hit her. Mark Sneddon. The *Western Chronicle*. The file Ford's pet DS, Troughton, had pulled together. She'd seen him slip a printout of a story from the *Westie* into it. She felt the calculations rush through her head, information crashing like waves onto the shore of her consciousness before she had a chance to process what it all meant. Studied Donna, even as she thought of how Ford had brushed aside her offers of help in looking into Tim Montgomery. Was this why? And, if so, how did it connect?

She took her glass of Coke. Swallowed a gulp to try to quench the sudden dryness she felt in her mouth. Rolled the dice in her head. Follow the lead or follow protocol?

Decided.

'Donna, tell me. Do you remember Mark ever mentioning a story he covered about a place called Drygrange?'

CHAPTER 18

The sky was a dead grey, the sun not even trying to break through. Connor watched as sleety rain peppered the patio doors, turning the garden beyond into an impressionist's smear. He opened the door, felt the chill of the morning rush into the flat. Strained to see into the bushes for any sign of Tom, felt a pang of something sharper and colder than the wind as he did so. Jen would hate the thought of Tom outside on a morning like this, cold and alone in the dark. She had always cared for the cat, encouraged Connor to try to win its trust.

'Tom will give you someone to talk to when I'm not here,' she had teased him one night, when they were sitting on the couch, a film forgotten on the TV in front of them. 'And, besides, you could do with another female in your life.'

Connor felt his grief overwhelm the humour of the memory. Typical Jen. Tom had never come close enough to the house for Connor to decide which sex the cat was, but Jen was in no doubt.

Would she ever find out now? It was a question he didn't want to face, let alone answer.

He sighed in frustration, put the door on a hasp so the wind wouldn't catch it, then turned back to the kitchen and set about making coffee - he was going to need it.

He had spent most of the previous evening talking with Ford, trying to see the connection between Tim Montgomery's murder, the message left with his body and the threat to Paulie King. The revelation that Paulie and Duncan MacKenzie had been interviewed as part of an investigation into the murders of three young girls gave them a clue to the letter Duncan had received – *I will take your daughter from you, just as mine was taken from me* – but what was the killer insinuating? That the police had missed something? That Paulie was a child killer? It was possible, but the thought didn't sit easily with Connor. He knew Paulie was many things – a psychopath with a penchant for violence, a sadist with an obsessive need to keep his car clean and his home tidy. But he had seen the other side of Paulie too, the almost avuncular tenderness with which he spoke of Jen. Connor was happy to concede he was too close to the situation, but he couldn't bring himself to believe that Paulie was a child killer. And even if he was, even if the killer was demanding some twisted retribution, how did that fit with Tim Montgomery's murder? And what about Dessie Banks and his claim that Paulie was about to rat out his empire to the police?

They had talked for hours, whisky forgotten, swapped for coffee and conjecture. Ford had initially been furious with Connor for not coming forward with what he knew about why Jen was hurt, his anger only ameliorated by the larger problem with which this knowledge presented him. There was a connection here between what had happened to Jen, a child-murder investigation from years ago and the slaying of a civil servant. The question was, what was it?

Connor could tell there was something Ford wasn't telling him, some strand of thought he wasn't willing to share. He let it slide. They both had their secrets – Connor omitting the small fact he had beaten the shit out of two men and discharged an unlicensed firearm from his recounting of events.

Eventually, they had come up with a plan that showed Connor, again, that Malcolm Ford was willing to sacrifice police procedure at the altar of cold pragmatism. Ford would delve into Operation Calderwood, find the full witness statements given by MacKenzie and King. He would also cross-check Montgomery with the investigation, see if he had been involved at any stage. And then there were the suspects to track down. If there was a link between Montgomery, Calderwood and Paulie, the letter MacKenzie had received, the reference to a lost daughter and the promise that *This is not murder. This is justice* gave Ford something to work on. The parents of the children murdered back in 1997 needed to be interviewed.

Connor had asked how the detective was going to introduce this line of enquiry into the investigation, Ford replying simply that he would 'handle it'. Meanwhile, Connor had agreed to talk to MacKenzie about the matter, see if he could remember anything that might help them both. He didn't tell Ford he had another lead to follow, one that might take him towards Edinburgh. After all, they both had secrets.

With the plan made, Ford had left, but not before extracting a promise from Connor that he would check in regularly. Connor had agreed, then tried to rest, sleep eluding him, his mind racing with possibilities and ideas. He had given up on the notion of sleep at just before 6 a.m., decided to start the day with a run. The weather he was seeing outside would make it more challenging, and that suited his mood.

He drank a cup of coffee, left some tuna out for Tom. Got changed and picked up his phone. Cursed under his breath when he read the display. One new message, left just ten minutes ago. Donna. He had forgotten to return her calls from the previous day. One more thing to do. He opened the message. Read it, then reread it, hastily recalculating the route for his run as he did so.

Working on this murder at SG building in Edinburgh. Maybe got a link to Mark. Feeling a bit shaken up. Could do with a talk. Any update on Jen?

Connor thumbed in a reply: *Your place? Twenty-five minutes? Nothing on Jen yet.* Hit send, then composed another message, this time to Duncan MacKenzie. They had agreed he would get in touch if there was any change in Jen's condition, but Connor saw no harm in pushing the question a little, especially in light of the conversation he planned on having with the man later in the day.

His phone pinged just as he hit send: Donna replying. *Take it you're running here? No probs, will get coffee on.*

CHAPTER 19

At the same time as Connor was heading into the sleet, Susie was cursing it as it spattered onto her windscreen in Edinburgh. The call had come in at just after 6.30 a.m., the news banishing any lingering weariness she felt from her late night with Donna. It took her about twenty minutes to get to Lothian Road – the long, concrete canyon that ran from Princes Street up to Marchmont, the Meadows and beyond – and Festival Square where the body had been found. A large concrete courtyard surrounded on three sides by office blocks and the glass-fronted entrance to a hotel, it had been a popular location during the festival, playing home to a range of market stalls and street performers looking to attract the eye of those visiting the Lyceum Theatre and Usher Hall, which sat directly opposite.

This morning, though, the square was screened off with SOCO barriers and police tape. A contraflow had been set up on Lothian Road, diverting traffic away from the pavement leading to the square, and Susie ground her teeth as she thought of the nightmare that would cause when rush-hour fully kicked in.

But it would be nothing, she knew, compared to the nightmare in the square itself.

Let through the vehicle cordon on the West Approach Road off Lothian Road, Susie found a space in the hotel car park, squeezing between two police vans. She flashed her ID at the outer cordon, ducked under the tape that fluttered in the cold morning breeze and took in the scene. The market stalls dotted around the square were shuttered and abandoned, their bright, cheerful colours made gaudy and tasteless by what had been found there. In front of the hotel there was what looked like a modern art installation: a series of stone spheres carved with random shapes clustered like mushrooms around a central display; a half-sphere sat in the centre of a section of scrub ground, its metal surface scored with deep channels carving out an almost geometric spider-web pattern. In front of the sphere, almost like an offering placed before an altar, stood a gurney, a twisted sheet laid across a shape on top of it, a shape Susie knew she didn't want to see but would have to face. It had been covered by an awning the SOCOs had hastily constructed: they were doing their best to preserve the scene despite the worsening weather.

Close to the gurney, Ford was watching the SOCOs flit around the scene. They looked like anaemic clowns to Susie, trying to contain the immediate locus, seal the area around the body as much as they could to preserve any evidence. With the rising wind and spattering sleet, Susie didn't fancy their chances much.

Ford turned as she approached him, the sound of her boots alerting him to her presence. 'Ah, Drummond,' he said, slightly bloodshot eyes flicking up as though looking for something. 'Took you long enough to get here, especially as you only had to come from town. I've had to drag my arse all the way here from Bridge of Allan.'

She took a breath, determined not to rise to the barb. 'Yes, sir. Sorry. Even at this time, city-centre traffic in Edinburgh isn't the easiest to get through. Not a problem I imagine you have to deal with in Stirling.'

Ford held up a hand, waving away her veiled insult. Made a show of looking over her shoulder. When he spoke again, his breath stank of old coffee and fresh exhaustion. 'I take it you've handled action assignments as I instructed.'

She nodded acknowledgement, kept her face emotionless, free of the questions that were bothering her. Ford had initially arrived from Stirling with Troughton in tow, his very own loyal go-fer to do his bidding. But when the call had come in about this, he had given Susie the job of passing out duties to other officers, but stipulated that

Troughton was not mobilised and remained in Stirling. Something about that bothered Susie almost as much as the implied insults Ford was hurling at her.

'Yes sir. Officers have been assigned to canvass for potential witness statements and a search of the immediate area, while DS Troughton is working from Randolphfield and checking CCTV footage of the area. He's pulling it from the council now, will call as soon as he has anything.'

Ford nodded, jaw working furiously, eyes again strobing over Susie. 'Good,' he muttered, after a moment. 'Well, you'd better see what we've got. Tennant is on the way, says he's stuck in traffic like you were.'

They approached the gurney, the SOCOs giving them furtive disapproving glances but no one daring to question Ford.

The sheet had an almost hypnotic effect, dragging Susie's gaze to it, making it impossible to resist. The note was pinned to the middle, a ragged piece of A4 paper, the words *This is not murder. This is justice* scrawled on it in a dark, angry red. She spotted a patch of blood on slabs below the gurney, shuddered as she realised it was the same colour as the words on the note.

'When was the initial report made?' she asked, her voice taking on the strange, distorted sound she had noticed it developed at crime scenes.

'Initial report was made at five a.m.,' Ford replied, tiredness giving his voice a slight slur. 'Clean-up crew from the hotel. They come out to clear up the square from the night before so the hotel guests don't see anything that puts them off their breakfast.' He nodded up towards a bank of windows. Susie could see tables and chairs behind them, knew from previous visits it was a large, thick-carpeted restaurant area. A sudden thought of her own dinner from the night before flashed through her mind, and her stomach lurched even as she felt her cheeks flush. She darted a glance at Ford, but he was too fixated on the horror in front of him to care.

'Anyway,' he went on, rummaging in his pockets, 'one of the poor bastards found this. So he has a look, pulls back the sheet and then . . .'

Susie's gaze fell back on the gurney, her stomach giving a sickening lurch. She hated this moment, when mind and body clenched, preparing for the blow of whatever horrors came next.

Ford drew a pair of latex gloves from his pocket and snapped them on, leaned towards the gurney.

Susie spoke before she could stop herself. 'Sir, shouldn't we wait for Dr Tennant before we disturb the . . .'

He turned, shot her a look as sour as his breath. 'The SOCOs have already taken their pictures, *Detective Sergeant*,' he hissed. 'And, besides, the cleaner who found this moved the sheet then replaced it when he saw what was under there. The weather is deteriorating. We've a limited window. So we use it. Unless you think Dr Tennant is going to do anything other than confirm the victim is deceased after he sees this?'

Ford drew the sheet back slowly, giving Susie time to take in the horror in front of her. The world seemed to grow brighter, harder, grey and cold as (*post-mortem pictures*, her mind whispered) she made sense of what was in front of her.

It was as though the victim had been forced to bite down on a hand-held blender. Clots of mangled crimson meat hung from the bottom of the head, held there only by the glinting white bone of what Susie realised was the bottom jaw, which had been split in half. The head was thrown back in a silent scream of frozen agony. Susie's legs weakened as she saw the eyes were open. They stared blankly up at the grey morning sky, the growing milky film that was creeping over them doing nothing to disguise the sheer terror and incomprehension in them.

Sleet is falling into those eyes, Susie thought, as her stomach heaved.

Tearing her gaze away from the head, she allowed her eyes to roam down the body, stopping abruptly when she got to the pale hand that hung from the side of the gurney. She felt her legs twitch, the need to run, get away from this insanity, suddenly seizing her, to feel the wind and sleet on her face. Anything that would tell her she was alive, anything, anything, but this.

'Is that . . .' she whispered. Tasted bile in the back of her throat. Coughed and started again. 'Sir, is that what I . . .'

Ford nodded, eyes following Susie. Pale fingers wrapped around a lump of blood-streaked gore that twisted back over the thin wrist, like a snake. The end was a ragged stump, the blood dark and somehow angry against the cooling blue-grey hue of decomposing flesh.

'We'll have to wait for Tennant to confirm,' Ford said, his voice as toneless as the drone of the traffic from Lothian Road, 'but, yes, Drummond. I believe that's the victim's tongue.'

CHAPTER 20

Darkness.

No, more than that. A complete lack of everything. An absence that rushed in, filling every pore like oil. Cloying. Stifling. Choking. But somehow comforting too. Familiar. Safe. Warm.

Had there ever been anything else? Something beyond this? An existence filled with light and colour? With sensation and chaos and noise? With a world turning upside down, view lurching head over heels as she flew through the air, feeling the strings that tethered her to her body being severed one at a time even as a pain unlike anything she had ever known rushed towards her, a ravenous, drooling monster intent on devouring her body and her sanity?

No. No. Better to remain here. In the darkness. Safe. Secure. Let it consume her. Let it take her. Let it end her.

But something, some urge deeper than the darkness itself, compelled her to reach out. Explore with her senses, find the edge of the darkness and tug, pull.

Fight.

A memory now. A voice she knew. Normally soft and gentle, made harsh and demanding by panic and terror.

'Breathe, Jen, for fuck's sake, breathe!'

She did as she was commanded, felt her body rebel at the effort. A massive weight seemed to press down on her even as an alarm began to sound, deafening and shrill as it shattered the peace of her darkness.

She was drowning. Something in her throat, making it impossible to breathe. Her eyes flew open, then screwed shut again at the harsh, stabbing light that attacked them. She flailed, felt something harsh and plastic protruding from her mouth. Clawed for it, tried to pull it free. Strong hands on hers now, even as a voice told her, 'Be calm, calm, sweetheart. You've had an accident. The tube is there to help you breathe. We'll get it. Just for now, be calm.'

She forced herself to obey the voice, with an effort, willed her hands to be still. Risked opening her eyes again, the world resolving slowly as she did so. Saw a woman with a pinched face and kind eyes leaning over her, readjusting the tube that had been rammed down her throat. Tried to turn her head. Fresh panic lancing through her like cold fire as she realised she couldn't. Swivelled her eyes. Saw her dad in the corner, arms folded over his chest, one hand clamped to his face, framing eyes made too large with tears.

In that moment, Jen knew. Knew what had happened. Knew what she had lost.

And she prayed for the darkness to take her again.

CHAPTER 21

Connor's meeting with Donna was like the espresso she offered him – short, intense and leaving a vaguely bitter aftertaste.

By the time he got to her flat, heaving for breath and feeling as if the driving sleet should be turning to steam the moment it touched his skin, he found Donna had mobilised her mother, who greeted him at the front door after buzzing him up.

'Ah, son, you'll catch your death like that,' Irene Blake said, as she ushered Connor into the flat, gesturing up the hall. 'You'll find Donna in the kitchen, son. We only arrived ten minutes ago, got the call that she has to go to work so we've to take Andrew.' Irene rolled her eyes, gave a sigh only a long-suffering and permanently disappointed parent could muster.

Connor knew Donna's mother disapproved of her daughter's career, knew also that she was looking for an ally in him. So he gave her a smile and a noncommittal nod, grateful when the sound of Andrew's laughter burst from behind the living-room door followed by his grandfather's voice, distracting Irene from further conversation.

He made his way to the kitchen, found Donna there, phone clamped to her ear as she hunched over an elaborate coffee machine. She turned and raised a finger as she saw him. One second, the gesture said.

'OK. Text me the address and I'll meet Keith there,' she said.

‘Thanks, Tony. I’ll check in with you later.’ She ended the call, offered Connor a smile. ‘Sorry, got the call from the desk just after you texted. Heading for Edinburgh now. Seems there’s been another murder.’

Connor kept his expression neutral. ‘What, you mean like the one at Victoria Quay yesterday? The one you said was linked to Mark?’

Something flashed in Donna’s eyes at the mention of the name, vanishing like the steam that rose from the cup she offered Connor. ‘Maybe. Patchy details at the moment. I’ve spoken to a pal in the police. All they could tell me was Ford was there and that it’s a bad one.’

‘Where?’ Connor asked, already making a mental note to call Ford. Two killings in two days in Edinburgh. Home of Dessie Banks. No coincidence, surely.

‘Centre of town, off Lothian Road,’ Donna said. ‘So someone is trying to send a message.’

Connor blinked away the sudden image of the letter sent to Duncan MacKenzie and the message it held. A message he was trying desperately to understand.

‘So, you said there was something about the murder at Victoria Quay that linked to Mark, something you wanted to talk to me about?’

‘Hmm?’ Donna said, distracted. Connor felt a wisp of irritation coil through him. This was pointless. Mark and whatever she had found were yesterday’s news. Now Donna had the scent of something fresh and, like a hunter, she was focused on tracking down today’s prey. Yesterday might as well have been a lifetime ago.

‘Oh, yeah, sorry,’ she said at last, pushing a folder that lay on the breakfast bar towards him. ‘A contact in the police said Ford was sniffing around this story in relation to Tim Montgomery, the guy who was found dead in Leith yesterday.’

Connor flipped open the file, skimmed the printout of the *Westie*’s front page on the suicide of Cameron Donald. Was this what Ford wasn’t telling him last night? At first glance, there was no link to Montgomery, Operation Calderwood, the message that had been sent to MacKenzie or left with Montgomery’s body. So what did it mean?

Too many questions. Not enough answers.

Donna flashed an apologetic smile. ‘Look, Connor, I know I asked you round here, but I really have to go. Need to get a report sorted and on-air ASAP.'

Connor smiled, drained his coffee. 'No bother,' he said. 'Got plenty to do myself. You OK if I keep this?' He gestured to the printout.

'Be my guest,' Donna replied. 'And let's catch up later, yeah? I want to know about Jen and hear what you think about all this.'

Connor nodded agreement. He thought that all roads seemed to be leading to Edinburgh. The question was, why?

CHAPTER 22

Questions. All he had were questions.

Everything had seemed to happen at once – an explosion of chaos in a room that had been as still and expectant as a church waiting for a funeral procession to arrive. Alarms began to scream, drowning out the hateful hiss and spit of the ventilator. Then Jen had started to buck and thrash in the bed, clawing for the tube they had put down her throat and making a guttural, terrified gagging noise that would haunt him for the rest of his days. He had made one stuttering step forward, but a nurse had grabbed him, pushed him aside more effectively than many so-called hard men he had known. He had watched them work as Jen awoke, the questions piling up in his mind as they did.

Would she be OK? Could she walk? Was she brain-damaged? And, as he saw one bloodshot, tear-rimmed eye swivel towards him, the final question. The one that demanded an answer above all others. The one he used to blot out his rage, his pain and his fear.

Who was he going to make pay for this?

He sat outside Jen's room now, having allowed the nurses to usher him out gently so they could work. Elbows on knees, head down, he tried to think, use the questions that were churning through his mind to anchor him to the spot, to keep him out of Jen's room, and quell the hysteria that seemed to be swelling in him, like a rising scream.

Who had done this?

The simple answer was Paulie. From what Fraser had told him, it was the most obvious solution. The car that had hit Jen was registered in his name, had been found at his home. And there had been no word from Paulie since the night the letter had arrived. The temptation to believe the narrative, to settle his rage on Paulie and scorch the earth to find him was compelling, especially with the revelation that Dessie Banks was looking for him as well. But Duncan found it impossible to believe. It was too neat. Paulie would die for Jen. After Hannah had died, he had effectively helped Duncan raise her. So why would he suddenly turn on her? It was as implausible as the notion that Paulie would rat out Dessie Banks. And, besides, what did he really know?

No, something else was going on here. Something linked to the death of a man's daughter. Duncan could think of only one thing. But it was impossible – the situation had been dealt with years ago: he and Paulie had seen to it as a duty and a matter of honour. The only other man who knew what had happened that night a lifetime ago was somewhere else in this hospital, still trapped by the same hissing monster Jen had just fought her way free from, breathing his life away in mechanical precision.

So . . . who?

He heard a door squeal open. Looked up into the eyes of the nurse who had pushed him aside so easily. Saw the same cool professionalism now, expression carefully neutral as she gestured to him to come and get an answer to one of his questions.

Problem was, Duncan wasn't sure he wanted it.

CHAPTER 23

Ford sat at his desk, the pathologist's report on the Lothian Road victim forgotten in front of him. It didn't hold any real surprises – the victim's jaw had been mostly pulped by a blow from a sharp, bladed instrument, which Dr Tennant had postulated was most probably an axe. Cause of death had been exsanguination from the wounds to the head and, as Ford had guessed, the victim had been left holding his own tongue.

'Gruesome, but fairly routine,' Walter Tennant had told Ford when he handed over the report. Ford had been forced to agree. To a point. What was not routine was the identity of the victim, which had been discovered when the body was searched and a wallet found in a jacket pocket. A double-check of the fingerprints had confirmed that the wallet did indeed belong to the man who had lost most of the lower half of his face, but Ford hadn't needed that confirmation to know it was right. After his visit to Connor Fraser last night, it made perfect sense.

Terry Glenn was known across the Central Belt as a long-term associate of Dessie Banks. With the nickname Terrier Tel, he was famed not only for his lack of stature, but the ferocity of his rage. If someone was foolish enough to cross Banks, Terry would be set on them, usually extracting monies owed, co-operation or silence with a toxic blend of violence, intimidation and a diseased, twisted imagination. Years ago Ford had heard a story about Glenn forcing a pub landlord who had fallen behind on his protection payments to grind a pint glass in a tea-towel then roll the shards around his own mouth. It was one of those urban legends that haunted police stations – never confirmed due to the fact that Glenn had allegedly threatened to cut off the nose of the landlord's wife if he didn't take his medicine like a good boy.

Now Glenn was dead. And Ford had questions buzzing around his head, angry and incessant. Was it a coincidence that one of Dessie Banks's most trusted lieutenants had died a day after Paulie King had gone missing, allegedly after threatening to divulge everything he knew about Banks's empire to the police? Was the fact that Glenn's tongue had been ripped out some kind of message? *This is what happens if you talk?* And then there was the other message: *This is not murder. This is justice.*

Ford dragged his notepad across the desk and grabbed a pen. Wrote down three names, then studied them. What the hell linked Jen MacKenzie, Tim Montgomery and now Terry Glenn? What made what had happened to them 'justice'?

He circled Montgomery's name, hoping Troughton was having more luck than he was. He had left him back in Stirling to give him the freedom to look quietly into the allegations made against Montgomery by Cameron Donald's wife. Allegations of sexual abuse leading to a man taking his own life should have been followed up by officers at the time. If they weren't, Ford wanted to know why. But he wanted to get those answers quietly. Dead-ending a potential line of enquiry, especially in such a high-profile suicide, would have taken power, authority. The last thing Ford needed was the chief constable knowing he was stirring up shit from almost three decades ago.

Not yet.

He pulled out his phone, glanced up at the door, then hit dial. Wrote another name on the notepad as he waited for Connor Fraser to answer his phone. Underlined it three times, then added a question mark at the end. Whatever was going on, Paulie King was at the heart of it.

CHAPTER 24

The ringing of the phone cut through the car, competing for a moment with the snarl of the V8. Connor risked a glance at the console, saw Ford's name. Mashed the decline key with his thumb, then tightened his grip on the steering wheel.

Later. He would deal with Ford later.

The message had arrived just as Connor had got back to the flat. It was as blunt and direct as the wave of panicked relief Connor felt when he read it: *They woke Jen up. Get here. Now.*

Connor had grabbed his keys, jumped into the car. Was almost at the entrance to the hospital when the call from Ford had come in. He made a mental note to call him back once he had seen Jen.

He parked and jumped out of the car. Took off towards the hospital, then stopped, whirled around, eyes strobing across the sleet-swept, dingy grey of the car park. What had he seen? No, not quite seen. Felt. Like a whisper carried on the wind, an echo of something. Something . . .

He shook his head. No time for that now. Turned and sprinted for the hospital.

He was met at the door of the ward by MacKenzie, who looked like he had aged fifteen years overnight. His skin was pallid and slack, grey peppering his stubble. But there was something in his eyes, an almost feverish glittering of hope that at once reassured Connor and terrified him. 'How is she?' he asked.

MacKenzie's face twitched into a smile, then fell serious. 'Awake,' he said, after a moment. 'Came up fighting, clawing to get the breathing tube out of her throat. They're booking her in for tests to see about her back but . . .' MacKenzie gave a shrug, eyes sliding from Connor's. *Don't get your hopes up*, the gesture said.

Connor blinked aside the memory of Jen flying through the air. None of it mattered. Not now. 'Can I see her?' he asked.

'Yeah, she's been asking for you,' MacKenzie said, something unrecognisable in his tone. 'But not long, OK? She's tired and, like I said, the doctors have a lot of work to do.'

Connor nodded understanding, followed MacKenzie into the ward. The last time he had been in this hospital, he had been fighting for his life, protecting a comatose man from his psychopathic son. He felt more terror now than he had then.

MacKenzie guided Connor down the corridor to Jen's room, opened the door for him. 'I'll leave you two alone,' he said. Turned to Connor, his voice growing as cold and hard as his eyes. 'Just take it easy, keep it quick. She's tired.'

Connor nodded. Now wasn't the time to get into a pissing match with MacKenzie.

He walked into the room, saw Jen give him a smile. Framed in the patchwork of bruises that dappled her skin, it was like watching a light flicker on and off as she fought the pain she was feeling when her cheeks pulled tight.

He crossed to the room, took her into a hug. She felt small, fragile, and his stomach lurched as he remembered the feeling of one of her ribs cracking as he fought to save her life. 'Jen, I'm sorry, I . . .'

Her hand was cool on his cheek. 'You've nothing to be sorry for,' she said, her voice a raspy whisper from the breathing tube that had been rammed down her throat. 'Dad told me what happened, that you probably saved my life.'

Connor's face reddened. 'What do you remember?'

Jen's eyes closed just long enough for Connor to regret the question. The last thing she needed was to be reminded of what had happened. Stupid, Connor, he thought. Stupid.

'Not a lot,' she said. 'I remember seeing you running towards me, then . . .' She closed her eyes again, as though trying to block out the memory. Connor saw a tear roll down her cheek, glistening against the bruises.

'Look, it doesn't matter,' he said, taking her hand, conscious of the tubes that snaked into the back of it. 'The important thing is you're here and awake. As for the rest of it . . .' He wasn't sure what to say. Watched as Jen's mouth tried to form words, failed. She smiled again, gave his hand a weak squeeze.

'It'll be OK,' she said. 'Doctors are coming to look at me soon, see how bad things are. But I know who I am and where I am, so that's something.' She smiled again, and Connor felt a twist of unease in his guts as he recognised Duncan MacKenzie in that smile. Cold. Empty. False.

He sat with her for a few more minutes, swapped inanities until he saw the weariness settle on her. Kissed her cheek and promised to visit again as soon as possible, then snuck out of the room. Found MacKenzie waiting for him.

'I want the bastard who did this,' he said.

'So do I,' Connor replied. 'And we need to talk about that. The name Tim Montgomery mean anything to you?'

'No, should it?' MacKenzie replied, his face blank and expressionless.

'Maybe,' Connor said. 'He was found in . . .'

MacKenzie raised a hand, impatience in his eyes as he looked over Connor's shoulder. 'Not now. I need to make sure Jen is OK. Doctors are seeing her in an hour. Depending on how that goes, we can catch up after that. You can tell me about this Montgomery prick then.'

Connor nodded agreement. He had other leads to follow and, now that he had seen Jen, the determination to do it. 'Fine. Call me when you're free,' he said, then headed for the door.

***

MacKenzie opened the door to Jen's room slowly, watching the sliver of light from the corridor sliding across the floor. She was propped up in bed, head turned to the window. He could see tears on her cheek, glistening in the pitiless, meagre light of the day.

'Did you tell him?' she said, her voice a cruel, misshapen caricature of her usual upbeat tone.

'Of course not,' he replied, anger and sorrow making his voice more clipped than he'd intended. He was more rattled than he would have liked. 'That's down to you.'

Jen nodded, jaw setting tight as though she was preparing for a blow. 'Yeah,' she whispered. 'It's all down to me now.'

CHAPTER 25

It didn't take long to spot the car tailing him. And, to be honest, Connor would have been angry with himself if it had. It wasn't as if they were being subtle about it – using the same high-end Range Rover he'd seen at Paulie's place the previous day and only staying one car behind him. Subtlety obviously wasn't in his pursuers' game plan.

Which, now he had seen Jen, was just fine with Connor.

He stayed on the A9, the road cutting through farmland and small towns as it made its way back towards Stirling. Spotted a layby and hit the accelerator, putting some distance between him and the car behind. Pulled in, grabbed the gun from its holster under his seat, then watched his rear-view mirror. He'd made his move, given those tailing him a choice. They could drive by, pretend they hadn't been following him in the first place, or they could take a more proactive approach and pull in behind him. If Mo was in the car, Connor guessed it would be the latter choice. Mo didn't strike him as a man who would let a broken nose go unanswered.

As expected, the Range Rover indicated and slid in behind Connor's car. He felt a cold thrill of adrenalin as he watched the car come to a halt, its hazard lights flicking on almost as soon as it did. Warning? Or signal of truce?

The driver's door swung open, Connor smiling despite himself as Mo emerged into a morning that looked barely more sullen than he did. He held up his hands as he moved towards Connor's window, waved them. Fine: so Mo wasn't carrying a weapon. Didn't mean whoever else was in the Range Rover wasn't. Connor waited.

He slid his window down when Mo tapped on it, letting in a blast of wind almost as icy as the glare Mo was giving him. His eyes glittered from sockets cushioned by black swellings, the bruising arching over a nose now sitting at an angle that was painful to look at.

'Morning, Mo,' Connor said, making no attempt to hide the gun in his lap. 'That looks nasty. How's Ewan? Bet he's not going to be running any marathons any time soon.'

Mo's entire face seemed to clench. Connor saw a knot of muscle flutter in his jaw, as though he was biting down on whatever he really wanted to say and found the words unpalatable.

'Here in peace,' he hissed, nodding back towards the Range Rover. 'Boss has an offer to make you.'

'Boss?' Connor blinked up at Mo. 'You mean Dessie Banks has ventured across the Forth? For me? I'm touched.'

'Course not, you daft fuck,' Mo said, the mask of enforced civility slipping. 'I'm going to reach into my pocket for a phone, OK? Don't get any fucking ideas with that cannon of yours.'

Connor nodded, curled his finger around the trigger. Saw Mo had spotted the subtle move. Message sent. 'Go on, then.'

Mo produced a phone, fingers dancing on the screen for a moment, then clamping it to his ear. 'Yes, boss, got him now. Hold on.' He offered the phone to Connor.

'Hello?'

'Connor Fraser?' The voice was flat and empty, no emotion. It was, Connor thought briefly, like one of those computerised junk calls telling you about a potential claim for an accident you were recently involved in.

'Speaking.'

'My name is Dessie Banks. I believe you know who I am. I want to discuss a business proposal with you.'

'Hey, it's your phone bill,' Connor said, eyes flicking between Mo and the rear-view mirror. All this for one phone call? Really?

'I believe you're looking for Paulie King in relation to what happened to Duncan MacKenzie's wee girl yesterday.'

'Let's just say I'd love to have a chat with him,' Connor said.

A laugh like stone being dragged across a cheese grater barked down the line. 'As would I, Mr Fraser. As I believe Mo told you, I am keen to discuss certain matters with Paulie myself.'

'Like him squealing to the police about you, yeah?' Connor said. 'Sorry, Mr Banks, but that sounds unlikely to me. Hardly in keeping with the Paulie I know.'

A soft smacking noise down the line, followed by a deep inhalation of breath. So Dessie was a smoker. 'I thought so too, Mr Fraser, but I have proof of Paulie's intentions. So I have a proposal for you.'

Connor ignored the line. 'Proof? What proof? And why would Paulie go to the police about you anyway?'

'You can ask that when you find him, Mr Fraser. And that is my proposal. Find him, bring him to me at least breathing, and I will not only pay you a hundred grand, but I will let you have what is left of Paulie when I have finished with him. You can extract whatever justice you want for the harming of Jennifer MacKenzie after that.'

Justice? The word jumped out at Connor. Coincidence? Or something more?

He bit back the questions he had, heard the phone ping, a notification that a text had arrived.

'I've just sent you the proof I referred to, Mr Fraser. Have you seen it?'

'Hold on,' Connor said, pulling the phone from his ear and opening the message. It was a picture of Paulie standing in what looked like a dockyard, a woman in front of him, auburn hair trailing out behind her in the wind.

'Who's that?' Connor asked, already knowing part of the answer. The way the woman was standing told him.

'Her name is Detective Sergeant Susie Drummond, Mr Fraser,' Banks replied, his voice warmed now by disgust. 'My understanding is she has been having several long chats with Paulie over the last month or so. I am told that Paulie is ready to give her some, ah, embarrassing information about my business.'

'OK, but even if that's true, why do you need me?' Connor asked.

Banks sighed down the line, as though Connor's stupidity was an annoyance to him. 'Obviously, I cannot be seen to be actively looking for Paulie, given DS Drummond's involvement. But you are an unknown in Edinburgh, Mr Fraser, so can act with an impunity I cannot. I have resources to help you. You can find Paulie. We can help each other. I will pay you handsomely, and may even forgive your trespass against my men. So, what do you say?'

Connor glanced out of the car window, smiled up at Mo. Felt his finger tighten on the trigger slightly. It made sense now. If you were going to offer to buy a man's life, the least you would want for that conversation was a phone you controlled and plausible deniability of ever meeting the man you were trying to employ.

'Tell me what you know,' he said.

CHAPTER 26

The weather was doing nothing to improve Ford's view of Mosshead. He'd never liked the place. Situated between Edinburgh and Glasgow, it was one of several new towns that could trace its origins back to just after the Second World War, when Germany had bombed Glasgow, and the laying of the M8 through vast tracts of the old city created a demand for some safe, affordable housing and creative thinking about how to provide it. To Ford, whoever had done the thinking around Mosshead was either drunk, mad or both. The town was a tangle of neighbourhoods connected by roads and roundabouts designed to confound anyone without an intimate knowledge of the area or state-of-the-art satnav, while the brutalist architecture made him think someone had given a child a Lego set made of concrete and told them to design the town.

He found the house he was looking for in the Blackmoor area, on a new-build estate that looked anonymously restrained compared to the nightmare of blunt concrete and grey harled walls Ford had just driven through. He pulled up at the kerb, double-checked his satnav with the address in the folder on his passenger seat. When Troughton had given him the background he had requested on Cameron Donald's suicide, this address had been in the file as the home of Donald's estranged wife, Victoria. According to what Troughton had been able to discover, she had taken the decision to move from the Borders to North Lanarkshire not long after Donald had taken his own life. It made sense to Ford. The last thing any parent would want was to raise their children in the shadow of the place their father had decided to die.

He flicked through the file, irritated again by what it didn't tell him. Troughton had done his usually thorough job, picking through the incident reports from the time of Donald's death, looking for anything that indicated an action had been ordered to look into Tim Montgomery after Victoria Donald's allegations that he had abused her husband, which had ultimately driven him to take his own life. But there was nothing apart from one solitary statement, which had been typed up, signed by Mrs Donald and countersigned by an officer with an illegible scrawl and a bad habit of not printing their name below that signature. Ford had smiled bitterly at that: it was an old copper's trick. Sign the statement with the equivalent of an X, don't put your full name on it, then file the report away to die. He had seen it happen too often in the past when officers wanted to make facts fit a case and inconvenient truths vanish.

The question was, what were the truths about Tim Montgomery? And who wanted them to disappear?

Satisfied that DS Troughton and the Edinburgh detective he had been assigned, Drummond, were both checking into the last movements of Terry Glenn before he had ended up mutilated and dumped on Lothian Road, Ford had got moving, glad to be out of Edinburgh. There was something about the city that unnerved and irritated him, as if it was playing a tune in the wrong key or speaking in a dialect he couldn't understand. Ford had never bought into the old East versus West, Glasgow versus Edinburgh mentality, but a few days of working in the east coast's capital had convinced him that living on neutral ground in Bridge of Allan was the right place to be.

He forced himself to focus on the task at hand, gathered his notes and put them back into the folder as he looked up the path that led to Victoria Donald's home. He had phoned ahead to arrange the meeting, could see she had made the place ready by switching on the porch light, which gave off a meagre, jaundiced glow that did nothing to dispel the chill gloom of the day. Ford had heard on the radio the weather forecasters predict snow and he wished it would hurry up and arrive. At least snow was clean, fresh. The slushy sleet that was spattering his windscreen now just made the world murky.

And cold.

He pulled his jacket tight, dashed for the front door and rang the bell. Heard footsteps approaching at the sound, felt a waft of warmth wash over him as the door swung open.

'Mrs Donald?' he asked, as he raised his warrant card. 'I'm DCI Malcolm Ford. We spoke on the phone earlier?'

She was a small, compact woman with dark eyes that seemed too large to be contained by the glasses she wore. Her skin was taut and pink, as though she had just been exercising, and Ford could see a thin bead of sweat on her brow. 'Ah, yes,' she said, voice matter-of-fact. 'Well, you'd better come away in. I've had the kettle on.'

Ford smiled, nodded his thanks and followed her into the house. It was like stepping into a sauna, the heat an almost physical presence that seemed to crowd in on him.

'Take your jacket, son?' Victoria asked.

'Yes, please,' Ford said, handing it over. She hung it over the banister of a flight of stairs opposite the front door.

'Come on, then,' she said.

He followed her along a short, narrow hallway to a large living room that was dominated by a huge sofa and the most elaborate armchair Ford had ever seen. It was a leather recliner mounted on a small stand, a cable connecting the left arm to what looked like a remote control.

'You take a seat, I'll get the tea,' Victoria Donald said, her voice the same toneless drone Ford had heard on the phone. He watched her shuffle out of the room, then cast his gaze around. Photos of her with two young men were dotted across the walls, interspersed with others of smiling children and women. Just another family, their history told in pictures, he thought.

All that was missing was any of the father, Cameron Donald.

He heard the soft clatter of china, turned to see Victoria re-enter the room carrying a tray cluttered with teapot, cups and biscuits.

'Sit down, sit down,' she said, vague impatience colouring her voice as she laid the tray on a coffee table in front of the throne-like armchair.

Ford did as he was told, perching on the oversized couch as Victoria eased herself into her recliner, hissing out her breath and wincing as she did so.

'Sorry,' she said, as she found a comfortable position. 'Arthritis, you see. The weather doesn't help with it.'

Ford nodded understanding. It explained why the heating was at full blast, as though she was trying to wrap a protective blanket around her body. He felt the urge to loosen his tie, fought it.

Victoria Donald took Ford's instruction on how he liked his tea, poured, then settled back in her seat, steam from her own cup crawling up her glasses. 'So, you wanted to talk to me about Cameron?' she said after a moment. 'Can't say I'm all that surprised after the news the other day.'

Ford nodded. Down to business. 'Yes, Mrs Donald. I found your statement to officers about Tim Montgomery, and the allegations you made that he abused your husband when he played for the junior football team in Galashiels. I wondered if you could tell me some more about that.'

'They weren't allegations, son,' she said, voice hardening. 'Cammy told me all about it. How that bastard would check on him in the showers, make sure those leg muscles weren't too knotted after practice by giving them "special sports rubs". He took Cammy aside for "special coaching", told him he had talent. He coached him, all right. On how to suck his cock or wank him off. Bastard. I hope he rots in hell.'

Ford took a sip of tea, playing for time as he gathered his thoughts. 'So why wasn't this reported at the time of the abuse? Why was nothing said before Cameron died?'

'You ever been to a small town in the Borders, son? It's different down there. The community is everything. And remember, this was more than forty years ago, the eighties, when it seemed like a child abuser was on the TV every other bloody day. Who knows? Cammy might have said something to his folks, it might have all been dealt with quietly. He only told me about it when James and Laurence came along. He'd buried it, tried to get on with his life, but something about having the boys brought it all back to the surface. It tortured him, and I think he was afraid history would repeat itself. It was why he moved out.'

Ford said nothing, stared into his cup. He knew where Victoria was going with this, didn't want to lead her there.

'Cammy would never have hurt the boys. Never. But I couldn't get him to see that. I think he took his own life to protect them. And when he did, I knew Montgomery had to pay.'

This is not murder. This is justice, Ford thought suddenly.

'So you went to the police after Cammy, ah, took his own life?' he asked. 'What happened, then?'

'Fuck-all,' Victoria said bluntly, the profanity made shocking by her mundane, resigned tone. 'I called the local station, made an appointment to see one of the officers. Was told I'd have to wait as someone from CID would have to come down from Glasgow to take the statement. Went in a couple of days later and told them what I knew. Then nothing.' She cleared her throat, looked at Ford, accusation in her eyes. 'I could have done more – maybe should have gone to the papers, forced you lot to take more notice. But I was a single mum with two boys who had just lost their dad. Life got away from me. So Montgomery went free. Until now.'

'Until now,' Ford agreed. 'Did you ever share any of this with your sons? Tell them what Cameron told you?'

'No, I bloody well did not,' Victoria replied. 'And don't you be thinking that my James or Laurence had anything to do with what happened to that bastard. They're good boys, not touched by any of this. The only person I ever told was that detective I spoke to in Galashiels.'

Ford jotted a note in his pad to look up James and Laurence Donald. Just in case. 'I don't suppose you remember what the name of that detective was?' he asked.

'Course I do,' Victoria replied, her voice taking on a vaguely satisfied tone now. 'It's my bones that are rotting, son, not my brain. His name was Dennis Morgan. Detective Inspector Dennis Morgan.'

CHAPTER 27

Good to his word, MacKenzie called Connor and arranged to meet him at Jen's flat in the Woodlands area of Stirling. 'She asked me to get her some things,' he said, the words sounding as though they were sticking in his throat. 'So meet me there.'

It didn't take Connor long to get to the flat – it was less than a mile from his place, and he was already halfway there after his layby chat with Dessie Banks. He parked up, saw no sign of MacKenzie's car. Thought about using the key he had and letting himself in, decided against it. Doing so would cross some undefined line in his head, encroach on territory that MacKenzie had rightfully claimed as Jen's father. Connor knew his attitude was out of date and vaguely ridiculous, but it was a line he would not cross. Not now. Not when he needed Duncan MacKenzie onside.

The tale Banks had told Connor had been brief – and bitter. Paulie had been acting as a go-between for Banks and MacKenzie Haulage as they worked out a supply route for certain items that might be 'frowned upon by the authorities'. While Banks refused to tell Connor what these items were, he did reveal that they were being delivered to MacKenzie Haulage, then loaded onto trucks and distributed around the country from there. It made a certain sense to Connor – MacKenzie had the distribution network, drivers who knew enough to stay quiet and Paulie as a general to oversee the whole operation. Plus, it bought him influence with one of Scotland's biggest gangsters, leverage that might come in useful if he ever got involved in more lucrative, less legal transport opportunities presented by Britain's departure from the European Union.

But what, Connor mused, had happened? What did all this have to do with Operation Calderwood, and what had driven Paulie to a meeting with a police detective? Connor made a note to check in with Ford about DS Susie Drummond. He had been tempted to get Robbie to run a background check on her, decided against it. He didn't know what was going on, yet, but he had a feeling that Sentinel shouldn't be anywhere near it.

That didn't mean he couldn't invite someone else to the party, though.

He was roused from his thoughts by the sound of another car arriving; MacKenzie flicking his hand up in a greeting as he parked. Connor took a deep breath, got out of his car, studied MacKenzie as the man emerged from his own. If anything, he looked worse than he had at the hospital, the exhaustion seeming to radiate from him.

'What did the doctors say?' Connor asked. It was too cold for small-talk, and he had no patience for it anyway.

'They're still working on her,' MacKenzie replied, as he rasped a hand across his chin. 'The good news is she's lucid and aware, can move her head and her arms. But . . .' He sighed, the rest of the sentence carried away in the plume of his breath.

Connor felt a twist of cold that was nothing to do with the sleet. 'But what?' he forced himself to ask.

'But . . .' MacKenzie sighed again, impotent anger flashing across his face, making him look somehow older yet more alive at the same time '. . . but they're not ruling out spinal damage, and there are other injuries they're worried about.'

'Other injuries? What—'

MacKenzie held up a hand. 'We'll know more later,' he said, as he made a show of rummaging in his pocket and producing a key. 'Let's get out of this fucking weather and find the stuff for Jen. We can talk while we work.'

They made their way up to the flat in silence, Connor remembering the first time he had met MacKenzie. It had been in this very hallway, MacKenzie stepping out of Jen's flat to size up the man who was daring to call on his daughter. He had been worried about Jen getting hurt, seen his world threaten her before. And now here they were.

Connor stepped into the flat, felt something like vertigo surge over him as he remembered the last time he was here. Just over a week ago, after Jen had finished late at the gym and he'd timed a workout to finish at the same time she did. They had picked up takeaway on the way back, eaten and then . . .

He shook the thought away. Not now. Saw MacKenzie standing in the middle of the room, a man adrift in his own thoughts. 'Duncan, we need to. . .'

MacKenzie gave a start, as though he was an old car on which the key had just been turned. 'Yeah, yeah,' he said, reaching for the remote on the coffee table and flicking on the TV. 'Too fucking quiet in here. Need something on in the background,' he muttered to himself.

Connor watched as the TV flared into life, a familiar face filling the screen. Donna Blake, hair dragged across her face by the wind, police officers buzzing around behind her, SOCO suits standing out bone white against the grey apathy of the day. Clearly, she'd made it to the crime scene she was talking about to Connor earlier that morning. It felt like another lifetime.

'While police have yet to confirm an identity, sources close to the investigation have told me that the victim is a figure known to the police here in Edinburgh. It's also been suggested that officers are linking this murder to the body found yesterday at the Scottish Government building less than five miles from this spot.'

Connor stared at the TV screen as it cut from a shot of Donna to a wide view of the plaza on Lothian Road. He knew the area well, had trained clients in the gym at that hotel before he had started work with Sentinel Securities. But it wasn't that which drew his attention. It was the officer he had seen on the left of the screen. Tall, lithe, standing talking to another officer, auburn hair trailing like streamers behind her, just like it had in the other picture he had seen of her less than an hour ago.

'Susie Drummond,' Connor said to himself.

'Who?' Duncan asked, head swivelling from the TV to Connor.

'Name not familiar to you?' Connor asked, even as he felt the questions begin to pile up in his mind. 'Should be. I saw a picture of her with Paulie earlier on. Dessie Banks showed it to me.'

'Dessie Banks?' Duncan blinked as if the name had been hurled at him, then snapped his head back to the TV. 'Haud on. Edinburgh. Known to the police. One of Dessie's men? What the fuck . . .?'

'Slow down,' Connor said, the pile-up in his head threatening to drown rational thought. He took a breath, forced himself to order his racing mind. Since Jen had been hurt, he'd been breaking his golden rule and reacting to the situation instead of evaluating, then taking proactive action. All he had to show for it was two badly injured men and a lot of unanswered questions.

Time to change that.

'We'll get to this,' he gestured to the TV, 'in a moment. But, first, I need to start at the beginning. I need you to think. Did the name I gave you earlier, Tim Montgomery, mean anything to you?'

MacKenzie blinked. Shrugged. 'Not really,' he said, defeat heavy in his voice. 'I mean, I know he's the guy they found in that government building yesterday but, before that, I'd never heard the name. Why?'

'One step at a time,' Connor said, the image of the note rising in his mind. *This is not murder. This is justice.* With the TV seeming to urge him on, he wanted to ask about MacKenzie's dealings with Dessie Banks and what they were planning to ship around the country. Forced himself to stop. Be patient. Try to be logical, build the picture slowly.

'Next question,' he said. 'About twenty-five years ago, you and Paulie were interviewed as part of an investigation into a series of child abductions and murders in Central Scotland. The investigation was called Operation Calderwood. Do you remember that?'

Something flitted across MacKenzie's face, a twitch Connor could almost dismiss as the man's exhaustion, Almost.

'Course I remember the killings,' he said. 'Every parent in Scotland at the time would. Fuck's sake, Fraser, wee girls were being abducted and killed. After that bastard Robert Black did his killing while driving freight around the country, it was only natural that the police would look at us. Paulie was ops manager at the time, was asked to give details of the drivers and the routes we took, match them up with the girls. I vaguely remember giving a statement, as the employer, about vetting drivers and the like. Nothing found linking the company to those lassies, and the investigation moved on. More than that, I cannae remember. But why the fuck is that important? And what does it have to do with what happened to Jen?'

This is not murder. This is justice.

Connor considered the couch, rejected the idea of sitting down. The last time he had sat on that couch, Jen had been with him. He wasn't going to sit there again until she did.

Instead he started talking, telling MacKenzie about the message left with Tim Montgomery's body, the same message that had been sent to Duncan with the demand to kill Paulie. About how he had asked a colleague to check police records on Paulie and Duncan, and how their statements to Operation Calderwood had come to light. Watched as rage fought with despair in Duncan's eyes as he told him what Dessie Banks had claimed about Paulie, and the meeting with Susie Drummond.

And as he spoke, Connor felt something shift in the corners of his mind, like a massive boulder grinding across the entrance to a cave, letting the vaguest shard of light shine through, giving him a hint at the shape he was trying to see, the monster he was destined to face.

CHAPTER 28

After checking in with Drummond that there had been no significant breakthroughs in tracing the last movements of Terry Glenn, Ford had left Mosshead and headed north for Stirling. He was breaking protocol by not returning to Edinburgh, found he didn't care.

One more thing to blame Dennis Morgan for.

Morgan had been a legend on the police force when Ford was learning the ropes, an old-school detective who had taken on the big drug barons of the west coast and won. He was a copper's copper, dedicated, intelligent, ruthless. Ford had first met him when he was involved in an investigation into the murder of two students from Stirling University - murders for which, he later discovered, he had helped Morgan frame a petty criminal while the real murderer went free. This revelation had come at a high cost: Ford's threat to quit Police Scotland and Morgan's permanent relocation to an ICU bed, where a machine breathed for him and he relived whatever dreams a man without a conscience could experience.

Ford hoped at least some of those dreams became nightmares.

The statement Victoria Donald had given, alleging Tim Montgomery was a child abuser, was, unsurprisingly, undated. But she recalled making it less than a month after her husband, Cameron, had died, which meant it was given at least six months after Ford and Morgan had watched as a false confession was beaten out of Dean Barrett, who was dealing drugs on the Stirling University campus.

Ford remembered Barrett, thin and pale and terrified, tied to a chair, tears mingling with blood and snot, Paulie King looming over him, the hard, flat sound of flesh being hit by wood filling the warehouse they were in.

A warehouse owned by Duncan MacKenzie.

Ford pulled off the motorway, considered heading for the university to surprise Mary with the offer of lunch. Decided against the idea – they had been married long enough for her to read his moods as easily as she read newspaper headlines and, right now, Ford felt nothing but frustration and anger. She would try to help him, coax him into talking, which would only widen the gulf between them. After all, what could he tell her? 'Sorry, love, the copper who trained me to be a detective was bent, fitted one kid up for murder and now it looks like he made an allegation of sex abuse against a civil servant disappear?' Hardly. But he needed to talk to someone, share what he knew, try to get perspective as he planned his next move.

Yet even as he dialled Connor Fraser's number, a familiar thought whispered to him; comforting, friendly, like an old song that brought with it good memories.

Just quit. Walk away. You've done your bit.

He shook his head, dismissed the thought for the fantasy it was, knew it wasn't really an answer. He had made his decision and stayed with the police. Partly to atone for past sins and partly, he was honest enough to admit to himself, to protect him and Mary from the void their lives would become if he ever went home and never left again.

He focused on the call, willed Fraser to answer. Whatever was going on, Duncan MacKenzie and Paulie King were at the heart of it. With Morgan tainting his history and stuffing his closet full of skeletons, Ford didn't know how he could follow this line of enquiry officially without being compromised himself.

Luckily enough, Connor Fraser didn't have a rule book he needed to follow.

CHAPTER 29

'So who the hell are we looking for here, Doctor Strange?'

Susie blinked at the monitor in front of her, which was filled with the face of DS John Troughton. Given the look on his face, he had just said something clever. Or thought he had. 'Excuse me?' Susie said.

'You know. Doctor Strange. Master of the Mystic Arts. Sorcerer Supreme. Our murderer is either him or Houdini. Must be some kind of bloody magician to dump two bodies the way he has and then disappear without a trace.'

Susie let Troughton's assumption that the killer was a man slide, focused on the job in hand. It had been her idea to have a virtual conference call with Troughton to compare notes and brainstorm where they were on the cases. She hadn't particularly wanted to do it but, with Ford taking himself off God knew where to follow 'different lines of enquiry' and Troughton stuck in Stirling on some top-secret mission for his boss, she was the only assigned detective on the ground in Edinburgh.

And she was damned if the investigation was going to drift because Ford couldn't keep his focus.

'Take it there was nothing on the CCTV from Lothian Road?' she asked, trying to get Troughton back on topic. She had questions she wanted to ask him, but first she had to get him talking, one colleague to another.

'Nothing yet, though I've sent the footage over to the specialists for frame-by-frame analysis. From what I can see, the only way the killer could have dumped Glenn was to get into the square from Chuckie Pend, no CCTV covering that, so it's a blind spot.'

Susie chewed her lip. She was beginning to hate the phrase 'blind spot'. It had come up once too often in this investigation already – first at the changing rooms leading to the pool where Tim Montgomery was found, and now at Chuckie Pend, a small, narrow vennel that ran from Morrison Street down into the square in front of the hotel where Glenn's body was found. And then there was the CCTV around the hotel itself. Blank. Maybe the killer was a magician after all.

'And nothing on Glenn's last movements?' she asked, impatience rising as she closed in on the question she wanted to ask.

'Officers are checking on that now and gathering statements,' Troughton said, looking down from the screen to his notes and giving Susie a glimpse of a widening bald patch. 'But it seems Glenn had a routine night. Finished work at the office on Forth Street that Banks uses for his property businesses, headed to the pub. He was last seen in a place called the Mitre at ten p.m., then headed off, walking up the Royal Mile, then down South Bridge towards Newington.'

Susie doodled on her notepad, made a noncommittal grunt of agreement. She knew the route Glenn would have taken well. The Mitre was a pub on the Royal Mile, popular with tourists and locals, its footfall only enhanced by the end of lockdown. It would have been a cold night for a walk through the stone canyon of the Royal Mile, then along South Bridge heading for his flat in Newington, but Glenn would probably have had a few whiskies inside him by then for insulation. Not that they had protected him from what had happened.

'OK, good, let's see if we can get anything from that. In the meantime, there was something else I wanted to discuss with you, John.'

'Go on,' Troughton said, an edge of wariness in his voice.

Understandable, Susie thought. She hadn't really been the most welcoming of colleagues given the circumstances, especially as it hadn't been Troughton's fault. After all, he was only following orders, going where his DCI told him to go, taking over from local officers with more experience of Edinburgh than he had. No, Troughton wasn't the problem. Ford was. What Susie wanted to know was how much of a problem the man really was.

'You pulled together a briefing for DCI Ford on Tim Montgomery, yeah?'

'Yeah,' Troughton replied, in a tone that told Susie she could probably fund a decent holiday from one night playing poker against him. Time to call his hand.

'I saw that. I also saw that one of the items you pulled was an old newspaper article on a suicide down in the Borders years back. Caught my eye as I'm from the Borders myself, started out in Hawick. But I was wondering, what has that got to do with Tim Montgomery or Terry Glenn?'

Susie wasn't expecting to be surprised by Troughton's reaction, but she was. Given what she had seen of her counterpart, she'd expected him to bluff, evade or slope his shoulders. But his reaction forced herself to rethink her plan to fleece him at the poker table any time soon.

'DS Drummond. Susie,' he said, his voice measured, clipped, as though he was giving an update at a case conference. 'DCI Ford asked me to look into background on Tim Montgomery and that was what I did. I'm here in Stirling looking into further leads the boss thinks could be pertinent to the case. DCI Ford has asked me not to discuss this with anyone until I've had a chance to update him, so I can't say any more.'

Susie felt her head bob up and down. So Ford was running his own investigation with Troughton and freezing her out? She felt cold anger roil in her guts. Made sense in one regard – high-profile murders, new turf: only made sense that Ford would use people he trusted to get the results. But that left the clear inference that Susie wasn't to be trusted, that she wasn't rated as a detective. Despite the advent of Me Too and lip service being paid to gender equality, she knew she was still competing on an uneven playing field, but she would be damned if her team captain was going to dig ditches in the pitch for her and set her up to fail. The question was, what was he on to? Donna had promised to call in some favours and dig into the *Westie*'s archives, see if there was anything else to the suicide story Mark had written up. But what could possibly link a suicide from years ago to two brutal murders today?

Troughton seemed to read her thoughts in her hardening gaze. 'Look, Susie, it's not personal,' he said. 'Ford can be a dinosaur in a lot of ways, but he's a bloody good police officer, OK? If he's doing this, it's for a reason. Talk to him. He respects someone who looks him in the eye and tells him how things really are.'

Susie wondered how many times Troughton had stared his boss straight in the eye and told him how things really were. 'Oh, I'll talk to him all right,' she said. 'In the meantime, let's keep digging, see if we can find a conversation stopper with either Montgomery or Glenn. You two are only visitors here, John, but Edinburgh is my home. And two murders on home turf is bad business for everyone.'

CHAPTER 30

Connor had never been much of a drinker. He was no puritan: his maternal grandfather had taught him an appreciation for a good pint of Guinness as well as how to do a hack squat back when Connor was living in Northern Ireland. But the Scottish taste for whisky had never really found a home in him. It was understandable. With his dad's aversion to the stuff, thanks to what it had unleashed in his own father, and Connor's love of heavy training at the gym, it was just something that had never been part of his life.

But now, with the gym off-limits, thanks to what had happened to Jen and the revelations of the last twenty-four hours, he was starting to rethink his life choices.

Malcolm Ford's current demeanour wasn't doing much to help him, either.

He'd picked up the messages from the policeman after leaving MacKenzie at Jen's place, arranged to meet him at his flat. Connor wasn't comfortable with having people in his home: he had bought the place as much for its seclusion as its comforts, but it seemed he had little choice at the moment, especially when Ford told him they needed to talk 'off the record'.

Ford stalked into the flat, dragging the chill of the day with him. Looking at him gave Connor a vague headache – he was like a walking illustration of stress, from the hunched shoulders and clenched jaw to the stiff back and eyes that couldn't seem to take in the room quickly enough.

Connor decided against whisky, started to make coffee instead.

'So what was it you wanted to talk to me about?' he asked as Ford stalked around the room, unwilling to sit down.

'You have any luck with MacKenzie?' Ford replied. Typical police tactic. Answer a question with a question. Dominate the conversation, get it going where you wanted it to. Fine. Connor had too many thoughts buzzing around his mind to take part in any verbal jousting with Ford. So he would let the policeman lead the way.

For the moment.

'Some,' he said, filling the cafetière with boiling water. 'Seems he remembers, vaguely, Operation Calderwood. The name of your first victim, Tim Montgomery, did nothing for him, though. He's heard nothing from Paulie, though it seems he was speaking to one of your lot before he disappeared.'

Ford walked across to the breakfast bar. 'Oh? Who?'

'Some detective sergeant. Susie Drummond? From what I'm told, he was speaking to her in relation to Dessie Banks.'

Ford froze at the mention of the name, the mug of coffee Connor had offered him stopping before his lips. The sight would almost have been comical if not for the look on the detective's face, which was as black as the coffee Connor had just poured.

'Dessie Banks. Fuck,' he muttered, shaking his head slowly.

'What?' Connor said, remembering MacKenzie's words now. *Haud on. Edinburgh. Known to the police. One of Dessie's men? What the fuck . . .?* 'Let me guess. The body you found this morning is connected to Dessie Banks somehow?'

Ford sighed, took a swig of his coffee, his expression telling Connor he should have offered him whisky after all. 'Aye,' he said. 'And there was another message, too. Same as the one that was sent to MacKenzie and left with Montgomery's body. *This is not murder. This is justice.*'

Connor let out a low whistle. 'Is the victim anyone I would know?'

'Huh?' Ford seemed startled from his thoughts. 'Hardly. Guy by the name of Terry Glenn. Was on Banks's payroll as an enforcer and adviser.' He gave a small, bitter laugh. 'Bit like Paulie was for MacKenzie.'

Was? The use of the word caught Connor's attention. The thought hadn't occurred to him. Could Paulie be dead? Had Banks already caught up with him and silenced him, his request for Connor to hunt him down nothing more than smoke and mirrors to provide himself with an alibi? It was possible - but likely? Connor had no love for Paulie. Their first meeting had turned into a fight Connor had goaded Paulie into, yet he knew the man was a force of nature. And the thought of that force gone, taken from the world by the likes of Dessie Banks, just did not compute for Connor.

'I take it you didn't know this DS Drummond was in contact with Paulie?' he asked, keen not to fall into the same trap as Ford and get caught up in his own thoughts. Right now, he needed answers, not theories or musings.

'No, no, I didn't, but I'll have a word with her. She's assigned to me at the moment for the Montgomery case.'

Connor nodded, satisfied. 'So what did you want to see me about? And why did it have to be so hush-hush?'

Ford blinked, and Connor raised his coffee mug to him in a small toast. Interview rule one: let the interviewee think they're in control, but always keep them off-balance. Connor's abrupt change of topic had done just that.

A smile played across Ford's lips and he gestured to one of the seats at the breakfast bar. Connor nodded, watched as the policeman settled into the chair, then seemed to fold himself around his coffee mug. In that instant he looked suddenly old to Connor, a man who had been ground down by a career of confronting violence and death. He knew Ford had considered resigning in the wake of the Colin Sanderson affair last year, wondered now if he regretted his decision to stay in the job. He looked as if he did.

'Remember Dennis Morgan?' Ford asked, eyes not leaving his coffee mug, as though he was unwilling to meet Connor's gaze.

'Christ,' Connor said, 'hard to forget.' The last time he had seen retired Detective Chief Inspector Dennis Morgan, Connor had been fighting for his life while trying to prevent Morgan's son, Michael, from caving his dad's head in with a tyre iron.

'Aye,' Ford said, as though reading Connor's thoughts. 'Look, Connor, what I'm about to tell you . . .'

Connor held up a hand. 'Forget it, sir. This is confidential. Between us.' He wondered what that made them. Partners? Co-conspirators? Ford had failed to report Paulie's disappearance or the link between two murders and what had happened to Jen. For his part, Connor had beaten the crap out of two men, broken into and then searched Paulie's home, discharged an illegal firearm and hidden evidence of a crime by not handing over Paulie's car to the police. The fact that Dennis Morgan was somehow wrapped up in all of this merely underlined that neither of them was overly concerned about how this case would be tried.

They were both interested in a simpler justice than that.

Ford took another sip of his coffee, his eyes finally settling on Connor's. There was resignation in those eyes, anger too. And something else, something Connor had not seen in Malcolm Ford before.

Shame.

'I found a report,' Ford began, 'alleging that Tim Montgomery had abused a kid while he was coaching an amateur football team down in the Borders. The kid ended up taking his own life by diving off a viaduct years later. His wife made a statement to the police naming Montgomery, alleging the abuse and claiming it was what drove her husband, a guy called Cameron Donald, to commit suicide. But the statement got lost. No further action was taken. And guess who the officer responsible was?'

'Dennis Morgan,' Connor said, more to himself than Ford. 'We both know Morgan was bent, but why would he cover up allegations of child abuse? Did he know Montgomery? Favour for a friend? Blackmail?'

Ford shook his head. 'I checked that. Can't find anything obvious that links Dennis to Tim Montgomery, either personally or professionally. I've got my DS, Troughton, going back through the records to double-check, and he's pulling the Operation Calderwood interviews and files as well, but I can't see why Dennis would make Victoria Donald's statement just vanish. I mean, what's in it for him?'

Connor shrugged, felt questions start to crowd in on his thoughts again. 'I don't know,' he admitted. 'But there has to be a reason. Morgan was a bent cop, and a ruthless one with it. If he made that allegation disappear, then it benefited him or someone close to him. I take it there were no other blemishes on Montgomery's record, no other hints of impropriety?'

'No,' Ford said, pushing his cup towards Connor, who turned to the kitchen counter to refill it. 'Nothing. Clean as a whistle. Would have to have been, what with him working at the government. They request security checks on all their staff as a matter of course.'

Something flashed across Connor's mind then, as though the boulder jammed in front of the cave mouth had shifted just slightly again. Something about security checks. Something . . .

He was startled from his thoughts by the ring of the doorbell. Saw Ford tense, smiled even as he felt a wave of relief wash over him – a purer stimulant than the coffee he and Ford were drinking.

He glanced at his watch. 'Relax, sir, should be a friend.' He moved for the door, careful not to let Ford see the blade he palmed from the knife block in the kitchen as he moved. He was expecting a friendly face, but if his caller was unfriendly, Connor would be prepared.

He swung the door open. Smiled. Took the person standing there in an embrace.

'Christ, Connor, you're gonna have to lay off those steroids, man. You near crushed me!'

Connor laughed, walked back into the flat. Saw Ford take in the newcomer in a way only a policeman could. 'DCI Ford, allow me to introduce you to Detective Inspector Simon McCartney of the PSNI. Simon was my partner back in the day.'

'Pleased to meet you, sir,' McCartney said, crossing the room and offering Ford his hand. 'I think we met briefly the last time I was in town. Hopefully be a less painful visit for me this time, eh?'

Connor smiled as he watched Simon work his easy charm on Ford, even as he felt the lie in his old friend's words. Pain was something none of them were going to be able to avoid.

CHAPTER 31

John Troughton was not normally troubled by what others thought of him. He was under no illusions – he knew what other officers' opinions of him were. Conservative with a capital and lower-case *c*, dedicated to procedure and protocol, willing to insert his tongue as far up DCI Malcolm Ford's arse as he deemed necessary to further his own career. He knew he had a reputation for being dour, loyal, a stick-to-the-rulebook copper who would have a long but dull career as he trudged his way through the ranks and up the corporate ladder until he was stopped by his own mediocrity.

Which suited Troughton just fine. He had spent a lifetime being underestimated, his unassuming manner and bland looks a camouflage that he used to help him get to where he wanted and needed to be. The opinions of others had never been part of the game plan.

Until now.

He was in Stirling, at Randolphfield police station, a dull, depressing building covered with pebbledash that looked like acne and small, narrow windows that seemed to squint suspiciously at the day. Normally, the façade of the building didn't bother him. It was just another place to work, another office to access the resources he needed to do his job. But today he felt the presence of other officers bear down on him like an almost physical force, as though they were all looking over his shoulder, judging him.

And it was all Susie Drummond's fault.

He should have expected it. When Ford had told him they were heading to Edinburgh and whom they would be working with, he had looked Drummond up. Her record and some less official gossip told him that she was an officer who had made more than her fair share of mistakes, including one with a married detective chief inspector that had nearly derailed her career, but that she was also a tenacious investigator. She had brought a miscarriage of justice involving a Gulf War veteran to light, caught a murderer and dragged the actions of a corrupt politician into the light of day. It was a score card Troughton was jealous of.

And it was why Drummond's opinion mattered to him.

He had vouched for Ford to her, assured her he was a good copper who was only interested in solving the murders of Tim Montgomery and Terry Glenn. But looking at the files strewn on the desk in front of him, Troughton was forced to question that opinion for the first time.

Ford had contacted him early, told him he was to stay in Stirling to 'pursue background on another potential line of enquiry'. He had then asked him to dig out files on an investigation from almost a quarter of a century ago into three child abductions and killings across Scotland. While he was too young to remember the story personally, it was one of those tales that had seeped into the country's collective unconscious. In the summer of 1997, as Cool Britannia ruled the airwaves and Tony Blair drove a stake into the heart of the Tories, a different monster began to stalk Scotland, a monster that fed on the fears and anxieties of parents by making their worst nightmares real. It first showed itself in Aviemore, in the Highlands, before moving on to Fort William on the west coast and finally Prestonview, a small, utilitarian town in East Lothian. In each of these towns, a child had disappeared, only to turn up dead hundreds of miles away days later, their bodies dumped by the side of the road like so much rubbish. But what, Troughton thought, did that have to do with the murders he and Ford were now investigating, and what had driven Ford to ask him to dig into this in the first place?

He found the answer in witness statements collected as part of Operation Calderwood. Given the huge distances between where the children had been snatched and where their bodies were discovered, a line of enquiry had quickly developed that the killer could be a long-distance driver. Troughton could see the logic of the theory. A decade earlier, a monster called Robert Black had kidnapped, violated and killed five children while working as a cross-country driver. As part of Calderwood, hauliers known to have routes passing through or close to the town were interviewed and vetted. And in those interviews, Troughton found an answer, and a question.

The name wasn't new to him: working in Stirling, every police officer knew the name Duncan MacKenzie and that of his firm, MacKenzie Haulage. Troughton had heard a lot of rumours about the company and the man, rumours that indicated he had been playing a very long, very successful game of cat and mouse with law-enforcement agencies across the country. Rumours that not all of his income came from legal sources.

But how, Troughton wondered, did that connect MacKenzie Haulage to the current killings? The statements he read from MacKenzie and the man who was his operations manager at the time, Paulie King, showed nothing out of the ordinary. Both men had gone out of their way to cooperate with the investigating officers at the time, and a vetting of the drivers employed by MacKenzie Haulage showed nothing untoward. So how did that connect to the murders of Tim Montgomery and Terry Glenn? He thought again of the single report he had found in the files on Tim Montgomery, the allegation of sexual abuse that seemed to dead-end after the victim's wife made a single statement claiming Montgomery was a paedophile. Was that somehow connected with Operation Calderwood? He flicked through the files, felt frustration well up in him, skin prickling as it did when he'd had one too many cups of coffee. None of the three victims in 1997 had been sexually assaulted: just grabbed, murdered then dumped.

So what connected them? What was Ford looking for? Troughton heard his own words to DS Drummond again – 'He's a good copper, I swear.' Wondered if that was a lie, if the boss had finally hit a brick wall.

He sighed, laid out the case files in front of him. Three children, all taken from three different locations, one in the Highlands, one on the west coast, one in . . .

. . . in . . .

Troughton lunged forward suddenly, grabbing for the file marked Tracy Westerly. Scanned it, felt his eyes start to throb in time with his pulse as he read. Then he turned to his computer, felt seconds crawl by as he punched in his password with numb fingers and navigated his way to Google Maps. Started dropping virtual pins, eyes darting between the files on his desk and the screen.

He studied the last pin he had dropped – Tracy Westerly. Nine years old. Went missing from Prestonview in East Lothian on 22 July 1997. Troughton knew the place: it was a small town, all naked brick and black slate roofs – a hard place that still bore the scars of its mining heritage. He grabbed for the copy of the news report he had printed for Ford, the report that detailed the death of Cameron Donald. Studied it again, eyes lingering on the picture of the viaduct that loomed from the front page, a depiction of doom rendered in stone and steel.

He took a moment, followed the chain of thought in his head, testing his logic. Found it sound, no weak links. Nodded to himself, then reached for the phone. He might not have found the answer for Ford, but he was sure he had found a big piece of the puzzle.

The question was, how did it all fit together?

CHAPTER 32

Susie had never been big on surprises. She hated things being sprung on her, an aversion bred into her by a career in the police, which had taught her that surprises were rarely pleasant, and more than likely to cause her trouble.

Case in point: the call she had just received from DCI Malcolm Ford.

After her conversation with Troughton, Susie was determined to confront Ford about the case, find out what he was hiding and what he had Troughton working on. She knew he was back in Stirling, whatever lead he was following conveniently putting him on a path home. She had decided to call him, demand a meeting, got as far as getting her phone in her hand before it went, Ford's name on the caller ID.

'Sir?' she answered, cursing herself. She should have expected this. Troughton would have played the obedient lapdog, probably called Ford as soon as he hung up on Susie. She made a mental note to take that up with Troughton later.

'Drummond,' Ford replied, his voice tight, formal. The tone of voice that heralded a bollocking, she thought. Fine. She had a few choice words to air herself.

'Look, first, I want to apologise to you. This investigation has taken a few left turns, some of which are somewhat, ah, close to home for me. I've read your record, know you're a good copper, you deserve better.'

Susie opened her mouth, closed it. Cleared her throat, tried to play for time. Surprises. They were never a good thing. 'Thank you, sir,' she heard herself say, wincing at the banality of the words. What the hell was going on?

'Good,' Ford said, voice gruff as he swatted away her gratitude. 'All that said, I need to ask you something, Drummond. It's against protocol and procedure, and while I know that's not always been your biggest concern, I need you to understand that this is a request, not an order. Are we clear?'

Not always been your biggest concern, she thought. Shit. Just what type of copper did Ford think she was? Sloppy? A rule-breaker? What? Was he looking for a detective . . . or an accomplice?

'Absolutely, sir,' she said, not sure she wanted to hear what was coming next.

'Good. In that case, Susie, I want you to get across to Stirling. I've arranged for you to meet with someone to discuss your conversations with one Paulie King. I can't go into it at the moment, but this might have material value to the investigations of both the Montgomery and Glenn murders, OK?'

Susie bit down on the expletive that was crawling up her throat, carried on a tide of adrenalised panic. Paulie? How the hell did Ford know she had been meeting Paulie? And if he knew about that, how much did he know about the rest of it? *Not always your biggest concern*, she thought.

'OK,' she said slowly, trying to think. 'Who is this person you want me to meet? And how is he connected to the case?'

'His name is Connor Fraser. He's a security consultant, used to be one of us. How he fits into the case, well, I'm hoping that's something we can ascertain after you've met with him.'

'Where am I meant to be meeting him, sir? Randolphfield?'

A crackle of static on the line, the sound of a hand being placed over the phone. Muffled voices, Ford and another man. She couldn't make out what they were saying, but it was enough to tell her that Ford was already with this Fraser character, whoever he was. Which raised the question, why did Ford want her to interview a person of interest he was already with?

'How quickly can you get over here?' Ford asked after a moment.

Susie glanced up at the clock on the wall, calculated. 'Say two hours, sir? I've got paperwork to file on the Glenn post-mortem, and actions to assign, but then I can get moving. I can book an interview room at Randolphfield.'

'That won't be necessary,' Ford replied, voice a patchwork of wariness and impatience. 'There's a café in the centre of town, on Bow Street. I'll text you the postcode so you can satnav it. You can meet Fraser there.'

'Sorry, what?' she asked, before she could bite back the words. Her DCI was asking her to talk to a person of interest who could have vital information relating to two murders – and he was asking her to do so not in a police interview room, but in a cosy café in the centre of Stirling? What the hell was going on?

A sigh down the line, all weariness and frustration. 'Drummond, just do it, please. I'll arrange to meet you later on, explain as much as I can, but for now, just get yourself to Stirling.'

'OK, sir,' Susie said, knowing it was pointless to argue. She could, of course, refuse, but then what? Sit filing paperwork, hoping some random fact would give them a clue as to what the hell was going on? Or take the chance, follow Ford's lead and see how much he knew about her involvement with Paulie King? No choice, really.

She ended the call, read the text that came through from Ford a moment later as she chewed her lip. Dragged her keyboard towards her, typed in the name Connor Fraser. Started reading the search results that came back. As Ford had said, Fraser was a consultant with some Edinburgh-based outfit called Sentinel Securities. Susie recognised the name of the company and the cases they had been involved in over the last couple of years. Whoever Fraser was, he certainly didn't like the quiet life.

She gave a small laugh as she read one of the reports, shook her head in resignation. She should have known. Grabbed for her phone, dialled and waited.

'Hello?'

'Donna, hiya, it's Susie. You got a minute? Good. Seems I'm heading your way in a wee while, and before I do I wondered if you could answer a few questions for me about a pal of yours, a man named Connor Fraser?'

CHAPTER 33

It twisted inside him, an impotent fury that whispered at him to lash out, pick up the chair he was sitting on and throw it through the window. Stamp his foot through the plywood coffee table in front of him, toss the rancid cup of boiled piss that dared to call itself coffee into the face of the next nurse or doctor who dared cross his path.

Instead, Duncan MacKenzie sat in the stagnant, cloying quiet of the hospital and did what he hated most of all. He waited.

They had taken Jen away half an hour ago - yet more tests and X-rays to ascertain the extent of her injuries. She had smiled at him, insisted it would be OK, that he should go home and get some rest. Duncan had brushed aside the suggestion with a you-know-better smile, the similarities between Jen and her mother, Hannah, tearing at his guts and burning at the back of his eyes.

It had started when Jen was just a child. Nothing big at first: Hannah complaining of headaches and a general feeling of tiredness. With MacKenzie Haulage starting finally to gain some traction and win serious business, and a boisterous daughter at home, Duncan and Hannah had dismissed these early warnings in typical Scottish fashion - with a joke and a smile. They were a married couple in a tough business with a child at home who was just on the cusp of her hormone-driven rebellion against everything her parents were trying to teach her. Who wouldn't have a headache and feel run-down amid all of that?

It wasn't until Hannah's first seizure, when Duncan had found her on their living-room floor, writhing and gasping for breath, eyes rolled back, hands palsied talons that clawed for the air, as if warding off invisible demons, that they took the matter seriously.

And by that time it was far too late.

The diagnosis was as swift as it was devastating. Hannah had a brain tumour. The doctor who broke the news, a cold, strangely angular man with dead brown eyes that glittered almost as brightly as the watch on his wrist, called it a grade-four glioblastoma. He spoke of treatments and projections, of decisions to be made and hope to be clung to. Duncan heard the words, but couldn't process them over the scream that was building in his mind as he felt Hannah's nails dig into the flesh above his knuckles.

The next three months passed in a blur of hospital appointments – Duncan relegated to waiting for Hannah just as he did for Jen now. The only difference was that Paulie was by his side for every treatment, every hospital appointment. No surprise, really: the three of them had been inseparable since school at Falkirk, a trio briefly made a quartet when Paulie had married Jane Landis, a temp who had come to work for MacKenzie Haulage and found more than shipping orders to file and mileage logs to complete. The marriage had lasted four years, until Jane's wandering eye fell on another man. A man Duncan had last seen sitting in a bloodied puddle of his own piss and shit, Paulie looming over him as he told him to take Jane and 'fuck off to whatever corner of the world the wee hoor wants to live in'. Duncan had been struck by two things that night – that Paulie had let the man, a property lawyer called Barry, live, and that he had given him ten grand to start a new life with Jane. It took him a long time to balance that equation, wondered sometimes if it would have been better if he never had.

Finally, on an August day that seemed too bright and full of life for the poison it carried, Hannah told Duncan that it was over. No more treatments, no more sitting for hours as chemicals were pumped into her, robbing her of what little strength and vitality she had left. She was going to die, and she was going to die as the woman she was, not a strung-out shell whose body had been turned toxic by the very treatments designed to keep her breathing just a little longer.

She died two weeks later, at home. Duncan remembered having to tell Jen when she came home from school, his heart breaking as he saw the war rage in his daughter's eyes between the need to sob and scream and mourn her mother and the desire to be strong for him. She knew her mother had been his world, the woman for whom he had made something of himself. Duncan had been at pains to stress that to her every chance he got once they found out that Hannah was ill. Knew also that, without her, her dad would be lost, vulnerable to his baser instincts.

But it wasn't Jen who ultimately saved Duncan from the bottle or the impulse to start a fight he could not finish. It was, in an ironic twist that reaffirmed MacKenzie's belief that any God who might exist had one hell of a sense of humour, Paulie. He sat with Duncan through the long nights when memories of Hannah would torture him, drank with him when he needed to, sobered him up the following day. Paulie became Duncan's shadow, a protector who could see when his boss needed to rage or to grieve. He was in Duncan's corner when the need to inflict his pain on someone else drove him to a bare-knuckle boxing match, patched him up when the bout went bad, paid off the other fighter if Duncan took things a step too far. They had always been close, brothers in all but blood, but Hannah's death, the loss of one of their trio, and the desire to protect Jen from as much of their world as possible, had forged a stronger bond between them. A bond that allowed them to commit unspeakable acts in Prestonview in 1997, safe in the knowledge that what they were doing was right.

It was not murder, it was justice.

He was startled from his thoughts by the trilling of his phone in his pocket. He looked up, caught a stern-faced nurse glaring at him from the admin desk, felt again the urge to throw the coffee he was cradling into the sour-faced bitch's face. Instead, he smiled an apology at her, took out his phone, frowned at the unrecognised number.

'Duncan MacKenzie.'

'Boss, it's me,' Paulie said, after a moment's pause. 'Can you get somewhere quiet? We need to talk.'

CHAPTER 34

Susie found the café with relative ease, nestled on Bow Street not far from the castle. She hadn't spent much time in Stirling, but it surprised her how much this part of the city reminded her of Edinburgh's Old Town, with narrow, cobbled streets and buildings hewn from granite, sandstone and lime. She could imagine the place being described as picturesque on a summer's day, with the sun warming the old stones of the buildings, giving them a welcoming glow. Unfortunately, at that moment, with the grey sky overhead and a wind that sleet had sharpened to a razor's edge, it was no one's idea of a tourist destination. Unless, of course, the tourist was looking for cold and oppressive, with a twist of underlying menace.

As arranged, Donna was waiting for her at the door of the cafè, only her eyes showing between a scarf, a turned-up collar and a beret. Even off-camera, she exuded a casual elegance that Susie envied: she never felt comfortable in the business suits she wore for work, hated having to wear a dress or make-up for a night out. She was happiest in her running gear or a pair of jogging bottoms and a hoodie. She wondered if Donna even had a pair of jogging bottoms in her wardrobe. Doubted it.

'Well, this made the day more interesting,' Donna said, as Susie approached, voice muffled by her scarf and dampened by the low wind.

'Hmm,' Susie replied, noncommittal. Donna had been more than happy to give her all the background she needed on Connor Fraser, background that made her wonder again what the hell Ford had got them into. But the information had come at a price: when she found out that Susie wasn't meeting Connor in an official capacity, she had insisted on coming along. Off the record, of course.

Donna seemed to read Susie's concerns in her tone, held up a gloved hand. 'Look, Susie. I meant it. Off the record for now, OK? I know Connor. He can be a hard-headed arse at times, but he's a good guy deep down. Me being here might help, or it might put him off balance enough for you to get the edge on him. You might need it – the man's no fool. I promise, anything I get from this and decide to put on camera, I'll run past you first.'

Susie studied Donna's eyes, wondered how far she could trust her. If her record with journalists was anything to go by, she was looking at a fifty-fifty chance that she was going to get screwed over somewhere along the way.

If she was lucky.

'Too bloody cold to be out here,' she said. 'Let's get inside.'

They opened the door, walked into a small, inviting café that seemed to have been carved out of the sandstone foundations of the building. It was a vaulted room, the naked stone glowing in soft light, a tartan carpet in the middle of a highly polished wooden floor. There were fewer than a dozen tables – at one, two old women sat huddled over scones and a pot of tea, talking in low, conspiratorial tones. At the other, two men began to stand as they saw Donna and Susie approach.

'Well, well, well,' Donna said, as she pulled her scarf down to reveal a smile. 'This day is just full of surprises. Simon McCartney. What the hell are you doing here?'

Susie watched as the taller of the two men returned Donna's smile and took her in a hug. He was lithe, with sandy hair and a face that Susie would almost have described as unremarkable if not for his smile, which seemed somehow lopsided, as though it was a jigsaw puzzle he hadn't quite managed to put together in the right order.

'Well, someone has to keep this eejit right, don't they?' Simon said, his accent telling Susie he was from Northern Ireland, Belfast most probably. Interesting.

'Detective Sergeant Drummond?' the other man said, offering a hand to her. Connor Fraser was wide where Simon was tall, the jumper he was wearing doing nothing to disguise his broad chest, pumped-up arms, and shoulders that looked as though they might have been cut from the walls of the café. Donna had told Susie that Connor was imposing, but there was something more. Almost as if the sheer mass and density of the man were exerting some low-level gravitational pull, commanding the attention of the room. Donna had described him as a hard-headed arse and Susie could see why. But there was something else as well: a quick intelligence in those jade-green eyes that seemed to defuse the inherent threat his build gave off.

'Connor Fraser, I presume,' she said, taking his outstretched hand. It was warm, gentler than she'd expected.

He flashed a smile, gestured for her to sit.

'When DCI Ford arranged for you to meet me, I doubt he thought we'd be doing so in front of his favourite reporter.' Connor paused, eyes straying from Susie to Donna, a small smile twitching his lips. 'Hi, Donna.'

'Ah, but wouldn't it piss him off if he did know?' Donna replied, amusement in her voice. 'Sorry, Connor. Susie called to ask me for some background about you, and when I heard you were meeting her, I thought I'd come along as a bit of moral support. Doesn't look like I'm the only one who thought a chaperone would be a good idea.'

Simon laughed. 'The day I can chaperone this one is the day I retire,' he said. 'I'm only here for the tea. Speaking of which, can I get you ladies anything?'

Donna asked for a coffee, Susie opting for tea. Simon nodded then got up, heading for the counter and the bored-looking waitress, who eyed him with a faint air of resignation.

'So, DCI Ford told me you may be able to help me with something I'm working on,' Connor said.

Susie sat back, considering. *Something I'm working on?* 'Hold on,' she said. 'I was under the impression you were helping DCI Ford. I'm not here to help you in an unauthorised investigation of a police matter, Mr Fraser.'

Connor raised his hands in a placatory motion. Susie could see thick ridges of calluses on his palms. Gym-goer. Definitely.

'Sorry,' he said. 'Poor choice of words on my behalf. I've worked with DCI Ford before. He's a good police officer. I'm investigating another, ah, incident, and it appears there might be overlap with your investigation, and some people you've recently been meeting.'

Donna spoke before Susie could reply. 'Hold on, another incident? You mean what happened to Jen? Jesus, Connor, I thought that was just an accident. You telling me you think otherwise?'

Susie could see pain in the tightening of Connor's jaw and the momentary narrowing of his eyes.

'Yeah,' he said, his voice almost impossibly soft for a man of his size. 'There's more to it than just a hit-and-run. And it looks like this might tie into the murders in Edinburgh.'

'Hold on,' Susie said. She needed to get this conversation back where she wanted it to go. 'Who is Jen, and what are we talking about here? A hit-and-run? Was it fatal?'

Tension flashed across Connor's face, eyes darkening. In that instant, Susie saw the man he could be if the mood took him. Knew that it would take more than the pepper spray and baton she was carrying to stop him.

'Jen MacKenzie,' he said slowly, just as Simon returned with a tray of coffee, tea and scones. 'My girlfriend. Daughter of Duncan MacKenzie. She was run down yesterday outside the gym she works at on Craigs Roundabout. Doctors are worried about potential spinal injuries. They're assessing her now. But I've got information that suggests it wasn't an accident, that she was targeted to send a message to her father, Duncan MacKenzie.'

'OK,' Susie said slowly, trying to put the pieces together in her head. 'But how does that connect with the murders of Tim Montgomery or Terry Glenn? Did she know either of them?'

'Not that I'm aware of,' Connor said. He paused for a moment, eyes darting to Donna, a quick calculation running through his mind as a decision was made. 'I'll get back to that, but first I'd like to know . . . why have you been meeting with Duncan MacKenzie's right-hand man, Paulie King?'

Susie felt a sudden stab of vertigo, as though she was standing on the edge of a cliff. Should she jump or back off? None of this was protocol, off-the-record chats with a potential person of interest, information freely shared, a DCI encouraging her to ignore procedure to get the job done. But where did that leave her? Her career record was hardly spotless, and a mess like this could prove to be fatal. But then she remembered the body bobbing in a pool of blood in a swimming-pool, and a pair of eyes staring sightlessly into the sky as sleet fell into them. What was it Troughton had said about Ford – *He's a bloody good cop.* He would have to be.

'OK,' she said, taking a sip of the tea Simon had just poured for her and turning to Donna. 'I need this to be totally off the record, OK, Donna? I'm taking one hell of a risk here, all because Ford has vouched for Connor.'

Donna nodded, face pale, eyes haunted. What Connor had told them about his girlfriend had rattled her more than she was trying to show.

'OK,' Susie said again. Decision time. 'Yes, I was meeting Paulie King. But it wasn't professionally. He's ah . . .' She looked down, away from Connor's gaze, which was now almost predatory. 'He's a friend of the family. He pushed some work my dad's way years ago, has kept in touch ever since. Last time I saw him - must have been two, three nights ago? - he said nothing relating to the cases we're investigating or your friend, ah, Jen, did you say?'

Connor's head twitched in response. 'He said nothing about Dessie Banks?' he asked, his voice as cold as his gaze. 'Didn't offer any information whatsoever that could have incriminated Banks or connected him to any criminal activity?'

'No, nothing,' Susie replied. 'I meet up with Paulie occasionally. Given his, ah, reputation, we do it quietly, somewhere out of the way. Go for a pint in a pub on the edge of town or a walk somewhere remote. He wanted to see me as my dad has been ill, wanted to know how he was, whether there was anything he could do to help. He's always been good like that. But what do you mean about Dessie Banks? And is that what you mean about the link? The man we found murdered on Lothian Road today was a known associate of

Banks. How does that tie in with your girlfriend?'

Something indescribably sad flitted across Connor's face, replaced by a puzzled look that somehow made him seem both younger and older at the same time.

'It's another connection, but it's not the one Ford and I have found, DS Drummond,' he said at last.

'Call me Susie,' she replied, impatience edging her voice. If she was going to go out on a limb for Ford, this man had better make it worth her while. 'So tell me, what is this link?'

'*This is not murder. This is justice*,' Connor said slowly, eyes searching Susie's as he did so. 'I believe you found that message on or near the bodies of Montgomery and Glenn. It was also part of a message sent to Duncan MacKenzie the night before Jen got hurt. The message demanded Duncan have Paulie killed or Jen would be killed instead. Next morning, Jen got run over and Paulie was in the wind.'

'Wait, what? Paulie's missing?' Susie heard the note of panic in her voice, ignored it. She could deal with self-recrimination later. 'Has he been hurt? When was he last seen? Why has none of this been reported officially? Look, Connor, what the hell is going on?'

'I don't know,' Connor said simply, massive shoulders rising and falling in a shrug that seemed too inadequate a gesture for a man of his size. 'MacKenzie tried to contact him when he got the message, couldn't find him. Nothing has been made official because, bluntly, I can go places and ask questions you and the police can't, Susie. Ford thought talking to you, and establishing your connection to Paulie, would be useful, might help find him.'

'Can it?' Donna asked, before Susie could speak.

'Possibly,' Connor replied, his coffee mug like a piece from a child's tea set as he rotated it slowly in his hand. 'It tells us one thing. Someone is trying their best to put a very big target on Paulie's head. First, there's the car that hit Jen being registered to him and stored in his garage. I almost would have bought that, but whoever tried it obviously doesn't know Paulie very well.'

'How so?' Susie asked, a vague image forming in her mind along with a realisation. If Ford was a good cop, then Connor Fraser must have been a great one.

Connor smiled. 'Junk,' he said simply. 'The car used to run over Jen was filled with juice bottles and a wrapper from McDonald's. No way Paulie would allow such mess in a car he used. Not in the man's nature. Then there's someone claiming he was meeting you to blab about Dessie Banks's criminal enterprises to the police. So someone is turning the heat up on Paulie, trying to paint him as the bad guy and get everyone looking for him. The question is . . . why?'

CHAPTER 35

Hiding was not in his nature.

Paulie King lived by a simple code – find a problem, confront it, resolve it. It was a lesson bred into him early when his dad would come home drunk and swing for his mother, determined to vent on her his frustrations at his life as a postman. Back then, there was a simple choice: hide and let his mother take a beating, or confront the problem and resolve it. These resolutions frequently led to Paulie missing school the following day due to bruises or, on one occasion, a broken bone. But Paulie never backed down, never hid. For him, the equation was simple – every blow he took was one less injury inflicted on his mother. So he took the punishment his father meted out, night after night, until he turned seventeen and he stopped the fight with a cricket bat to his father's jaw and a simple promise: 'Hit her or me once more and I will kill you.'

His father never raised a hand to his mother again.

But now here he was, hiding. He had seen the news reports, knew that his decision not to confront the problem straight on had caused pain and suffering. He didn't give a fuck about Montgomery or Glenn, they had got what they deserved, but the fact that Jen had been seriously hurt drove needles of glass into his guts and demanded retribution. That had never been part of the plan, or the agreement.

He had got as far as the front door, car keys in one hand, a heavy kitbag in the other, when he had come to his senses and stopped himself. This was, after all, his own fault. The consequence of a decision made years ago. A decision that, despite all the pain it had subsequently caused, he couldn't quite bring himself to regret.

He had a plan, knew he had to follow it. Stay hidden, wait for his moment, hope Duncan would go along with what he had asked of him. It was a huge request, and one that Duncan would never honour if he knew the truth about *that* night, but Paulie had no other option. What was done could not be undone. But he would get justice for Jen. If the cost of that justice was his own life, that was a price Paulie was willing to pay. It was a price he had agreed on that night all those years ago. A price he would pay ten times over for one more moment, one more chance.

One more night.

So he would wait. Strike when the time was right. Finish what had begun what felt like a lifetime ago. And when he acted, it would not be murder. It would be justice.

CHAPTER 36

After meeting with Fraser, all Ford wanted to do was go home. The arrival of Simon McCartney underlined a simple fact that Ford had known in his gut for a while but did not want to acknowledge to himself: that whatever was going on, it was going to get bloody. He knew Fraser felt it as well. That was why he was calling in reinforcements. It was like looking at a darkening sky, feeling the static of pending lightning in the air, knowing a storm was on the way. With everything he had learned, Ford knew that a storm was coming. And he wanted to get home before it broke.

Unfortunately, Troughton had different ideas. The call had come when Ford was halfway back to Bridge of Allan, the young officer telling him that he had made a breakthrough in his research into Tim Montgomery, Cameron Donald and Operation Calderwood. Ford had asked him to explain, but Troughton had refused, insisting, 'It would be better if I show you in person.'

So he had, reluctantly, turned the car around and headed for Randolphfield. The station loomed like an ugly sentinel in the darkening day, a pebble-dashed Pandora's box that held nothing but misery and pain, any hope leaking from it consumed by shadows as the day grew ever more sullen.

Ford went to his office, with a brief pit stop in the canteen for coffee. He got the feeling it wouldn't be the only bitter thing he was about to swallow.

Troughton bustled in a few minutes later, his demeanour making Ford wonder if he should have a word with the canteen staff about the amount of sugar they were letting the junior officers have. Surely, he thought, he had never been that enthusiastic. Or young.

'Right then, Troughton, enthral me,' Ford said, as he settled into his seat and watched his DS dump folders and files onto the desk between them.

'Yes, sir,' he said. 'As you requested, I looked back at the Operation Calderwood files, with particular reference to MacKenzie Haulage and Tim Montgomery. It took a while, and it's a bit of a leap, but I think I might have found something.'

A bit of a leap? Ford hated the guilty stab of relief he felt at those words. 'Go on, then,' he said.

'Yes, sir,' Troughton said, reddening suddenly. 'But if you don't mind, I'll ah . . . I'll need your computer.'

Ford grumbled, got up. It was impossible to get comfortable anyway. 'All yours,' he said, with a flourish, before doing an awkward dance to squeeze past Troughton and arrange himself in the visitor's chair at the opposite side of the desk.

'Great, thanks,' Troughton said, as he eased himself into the chair. Ford had to admit, it suited the young detective. Was this it? Was he looking at the future of Police Scotland and his own replacement?

The soft chatter of keys, light from the screen washing over Troughton's face. 'So,' he said, his voice becoming calm, almost distant, as he spoke. 'I looked back at Operation Calderwood, in particular the interviews and statements given by Paulie King and Duncan MacKenzie. I then went back and cross-referenced that with the kids who were taken, and that's where things get interesting.'

'Go on,' Ford said, impatience mixing with trepidation. Again, the thought of a Pandora's box flashed through his mind. Was this really something he wanted to open?

'Well, I plotted out the sites of the abductions, and where the victims were found, with the haulage companies interviewed because they drove routes in or near either area. And that's when I found this . . .'

Troughton swivelled the computer screen around so Ford could see it. It was a map of east Scotland, zoomed in on the area from the

Forth Estuary to the Border and Berwick. On the map were three dots, like pins driven into an old-fashioned wall map.

'OK,' Ford said slowly. 'So what am I looking at?'

Troughton tried and failed to suppress a small smile, obviously proud of his work. He picked up a pen, tapped the screen gently, indicating a pin on the shoulder of the map, not far from North Berwick. 'This is Prestonview,' he said. 'Tracy Westerly was the second child taken. Disappeared while walking home on July the twenty-second, 1997. Last reported seen on Prestonview high street, having just been into the newsagent's for a bag of sweets – she picked them up every Tuesday to take to her grandparents, whom she visited on the way home from school. MacKenzie Haulage was identified as they had a shipping yard in an industrial estate just outside Prestonview.'

'Aye, OK,' Ford said, as he sipped his coffee. 'So far, so standard. That was the point of Calderwood, to rule out hauliers in the locus of the victims.'

Troughton nodded agreement. 'Yes, sir, but look at this.' He tapped his pen on a second pin, further inland, about two-thirds of the way to the border with England, which was marked in yellow. Ford leaned forward, the first vague echoes of an alarm starting to stir in his head as he heard old box hinges creak open.

'This is Fountainlow. A wee village just off the A68. Pretty unremarkable place, apart from the fact that Tracy Westerly's body was found dumped in a layby just outside it on August the eighteenth, 1997. Post-mortem examination found she had been beaten and strangled. Like the other victims, no sign of sexual assault.'

Ford nodded, his eyes drawn to the third pin, which was closer again to the border. He could see it now. It was all so obvious that Troughton had literally drawn him a map and connected the dots.

'That third location,' he said, a bitterness that was nothing to do with his coffee flooding his mouth, 'that's . . .'

'Yes, boss,' Troughton said, his voice flat now, a doctor delivering bad news. 'That's Drybridge, where Cameron Donald took his own life. Given the report we had from his wife alleging Tim Montgomery abused him, there's one link to the cases we're working on at the moment. But as we don't know who took that statement, it's all a bit of a leap, like I said.'

'Morgan,' Ford said, almost to himself, his eyes strafing across the map, following the pins. It made perfect sense. Like a lot of haulage firms back in the late nineties, MacKenzie Haulage would have used the A68 to transport goods from Edinburgh and the east coast down through the Borders to England. And the three locations were directly on or within spitting distance of that road. But what did it . . .

'Sir?'

Ford looked up, realised Troughton had been speaking. 'Sorry, Troughton, was lost in my own thoughts there. You were saying?'

'You said "Morgan".' Troughton's voice was wary now, face pale. 'That's not Detective Chief Inspector Dennis Morgan by any chance? Your old boss?'

Ford felt something cold and scaly flip lazily in his stomach as the Pandora's box in his mind squealed open another inch, foetid light spilling from it. Knew that, unlike Pandora's box, there would be no hope released here. 'Yes,' he said. 'Why?'

Troughton shuffled the files on the desk, found one and handed it to Ford. 'Those are the statements taken from Duncan MacKenzie and Paulie King, sir. Look at the recording officer.'

Ford flicked through the report, found what he knew he would. It was a neater signature than he had seen on Victoria Donald's statement, but the similarity was undeniable. Ford didn't need the name and rank of the officer printed below the signature to tell him whose it was.

Dennis Morgan.

CHAPTER 37

They spotted them on Corn Exchange Road, which connected Spittal Street and the heart of historic Stirling to the residential area surrounding the Albert Halls and lining Dumbarton Road. It was only a five-minute drive from Connor's flat to the café, but Simon had insisted on taking his car. He claimed it was because of the weather, but when they had left the flat and Connor had seen the small, gleaming hot hatch Simon had brought with him on the ferry from Belfast, he knew there was another explanation.

'Two cars back, making a right fucking mess of it,' Simon said, eyes flicking between the rear-view mirror and the road in front of him.

Connor leaned forward as best he could in the cramped front seat, his shoulders and back too wide for the sports seats that seemed to be trying to rearrange his spine. He studied the wing mirror and the street behind him. Smiled. 'Black BMW? Three series?' he said, eyes drawn to the car behind them.

'Aye, that's the one. Spotted them when we got out of the café. Fucking amateur. He keeps on either nosing the car out or trying to kerb it to make sure he keeps us in his eyeline. He might as well flash his headlights at us. How do you want to play this?'

Connor studied the street in front of them: black and sleek, like oil, from the falling sleet, lined with naked trees that stretched dark and skeletal into a sky that looked a lot like Connor was feeling. 'Turn right at the junction,' he said, jutting his jaw ahead. 'We'll take them for a bit of a ride, see what they do.'

'Fair enough. You thinking they're this character Banks's men?'

Connor considered. Made sense. Banks had put a price on Paulie's head, asked Connor to bring him in. But if Banks's men followed Connor, and he led them to Paulie, why not cut out the middle man and save a few quid? It would also balance the books in Banks's mind, allow him to avenge the outrage Connor had inflicted on him by taking out two of his men so easily. 'Aye,' he said. 'Probably. But either way, I'm not in the mood for this shite. You?'

Simon grinned, mischief in his eyes. 'Fucking right,' he said. 'Let's have a wee bit of fun. Frog march?'

Connor found himself smiling now, remembering the move from their time in Belfast. 'Why not? Just like old times.'

Simon drove to the junction at the foot of the road, brought the car to a halt. Left would take them back towards the centre of town, right out onto Dumbarton Road and, ultimately, the castle and main arterial roads connecting Stirling to Edinburgh and Glasgow. Not that they would need to go that far.

He sat, patiently watching the traffic crawl past, the little Renault's engine burbling restlessly. It was, Connor thought, a car built for Simon. Small, powerful and incredibly fast, it was a turbo-charged predator disguised as a house pet.

Cars approaching from both directions, Simon hammered the accelerator. The engine roared and the car took off, back end fishtailing slightly on the sleet-slickened road. Ignoring the sudden blare of horns and Simon's laughter, Connor swivelled in his seat, just in time to see the BMW dart from the junction, narrowly avoiding a cyclist, who swerved and lurched precariously from side to side before regaining their balance.

'Hit it,' he said to Simon, trying to ignore the sudden surge of hungry excitement in his guts. After all the frustration of the last couple of days, this was what he needed.

Watch that Fraser temper, son, he heard his dad whisper in his mind.

Fuck. That.

Simon gunned the engine, a small, squat church blurring past on the right as they picked up speed. Connor looked into the wing mirror again, spotted the BMW. Calculated. 'Up here, on the right,' he said. 'Turn onto Victoria Road. The road dead ends. We can have a little word with these jokers there.'

Simon nodded, the car swinging in as instructed. The street was typical well-heeled Stirling, all stone-built villas with large white-framed windows and dark slate roofs. Simon accelerated up a gentle hill, then pulled off the road where it widened and gave way to a large wooded area bisected by a broad pedestrian walkway. He turned the car quickly so they were pointing back down the street they had just driven up, obscured from it by the curve in the road.

They waited, saying nothing, engine burbling quietly. A moment later, the BMW appeared, two occupants visible. Simon waited until they passed then floored the Renault, surging forward in a spray of mud and scree that hit the underside of the car, like gunfire. He pulled alongside the BMW then drifted in, forcing it into the kerb, where it came to a stop in a squeal of alloys hitting concrete.

They jumped out of the car, Connor circling behind the BMW, Simon taking the front as the doors swung open. A Glock appeared in Simon's hands, as easily as a magician pulling a card from a deck, and he closed in on the car. In that instant, Connor realised Simon hadn't driven here to show off his new toy. No, he had driven because it made it easier to bring his armoury with him.

'Out the fucking car, boys. Now,' Simon said, his voice as dark and foreboding as the barrel of his gun.

The BMW's driver and passenger doors swung open, two men stepping out.

'Afternoon, fellas,' Simon said. 'Hell of a day for a wee drive. Want to tell us what this is all about?'

The driver of the BMW glared at Simon, as though his gaze could somehow melt the weapon that was pointed at him. He was a small, squat man with ears and a face that were obviously no strangers to a boxing ring. He held up two massive hands, and Connor noticed that the ring finger on the left stopped at the second knuckle.

'Got a message for him,' he spat, jutting his jaw at Connor as though he could strike him with it. At the passenger side of the vehicle, a tall, wiry man with sharp eyes tilted his head towards Connor, as though he was some new species of human he had never seen before.

'Go on,' Connor said.

'Mr MacKenzie sent us. Wanted us to keep an eye on you, in case Banks's people tried anything.'

Connor masked his surprise. He had been expecting Banks's goons. Not this. 'Very kind of him,' he replied. 'But tell your boss I don't need any babysitters. I'll be in touch with him when I need to be.'

The wiry man snorted a laugh, cruelty given vocal expression. 'Tell him yer fucking self,' he said, head shaking. 'Boss wants to see you, pronto. Got some news for you about an, ah, mutual friend you've been looking for. Says he'll see you at the yard in an hour. Ah wouldnae be fucking late.'

CHAPTER 38

The decision facing Ford was as simple as it was unpleasant. Which variation of the classic shit sandwich was he prepared to swallow?

He had come to this conclusion after his meeting with Troughton, which had left him with a simple choice – follow procedure, make everything official and get all that Troughton had discovered on the record, or keep quiet and try to figure out what the hell was going on? If he followed protocol, there was no way that would happen; the high heidyins would yank him from active duty before the words 'bent copper' or 'potential cover-up' could be uttered.

Whatever was going on, DCI Dennis Morgan was at the heart of it, like a bloated, comatose spider at the centre of a tangled web, the answers locked away in a brain that had retreated from the world as a machine forced his body to breathe. He had been in a coma for more than a year now, the doctors warning Ford that any form of recovery was increasingly unlikely.

None of which helped Ford now.

He was sitting at his dining-room table, listening as sleet tapped at the patio windows, impatient and insistent, like his thoughts. He closed his eyes, forced himself to take one piece of information at a time and forge them into a logical sequence. Gave a bitter laugh as he realised it was Morgan who had taught him this technique.

What did he know? That his former boss, Dennis Morgan, had taken and then conveniently lost a witness statement alleging that Tim Montgomery had been a paedophile and that his victim, Cameron Donald, had taken his own life less than five miles from where the body of a young girl, Tracy Westerly, had been found. Thanks to Troughton, he also knew that Morgan had been involved in the investigation of Tracy's death as part of Operation Calderwood, which had been set up in 1997 to look into the disappearance and murder of three young children across Scotland. During this investigation, Morgan had taken statements from Duncan MacKenzie and Paulie King, men from whom he had called in favours in the past.

But what did it mean? What did Morgan have to gain by making allegations against Montgomery vanish – and how did Operation Calderwood fit into it? None of the victims in that case had been sexually abused, just grabbed, killed and dumped, which did not fit Montgomery's profile, if that was the connection.

Or was there something else? Something more that he had yet to see? Something to do with MacKenzie Haulage and Paulie King who, according to Connor Fraser, had now disappeared after being spotted with DS Drummond?

He sighed, frustrated. There was no way he could make this official. Yet. The fact that he had sent Drummond to meet Fraser and effectively let him run a shadow investigation for his own ends was proof of that. And there was something else, a simpler reason that he saw in his eyes every time he looked into a mirror: guilt.

He had colluded with Morgan once, allowed himself to be led astray by the senior officer and cut corners on another case they had worked on. That had led to one miscarriage of justice, and he would not allow Morgan to be responsible for another. If he had helped Montgomery evade justice all those years ago by covering up his abuse of Cameron Donald, then Ford would expose that, damage to the service or his own reputation be damned.

He froze, random thoughts crashing together in his mind, fused by one simple word.

Guilt.

He scrabbled around the table, found the crime-scene photograph from Victoria Quay and the message daubed on the wall in blood.

This is not murder. This is justice.

Flicked through the files, found another. Opened it. Read. Felt spider-like legs of cold skitter across his spine. Understood, in that instant, not only the message but, finally, who it was for and what it might really mean.

CHAPTER 39

'This is what I like about visiting Scotland,' Simon said, as he brought the car to a halt. 'The scenery is always spectacular.'

Connor laughed as he peered out of the window. A remote industrial estate, sleet-dampened tarmac glistening like whale skin in the waning light of a day that seemed to have given up any pretence of good humour. Jaundiced light spilled from the office building that squatted low and ugly in the centre of the yard, bracketed by two large warehouses. Connor had only visited MacKenzie Haulage twice before, and neither of those visits had been particularly pleasant. He doubted it would be a case of third time lucky.

'How do you want to play this?' Simon asked, as he killed the engine.

'Straight on,' Connor replied, gaze not leaving the office block. 'No point in pissing about. MacKenzie wants to see us, I want to have a word with him about having his goons follow us about. We go in, see what he has to say. Things go sideways, well . . .' He didn't need to finish the sentence. Simon merely nodded agreement, took a deep breath then swung the car door open and stepped into the yard.

They were met at the front door of the office block by a man Connor thought was vaguely familiar. Or maybe it was just that MacKenzie got a bulk discount for hiring shaven-headed, heavy-set men with faces that had been rearranged over the years by fists, feet and other blunt-force trauma.

'Boss will see you in his office,' the man said, voice little more than a whisper as his eyes flicked over Simon. 'Alone. Yer boyfriend can wait outside.'

'What? You want to have some fun while the men talk, that it?' Simon said, taking a half-step forward as the rent-a-thug bridled and squared his shoulders.

'He comes with me,' Connor said, tone conversational, friendly, even as he focused on the soft spot just below the thug's ear that he would hit to knock him out if needed.

'It's all right, Marty. Let them come in.'

Connor turned, saw Duncan MacKenzie framed in the door to his office. He looked better than when Connor had last seen him, the weary exhaustion replaced by a focus that glittered in his eyes and radiated from his ramrod-straight back.

Somehow, Connor didn't find the change in demeanour comforting.

MacKenzie gestured them into his office, then closed the door behind them. 'Duncan MacKenzie,' he said, thrusting his hand towards Simon, who took it with a smile and a nod.

'Simon McCartney. Friend of Connor's here. I heard about what happened to Jen. I'm sorry, Mr MacKenzie.'

MacKenzie's eyes flinched for an instant as the thick vein in his neck pulsed. Connor bit back a flash of panic at the sight. Had something happened to Jen? Was that why they were here? But if so, why not meet at the hospital?

Unless . . .

MacKenzie seemed to read the thoughts in Connor's face. 'She's fine,' he said, before turning his attention back to Simon. 'Thank you, Simon, it's appreciated.'

'Why are you having us followed?' Connor asked, cursing himself for allowing MacKenzie to read him so easily. 'And what makes you think Dessie Banks is going to try something? Doesn't make much sense, given he's asked me to look for Paulie.'

MacKenzie considered Connor for a second, as though evaluating him. Then he shrugged and stepped around his desk to sit in the oversized leather chair: the king taking his throne. He gestured for Connor and Simon to sit.

Neither did.

MacKenzie sighed. 'Fine,' he muttered. 'I wanted to see you because Paulie has been in touch. And some of what he told me makes me think you might be in danger. If not from Banks, then from other interested parties.'

Connor felt pressure build behind his eyes, as though all the questions he had were crowding forward in his head and trying to escape. 'Hold on, Paulie's been in touch? Where is he? Why did he pull a disappearing act? And does he know what the hell is going on and why Jen got hurt?'

MacKenzie laid his hands on his desk, rocked back in his chair. 'He called me earlier,' he said, after a moment. 'He doesn't know why Jen was attacked, or what all the this-is-not-murder-this-is-justice shite is, but he did tell me why he disappeared. I'd probably have done the same in his shoes. It also explains why Banks is so keen to find him.'

'Go on,' Connor said.

'It seems Mr Banks has been playing me for a fool,' MacKenzie said, the old weariness returning to his voice as he spoke. 'You know Paulie was arranging for us to transport certain items for Banks, yes?'

'Yeah, but you conveniently never told me what those items were.'

MacKenzie gave a wistful smile. 'Hardly matters now, but we were moving prescription drugs, Fraser. You know, cancer drugs, Parkinson's treatments, glaucoma drugs, certain antibiotics. All the stuff you either can't get now in this country or has been made astronomically expensive due to Brexit. You'd be amazed what that's done for my business, Connor, both on and off the books.'

'OK,' Connor said slowly. 'So you and Banks are humanitarians, bringing hope to the hopeless and charging for the service. I don't see how that drives Paulie into hiding and Jen into a fucking hospital bed.'

Cold hate glittered in MacKenzie's eyes. He chewed his lip, then pulled his face into an expression that was more snarl than smile. 'It turns out,' he said, his voice now a cold, dead thing that seemed to make the air in the room somehow heavy, 'that Banks wasn't just using our lorries for the agreed drugs shipments. He was also using our drivers to transport more, ah, exotic items for other clients.'

'Exotic items,' Simon said, taking a step towards MacKenzie's desk. 'Drugs, porn or firearms?'

MacKenzie grunted a laugh. 'Very good, Simon. I can see why Connor likes having you around. But you're right, Paulie had a . . . a chat, shall we say, with one of our drivers, who was being a little too splashy with his cash. He thought he might be skimming from us, but it turned out he was just earning on the side by working for Banks. The bastard has been using our deal as a Trojan horse to access my men and my network.'

'To distribute what?' Connor said, doing nothing to keep the impatience from his voice.

MacKenzie looked down, hatred replaced by something else now. Something Connor had last seen in DCI Malcolm Ford's eyes.

Shame.

'Pornography,' MacKenzie said, knuckles flashing white as he gripped the desk. 'Specifically, extreme pornography. You know, the stuff they don't want to put online, the stuff even the dark web rarely touches as it's too hot and traceable. Sadism. Torture porn and the like. It seems there's a particular breed of sick cunt out there who wants their perversion in untraceable hard copy, and Banks was using my business to transport it.'

'So why did Paulie go dark?' Connor asked, as he tried to think past his revulsion. 'Why not just come straight to you or, even better, confront Banks about all this? Why set him up, why get everyone looking for him, me included?'

MacKenzie leaned forward, steepled his hands on the desk in front of him. 'Think about it,' he said. 'Banks is supplying the most abhorrent, depraved material out there to people who will pay not only for their perversion but also their privacy. Paulie finds out about this, and who is asking for the stuff, so what would Banks do?'

'Protect his business and his clients,' Connor said slowly, the pieces slotting together in his mind. 'He'd want to shut Paulie up, and discredit him in front of you in the process. Is that why he gave you the picture of Paulie with that detective? Christ, did Banks frame Paulie for what happened to Jen?'

'I don't think so,' MacKenzie said, his tone telling Connor he had already thought all this through. 'Banks isn't known for being subtle. He thinks he's got you on Paulie's tail, all thanks to this he's-about-to-run-to-the-police bullshit. But to get to Paulie through Jen? No, doesn't make any sense.'

An idea flashed across Connor's mind then, unconnected thoughts clashing together to give off the briefest spark of light. But then it was gone, replaced by more immediate concerns. 'So where is he?' he asked. 'I need to speak to him about Jen, see if and how this all ties into these murders. I take it Paulie didn't have anything to say about them?'

'No, and he didn't tell me where he was either. Just that he's staying off the radar for the moment while he tries to resolve all this.'

'And will that be with a shotgun or a flamethrower?' Simon asked. 'No way you're going to the police about any of this, so that doesn't leave either of you with many options. Only real question is how messy all this is going to get, and what you expect Connor and me to do about it?'

MacKenzie tilted his head to the side, acknowledging Simon's assessment of the situation. 'You're right, of course,' he said. 'That bastard Banks has been using my business to transport this filth. He'll answer for that. To me. Paulie has asked for certain, ah, items to be made available to him, and I'll arrange for that to happen. Which is another reason I wanted to meet you here, Connor. Paulie asked that you deliver the items to him.'

'Aye, right,' Connor said, incredulous. Working outside the margins to find out what had happened to Jen was one thing, but turning gun-runner for MacKenzie and Paulie to wage their own private little war? Forget it.

MacKenzie flashed his empty smile again, as though he was laughing at a punchline only he could hear. 'It's not what you think, Connor. Look, I'm getting things organised at the moment, should take a couple of hours.' He paused, his face darkening, like a sky suddenly marred by rain clouds.

'In the meantime, you should head to the hospital, visit Jen. I spoke to her before you arrived. She wants to see you.'

CHAPTER 40

After her meeting with Connor and Donna, Susie's first move had been to try to contact Paulie. She wasn't surprised when he didn't answer: the story that Connor had told her made it almost inevitable that, after a few rings, the call would divert to Paulie's gruff voice as he told her to 'leave a message if you want to'.

She hesitated, the thought of leaving a recording of her voice on his phone ringing a vague alarm bell, knew it was too late for that. The call was logged: if the police ever got wind of any of this and looked into Paulie's movements, they would find her number there.

She left a perfunctory message for Paulie, then killed the call and sat in the car, staring unseeingly out into the day. *The police.* When had she started to think of herself as on the other side of the fence from them? Was it when she had learned that her DCI was running lines of enquiry that were parallel to the official investigation? When she had agreed to meet and be effectively interviewed by a former police officer who seemed to know more about what was going on than she did? Or was it earlier than that, when she had answered Paulie King's call a week ago and agreed to meet him in Leith Docks?

What she had told Donna and Connor about Paulie was true . . . to a point. Her dad, Ian, had met Paulie years ago when he was working as a mechanic in a small garage he had opened in Hawick. He had taken on some jobs with Paulie, who was working for a haulage firm that had a depot nearby at the time, and the two men had bonded over a shared love of classic cars and anything that ran on diesel or petrol. A typically Scottish friendship had evolved – long periods of silence interspersed with catch-ups, nights at the pub and promises to stay in more regular contact.

And slowly, as Paulie and Ian had got to know each other, extra work began arriving. Small jobs at first – a bodywork repair here, an engine remapping there. All handled quietly and discreetly at the small garage in an out-of-the-way Borders town. Looking back on it now, Susie could see the appeal – a place for Paulie to get some no-questions-asked work done and a steady stream of income for her father.

It was only years later, when she applied to become a police officer, that her father had taken her aside and told her what some of the jobs really were. VIN, or chassis, number changes, paint jobs for cars that had been stolen and resold, repair work to vehicles that had been used when quick withdrawals and quicker getaways from the bank were necessary. She still remembered the look on her dad's face as he told her what he had been doing, earnest and grave, but laced with a sly we-got-away-with-it humour.

He said he had told her because she had 'a right to know' and didn't have to worry that anything would ever be traced back to the family business that could make her new career problematic, but Susie knew the real reason. Her father, who had come from a time when police had charged down striking miners on horseback and elicited more than a few confessions with the aid of a slippery set of stairs, hated the police. And telling his daughter, who was about to join their ranks, about his work with Paulie was his way of giving the establishment a one-fingered salute.

But despite all this, she kept in touch with Paulie. He had been a sporadic presence in her life, always a little distant, but gentle and kind whenever they met. And he had mastered a skill that Susie had seen elude hundreds of her father's customers over the years – showing simple respect and courtesy. So she had kept in touch with him and, when her dad had suffered one of his increasingly frequent bouts of angina, had agreed to meet Paulie to tell him what was going on.

The question now was, who had been watching that meeting? And why?

She let out a frustrated sigh. Paulie. This all came down to Paulie. Until he got in touch, there wasn't much she could do. And in the meantime two men were dead, bodies dumped with a message that seemed to connect the killings to an attack on Jen MacKenzie.

What was it Troughton had said? Are we looking for Doctor Strange? She was forced to admit he was right. How could someone get into a government building, evade all the security checks and cameras, kill Tim Montgomery, leave their gruesome calling-card message and disappear without a trace? She thought back to the man who had discovered the body, Martin Christopher, with his regulation civil-service haircut and glasses that winked in the overhead lights every time he moved his head.

Lights . . .

Who are we looking for? Doctor Strange?

Susie stopped, stared out of the windscreen, as though the answer was there, beyond the smear of sleet. Something about lights. What was it Christopher had said? *The lights came on and I didn't understand what I was seeing at first.*

She chewed her lip, ignoring the pain as she bit down harder than she intended, almost as though she could stop the nebulous thoughts forming in her mind escaping by sinking her teeth into it.

Lights . . .

Didn't understand what I was seeing at first . . .

And something else. Something Connor had said. *I can go places and ask questions you and the police can't, Susie.*

She reached into her pocket for her phone, dialled Troughton. The idea was there, fragile, like thin ice on the surface of a pond. Too much pressure and it would shatter, but maybe, maybe . . .

'Troughton,' she said, as he answered the phone. 'It's me. Meet me at Victoria Quay in ninety minutes' time, will you? Bring Martin Christopher's statement and the crime-scene analysis. I think maybe I've got an idea.'

CHAPTER 41

It hadn't been easy getting in to see Jen. She had been moved from critical care to a private room, which Connor took as a positive sign. The problem was that she was being guarded by a ward sister Connor suspected was moonlighting as a bouncer at some of Stirling's less gentrified establishments. He eventually managed to charm his way past her, feeling ever more uncomfortable as he resorted to worried-boyfriend theatrics and promises not to be in there for long.

The moment he stepped into the room, Connor knew he was right. He wasn't going to be in there for long.

She was sitting in the bed, which had been angled to prop her up. The bleached white of the sheets only accentuated the bruises that seemed stained across every inch of exposed skin, a riot of purples, dusky reds and gangrenous green patches that made Connor's stomach give an oily twist. When she looked at him, Connor briefly thought the bruises had bled into her eyes, the thought quickly dispelled by a realisation that gave his stomach another sickly squeeze: seeing him had somehow hurt her.

'Hey,' he said, his voice sounding too loud and strident for the somehow breathless silence that filled the room. 'Your dad told me you wanted to see me. Came as soon as I could.'

She flashed a weak smile at him, the perfection of her teeth somehow rendered perverse by the ruin of the face surrounding them. One arm twitched up as she gestured for him, and Connor felt a wave of relief swell in him. Whatever injuries she had endured, she was moving. That was a start.

'Hiya,' she said, as he took her hand in his. It felt warm, clammy, but he did nothing to move his grip.

'I see your dad dropped off the stuff from your flat,' he said as he sat down, gesturing to the various pictures that were crammed onto the bedside table. He recognised a couple of the pictures from her flat, one of him and Jen at the gym, another from the weekend they had spent together in Aviemore. They surrounded another picture he didn't recognise – bigger than the others in an elegant metal frame. Jen as a child, her mum and her dad, all smiling into the camera, unaware of the pain that life was preparing to inflict on them.

'Yeah, he was in earlier,' she said, a flatness to her voice that seemed to resonate with the heavy silence in the room.

Connor dragged his eyes from the pictures, focused on Jen. Could see something flit across her eyes as she studied his face and he felt his lips contort into something akin to a smile in return. 'So,' he said, after a moment, 'what's the latest?'

She blinked, her gaze hardening as the smile faded from her lips. 'Well, I'm not going to be running any marathons any time soon, and I can kiss goodbye to my personal training clients for a while as well,' she said, her eyes straying from Connor and down the bed to her legs. She took a breath. Held it. Connor felt her grip tighten on his hand momentarily, as though she had felt sudden pain.

'You OK?' he asked. 'Want me to get . . .' He trailed off as he saw the tears that were beginning to form in her eyes. 'Jen, what is it? I . . .'

Her jaw tightened and she nodded once, as though confirming a decision to herself. 'I was pregnant,' she said, the words as dead and empty as her eyes.

Connor felt as though he had been slammed in the guts with a sledgehammer. He couldn't breathe, as though the sudden onslaught of questions and thoughts screaming through his mind were a tidal wave that was forcing his head under water. Could a man drown in his own thoughts? 'Jen, what – what do you . . .?' he heard a voice he vaguely recognised as his own. At least, that was what he thought it said. It was hard to hear over the hammering thud of his blood in his ears.

'I was going to tell you that morning,' she said. 'I was eight weeks gone. I was going to keep it, wanted to tell you, see what you would say.' Her grip on his hand eased. 'Doesn't matter now, though. I lost it in the, ah, accident.'

Connor felt his mouth fall open. Closed it. Focused on keeping himself breathing. Searched Jen's face for any kind of hint as to what to say next, found none. A kaleidoscope of images and thoughts and memories flashed through his mind in a panicked jumble: Jen flying into the air as the car hit her . . .

pregnant

the feel of her beneath him in bed

I was going to tell you that morning

her rib snapping under his hands like a twig as he forced life back into her body after she had been run over.

I was going to keep it.

He could feel himself going into shock, his overloaded mind crying out for the numbness it would bring. Strangled the thought, forced himself to think, breathe. She needed him. Now. He could process this later. 'Jen, I . . .'

She shook her head, the sound of her hair rubbing across the cheap hospital pillow like static. 'Connor, I told you because I needed you to know. I needed to be honest. I'm facing a long road back here, and I don't want you sticking around out of some kind of feeling of obligation or guilt, OK?'

He nodded dumbly, gaze unconsciously moving to her stomach. Felt sudden heat burning behind his eyes, crying out to be free. Coughed, straightened his back, swallowed the pain and grief that threatened to overwhelm him. He understood her pain now, wished to hell he didn't.

I was going to keep it.

'Look, Jen, you know that whatever happens, I . . .' He felt like he was adrift at sea, grasping for words as though they were flotsam from the wreck of his life and the right ones would keep him afloat.

'You didn't sign up for this,' she said, her voice cool, even. 'I wasn't expecting any grand commitment when I told you about the baby, but I wanted you to know either way. And I need you to know now. No secrets. No guilt. I don't have time for any of that now.'

'Jen, you know I'm here no matter what,' he said, pushing down the flash of guilt he felt even as he remembered walking around his flat, wondering if and how he would adapt it for Jen. Did he mean that? Really? Or were they just words he thought Jen wanted to hear?

She studied him for a moment, the façade starting to buckle, tears and grief flooding into her eyes, as toxic as oil polluting a mountain spring. 'I'm sorry,' she whispered.

Connor shook his head, leaned forward. Took her gently in his arms as he felt her body begin to heave with tears. Bit down on his bottom lip as he fought to keep his own emotions in check. When he made the decision, he clung to it desperately, focused on it, used it to drown out the grief and sorrow he felt.

He would find whoever had run Jen over. And when he did, he would kill them, just as they had killed his unborn child.

CHAPTER 42

The journey to Victoria Quay wasn't as much of a drive as it was a rolling battle with her own self-doubt. Susie had spent the trip going over her idea, attacking it from every possible angle. It was a hell of a leap and, looked at coldly, it could almost be described as ludicrous. But it was the only solution that fitted all the facts.

And there was something else. Something that told her she was right. Connor Fraser's voice, urging her on – *I can go places you can't.*

But she had to be sure. And she wanted Troughton's opinion. He had shown her he wasn't just the yes-man she had first thought he was when he had stood up to her about Ford. She just hoped he would be as candid when he heard her theory.

They met at the main entrance, Troughton's curt nod in greeting doing nothing to mask the excitement in his eyes, like he was a kid about to be shown a magic trick.

Susie hoped she was up to it.

'Thanks for coming,' she said, as he fell into step beside her. 'Let's take a walk, shall we?'

They showed their warrant cards at the main desk, Susie earning a puzzled scowl as she asked the woman behind it if she could borrow an access pass for the building. 'You'll no' need it, love,' she said, voice and demeanour telegraphing vague impatience in the way only Edinburghers can. 'Your police IDs are enough. I'll buzz you in now.'

Susie smiled, counted to five in her head. 'Please, it'll help with our enquiries,' she said.

The woman behind the desk shrugged. 'Aye, all right,' she said, passing Susie a credit-card-sized piece of plastic attached to a faded red lanyard. 'But ye'll have to sign for it.'

After filling in the necessary paperwork, they were buzzed through a security door and into the main atrium. Susie could hear the vague whistle of the wind from outside as it echoed through the cavernous glass and steel skeleton of the building, as though the whole place was shivering in the bad weather.

They turned right, heading for the swimming-pool where Montgomery was found. Susie stopped in a seating area that was directly across from the main canteen, where she had interviewed Martin Christopher only two days ago. Remembered his glasses winking in the light as he fiddled with them. It had seemed like a nervous tic at the time, the self-soothing gesture of a man who was deep in shock. But was it? Or was it something more?

And then there were Connor Fraser's words. *I can go places you can't.*

They followed a narrow corridor, coming to the door that led to the changing rooms and, ultimately, the swimming-pool. Susie looked down at the small security-card scanner sitting next to the door, felt self-doubt rise in her mind again. Maybe she should walk away now, look at the whole thing again, keep her mouth shut until . . .

'Let's go through this a step at a time,' she said suddenly, speaking before her thoughts overwhelmed her.

'What have we got? Tim Montgomery has his throat slashed in this pool, his blood used to daub a message on the wall. But we've got no record of anyone but Montgomery leaving or entering the pool area until he's found by Martin Christopher, right?'

Troughton retrieved a tablet from his shoulder bag, started swiping and tapping as he called up the relevant reports and statements. 'Yup, that's correct,' he said, not looking up. 'Montgomery's card was swiped here at six twenty-seven a.m., giving him access to the changing rooms and the pool. Nothing else until Mr Christopher swiped in at seven forty-three a.m. Bilston Glen got the 999 call from the front desk here at seven fifty-nine a.m, which is consistent with him finding the body, tearing along to the front desk and getting them to call us.'

'OK,' Susie said. 'So far, so simple. Montgomery swipes in. In the hour and a half between then and Martin Christopher swiping in to find the body, our unknown killer somehow gets past this locked door, cuts Montgomery's throat and then disappears. Agreed?'

Troughton's face contorted into a confused scowl. 'That's what fits the facts,' he said. 'No murder weapon found on the scene, nothing found on Mr Christopher either, which could indicate he was somehow involved.'

Despite herself, Susie smiled. 'You're forgetting one thing,' she said, after a moment.

'Go on,' Troughton said, impatience frosting his voice as the scowl on his face deepened.

'Christopher was sick,' Susie said.

'Huh? Susie, what the hell does that mean? He'd just found a man floating in a pool of his own blood. In those circumstances, I'd probably be sick myself.'

Susie nodded, felt her self-doubt dissipate, like clouds after a storm. She was right, she was sure of it.

I can go places you can't.

She held up the card she had been given at the front desk, tapped it against the reader. Heard the click as the door unlocked, pushed it open, the lights in the changing room automatically flicking into life.

'Christopher said these lights were out when he walked in here,' she said, more to herself now. 'But when we checked the boards, everything was fine. No blown fuses, no signs of tampering. So either it was a one-in-a-million coincidental fault or . . .'

'He was lying,' Troughton said. 'Fair enough, but why lie about that? The lights here being on or off didn't affect him getting to the pool, finding Montgomery or him being sick, which I still don't bloody understand by the way.'

'I'll get to it,' Susie replied. 'Give me a minute to walk this through. We've been assuming that this all played out the way Christopher told us it did because the security-card swipe logs and the CCTV footage we managed to pull confirmed it, right? But what if you were right all along? What if we are looking for Doctor Strange all this time?'

Troughton's scowl collapsed, replaced by naked impatience. 'OK, I'm bloody lost,' he said. 'Doctor Strange, Christopher throwing his guts up and lying about lights. DS Drummond, Susie, what the hell are you trying to get at?'

'First rule of magic,' she said, stepping into the changing room. 'Always distract the audience so they don't see what you're really doing. Christopher telling us about the lights was a nice little detail, something to give colour to his story, and subtly shift us into thinking someone else was involved. The lights were out. The big bad killer must have fiddled with them before he attacked Montgomery. And while we're looking for that killer, we're not looking too closely at Christopher's story and the rest of the facts.'

'What bloody facts?' Troughton snapped.

'It's all about these,' Susie said, holding up the security pass. 'They let you go to places other people aren't allowed to. Other than through the changing rooms, the only other way you can get into or out of the pool is by the fire exit, which is alarmed. So whoever killed Montgomery must have had a card, yes?'

'OK, but I still don't see . . .'

Susie waved aside his words. 'You got the pictures of Christopher's personal effects? SOCOs would have taken them from him when he was processed. Find his security card, will you?'

Troughton tutted, glanced back down at the tablet. Turned it to Susie as he found the file he was looking for – four images of Christopher's security pass, front, back, in its lanyard holder and the holder on its own.

Susie took the tablet, pinched and swiped until she found what she was looking for. Grinned.

Bingo.

'OK, try this for an alternative view. We know the killer had to have had access to a security card and the pool. So either someone swiped in days ago and lay in wait for Montgomery, or Christopher is our man.'

'But how can he be?' Troughton asked, his voice taking on a

pleading tone now. 'We checked his personal items. Nothing that could be used as a murder weapon, traces of the victim's blood on him from the water in the . . .'

Troughton trailed off, a light coming on in his eyes as Susie saw the idea begin to form for him.

'As he was sick into the pool, right? He got to his knees and puked into the pool. Which, if he was involved, gave him the chance to not only mess up the crime scene by getting his trace evidence all over it, but also the perfect opportunity to wash his hands – and the murder weapon.'

'Aye, OK, maybe,' Troughton said. 'I get the hands, the water wouldn't have been totally polluted by Montgomery's blood immediately, so there would be trace but not arterial spray. But that still leaves us with a murder weapon.'

Susie pointed to the tablet and the image showing the back of Christopher's card. It was scored with small scratch marks, and something else, small blue blobs in a tight cluster.

'Blu-tack,' she said. 'You've seen everyone here, they have to wear their ID badges around their necks on lanyards. I noticed that Christopher had his clipped to a tie pin, to make sure it always pointed picture-side forward. Thought it was just an affectation, but what if he was hiding something on the back of the card? Something like a razor blade, something that would score the card, something that would be just big enough that he could hide, something that was lethal enough to open Montgomery's throat?'

Troughton did nothing to hide his scepticism. 'So you're claiming Christopher swiped in with a concealed blade, slashed Montgomery's throat, wrote the message, cleaned his hands of the worst of the blood, then ran for security to call us? It makes a kind of sense, Susie, but without a murder weapon, it's only a theory. And then there's the bigger question. Why? What's the motive?'

'That I don't know. Yet. As for the murder weapon, I had an idea about that. Take a look at this.' She tapped the tablet, found the file she was looking for, Troughton stepping towards her as she began to play the CCTV footage from outside the pool. Christopher exploding out of the doors, sprinting down the hallway and out of shot. A jump as the camera changed, the new view showing Christopher as he swiped back through the security doors at the main entrance and sprinted to the security desk. He grabbed for it, like a man holding onto a life raft, then began waving wildly back the way he had just come.

'Just as he described,' Troughton said. 'He found the body, puked, ran like hell for Reception to sound the alarm.'

'You didn't see it, did you?' Susie asked again. 'Doctor Strange himself and you missed it.'

She replayed the last few seconds of the footage, heard Troughton hiss beside her.

'Fuck me,' he whispered. 'Forget Doctor Strange. That's worthy of Houdini.'

'Let's go see if we're right,' Susie said.

They headed back for the reception desk, not quite running, both of them wanting to. Susie could feel the excitement build in her, like it was Christmas morning and she was bolting downstairs to see what Santa had left her. She used the pass to get them through the main door, then got to the security desk, ignoring the quizzical glance from the woman she had spoken to earlier.

Susie glanced at the pad. 'He was here,' she said, taking up the position Christopher had occupied in the CCTV footage.

Troughton nodded, moved behind the desk, ignoring the increasingly colourful objections of the security guard. He bent down, disappearing from view. Susie found herself holding her breath, willing him to speak.

'Susie,' he said at last, his voice betraying nothing. 'You'd better take a look at this.'

Susie rushed behind the desk, knelt beside Troughton. Looked up, following the lip of the desk as it curved round and into a void space. They had never thought to look here. Why would they? They didn't know what to look for, and the immediate crime scene was secured and sealed off as SOCOs picked it apart. Christopher had been searched, his belongings catalogued. So why look at the reception desk?

Susie took out her phone and snapped a picture of what Troughton had found. Tucked into the corner of the recess, where Christopher had reached into when he had grabbed the desk, was a small blob of Blu-tack. And at the centre of that Blu-tack, glinting in the light from Susie's phone, was a blade. Susie recognised it immediately – she had seen her father change the blades on his Stanley knife on countless occasions over the years. Less than three inches long, but wickedly sharp, it could cut almost anything.

Including, she thought with a shudder, Tim Montgomery's throat.

But why?

CHAPTER 43

'Connor! Connor, for fuck's sake, man, slow up!'

It was as though Simon was shouting at him in a foreign language. Connor heard the words but couldn't comprehend them: they were background noise lost in the screaming cacophony of thoughts tumbling through his brain.

After visiting Jen, he had asked Simon to drive him back to the MacKenzie Haulage yard. He had seen the questions in his friend's eyes, mixed with concern and something simpler and uglier, something that threatened to penetrate the cocoon of rage Connor had wrapped around his soul.

Fear.

They had driven back in silence, Connor's hands clamped to the sides of the too-small passenger seat of the Renault. He was out of the car before Simon had fully stopped, marching directly for the front door of the office. As he approached, the thug from earlier stepped out of the glass doors, scowling into the fading light of the day, his stance growing rigid as he read Connor's intent in his relentless march.

'He's busy,' Marty said, voice as blunt as the sound of Connor's feet on the tarmac. 'You're back too early anyway. You shouldn't be here for another hour.'

Connor didn't speak, just kept on walking. Saw Marty take a half-step forward, one arm outstretched in a 'stop' motion as the other reached back and behind into his waistband. He could have been going for a weapon, Connor thought.

Good enough.

Connor grabbed Marty's outstretched arm, thumb digging into the palm and pushing up, bending his wrist back at an impossible angle. He kept moving, using his momentum to drive the man back even as the right hook crashed into his temple and dropped him to the floor. He let him down gently, holding him, like a doll, by the arm, even as he heard Simon shout from behind him.

'Christ, Connor! Slow the fuck down, just . . .'

He ignored it, swung open the door to the offices. Stepped in. Marched down the hallway to MacKenzie's office. He reached out and, just as he grabbed the handle, felt a hand land on his shoulder.

'Connor, fuck's sake man! Calm down! What the hell's going on? You flattened that poor boy outside, now you want to, what, kill Jen's dad? Come on, man, talk to me. What the bloody hell is going on?'

Connor turned to his friend, whose face was a mask of wary concern. He opened his mouth, closed it, unable to form the words. Felt the rage he had clutched, like a life vest, since Jen had told him she was pregnant fall away, like dried leaves ripped from a tree by the hurricane of grief that screamed through his mind. He felt Simon's hand grip his shoulder tighter, as though trying to transfuse his own strength into him.

'Connor, what is . . .?'

'She was pregnant,' Connor said, watching as the words hit Simon harder than any uppercut ever would. 'Jen. She was pregnant when she was run over. Lost it. That's why she wanted to see me. To tell me. And the piece of shit in there,' he threw a thumb over his shoulder at MacKenzie's door, 'knew.'

'Connor, Jesus, man, I'm so sorry,' Simon whispered, his eyes reflecting Connor's own pain. 'But this does no good. So her dad knew. So what? Wasn't his place to tell you, though, was it? This was your and Jen's business. So what you going to do? Take her da apart because you're hurting? What's that going to achieve?'

Connor felt his shoulders collapse, as though Simon's words had physical weight and were pressing down on him. One more burden to endure. 'Aye,' he replied, knowing it was inadequate, but unable to articulate his thoughts to his friend. He had never seriously considered fatherhood, but the sudden loss of it left a void in the centre of him. His father had been a terrible parent: would Connor have been as bad? Or would he have followed his gran's path, nurtured and supported the child as she had him when he had found the door to his father's love closed to him?

He took a deep breath, blinked the thought away. Gave Simon what he hoped was a reassuring smile. 'You're right. Sorry, man, got a bit caught up. Kicking MacKenzie's head in won't help, but he does have answers, I'm sure of it. So we get them. For Jen. You with me?'

'Always,' Simon said, eyes not leaving Connor's.

Connor nodded, glad to be able to turn back to the door and away from his friend's gaze, the unflinching loyalty he saw in it. Simon deserved a better friend than he was. The question was, could he do anything about it?

He grabbed the door handle, thrust the door open.

MacKenzie stood up from behind his desk as though his chair had been electrified, a storm of outrage and fear scudding across his features, chased by something uglier. Resignation. 'So she told you,' he said, a statement, not a question, as he lowered his gaze. 'I'm sorry, Fraser – Connor. Really. I know you're pissed off but it wasn't my place to tell you. Jen wanted to tell you herself, in her own time, her own way.' He paused, shook his head, then looked up, anger now flashing in his eyes. 'Fuck's sake, Fraser, you think this only affects you? Jen lost a child. I lost a fucking grandchild.'

Grandchild. The word sliced through Connor's mind. What was it Jen had said? *I was going to keep it.* It. A boy or a girl, she hadn't said, and Connor hadn't asked. Would they have known at two months? Or was the son or daughter that never was another possibility snatched away from them by whoever had run Jen down? Connor felt a sudden wave of exhaustion crash over him, fought the urge to collapse into the chair opposite MacKenzie.

'No more bullshit,' he said, as he faced MacKenzie straight on. 'What the fuck is going on? There's more to this than Banks using your trucks to smuggle high-end porn and God knows what else to clients. That message to you, *This is not murder. This is justice*? That's personal. Why does someone want Paulie dead? Why was Jen targeted? And what has this got to do with the murders of Tim Montgomery or Terry Glenn? You know something, Duncan, and I swear to Christ you're going to tell me or I'll—'

'You'll what?'

Connor whirled around, saw DCI Malcolm Ford standing in the door to the office, calmly taking in the scene.

'I assume that the unconscious man who's been left in the recovery position in reception is your work?' Ford said, eyes darting between Connor and Simon.

'Sir, I . . .' Connor fumbled for the words. The sudden appearance of the policeman had thrown him, as though he was putting together a cabinet and had come to the end of the job, only to find a piece was left out.

Ford smiled, held up a hand. 'The commission of violence before I got here is not my business,' he said, his voice growing cold. 'But what happens now that I am here is very much my business.' He stepped more fully into the office so he could see past Connor and to Duncan MacKenzie.

'Duncan,' Ford said, 'looks like you've had a wee bit of an afternoon. But Fraser here was on the right track with his questions, wasn't he? So here's another. And believe me, Duncan, you're going to want to answer this one.'

Connor watched as MacKenzie sat back into his chair: the king on his throne, trying not to show that recent events had knocked his crown perilously squint.

'If I'm going to talk to the police, I'll want my lawyer present,' he said, one hand reaching for the phone on his desk. Connor noticed the hand was shaking slightly, relished the fact.

'That's fine,' Ford said. 'Probably better he's here anyway. After all, you're going to tell us all about your yard at Prestonview, your statements to Dennis Morgan regarding Tracy Westerly, aren't you? I don't know all of it, but I know enough to be sure you'll want to get it right, so a lawyer is probably a good idea.'

MacKenzie sagged in his chair, hand retreating from the phone and finding its way to his rapidly reddening neck. 'It can't be that,' he whispered, more to himself than anyone else in the room. 'We dealt with that years ago, the three of us. And what we did, I'd do again.'

Connor watched as Ford nodded slowly, grudging agreement in the gesture. Again, he felt the weariness threaten to overwhelm his body, just as questions threatened to overwhelm his mind. 'What the hell is going on?' he said. 'No more bullshit. No more games. Tell us what you know, Duncan. Now.'

MacKenzie looked up at him, the old defiant anger flashing in his eyes. It was dampened by a sudden cough that seemed to rattle his whole body. 'OK,' he said.

And then he started talking. As he did, Connor felt the shadows in the room deepen and grow colder. When MacKenzie had finished, the four men stood in silence, each alone with his thoughts. Each coming to the same inescapable conclusion.

It had been justice after all. A justice of another time. A more savage time, one ruled by a code that was underpinned by the notion of 'eye for an eye, tooth for a tooth'. But justice nonetheless.

CHAPTER 44

After the discovery of the Stanley knife blade, the Montgomery investigation swung into a routine that Troughton found at once comforting and maddening. The blade had been taken away for forensic testing, while Martin Christopher had been flagged as a leading suspect in the inquiry and all efforts were being made to locate him.

The problem was, Martin Christopher had pulled another magic trick and disappeared.

Scottish Government records, council tax and local voting rolls all showed that Martin Christopher resided in Dalgety Bay in Fife. Troughton knew the place well: he had visited another murderer there a few years ago. It was a typical commuter town that had started to develop in the sixties just as Edinburgh prices began to drive people further out of the city. Just over the Forth, visible from Victoria Quay and looking back on Edinburgh, Dalgety Bay was effectively a massive housing development that had sprouted a few small business parks, restaurants and pubs as it grew. It wasn't the most affluent of locations, but neither was it particularly down at heel. It was anonymous. Forgettable, even.

Just like Martin Christopher.

Officers dispatched to his listed address along with DS Drummond found a typical detached home in a neat cul-de-sac. Troughton had thought about arguing for his place on the team, then kept his mouth shut. Susie had figured out the murder: it was her hard work that had led them to the murder weapon. Troughton had been impressed, and found it hard to begrudge her the follow-up. But when she and the other officers forced entry, they found a drift of mail behind the door, empty cupboards and a kitchen that was bare, apart from a few forgotten tins of beans and fruit. The house was still full of furniture, and pictures still adorned the walls, but it was clear it had not been a home for some time. Co-ordinating the search for Christopher from Edinburgh, Troughton was frustrated at not being on the scene. Even if the house had been abandoned, he had a feeling he could get a sense of Christopher and his possible movements not only from what was missing, but from what had been left behind.

Troughton reread Susie's notes on her initial interview with Christopher. She had proven to be an insightful and resourceful police officer, yet there was nothing in her notes to suggest Christopher had been anything more to her than he had pretended to be – a man who had been deeply traumatised by what he had found. How, Troughton wondered, was Susie dealing with that? With the knowledge that a killer had been sitting across from her, telling her everything she wanted to hear, secretly laughing at her from behind the façade he had constructed? If she was anything like the person he was coming to know, Troughton got the feeling that it would spur her on to find Christopher, no matter what she had to do.

But where had he gone? There were no other addresses listed for him with the Scottish Government, and while local authority records were being searched for other Martin Christophers, Troughton wasn't hopeful of success. The man was meticulous: he was hardly going to leave a forwarding address. But had he left something else?

Troughton skimmed back through the notes. Yes. There. When Susie had asked Christopher if anyone could meet him at home, he had said one name – Gina. Who was that? Troughton flicked through the government's personnel records, found no listing of a Gina in the department Christopher had worked. So who was she? A friend? A relation? A lover? Troughton leaned forward, tapping away at the computer until another file appeared on screen. Christopher was listed as a widower. No other family members were on file.

. . . family . . .

Troughton tossed the idea around for a moment, then shrugged, turned to his computer and accessed the Scottish Government's personnel file on Christopher. He clicked through to emergency contacts, hoping that some distant relative or even a friend might be listed, giving him something, anything, to work on. Felt disappointment as the file returned a 'no details found' message.

He sighed, frustrated. Stared at the screen, which seemed to mock him. 'No details' – that was something he was getting all too used to. Idly, he scrolled across the page, noticed a small box flick up when he hovered over the message: 'File last updated 21/5/16. 13:57.'

He leaned forward slowly, like a reluctant child settling down to homework they really didn't want to do. Hit some keys, calling up the previous versions of the file. He knew what he was doing wasn't strictly by the book, but from the way Ford had been running the investigation, he doubted the guv would mind and, besides, what did a little low-level hacking matter when it was going to be another dead end?

But then the previous version of the file loaded, and Troughton's world stopped.

He read the name once, then twice. Scrambled for another file he had found earlier in the day, a file requested by DCI Ford. Felt excitement prickle his skin even as he reached for the phone to call Ford. As he dialled the number, his eyes were drawn back to the computer screen, and the name of the emergency contact that Martin Christopher or someone else had attempted to remove from his file. A name that forged another link in a chain Troughton was just starting to understand.

Gina Westerly. The now-deceased mother of Tracy Westerly.

CHAPTER 45

Donna wasn't sure what surprised her more – the request that had been made of her or her mother's single-minded dedication to making sure she could honour it.

After her meeting with Connor, Susie and Simon, Donna had been left in limbo. If Connor was right, she had the inside track on the biggest story in town – two brutal murders were somehow linked to a hit on the daughter of a local businessman who had a reputation for being a little more than just another pillar of the community. The problem was, what could she actually report? Unlike the keyboard warriors, and everyone out there who thought that an internet connection and a social-media account made them journalists, Donna had rules to follow. She needed facts, corroboration, concrete evidence of what she was reporting. Yes, she could confirm that the deaths of Tim Montgomery and Terry Glenn were somehow linked due to police contacts confirming that the same message, *This is not murder. This is justice*, was found at both crime scenes. But she didn't have such confirmation with Jen. She doubted Duncan MacKenzie would confirm the existence of the note Connor had mentioned, and she had promised Susie that she would keep her relationship with Paulie King off the record.

For now.

Frustrated, she had checked in with the news desk to see if any new lines on the murders had been issued, then headed home to work.

Thankfully, her mother, Irene, was already at the flat with Andrew, so she ignored the disapproving stares when she got home and told her mum she 'had to work' then retreated into the small spare bedroom she had converted into a study. It had seemed like an indulgence when she had moved into the flat with Andrew, and her mother had made no secret of her contempt for this outpost of journalism in her daughter's home, but Donna loved the room. It was a sanctuary, a retreat. A place where she could shut out all her problems, mistakes and regrets, and focus on the job that both maddened and inspired her. About a year ago, she had been offered the chance to make a change: swap reporting for writing a book based on her encounter with a killer, then take a plum position at a PR company. The hours were better, the money even more so, but Donna had declined both offers. She wanted to make the news, not be it, and spinning the truth into a neat little headline for someone else's benefit had never been her style. Donna knew she had been ruthless in her career, had jumped on opportunities when they arose, despite the potential fallout, but she also knew she was honest. She had lived a lie once before, when she had believed she had a future with Mark Sneddon, Andrew's late father, and she had vowed to herself that she would never do that again. She was a reporter, a journalist, only ever happy when she was breaking the news or scooping the competition.

She had been at the computer for about half an hour searching for anything she could find on Dessie Banks, Paulie King and Duncan MacKenzie, when her phone buzzed on the desk beside her. She picked it up, frowning slightly at the 'no caller ID' message on the screen. Probably a junk call about a car accident she hadn't been in, or a nutter with information on the lizard overlords that were secretly manipulating mankind with 5G.

She considered ignoring the call, had the phone to her ear before she realised the decision had been made.

'Donna Blake,' she said, keeping her voice cool and clipped.

A pause on the line, then a voice. Familiar, but rougher than Donna remembered, like a picture that had had sandpaper rubbed over it.

'Donna? Donna, it's Jen MacKenzie. Sorry for calling you out of the blue. Can you talk?'

Donna remembered Connor's words in the café: *She suffered spinal injuries, they're assessing her now.* Felt something between relief and terror flash across her mind. 'Jen, bloody hell. It's good to hear your voice. Connor told me what happened. How . . . how are you?' Donna winced even as she spoke the words. What the hell was her follow-up going to be? *You calling to see if I'm free to go dancing on Friday? Aye, sure, no problem.*

Idiot.

'I'm . . . I'm OK,' Jen said, the rough, dead tone in her voice telling Donna the absolute opposite was true. 'Donna, I'm calling because I need a favour. If you're free any time today, is there any chance you could come and see me?'

Donna blinked, stared around the room, mind racing. What the hell could Jen possibly want to see her for? They were hardly close, knowing each other solely through Connor, so why . . .? 'Yeah, no problem,' she said, snapping off the thoughts as she calculated times in her head. 'I'm free just now, can be there in about half an hour, if that works with visiting times?'

'Don't worry about that,' Jen said. 'The nurse here has taken a bit of a shine to me. She'll let you in if you ask for me.'

Jen gave Donna the details of the ward she was in, then ended the call with a 'thank you' so perfunctory it might have been delivered by a politician. Donna chewed her lip for a minute, then headed through to the living room, bracing for a fight with her mum. Now that Donna was home, her mother would expect her to do her work, then take over with Andrew. It wasn't an unreasonable expectation, and Donna had been looking forward to spending time with her son, even though he seemed to look a bit more like his father every day.

She stepped into the living room, Andrew crashing into her legs as she did so with an excited cry of 'Mummy, Mummy!' which quickly degenerated into growls and snaps as the plastic dinosaur he was holding tried to eat her.

Donna gave Andrew a hug, then looked up at her mum, whose pinched face and hard eyes told her she knew what was coming. 'Mum, it'll only be a couple of hours,' Donna said, hoping that getting the rebuttal in quickly would somehow make this go easier. She hated needing to rely on her mother like this, but with the cost of childcare being what it was, she didn't always have many other options.

'Donna, this can't go on,' Irene said, folding her arms. 'Your father and I love seeing Andrew, you know that. But he needs his mother, and this . . .'

'It's about the girl who got run over the other day in town,' Donna said, hating herself for playing the emotional-blackmail card, not having time to worry about it. 'I know her a bit. Anyway, she just called. Wants to see me. I'm not even sure it's work-related, but I said I'd go.'

Something seemed to shift and relax in Irene Blake's features, as if the words 'not even sure it's work-related' were a balm to some pain she was trying to keep hidden. Her posture relaxed, and the stern expression on her face turned into one Donna hadn't see a lot over the years. Maternal.

'Och, why didn't you say?' Irene said. 'I read your report. That poor wee lassie. If she needs a friend, you go on, do what you can to help. Your dad can come round here, we'll look after Andrew.'

Ten minutes later, Donna was on the road to Forth Valley Hospital, which was south of Stirling, on the road to Falkirk. She thought of Connor and his gran as she passed the signs for Bannockburn, wondered again how he was coping with all of this. Despite his imposing stature, she had seen something in him at the café, a nervous fragility hiding behind the hard-man resolve he had projected so many times before. The realisation brought an unexpected pang of jealousy, faint like the aching of an old scar in bad weather, but undeniable. She pushed it aside, concentrated on driving in the worsening weather.

Thoughts like that were for another time. Definitely not now.

Arriving at the hospital, Donna found her way to the ward Jen had described. She knew the place, vaguely, from past stories she had done on the hospital. The ward was, unofficially, known as a close-observation unit, where patients who were deemed stable enough to be released from the critical care unit were taken to be treated, monitored and assessed. The forced near-silence, punctuated only by the bleeps of monitors and the soft squeal of soles on the heavily polished floors, unnerved Donna, reminded her of the hours after she had given birth to Andrew when she had looked at him in the cot beside her bed and wondered at the responsibility of having a life entrusted to her, even as her fears and doubts crowded into the quiet of the ward and wrestled with her love for her son.

Just as Jen said, the ward nurse Donna encountered, a slight, almost fragile-looking brunette, with a blade-like nose and cold blue eyes, flashed a sullen smile when she heard Jen's name, and ushered her to a room halfway down a long, narrow corridor. Donna thanked her, watched her retrace her steps along the hallway, then took a deep breath and stepped into the room.

Jen was sitting up in bed, light from a laptop playing across her face. Donna felt a stab of panic, the urge to step back out of the room scrabbling up her spine with cold, skeletal fingers. She had always admired and, if she was honest, resented Jen's natural good looks and flawless complexion. But that was gone now, replaced with a patchwork of lurid greens and blacks and purples, as though the devil himself had applied her make-up. Jen looked up, the bruising around her eyes making it look as if two black, empty pits were staring at Donna. The illusion was broken by the sudden flash of perfect white teeth as Jen smiled a welcome. There was nothing comforting in that smile.

'Thanks for coming,' Jen said, as she laid aside the laptop, wincing as she moved.

'No problem,' Donna said, as she stepped into the room, cheeks reddening slightly as she realised she had been so intent on getting there that she hadn't even thought about stopping for flowers or another traditional get-well-soon gift.

Jen seemed to read the thought in Donna's expression, eyes flitting to the bedside table, which was cluttered with pictures. Donna vaguely wondered if any of them had come from Connor.

She sat down beside the bed, took her time arranging her bag and smoothing her trousers, willing Jen to speak first, not wanting to repeat her mistake on the phone with a general 'how you doing' query.

One look told Donna the answer to that. And it wasn't a pretty one.

'I need you to do me a favour,' Jen said, after a moment. Donna heard pain in her voice, but something else as well – a resolve that she had heard in her own voice on more than one occasion when she had decided on a course of action and was trying to persuade everyone around her to follow her lead.

'Go on,' she said slowly, not sure she really meant it. After all, she hardly knew the woman, what was she doing here, by her bed?

'This,' Jen said, raising her arms and gesturing down the bed to her legs, 'this is going to change things for me, Donna, Connor too. It . . .' She stopped, took a deep hitching breath that threatened tears. 'It took something from me. From Connor and me. And whoever did this is out there now, free to walk about while I . . .' another breath '. . . I lie here. That's not fair, Donna. It's not right. And I need your help to fix that.'

Donna's thoughts flashed back to the café and Connor's words. *There's more to it than just a hit-and-run.* What did Jen know? What did she want? How did . . .

Jen spoke again, voice harder now. 'I've read what you wrote about what happened, but I want to do more. The police don't have the time or the manpower to look for a snot-nosed kid who ran me over in a car that was probably stolen, but I need them found, Donna. They . . .' Her voice trailed off, and Donna saw tears in her eyes. It was like looking at droplets of moisture glistening on a knife blade. 'They need to pay for this. For what they've taken from me.'

'And what can I do?' Donna asked. She knew the answer, knew what Jen wanted. It was obvious really. But she needed to hear the words.

'I want you to interview me. Put me on camera. "Hit-and-run victim appeals for witnesses from hospital bed". You know, that sort of thing. Must be worth a headline for you, surely.'

Donna felt a bolt of excitement flash up her throat, swallowed it. Yes, it was a hell of a human-interest story, and an exclusive. She could widen it out, talk about hit-and-run statistics, Jen the wounded, photogenic tip of a spear that could be driven right into the heart of road safety across Scotland. It could be a series of reports and interviews, an investigation into . . .

Donna forced the thoughts back, felt a pang of shame. There it was again, the ruthlessness she needed but despised. Here was a young woman, in obvious pain, asking for help to make sense of what had happened to her. And what was Donna's first response? See it as a headline, as a story that would advance her career.

Connor's words now: *There's more to it than just a hit-and-run*. But that's what Jen had just called it. So she didn't know.

Donna took a deep breath. 'Look, Jen,' she said slowly, forcing herself not to look away from Jen's eyes, 'I know you're hurt. Angry, even. But what you're asking is . . . well, it's . . .'

'Fair,' Jen said. Her voice flat as her hands folded across her stomach almost protectively. 'Someone did this to me, Donna. I have to know who.'

Donna took a breath. Closed her eyes, saw headlines flash across her mind's eye. Felt a surge of panic. Here it was, a moment of decision. Would she look back on it as a missed opportunity, a mistake or a decision well made?

There's more to it than just a hit-and-run.

She swallowed. Decision made. 'Jen, there's more to all this than maybe you know. Things that might make you think again about all of this. Maybe you should speak to Connor, see—'

'Connor's not here,' Jen snapped, pain etching itself into her face as she tried to move in the bed. 'If there's something going on here, I need to know, Donna, so tell me. Please.'

Donna studied Jen's face, saw pain and determination wage a guerrilla war under the camouflage of bruises. Saw something else too – an echoing grief that somehow made her bruises seem darker. What was it she had said? *They need to pay for what they've taken from me.* But if they went through with this, how much more could Jen lose?

Donna sighed, then slowly began talking. She told Jen about her meeting with Connor and Susie Drummond, about the note that had been sent to her father and the two men who had been murdered in Edinburgh. She told her about Paulie being missing and Connor's efforts to track him down. And as she spoke, Jen became increasingly still, as though Donna's words were an incantation slowly turning her to stone, making everything that was bruised and broken and brittle somehow hard and uncaring.

'So you see,' Donna said at last, 'going on camera might not be the best idea. If you were deliberately targeted, you being on camera will be a red rag to a bull. It could put you in real danger, Jen. I don't want that, and I bet Connor wouldn't either.'

Something flashed across Jen's face then, something at once defiant and predatory. She stared at Donna for a long moment, then nodded, as though confirming a decision to herself. 'I'm doing it,' she said. 'If you won't take the story, then fine, someone else will.' She gestured to the laptop sitting beside her. 'If it brings whoever did this to me here, then good. The thugs my dad has watching the place will kill the fucker, or I will. So you've got a decision to make, Donna. Do you want to be part of this, or not?'

CHAPTER 46

Duncan MacKenzie sat alone in his office, the light from the spotlights in the yard sliced into thin fingers of shade by the Venetian blinds. He raised a glass of whisky in silent toast to the sleet that spattered against the window, filling the room with intermittent static.

The office was silent now, Ford, Fraser and his little pal, Simon, having left, and Marty, once he regained consciousness, dispatched to recover at home. He'd been lucky: Fraser had stopped short of breaking his jaw, but Duncan could see from the discoloration and bruising that Marty wasn't going to be eating anything solid for the next few weeks.

One more insult to add to Connor Fraser's tally. One more wrong to right.

He gave a bitter laugh. Righting wrongs had been what had got him into this mess in the first place. They had thought they were doing the right thing, ensuring justice was done. It had seemed that way at the time, all those years ago, when the decision was made. Even now, with Ford's discovery of the truth, a truth he had shared with Fraser and McCartney, MacKenzie could not bring himself to regret what they had done, the actions they had taken.

But what had those actions led to? He remembered an old saying favoured by his mum, a devout, almost fanatical Catholic, who feared God almost as much as her husband feared her temper. 'Your sins will find you out, Duncan,' she would say, when he came home late or had been sent home from school with a note from his teacher, usually limping from the beating he had received. Was that what was happening now? Had his sins found him out? And was Jen suffering for them? Would he? He took a sip of whisky, swilled it around his mouth as he swirled ideas and possibilities around in his mind. So Ford knew what he, Paulie and his old boss, DCI Morgan, had conspired to do in Prestonview. He could see in the man's eyes that, somewhere deep down, somewhere primal, somewhere polite people would deny existed within them, the policeman agreed with their decision. And it was that agreement Duncan believed would save him. If Ford were to go to the authorities now with what he had discovered, every conviction Dennis Morgan had ever secured would be up for examination. Appeals, compensation claims, negative press, it would be devastating for Police Scotland, even ruinous. And Duncan knew that, above everything else, Malcolm Ford was a pragmatist. He wouldn't sacrifice three decades of policing for one moment of restorative justice.

Would he?

But what would Fraser do? MacKenzie had stayed his hand with the man, even come to develop a grudging respect for him and the way he cared for Jen. But things were different now. Jen had lost a child, faced months if not years of recovery from what had happened to her. Would Fraser stick with her, protect her, offer her comfort and security in a way MacKenzie had failed to do? Or would he put himself first, walk away, find easier prey? The mere thought of it filled MacKenzie with a cold rage he could barely suppress. Jen's condition gave Fraser a stay of execution, nothing more. If he supported Jen through this, he would live until she was strong enough to bear his loss. If he walked away, he would die immediately. Fraser's death was inevitable. Only the timetable was in doubt. That had become an immutable fact the moment Fraser had dared lay his hands on one of MacKenzie's men.

He was stirred from his thoughts by the chime of his computer on the desk, which was echoed a moment later by his phone. He reached forward, felt the world sway lightly as the whisky made its presence felt. Squinted at his phone and then, with a curse, tossed it aside in favour of his computer. He found it increasingly difficult to read the small, cramped text on his phone, but he was damned if he was going to lose that battle with time and get glasses. Not when he had people who could read things for him. Or a computer with larger fonts.

He clicked into his work email, telling himself it was vital that he kept on top of the business and that his sudden attentiveness was nothing to do with fending off thoughts of Connor Fraser. Got to his inbox, saw a new email. Stopped when he read the sender and the subject line, the whisky fug in his head vanishing, replaced with a mouth that was too dry and a mind that felt it had been turbocharged. The spatter of sleet on the window was suddenly a riot of sound.

From: Prestonviewcalling@gmail.com

Subject: This is not murder, and this is why

Duncan looked up suddenly, as if the sender of the email was waiting to jump through the office door the moment he read the subject line. But no one appeared, and he heard nothing but the cooling tick of the radiators and the tap-tapping of sleet. He waited for a moment. Then, with a hand he couldn't feel, he moved the mouse to the email and clicked it open. It was short, only twelve sentences, with a .MOV attachment at the end.

Mr MacKenzie,

As a father myself, I felt it was important I write to you to explain my actions and, more importantly, to explain why I attacked your daughter. I apologise for this but, in my defence, I can say that it was not my fault. It was, as with everything that has happened so far, the fault of Paulie King. I am sorry to say that he lied to us both, Mr MacKenzie, and now Jennifer must pay for that lie. I do not expect you to take my word for this. Please watch the attached video. It is not for the faint of heart but it is, I'm afraid, a necessary evil which we must use to get to the truth. And that truth is this. I am not a murderer. I am acting in the only way any father would. Timing is everything, Mr MacKenzie, and this video proves that. My question is, how much time do you think Paulie has left?

MacKenzie read the email again, felt confusion and irritation clamour into his thoughts even as his eyes drifted to the attachment. He hesitated, then clicked on it. Watched it for a moment, felt terror rise in his chest, cold and pure and scalding, as he realised what the grainy footage was showing him. Turned away and vomited as the small, brittle sounds of screams filled the office, then turned back, forced himself to watch even as he felt tears roll down his face and his hand clamp to his mouth.

When it ended, the sudden silence of the room shrieked at him. He wanted to get up, get away from what he had just seen, knew his legs would not carry him. Grabbed the bottle of whisky, drank from it, trying to use the alcohol to scour his insides of the evil he had just ingested.

Timing is everything, Mr MacKenzie, and this video proves that. My question is, how much time do you think Paulie has left?

His hand was moving before he realised what he was doing, the video playing again. His eyes strayed from the screen to the picture on his desk of himself, Jen, Paulie and Hannah then flicked away, as though he could not look at them in the face of such horror. And, in that instant, he understood.

He leaned forward, swiped the computer monitor from the desk and to the floor, the sound of it shattering seeming to echo what he was feeling as he grabbed for the photo and studied it.

Timing was everything. Absolutely everything.

Was his time finally up?

CHAPTER 47

The address listed for Gina Westerly's home was in one of the housing estates that had cropped up around Prestonview, developers lured to the area by cheap land and the promise of marketing a life that gave 'easy access to Edinburgh and central Scotland'.

Given what he had seen driving in, Ford wondered why anyone would want to access central Scotland if this was what was on offer: a high street with more vacant shops than occupied, the only businesses seeming to have any success hairdressers, corner shops and pubs. An effort had been made to modernise the town centre with a bronze plinthed statue of a miner, light in hand, jaw set defiantly as he stared bravely up Prestonview's main street. Some artistically minded local had obviously thought the statue too dull for the town's vibrant aesthetic and had improved it with lurid swirls of neon green and white that snaked from the plinth to the miner's helmet.

Ah, progress.

Ford pulled up in front of Westerly's home, the pavements already crammed with a SOCO van, two patrol cars and an anonymous hatchback he recognised as Troughton's. He stared up at the house for a moment, fought back the urge to keep driving. After his confrontation with Duncan MacKenzie, and what he had learned about Tracy Westerly's death, he knew nothing good could come from stepping into that house.

He was torn from his thoughts by a tapping at his window.

Troughton, cheeks red from the cold. Ford sighed, realised the decision had been taken from him. He swung the car door open, then got out, wrapping his jacket around him against the cold. 'What have we got?' he asked.

'Sir,' Troughton said, voice wavering slightly as he fought the cold, 'officers were dispatched after we identified the link between Christopher and Gina Westerly. Nobody at home, neighbours last remember seeing a man fitting Christopher's description here two days ago.'

Ford nodded. 'After Tim Montgomery was murdered,' he said. Troughton had filled him in on Drummond's discovery when he'd called him with the link to Westerly. He was forced to admit it was a damn good piece of police work. The type of work he used to aspire to do before . . .

'So how exactly is our man Christopher linked to the Westerlys?' he asked, pushing the thought aside.

'He was Gina Westerly's second husband,' Troughton said. 'She died about six months ago. Seems they were separated for a year before that time.'

'Ah,' Ford said. It explained the separate addresses, Christopher in Dalgety Bay, Westerly here. But why come back to the town where her daughter had been snatched? And why, if they were separated, was Christopher using his estranged wife's home?

Troughton seemed to read Ford's thoughts. 'SOCOs have made a first sweep of the property, sir. Seems like Christopher was using this place as a base. Makes sense, I suppose. If he was planning to murder Tim Montgomery, he'd want a place we wouldn't immediately look. We only found this place as I managed to dig into his file and found Mrs Westerly listed as an old emergency contact.'

'Uh-huh,' Ford muttered, ignoring the note of pride in Troughton's voice. 'And what was it that Mrs Westerly died of exactly?'

Troughton produced a notepad from his pocket, squinted at it in the wind as he riffled through the pages. 'Alcohol-induced liver failure, sir,' he said, after a moment. 'Seems Mrs Westerly had a drinking problem. She was listed as being hospitalised on several occasions over the years, and it finally killed her.'

Ford chewed on the thought. Made sense. Had losing her daughter driven Gina Westerly to seek solace at the bottom of a bottle? He and Mary had been unable to have children, but Ford had still mourned the loss of a life never lived with too much whisky and too much regret. When things were bad with Mary and the silence of the house taunted them with the absence of what might have been, he had developed a thirst that seemed to call to him. How much worse would it have been for Gina Westerly? To have lived that life, to have a home filled with the sounds and smells and sights of your child's life, only to have it snatched away in one moment of evil? If it had driven her to seek the oblivion of booze, Ford could understand that impulse. But, he was forced to ask himself, would the knowledge of what MacKenzie, King and his old boss, Dennis Morgan, had done after Tracy was murdered have brought Gina Westerly any peace? Might it have cauterised the wound she had tried to salve with drink, given her a shot at life, a chance of peace?

This is not murder, this is justice.

'Fuck it,' Ford barked, his voice gruff. He hadn't realised until he had spoken how close he was to tears. 'Too fucking cold out here. Let's get in, have a look around.'

They made their way past the cordon, the uniform there radioing into the house and the SOCO team to tell them they were on their way. As they approached the front door, a large man appeared from the gloom, pulling at the mask covering his face to reveal an expansive ginger beard that looked as if it had been flecked with white paint.

Despite himself, Ford smiled. 'Jim,' he said. 'You get around a bit. How you getting on?'

Jim Dexter stood up to his full height, the protective suit he was wearing rustling in protest. Ford had known the forensic specialist for years, had worked with him on several cases. And in each instance, he had been glad to have Jim with him. There was something about the man's imposing bulk, calm nature and almost avuncular charm that calmed Ford, and reassured him.

And if he ever needed reassurance, it was now.

'Ah, Malcolm,' Jim replied. 'Good to see you. Bit of a quiet one this, I'm afraid. House is clean, almost obsessively so. If I didn't know better, I'd think he'd had a professional cleaner in. There are some basic supplies in the kitchen, some toiletries, which we can use for forensic matching, in the bathroom. Apart from that, you could take a few pictures and put the for-sale sign up in the front garden tomorrow. This place is good to go.'

Ford grunted. What had they been expecting? Bloodied knives, pictures of potential victims pinned to the walls, their eyes gouged out? No, everything they had learned about Martin Christopher told them he was a methodical, meticulous killer. He had a plan and he was following it. Even the theatrics with Tim Montgomery and the message daubed in blood on the swimming-pool wall had been part of it.

But where was Christopher now? And what was his end game?

Another SOCO appeared at Jim's shoulder, eyes darting between his boss and the two policemen, as though unsure of whom to address first.

'Ah, sir,' she said, finally deciding to address the space above the three men's heads. 'We've found something. In the garage. You may want to see this.'

Jim raised his eyebrows. 'Lead on, Ellen,' he said, standing aside to let the younger SOCO step onto the front doorstep.

'It's easier to go this way than back through the house,' Ellen said, following a narrow path that led towards a drive. Set back from the house was a small, squat garage. Ford could see that the side door, which was parallel to the back of the main building, was open, SOCOs buzzing around it like ghostly flies.

'We can get the main door open – had a look at it from the inside, doesn't appear locked,' Ellen said. She stepped forward, grabbed the garage door and swung it up, the hinges giving an unhappy squeal as she did so.

The garage was in the same condition as Jim had described the house – obsessively neat. The walls were lined with shelving units on which tins of paint and other decorating materials sat. At the far end of the garage was a workbench, beside which two toolkits were neatly stacked.

Ellen took a step forward, gesturing to the workbench, the SOCO who was flitting around it with a camera backing off as she approached. 'We found it in the bottom drawer,' Ellen said. 'Wasn't locked, so we took it out and had a look.'

Ford, Troughton and Jim followed Ellen, crowded around the workbench. On it sat a small lockbox, which had been thrown open. Ford exchanged a glance with Dexter, who nodded agreement, then snapped on a pair of nitrile gloves and reached into the box.

The first sheet of paper was a printed-out hotel booking confirmation, for the same hotel as Terry Glenn's body had been dumped in front of. The room had been booked remotely, the name on the booking Moira Christopher, the card that had been used to pay for it in the same name.

'Who the hell is Moira Christopher?' Ford muttered. An accomplice? A relative? Possible, but Martin Christopher was listed as an only child. So who? The dates showed that the booking was for one night only – the night Terry Glenn had died. It made sense. Book a room at the murder scene, use it to case out the place you wanted to dump the body, stow your getaway vehicle in the hotel car park. And with its easy access to the West Approach Road and other routes out of Edinburgh, it made getting away before the police arrived very, very convenient.

Ford passed the printout to Troughton, dug back into the box. There was one other item there and he pulled it out. An old-style Kodak photograph print, most likely taken on one of those instant cameras that were so popular before the advent of mobile phones had turned everyone into a wannabe David Bailey or Rankin.

Ford flipped the photo over, felt bile flood the back of his throat. Bit back the sudden urge to swear. It was an image of a man lying crumpled on a floor. His feet were bare, his front a riot of blood that was almost black in the harsh glare of the cheap flash. The hectic angles of his legs and arms told Ford he was dead. The injuries to his face, hands and arms told him he had suffered before he died.

'Jesus Christ,' Jim Dexter whispered, as he looked over Ford's shoulder. 'Who the fuck is that poor bastard? Another of this guy's victims?'

Ford shook his head slowly, MacKenzie's words echoing through his mind, taunting him. *Tell me, Malcolm, and be honest with me. Did we do the wrong thing? Really? Or did your boss have the right idea all along?*

He took a breath, held it. Closed his eyes, found no respite in that darkness. Opened them. 'That,' he said, after a moment, 'is John Peterson. They used to call him Jittery John, I think. Not that it really matters. What matters is, he's the bastard that killed Tracy Westerly and those other kids back in 'ninety-seven. He's the man Operation Calderwood could never find.'

CHAPTER 48

Connor found Paulie in the garage at his home, staring blankly at the car that had been used to run over Jen. The sleet had given way to snow, which was beginning to frost the eaves of the house and outbuildings and lie on the ground. Normally, Connor preferred snow to rain or sleet; he hated being soaked by the rain.

Not today.

Paulie turned slowly as Connor approached, no surprise or wariness in his movement. His appearance was unchanged from the last time Connor had seen him: the same pendulous gut, slab-like arms and bull neck all squeezed into an open-necked suit that looked as though it had been carefully hung on the floor in a tight bundle before Paulie had pulled it on. But Connor knew Paulie better now, knew who he really was, thanks to MacKenzie's revelation, and it caused him to pause. In the past, his natural reaction to any meeting with Paulie had always been a defensive alertness, up on the balls of his feet, shoulders tensed, waiting to respond in kind to any move Paulie could make. But now he knew what moves Paulie was truly capable of. And it caused Connor to ask himself a simple question: if it came to it, could he match those moves? Would he?

'Fraser,' Paulie said, his voice betraying an exhaustion he had managed to hide in his posture. 'Thanks for coming. How is she?'

The sudden flash of rage Connor felt burned away his fear, his doubts. Jen had been an innocent victim in all of this, their child even more so. He took a step forward, fists balling. 'How do you think she is, Paulie?' he said, the words a hiss through gritted teeth. 'She's in fucking hospital, facing a long, hard recovery because someone ran her over with that car to get at you and her dad. So how the fuck do you think she really is?'

Paulie's posture eased, slackened by the sudden grief that seeped into his eyes. In that instant, Connor found himself face to face with the man Paulie could have been, rather than the monster he had become.

And he wasn't sure which one he feared more.

'Aye, stupid question,' Paulie said, as he ran a hand over the silvering stubble that bristled on his head, the sound like sandpaper on wood. 'Look, Fraser. Connor. I know this doesn't mean fuck-all, but I never wanted Jen to get hurt in any of this. That wee lassie, she, ah, she . . .' something dark and conflicted cut through the weary grief in his face, like a searchlight that had been flicked on for a second and then blown its bulb ' . . . she means the world to me. I promised her mum, Hannah, I would look after her, and now look . . .' He raised his massive hands into the air, as though conducting a symphony only he could hear.

'She's in hospital, getting the best care she can get,' Connor said, the lie of the words bitter in his mouth even as he spoke them. 'She's young. Strong. A fighter.'

'Aye, just like her mum,' Paulie said, a small smile twisting the corners of his mouth. 'And you'll be there for her, won't you, Connor? I've seen the way the lass looks at you. She'll need you now.'

Connor nodded, even as Jen's words echoed through his mind. *I'm facing a long road back here and I don't want you sticking around out of some kind of feeling of obligation or guilt, OK?* The loss crowded in on him, thick and rancid and viscous, and he fought to breathe through it. Considered sharing the pain with Paulie, twisting the knife. But no. No. The baby, his son or daughter, was an intimacy for him and Jen. Sharing it with Paulie felt wrong, as though it would somehow betray the child that would now never be.

'Can we just get on with this?' Connor asked, as he pulled his thoughts back to the present.

'Aye,' Paulie said, more to himself than Connor. He looked over his shoulder briefly at the car, his expression telling Connor that it would soon be resting at the bottom of a deserted quarry or torn apart by Paulie's own two hands. 'You got what I asked for?'

Connor reached into the shoulder bag he was carrying, produced what looked like a standard iPad, which had been encased in an industrial protective shell. 'Just as you wanted,' he said, powering the device up and handing it to Paulie. 'The tracker's been fitted to the truck making the next run with Banks's driver and the extra merchandise. You can track it all from that, see where he goes, where the driver makes the delivery. Though I'm still not sure how that's going to solve any of this or get the bastard who hurt Jen.'

Paulie looked up, as though Connor had startled him from his thoughts. He gave a smile that was somewhere between cruel and sad, pursed his lips. 'You let me worry about that, Fraser,' he said. 'The drivers leave our depot clean. We always make sure of that. So they must be either meeting Banks's people on the road or being directed to a drop site close to the main truck route. It can't be that far out of the way or the extra miles would show up on the truck's odometers. So we find out how the operation works, then we take it apart. And Banks either backs the fuck off or we burn him to the ground as well.'

'Is Susie Drummond part of that plan?' Connor asked blankly.

Disgust creased Paulie's features. 'No fucking way,' he said. 'Susie is just an old family friend is all. Despite the shite Banks is putting around, I'm no grass, and he's a soft cunt for using Susie to try to make me out to be one. We deal with this old school, the right way.'

'The right way.' Connor almost laughed. 'Aye, OK. But you still haven't answered my other question. How the hell does this get us any closer to who hurt Jen? And, more importantly, why did they hurt her? Seems to me that they would be grateful after what you did.'

Paulie took a step forward, stopped himself. His features twitched, as though the thunderstorm of emotions he was feeling was shorting out his muscles and causing them to move of their own volition. 'Grateful,' he spat. 'Aye, everyone's fucking grateful. Everyone . . .'

His head darted up as Simon sprinted into the garage. 'Who the fuck are you?' Paulie hissed, the iPad falling to the floor as he balled his fists. 'Fraser, you cunt. If you've . . .'

Connor held up his hands, gaze darting between Simon and Paulie. 'He's a friend. Promise. He's here as lookout only.' He turned to Simon. 'What's . . .?'

'Sorry,' Simon said, his pale face and tight jaw twisting a needle of panic in Connor's guts. He raised his phone, handed it to Connor. 'This just popped up on the news apps. Thought you'd want to see it as soon as. Seems our pal Donna has been busy since we last met.'

CHAPTER 49

Ford requisitioned a conference room at Prestonview police stati had Troughton call DS Drummond and get her to meet them t They all seemed to have different pieces of the same jigsaw pu was time to put them together and see what the big picture matter how ugly that picture turned out to be.

They waited in silence for Drummond to arrive, Troughto ping away at a laptop, Ford pacing around the conference taking in the surroundings. The room was an unhappy collis the old and the new: cheap, scarred tables, whiteboard and ar worn carpet crashing together with a wall-mounted TV that tra cables like entrails, a conference phone system that squatted in t middle of the old table, like some technological gargoyle, and a larg fish-eye video camera that sat atop the monitor, as though Big Brothe really was watching them.

Ford wandered over to the control panel on the side of the wall, made sure all the switches showed that the conferencing facilities were turned off. With Troughton watching, he unplugged the camera and conference phone as well.

'Take it this one is going to be off the record, then, guv,' Troughton said, in a tone that made Ford look at the young officer in a different light. He had always thought him to be a careerist arse-licker, educated with books and theory, and precious little time on the street. But on every case they had worked on, Troughton had proven himself

a competent investigator. His recent work with Drummond had underlined this and Ford was forced to admit that Troughton could have a bright career.

Question was, would he decide to start that career by reporting his current DCI to the chief constable and any lawyer he could find?

Drummond arrived ten minutes later, hair and shoulders glistening with snow. Troughton nodded a greeting, offered her a cup of coffee from the pot he had managed to scrounge from somewhere in the building.

'Right,' Ford said, clapping his hands together as he stood. He didn't want to do this sitting down. 'Drummond, thanks for coming. I think it's past time we all got on the same page here. But,' he paused, gave Troughton a long, pointed stare, 'this briefing is off the record. I have some things you need to hear. You're both good officers who have done fine work on this case, and I'll leave it to your judgement as to what you do with what I'm about to tell you, clear?'

Drummond and Troughton exchanged a glance, some unspoken conversation passing between them. Then Troughton dipped his chin to his chest and Drummond spoke. 'Understood, guv,' she said, her voice level.

'OK,' Ford said, taking a deep breath. No going back now.

'Here's what we know. Tim Montgomery was murdered in a Scottish Government building in Edinburgh two days ago, followed by Terry Glenn, a known associate of Dessie Banks, a day later. Thanks to your work, Drummond, we now know that Martin Christopher murdered Montgomery and, based on evidence Troughton and I found at the home of Gina Westerly, is the leading suspect in the murder of Terry Glenn as well.'

'OK,' Drummond said, her tone telling Ford she wasn't going to be distracted by his compliments. 'We get that. But what we don't know is why. What does that *This is not murder. This is justice* crap mean, why are Jen MacKenzie and her dad involved in all of this and,' her jaw tightened, 'what the hell has all this to do with a suicide in the Borders?'

Ford shot a glance at Troughton, who held his gaze and shrugged. 'She saw the newspaper clipping in the file I prepped for you, boss. I told her to talk to you about the rest of it. And I have a question of my own. How does John Peterson fit into all this, and how do you know he killed Tracy Westerly and those other kids in the 1990s?'

Drummond gave Troughton a puzzled glance. 'Wait. What . . .?'

Ford held up a hand, silencing her, even as he felt something cold lurch in his guts. 'Let's take that first. John Peterson was a driver for MacKenzie Haulage back in the nineties. He worked for them, briefly, at their depot here in Prestonview before being let go. Troughton, you have the statements from Duncan MacKenzie and Paulie King at the time that detail it, don't you?'

'Yes, boss,' Troughton said, his voice distracted and vague as he punched keys on his laptop. 'Here we go. A statement by Paulie King, operations manager for MacKenzie Haulage. "Peterson worked for us for a month but we let him go because, although he was a great driver, he was a pig in the cabin. The lorries came back constantly filthy, filled with litter, food wrappers and other detritus. The fluids weren't checked on the rig and the other drivers didn't want to use his rigs after he'd had them, so we terminated his employment."'

Let him go, Ford thought. *Aye, you let him go all right.*

'And who took that statement, Troughton?' Ford asked.

'You already know, sir,' Troughton said. 'Then-DI Dennis Morgan, your old guv.'

Ford nodded, felt shards of glass grind in his throat as he swallowed. Too late to stop now. Wasn't sure he could either. 'Right,' he said, as he turned to the part of the conference table where he had dumped his briefcase and notes. Took a moment to fish out the file he was looking for, stared at it, then handed it to Drummond.

'That's the forensic report on Tracy Westerly's body,' he said, voice cold now. 'Can you read out what was found on her body, Susie?'

She cleared her throat, flicked through the file until she found the page she needed. 'Yeah, here it is. "The deceased was found in a prone position in a layby which comprised of soft earth, stones and grass clippings. Personal effects on the body included one rainbow hair clip, a My Little Pony doll and a paper bag branded from Sweet Treets, a confectionery store in Prestonview Tracy was known to frequent."'

Ford closed his eyes, bit down on the sudden wave of nausea that scalded up his throat. Felt tears threaten, forced them down.

'Guv, what?'

'Morgan was a bad copper,' he said at last. 'He would plant evidence, coerce confessions. Do what he thought necessary to get a result and make sure the bastards he was hunting got what they deserved. You've both heard the stories about his clashes with organised crime on the west coast, know that you don't tangle with that type of criminal without getting your hands dirty.'

'Well and good,' Drummond said slowly. 'But what does that have to do with this and . . .'

'Think, Susie,' Ford said. 'Troughton just read it out. What did Paulie's statement say? *The lorries came back constantly filthy, filled with litter, food wrappers and other detritus. The fluids weren't checked on the rig and the other drivers didn't want to use his rigs after he'd had them, so we terminated his employment.* Something seem wrong about that to you?'

She made no attempt to hide her frustration. 'No, sir, it doesn't,' she said at last.

'"Detritus",' Troughton said, his voice small, a child afraid of giving the wrong answer in class. 'And "terminated his employment". Awfully precise language when you consider the rest of the statement and Paulie King as a whole. And if Morgan was bent, then . . .'

Ford nodded, felt a weight lift from his shoulders. Finally, it wasn't just his secret any more. 'He changed the statements,' he said. 'Before coming here, I confronted MacKenzie about it and he confirmed it. What was it they found on Tracy Westerly, Susie? A rainbow hair clip, a My Little Pony toy and a bag from Sweet Treets? Well, guess what they found in Peterson's cab, which Morgan omitted from the report.'

'No, they couldn't . . .'

'Yes, they could. And they did. Paulie's first statement detailed the discovery of a My Little Pony toy cardboard box and a bag from Sweet Treets.'

'Holy shit,' Drummond said, her voice suddenly very loud in the oppressive silence of the room. 'You're telling us that Morgan tampered with evidence and conspired with MacKenzie and King to let Peterson go free? But that means . . .'

'No,' Troughton said, his voice giving a hint of the man he would become in twenty years' time. 'That photograph we found at Westerly's house. Morgan didn't tamper with the evidence to let him go, did he, guv? It's worse than that. Morgan fixed the evidence so Peterson would be killed.'

'*This is not murder. This is justice*,' Ford said. 'MacKenzie admitted it. He, Paulie and Morgan conspired to keep Peterson free, only for Paulie to scoop him up and kill him at a later date, mete out their own brand of justice.'

'Judge, jury and executioner,' Drummond whispered. 'Jesus. If this ever got out . . .'

'Aye,' Ford said. 'A copper setting up a murder. Every case Morgan made would be under the spotlight. No conviction would be safe. And Police Scotland's reputation would be blasted back to the bloody stone age.'

'Forget that for the moment,' she said, her voice hollow, as though she was a computer working through a task. In some ways, Ford thought, she was. 'If this is true, then what? *This is not murder. This is justice* is a message that the killer understands Morgan's twisted brand of justice? But why Montgomery and Glenn? And why Jen MacKenzie? Wouldn't Martin Christopher be grateful for what Paulie and the rest of them had done? The man who murdered his stepdaughter was dead, and from what you're saying, Paulie made sure he suffered before he died. So why the other killings?'

Ford turned back to his briefcase, found the statement from Victoria Donald that accused Tim Montgomery of sexually abusing her late husband, Cameron. 'This is why Troughton had that newspaper clipping for me,' he said. 'It's a statement that Morgan suppressed at the time. It alleges that Montgomery sexually abused a child while he was coaching a football team in Galashiels, which later drove the boy to kill himself.'

Drummond's eyes darted across the page as she read, mouth moving silently. It made her look impossibly young, Ford thought. Too young for this.

'OK,' she said slowly. 'I can almost see a link. But if I remember rightly, neither Tracy Westerly nor the other Calderwood victims were sexually abused. So how does this fit in, and why did Morgan suppress it?'

'I don't know,' Ford said. 'Now you know everything I do. If you want to go to the chief with it, fine. I was Morgan's junior for long enough to know what he was. But I want this done with. Martin Christopher is still out there, somewhere, and he has the answers we need. But I can't find him if we're on the sidelines while Professional Standards crawl up our arses. So, your call.' He glanced between Drummond and Troughton. 'We're in this together now. I have a pension and a way out, but you don't. What we do next is up to you.'

Another look between Troughton and Drummond, another unspoken conversation. Another moment when Ford knew the two of them would make each other better police officers.

'What we do is find Paulie King and Martin Christopher,' Drummond said at last. 'And then we get answers for everyone. Once and for all.'

CHAPTER 50

'Do you have any bloody idea what this means? What could happen? Jesus, Jen.'

Jen looked up at Connor from her bed, jaw set. She looked like a boxer who had been put on the canvas again in the eleventh round of a bloodbath bout, but refused to stay down. 'Actually, Connor,' she said, her voice as hard as her eyes, 'I've got a very good idea of what *I*'ve just done.'

Connor caught the emphasis on 'I've', raised his hands. Obviously confrontation wasn't going to get him anywhere. Jen had made up her mind, taken a course of action. He might as well wade into the Forth and command the waves to turn back for all the good it would do. But he needed her to understand, realise what was at stake.

He was still debating how he was going to do this when Simon peeled himself from the wall he was leaning on and ambled towards Jen's bed. 'Forgive him for being an eejit, Jen,' he said, dialling up his accent as he widened his smile, 'but Connor's right, this could be serious. This interview could attract some, ah, unwanted attention.'

'I know,' Jen said, eyes not leaving Connor. 'Don't worry, Donna filled me in about the threat to me and the note sent to my dad. Unlike you, Connor, she thought it was important for me to hear the full story, not just the edited highlights.'

'Look, Jen, I'm sorry,' Connor said, fumbling for words. 'I was just trying to do what I thought was right to keep you safe. You've already been through so much, I just wanted to—'

'What? Wrap me up in cotton wool and keep me in the dark?' Jen snapped. 'Look at me, Connor. You're right, I have been through a lot. And I've lost a lot too. And the thought of whoever did this to me being out there now, free, makes me want to scream. So if the interview I gave Donna helps lure that bastard out, then so be it.'

Connor had to admit she had a point. He had watched the interview as Simon had driven them to the hospital, Donna giving the details of the incident in a voiceover accompanied by footage of the gym and the road where Jen had been run over. Then it cut to Jen, staring defiantly at the camera, the shot lit and framed to show off her injuries to maximum effect. A few preamble questions, and then the killer quote from Jen: 'Whoever did this to me, whoever ran me over and then drove off, is nothing more than a coward. But I've got news for them. I'm still here, and I will not stop looking for you until I get the justice I deserve.'

The justice I deserve, Connor thought. She might have been more subtle if she had got Donna to put a caption reading 'Come and get me, motherfucker' at the bottom of the screen.

'Look, Jen,' Connor said, trying to reset his thoughts and the conversation. 'Everyone here wants to get the bastard who did this to you, no one more so than me. And I'm doing everything I can to find him. But with the threat your dad received, this is a big risk. What if this sicko makes a move on you?'

Jen looked at him for a long moment, as though seeing something new in him and trying to decide if she liked what she had found or not. When she spoke her voice was cold, almost clinical, a world away from the warm, husky voice he had become used to. 'You've got your pal in the police, talk to him, I'm sure he'll get some officers to watch the place. Plus, Dad's got his goon squad prowling the hospital. But if you're really worried that whoever did this can get past them, I'm sure Simon will stay and keep me company.'

Connor exchanged a glance with Simon, who merely shrugged in response. 'No, Jen, wait. I'll stay with you, make sure—'

She held up a hand, silencing him, the IV tubes that snaked into the crook of her arm catching in the light as she moved. 'No, Connor. You said it yourself. You're already doing everything you can to find whoever did this, so you've got some plan already in action. Go. Do what you were going to do. Do it now, before this bastard ever gets here.'

Connor exchanged another glance with Simon. It made sense. Leaving him here, he knew Jen would be safe, and it would allow him to concentrate on Paulie, and whatever he was scheming to bring whoever had targeted Jen into the light.

But still . . .

'Go,' Simon said. 'I'll come out to the car with you, get a few of me things. Then you can take it, go and do what you need to do. I'll keep her safe, Connor, I promise I will.'

In the bed, Jen nodded gently.

'OK,' Connor said reluctantly. 'I'll call Ford, see if he can get some officers here. But promise me, both of you, you'll contact me if there's even the hint of trouble.'

Jen smiled, some warmth finally bleeding into her eyes as her expression relaxed. Connor could see weariness in her posture, wondered how much this show of strength and resolve had really taken out of her.

He crossed to the bed, kissed her gently on the forehead. Felt the almost haphazard heat of her brow on his lips, ran a hand through hair that was damp with sweat. Swore that whoever had done this would pay. No matter the cost.

CHAPTER 51

Night had fallen by the time Ford got back to Stirling, but the day showed no sign of ending. After his meeting with Troughton and Drummond, it was decided that they would look into Martin Christopher's background for possible clues to his current location, while Ford would check in with his contacts to see if they had any information that might lead them to Paulie King. Drummond had bridled at that, seemed on the verge of saying something, then gave up and merely nodded her agreement. Whether she was about to object to involving Connor Fraser, or make some other point about Paulie, Ford couldn't tell.

The call came as he was driving through West Lothian, squinting into a flurry of snow that seemed to be getting heavier the closer to home he got, as though the weather was trying to dissuade him from getting back to Stirling. Despite himself, Ford smiled when he saw the caller ID. He had a complicated case to deal with, Paulie King and Duncan MacKenzie were involved in it up to their necks, so who else would be calling but Connor Fraser? They arranged to meet at Fraser's flat, the man's tone telling Ford that he was none too happy about another intrusion into his privacy but was too distracted by other matters to do anything about it.

He declined the whisky Fraser offered him after he stepped inside, his mind drifting back to Gina Westerly and how she had died. He wondered briefly if that memory would give him similar pause when he got home to the bottle of Glenfiddich in his own drinks cabinet, knew deep down it wouldn't.

'Thanks for agreeing to meet me,' Fraser said. Ford could see weariness weighing down his features and his shoulders.

'Actually, it's fortunate you called me. I needed to see you anyway, see if you had any information about the possible whereabouts of Paulie King. The investigation into the murders in Edinburgh has made some real progress, but I need to speak to King to try to make sense of it all.'

Fraser's gaze hardened, calculations flitting across his mind. He straightened his back, as though the gesture could shrug off the tiredness. 'Oh? How so?' he said.

Ford sighed, felt the exhaustion he had seen in Fraser settle on him, as though it had been floating around the room, looking for a new home. He wasn't in the mood for jousting or game-playing. He had a killer on the loose, and too many unanswered questions. 'Off the record?' he said.

'Always,' Fraser replied, his face impassive.

So Ford told him. About Martin Christopher, him being Tracy Westerly's stepdad and the discovery of the photograph of John Peterson's picture at Gina Westerly's home. About the allegations of abuse made against Tim Montgomery, and how Morgan had made them quietly vanish.

Fraser was silent for a moment after Ford stopped talking, as though he was trying to absorb what he had just been told. Then he gave a snort of frustration. 'OK, so this guy Christopher kills Tim Montgomery and Terry Glenn, presumably for the same reason that he targeted Jen – to get revenge for the loss of Tracy Westerly. He said as much in that note that was sent to MacKenzie – "Kill Paulie King or I will take your daughter from you, just as mine was taken from me." So he blames Paulie for Tracy's death somehow. But we know that Peterson was Tracy's killer and Morgan conspired with Paulie and MacKenzie to kill him as a result. So, what? We're saying Paulie set up Peterson to take the fall for him and he really killed Tracy?' He fell silent for a moment, shook his head again. 'Sorry, no, can't see it.'

'Why?' Ford replied. 'Is it possible you're too close to this? That your, ah, personal relationship with Paulie and the MacKenzies isn't letting you see the bigger picture?'

Fraser looked up at Ford suddenly, as though he had whistled a familiar tune whose title he couldn't quite remember. Then the look faded, replaced by a frown so deep it might have been painful. 'No, it's not that,' he said. 'Yes, I admit, I'm too close to all of this. That my, ah, relationship with Paulie and the MacKenzies could complicate matters. But I know Paulie. He's a killer all right, and dangerous. But a child killer? I don't think so. There's something we're missing here. Some information this guy Christopher is working on that we don't know. But we might get a chance soon, thanks to Jen.'

'Oh? How's that?' Ford asked.

Fraser outlined Jen's interview with Donna Blake, and her jibe to Christopher that he was a coward and she was waiting for him. Ford rubbed his eyes with his fingers, sparks scudding across the darkness, the taste of whisky strong in his mouth now as he planned his drive home. 'Blake,' he whispered. 'Donna bloody Blake.'

'Yes,' Fraser agreed. 'Donna Blake. But it was Jen's choice, her idea. I've got my friend Simon with her now. But if Martin Christopher is driven enough to kill two men, he's not going to stop until he finishes the job with Jen. Any chance you could get some uniforms at the hospital? MacKenzie has his goon squad there, but I'd feel better if Simon had some professional back-up.'

Ford ignored the sting of irritation he felt at the insinuation that professional police officers were being relegated to mere back-up, focused on the task in hand. 'Fair enough, I'll see what I can do. But, tell me, Fraser, it's not like you to sit on the sidelines, especially with what's at stake. So what are you going to be doing when all this is happening?'

'Making sure there are no loose ends,' Fraser replied, his voice hardening. 'And when I'm done, I'll deliver Paulie to you personally, no questions asked.'

CHAPTER 52

The link between Tracy Westerly and Martin Christopher might not have given Susie much of a clue as to where the man might be, but it did allow her to see his life and work from a different perspective. The problem was, that perspective made no sense.

She was at home, having decided to head there after the meeting with Troughton and Ford. She had made the excuse that it was more efficient for her to go home and work rather than back to the office in Edinburgh or go to Stirling when she could merely boot up her laptop and start working. It was one of the few things she could thank the pandemic for – working from home had become an accepted norm, even for the police. But the truth was, Susie wanted to be alone for a while, gather her thoughts. A man she knew had been proven to be a killer, she was working for a DCI who seemed happy to bid protocol or proper procedure a cheery goodbye as they sailed over the horizon, and she had a growing sense of unease about where this case was going.

Back at her flat, she showered, poured a glass of wine, then cracked the laptop. After an argument over confidentiality and commercial sensitivity, the powers that be at the Scottish Government had, reluctantly, turned over access to Martin Christopher's email account and documents he was working on. And this was where Susie's perspective had started to shift.

As she had seen in the performance reviews she had read when she first interviewed him, he was a diligent, methodical civil servant who quietly got on with the work that was assigned to him. He had initially started as a policy development officer in education, but had transferred to the justice directorate in 1998. In light of what they now knew about Tracy Westerly being his stepdaughter, the move made sense to Susie: Martin Christopher had sought out work that allowed him to develop policy on child care and social justice. Again, his reviews told of a diligent man who worked hard and delivered tangible results to help keep kids safe. From what Susie could see, he had taken his pain at the loss of Tracy and harnessed it, used it to fuel his work to try and make an increasingly complicated and dangerous world a little safer for the children growing up in it. The last project he was working on, developing new policy to protect kids from potential abusers and harmful content online, was testament to that. The policy suggestions and notes Susie could access showed a thoughtful, intelligent man who could see the big picture and was doing his best to change it.

So how, then, did a man driven to do good become the savage killer she was now hunting?

She sighed, took another sip of wine. Contemplated getting her phone and making the call she had promised herself she wouldn't. After all, what could it hurt? If anyone could help her make sense of this, it was Doug McGregor, a reporter with a talent for sniffing out stories and trouble so raw it was almost supernatural. 'Attack it like a story,' she could almost hear him say. 'Answer the basic questions – who, what, when, where, how and, most importantly, why. That's all you ever need to know.'

She smiled, pushed the thought aside. As much as she could use his help, and the sound of his voice, Doug was dealing with his own issues at the moment. She had promised to give him the time and space to do that, and she would.

Still the question nagged at her. Why? Why would Martin Christopher suddenly snap and go on a murderous rampage? Why target Jen MacKenzie? Why now?

Frustrated, she turned back to the laptop, clicked back into the file marked 'Real-world risks'. It opened up to show a raft of email chains, conversations across government about potential dangers to young children. They were titled according to area of discussion: marketing, advertising, sexualised imagery, alcohol, drugs. She clicked on one chain at random, marvelled at the sheer number of people who were copied into the conversation. It was bewildering, dozens of people having a conversation via email, with other people getting randomly copied in 'for awareness' or asking to be dropped out as it was no longer relevant to them. She had thought Police Scotland was a bureaucratic nightmare, could see now where it had picked up the bad habit.

She clicked out of the email chain, kept scrolling. Cinemas, shopping centres, festivals, airports, public spaces, railway stations. Hold on. Susie stopped, scrolled back, felt her pulse quicken. Flicked into another file, read. There. Just as Donna had said after Tim Montgomery's body had been found. 'He's a high-up official in culture and external affairs, runs the funding operation for major festivals, including Edinburgh.'

Susie opened the folder marked 'Festival', was confronted by the same long catalogue of email conversations. Clicked on one, saw a massive copy list clog the 'To' and 'CC' fields in the email. Squinted at one, then hit Control F to bring up the search function. Typed in Tim Montgomery's name, not realising she was holding her breath as she hit the return key. Nothing. No matches. Susie sighed. No luck, but there was something here, she could feel it. She repeated the process with four more emails, had no luck. But then, on the fifth, just as she was beginning to give up hope, she got a match. There, highlighted in blue in the blizzard of names the email had been sent to, was Tim Montgomery. Susie felt excitement crawl up her throat. Swallowed it with a slug of wine as she read the email. She went to another email, followed the chain. And as she read, a glimmer of understanding winked at her through the confusion. She almost missed it, would have if she hadn't been briefed by Ford earlier that evening.

My Little Pony. And a rainbow hair clip. Two small, innocuous items. Two items that gave Susie the answer she had been seeking. The answer to the question Doug always insisted was the most important of all, the one that made sense of everything else.

Why.

CHAPTER 53

'So, explain to me again how this is going to work? And how it's going to get me Martin Christopher.'

Paulie's anger at the question was written all over his back. They were at his house on the outskirts of Stirling, Connor returning there after his visit to the hospital to see Jen. On an impulse, he had checked the garage as he approached the house: as he had suspected, the car that had hit Jen was gone.

'It's bloody simple,' Paulie said, turning slowly, the two crystal glasses he was holding looking impossibly fragile in his bear-like paws. He held one out, shrugged when Connor didn't make a move to take it.

'Suit yourself. Missing out on a good whisky,' he muttered before sipping from his own glass.

'You haven't answered my question, Paulie,' Connor said. 'How does this get us Martin Christopher? And why did he want Duncan to kill you and then target Jen? Seems to me . . .' he paused, the words sour in his mouth '. . . you did him a favour in your own twisted way.'

Paulie's eyes glittered, as though the crystal from the glass had somehow leached into his skin and become part of him. His face hardened, then softened, reacting to something only he could see. 'I don't bloody know,' he said at last, voice impassive. 'Guy lost his kid, for fuck's sake. Watched his wife drink herself to death because of it. Grief like that changes you. Trust me, I fucking know.'

Interesting, Connor thought, realising again how much he didn't really know about the man in front of him, the man who could be killer one minute, protector the next. The man who dressed as though the concept of proper sizing or tailoring was alien to him, yet showed enough flair for interior design to earn a spread in a property magazine.

'OK,' Connor said, changing tack. 'So what's the plan? We wait? Not the best idea, especially now that Jen has put herself back on Christopher's radar with that sodding interview.'

Paulie drained his glass, looked down. Surprised Connor with a smile that was strangely wistful. 'Aye,' he said, his voice soft now, as though warmed by the whisky. 'She always was a headstrong one, was Jen. Gets it from her mother. Hannah was the same. She wanted something, she got it. It was her way or no way. And fuck the consequences.'

'It's the consequences I'm worried about,' Connor replied. 'If you're wrong about this, if Christopher decides to finish what he started with her instead of playing along with whatever you've got . . .' Connor trailed off, the thought crashing into his mind. Stupid. Fucking stupid, Connor.

'You're not overly worried about Jen because you know where Martin Christopher is,' he said. Paulie had effectively told him what was really going on the last time they had met – *I never wanted Jen to get hurt in any of this . . .*

Any of this. Paulie had been planning it all along.

Paulie shrugged again, the smile on his face growing cruel now, cold. 'This has been a long time coming, Fraser. A long fucking time. And you're not going to mess it up. I told you, Banks will be dealt with old school for peddling this filth, just like Peterson was. It's what he deserves. What Christopher deserves too, really. What father wouldn't want that? But then . . .'

He moved almost too quickly for Connor to react. Surging forward, he dropped the whisky glass, which shattered as it hit the floor. Connor barely managed to turn away from the charge, Paulie catching his side instead of straight in the stomach as he had intended. He drove an elbow into the exposed back of Paulie's neck, the blow robbed of any real power by his desperate struggle to stay upright.

Paulie grunted, staggered forward. Reared up to his full height. Connor could see murder glint in his eyes, wondered if that was the look John Peterson had seen before Paulie had killed him. He wrapped the thought in his rising fear and buried it. Fear meant hesitation. And hesitation would very likely prove fatal.

'Right, then,' Paulie said. 'I was going to try and do this quiet for Jen, send you on a wild-goose chase while I did what needed to be done. But, no, you had to be the smartarse, didn't you, had to figure it out? Too bad for you, Connor. See, I can't let you stop this. There's too much at stake.'

He raised his fists, danced forward slowly – a bare-knuckle boxer approaching his opponent. Connor took a half-step back, trying to assess targets. Realised he had only one option with an opponent like Paulie – a man who wore his bulk like body armour and had spent a lifetime honing his skills.

Paulie snapped out a jab and Connor feinted to the left, ducking low and stepping into Paulie's arm reach. Smelt rich, smoky whisky as he telegraphed a blow aimed at Paulie's chin, then turned and smashed his foot into Paulie's knee instead. The only way to win this was to incapacitate Paulie. Trading blows would be suicide.

'Fucking BASTARD!' Paulie bellowed, backing off in a staggering lurch as his knee refused to take his weight.

'Paulie, I—'

Too late. Paulie charged forward again, his speed almost supernatural for a man so large. Connor dodged away, but Paulie was familiar with the move now, adjusted mid-leap to compensate. Caught Connor around the waist and drove him back, pain exploding in him, the smashing of picture frames almost an accompaniment to the agony as his waist collided with the drinks table and he was bent backwards over it.

Paulie's hand skittered up his front, fingers huge blunt things that dug into Connor's chest as though he was a rock-climber seeking purchase. Connor aimed blows at Paulie's sides and head as he fought desperately to regain his balance, throw Paulie off him. But it was impossible. Paulie's bulk had him pinned, gave him no chance to get a firm footing and use his weight against him.

Hot, desperate heat as Paulie's hands scrabbled over Connor's throat and squeezed. Connor thrashed manically as his eyes began to bulge. It was like his head was a tyre that was being overinflated – pressure building, building, a rising scream in his lungs echoing through his mind as his field of vision dimmed and darkened. He saw Jen in the darkness, felt something deeper than loss.

Paulie smiled; a leering devil in a fading world. Connor's hand scrabbled across the table, looking for something, anything, he could use. Anything. Something hard and cold brushed across his fingers and he grasped for it. Got a grip with a hand he couldn't really feel. Prayed and swung.

The picture frame sliced across Paulie's face and he roared again as blood gouted from the wound. Despite everything, Connor felt a savage flash of satisfaction – at least the bastard would walk away bloody.

'You stupid fucking cunt,' Paulie hissed. Then he drew his head back and drove it forward, his forehead a sledgehammer. Connor felt the vibration of the impact as his nose broke, but the pain was drowned out by the growing darkness. Felt his eyes roll back, the world shifting, tilting as he retreated from it. Knew he was falling, couldn't get his body to respond to his commands to stop. Tried to picture Jen in his mind, hold on for her, felt some splinter of an idea spark briefly, like a lighthouse beacon in the encroaching fog.

And then there was nothing. Nothing but a welcoming blackness that engulfed Connor Fraser's world.

CHAPTER 54

Troughton sighed, took a swig of the wine Susie had poured him, the action sharp, impatient. 'Nope, sorry, not seeing it,' he said. 'What the hell am I looking at anyway?'

Susie felt a smile twitch her lips, stifled it. Despite everything, she was growing to like Troughton: he was a non-nonsense police officer with a flair for investigation and a loyalty to his boss that was tempered with a clear-eyed pragmatism. None of which meant she couldn't enjoy getting one over on him.

She took the laptop from him, clicked through the files to the emails she had found. Initially Tim Montgomery had been one name in dozens that emails were sent to, but digging deeper into the trails showed that, over time, more personal exchanges had developed between Montgomery and Martin Christopher. She found one such email, titled 'RE: RE: RE: RE: Festival advertising – potential risks', opened it, scrolled to the bottom, then turned the screen back to Troughton.

'OK,' he said slowly. 'Fairly standard. Looks like Christopher was checking with Montgomery about festival acts and how their street marketing and flyering were handled. Makes sense, summer in Edinburgh, all those families and kids milling around the Mile, plenty of chances for kids to be exposed to acts or marketing stuff that wasn't age appropriate.'

'Yeah,' Susie said, taking a sip of her own wine and swilling it around her mouth, trying to get rid of a bad taste she knew deep down no wine could ever mask. 'Fairly standard. But keep reading up the chain, as the conversation progresses.'

Troughton did as she requested. Then stopped, turned to her, then back to the computer screen. Susie thought the effect was almost comical, like a cartoon character doing a double-take.

But there was nothing comical about what she had found.

'Fucking hell,' Troughton whispered, eyes searching hers for a moment, then turning back to the screen. 'Surely he wouldn't be that blatant, would he?'

Susie nodded. It made sense. She had worked enough cases to know that abusers loved the power their abuse brought them – their web of victims and the effect they had spreading like a crack in a sheet of glass, radiating from the first point of impact with the person who was abused. She had seen rapists force their victims to give evidence in court to satisfy this twisted desire for power and control, watched as women endured the ordeal of reliving their nightmare in front of a room of strangers. Montgomery, she felt, was no different. Another abuser, drunk on his own power, his feelings of superiority and invulnerability only magnified by the fact he had a police officer in his corner to make all his problems go away.

The email was the penultimate one in the chain, Montgomery's reply to a point Christopher had made about the complexities of monitoring and regulating marketing content in an age when anything you wanted was only the click of a mouse or a social-media post away. Reading it, Susie felt a dull, ill-formed rage well up inside her.

> I agree, Montgomery had written, It's a different world from the one I know, I'm afraid, when the latest My Little Pony was the big thing for my little girl and most problems could be solved by a trip to the sweet shop or a new hairband. But there are monsters out there now, we know this, and the police cannot always be relied upon to catch them or even recognise them.

'Jesus,' Troughton whispered, leaning forward and putting the laptop on Susie's coffee table, as though he didn't want it near him. Susie understood the feeling. 'He's more or less rubbing Christopher's face in it, isn't he? My Little Pony and a trip to the sweet shop? Fuck me. But I don't get it. We know Montgomery was a child abuser. Know that he had Morgan cover up what he did to Cameron Donald. But how does that connect with the murder of Tracy Westerly? She was snatched from Prestonview, years after Montgomery attacked Donald. So how does he know the details of Tracy's murder, and why would he be so blatant about it with Christopher?'

'Power,' Susie said, almost absently. 'You know what these bastards are like. Think about it. That email is close to the bone, but there's nothing there that could be used to directly implicate Montgomery in what happened. He's torturing Christopher, letting him know he knows about Tracy. Must have thought that, if it got nasty, his friendly polis could take care of the problem for him.'

'OK, so let's say that's the case. Christopher gets this,' Troughton pointed at the laptop, 'knows or strongly suspects that Montgomery knows something about Tracy's death. Why did he wait,' he leaned forward, peering at the screen, 'for more than three months to kill the man, and why do it so publicly? Why the message on the wall? And how does Terry Glenn fit into all of this?'

'I'm not sure,' Susie said. But even as she spoke, an ugly suspicion was forming in her mind, like an old-fashioned photograph being developed to reveal a picture of something unspeakably ugly. What was it Ford had said?

Morgan was a bad copper. He would plant evidence, coerce confessions. Do what he thought necessary to get a result and make sure the bastards he was hunting got what they deserved.

'What he thought necessary to get a result,' she said. And then another thought. The last line of Montgomery's email to Christopher. *The police cannot always be relied upon to catch them or even recognise them.*

Susie sat, chewing her lip, thinking it through. Gave a grunt halfway between a cough and a laugh as she felt her theory solidify into certainty.

'Huh?' Troughton said, almost reflexively.

Susie shook her head, cleared the thought away. 'We need to get to Stirling,' she said at last. 'I think I know what this is about, but we're not going to confirm it sitting here.' She looked down at the wine glass in her hand, calculated. She'd had about two, was probably OK to drive, or would be by the time they got on the road. Gave a laugh despite herself even as she put down the wine. After all, what difference would one more broken law make now?

CHAPTER 55

Simon's car felt a lot like the inside of Connor's head – cramped, unforgiving and noisy with thoughts.

He had awoken to a world of pain, crumpled on the floor of Paulie's living room, blood crusting around his lips and cheek as it leaked from his nose. His throat felt like it was coated with ground glass, thanks to Paulie's attempts to choke him to death, while touching his nose was like detonating a bomb, sending shrapnel shards of agony stabbing through his head as bone ground against bone.

He rose stiffly, slowly, his aching sides telling him that Paulie had delivered a few extra kicks to his ribs after he had passed out. He surveyed the devastation around him, shattered picture frames, and glass twinkling up from the carpet like obscene jewels. Yet the drinks table had been left perfectly square, one surviving picture, of Paulie, Duncan, Jen and her mother, Hannah, propped against the crystal whisky decanter.

A parting touch from Paulie, Connor thought. Not really surprising from a man who was almost pathological in his need for order and neatness. Despite himself, Connor gave a bitter laugh – leaving this place in such a chaotic mess must have been torture for Paulie.

Fuck him.

Trying to shake off the snarling pain that had infested his head, Connor moved slowly through the house, searching room after room.

As he expected, Paulie was long gone, but questions rushed into his mind, drowning out the silence of the now-abandoned home.

What was it Paulie had said? *This has been a long time coming, Fraser. A long fucking time. And you're not going to mess it up. I told you, Banks will be dealt with old school for peddling this filth, just like Peterson was. It's what he deserves. What Christopher deserves too, really. What father wouldn't?*

So Paulie was working with Martin Christopher. That would at least explain where the car used to run Jen over had gone: Christopher had presumably been here and taken it. But why? Why was Paulie helping the man who had almost killed Jen? And what 'old school' reckoning did he have planned for Dessie Banks?

Forcing aside the pain that was settling over him like a shroud, Connor grabbed his phone and called Duncan MacKenzie.

'Hello?'

The slurred numbness of his voice caused Connor to forget his pain for a moment, fear curling in his gut as he thought something must have happened to Jen. 'Duncan, Jen. Is she OK?'

'What?' Confusion coloured MacKenzie's voice for a second. 'No, no. She . . . she's fine. What do you want, Fraser?'

'Did you know?' Connor asked, the pain starting to seep back into his body now, almost welcome after the paralysing fear that something had happened to Jen.

'Know what?' MacKenzie asked There was an absence in his voice, a disinterest that unsettled Connor more than the gnawing pain radiating from his ribs.

'That Paulie had set me up? That he was working with Martin Christopher all along? I swear, Duncan, if this is your twisted idea of some sort—'

An ugly laugh grated down the phone, the sound of knives being sharpened on an old, dull stone.

'Well, well, the surprises never end. No, I didn't know, Fraser. Doesn't really surprise me, though. Two of them deserve each other.'

'What?' Connor felt the world surge and tilt as the vice around his head tightened and his vision darkened. He took a breath, ran a finger across his nose. The pain was instant and electric, jolting him back to consciousness.

MacKenzie sighed, almost bored now. But something in that sigh gave Connor the insight he was missing. Shock. Whatever was going on, MacKenzie was in shock.

'Where are you now? The yard?' Connor asked.

'What? No, no, I'm . . .' another bark of humourless laughter '. . . I'm at home. Was going to see Jen in a while, but not yet. No, not yet. Need to get my head straight first. Come and see me if you want. We can go and visit Jen together.'

Connor took one last glance around the room, saw nothing to interest him. Got moving, calculating the fastest route to Cambusbarron, and the virtual palace Duncan MacKenzie called home.

The snow had become heavier in the time Connor had been unconscious, the outline of Simon's car sketched out in white, like chalk on the charcoal of the deepening night. Connor looked at the car, then walked around it, inspecting, a growing sense of unease warring with the pain in his head for dominance. Something about this was very wrong. Paulie had said he wouldn't let Connor get in the way of whatever he was planning, yet he had left him alive and, from what he was seeing, with viable transport.

Something snarled in his mind as he fired the engine of the little Renault, the rough bark of the exhausts seeming to seek out the worst pains in his body and prod them.

The drive to Cambusbarron, a small, affluent village south-west of Stirling, was uneventful, the car's beams turning the snow into a field of static in the windscreen. As he drove, Connor tried to organise what he knew, see the bigger picture. He was reminded of a time in his childhood when he had lost one of his baby teeth and couldn't resist prodding the alien gap with his tongue. He felt he was doing that now mentally, prodding at a gap, feeling a familiar geography turned suddenly alien. He knew what he was missing, somewhere, just couldn't quite drag it to the front of his consciousness.

MacKenzie's house was an imposing Victorian manor on the edge of the village, the snow giving the limestone walls a cold bluntness that somehow reflected the personality of the man who lived there.

Connor expected one of MacKenzie's thugs to be on duty, but was surprised when the man himself answered the front door bell.

'Ah, Fraser,' he said, eyes roving over Connor's face, a lazy smile playing over his own as he inventoried the injuries. 'Looks like you've had a bit of a night. Come on in, have one of these.' He gestured with one hand, a glass brimming with amber liquid glinting in the light spilling from the house.

Connor followed MacKenzie inside, took in the house. Felt something catch at the corner of his thoughts as he saw the muted pastel walls, tasteful works of art and heavy drapes that framed the huge bay windows. And then there was something else. That glass MacKenzie was holding. Almost like . . .

Connor snapped his attention ahead as MacKenzie marched down a long hallway, then took a sharp left. Connor followed him, hanging back slowly, letting the door open enough to see where he was going. For all he knew, Paulie could be behind that door, waiting.

He stepped into a large study, the walls lined with books, industry awards and pictures. MacKenzie had taken a seat behind a desk that was almost identical to the one in his office at the haulage yard. The only difference was that the chair behind this desk was even grander - a true throne for a king.

But, Connor thought, was this king mad?

'So, what the fuck happened to you?' MacKenzie asked, his voice taking on its previous anaemic tone as he settled into his chair. 'You and Paulie finally get round to having that pissing contest you both wanted? Seems like he hosed you.'

Connor swiped the insult aside, told MacKenzie what had happened. Watched as MacKenzie took in the information, his eyes stealing between the glass in front of him and the open laptop on the desk as he listened.

'So do you know what's going on?' Connor asked, after a pause that MacKenzie clearly had no intention of filling. 'What's Paulie really up to? And what possible reason could he have for working with Martin Christopher?'

MacKenzie pulled his face into an empty sneer, teeth glistening in the glare from the laptop screen. 'Ah, questions. The truth is, Connor,

I don't think I know Paulie as well as I thought I did. As for what he's doing with Martin Christopher . . .' The leather of his chair sighed softly as he shrugged.

Connor felt the sudden urge to grab MacKenzie from that chair, squeeze the answers from him.

MacKenzie seemed to read the intent in his eyes, raised his hands in a placatory gesture. 'Here,' he said, his tone colder now, wary, as he lowered his hands to the laptop. 'This might answer some questions.' A fast rattle of keys, then MacKenzie slid the laptop across the table towards Connor, a harsh, jerky motion as if the computer was somehow hot or unpleasant to touch.

Connor looked down, saw MacKenzie had opened an email. Skimmed the contents.

Mr MacKenzie,

As a father myself, I felt it was important I write to you to explain my actions and, more importantly, to explain why I attacked your daughter. I apologise for this but, in my defence, I can say that it was not my fault. It was, as with everything that has happened so far, the fault of Paulie King. I am sorry to say that he lied to us both, Mr MacKenzie, and now Jennifer must pay for that lie. I do not expect you to take my word for this. Please watch the attached video. It is not for the faint of heart but it is, I'm afraid, a necessary evil which we must use to get to the truth. And that truth is this. I am not a murderer, I am acting in the only way any father would. Timing is everything, Mr MacKenzie, and this video proves that. My question is, how much time do you think Paulie has left?

He looked up, the questions forming in his mouth dying in the glare of MacKenzie's eyes. They were empty, haunted, the eyes of man who had seen untold horrors and had been hollowed out by them.

'Play the movie,' he said, voice as dead as his eyes.

Connor suddenly wanted to be out of that room, away from Duncan and his dead man's gaze. Wanted nothing more to do with Paulie and Christopher and whatever the hell was going on.

He clicked the mousepad, finger numb. Watched.

It was a grainy video of some kind of storage room, the walls utilitarian, dotted with shelves filled with what looked like car parts. The vantage point of the camera, looking down on the scene, told Connor it had been mounted to get the best angle on a tight space. He felt his breath catch in his throat as a small boy stumbled into the frame and bounced off one of the shelving units, obviously thrown roughly into the room. He sat in a heap and, to his horror, Connor realised that the video had sound.

He could hear the boy crying.

The child looked up, small face ghostly white in the harsh lighting of the room, tears glittering on his face. He shrank away, almost trying to merge into the wall, feet kicking uselessly on the concrete floor, as another figure entered the image. Older. A man, tall, rangy, a tangle of tattoos snaking up arms corded with muscles.

Connor jumped when MacKenzie spoke. 'That's John Peterson,' he said, the lack of emotion in his tone underlining the horror of what Connor was seeing.

He watched as Peterson closed in on the boy, his back obscuring the child. But Connor could still hear the small, birdlike screams, the choking, the increasingly frantic drum of feet on concrete. He felt tears scald their way down his face as he grabbed the side of the table and closed his grip on it, as though he could somehow send his strength to the dying boy. An impotent fury coiled its way around his heart and, in that instant, he thought of Jen and the child who had never been. He watched, unable to take his eyes from the screen. A moment later, Peterson backed off, and Connor bit back a choking wail as he saw the boy lying propped up against the shelving unit. He stared at the screen, willing the boy's chest to rise, fall, *just fucking move*. Knew it never would. A moment later, Peterson turned, leered at the camera and ticked off a small salute before the screen went dead.

The silence seemed to scream at Connor. He was unable to take his eyes from the screen. He felt the urge to vomit, to grab the laptop, smash it into MacKenzie's face, scar him the way Connor felt his own soul had just been scarred. He closed his eyes, dropped his head. Forced himself to breathe, using the pain this ignited in his sides to anchor himself in something approaching sanity.

'Why would you show me that?' he heard a voice say. It took a moment to realise it was his own.

He heard the laptop scrape across the desk, looked up to see MacKenzie typing, tears in his own eyes. He glanced at the screen then looked away, jaw working as he did so.

'This is a message,' he said at last. 'Took me a little time to get it, but it's there in the email. *Timing is everything, Mr MacKenzie.*'

'What . . .' Connor found it difficult to talk over the sound of the boy's cries echoing in his mind '. . . what the fuck do you mean?'

MacKenzie tapped some keys then whirled the laptop around to Connor, the image frozen with Peterson's back to the screen. 'Look at this,' MacKenzie whispered, tapping the screen at the frame where he had paused it. 'Look.'

Connor swallowed bile, reluctantly looked at where MacKenzie was pointing. In the top right corner of the image was a time and date stamp – '03:47, 15/9/97'.

'So what?' Connor said, a sudden exhaustion overcoming him, even though he knew that dreamless sleep was something he might never experience again.

'Three forty-seven,' MacKenzie said, raising his glass to his lips. 'On the morning of the fifteenth of September 1997.'

'So what?' Connor said again, eyes drifting back to the screen unwillingly; the passing driver unable to resist the lure of the car crash.

'So what?' MacKenzie said, tasting the words in the same way he was tasting his whisky. 'So this is on Monday, the fifteenth of September. But Paulie, Morgan and I agreed Paulie would kill Peterson the night before, on the Sunday, and Paulie told us he'd done so. So why do you think Paulie lied about that, Connor, and why did that poor wee shite in the video have to die for that lie?'

Connor turned away from the screen, eyes seeking something, anything that was normal in a world that had suddenly turned dark and predatory. His eyes roved around the room, falling on the pictures on the wall, a happy family smiling for the cameras, unaware that true evil existed.

Pictures.

He felt his breath catch in his throat, head feeling as though it might explode as random, unrelated facts clashed together, knitted, became something new. A sudden memory of Paulie's place, the perfectly muted décor, the expensive picture frames. The same frames he saw at the side of Jen's bed.

What was it Paulie had said? *She always was a headstrong one, was Jen. Gets it from her mother. Hannah was the same. She wanted something, she got it. It was her way or no way. And fuck the consequences.*

He turned. Saw the crystal tumbler in Duncan's hand, felt another click of recognition. Asked the only question he could.

'Tell me, Duncan, who decorated this place?'

CHAPTER 56

Susie had Troughton crack the laptop as they drove for Forth Valley Hospital, Ford saying he didn't want to leave Jen MacKenzie alone after her appearance on TV. A uniformed officer had been assigned to offer a visible presence at the hospital, but Susie knew the man well enough now to know that wouldn't satisfy him. She hoped what she had found would.

Troughton had initially complained about using the laptop while driving, saying it made him car sick. But when Susie told him what she suspected, and what she was looking for, his reservations were replaced by an almost childlike enthusiasm that Susie couldn't help but appreciate – and envy. She told him what she was looking for, the documents they needed, gripped the steering wheel hard as she waited, Troughton's laptop and his poor mobile-phone signal slowing their progress. But it couldn't stop it and, by the time they arrived at the hospital, the snow starting to drift against the walls, Susie had everything they needed. The who, the what, the when, the where, the how and, most importantly, the why. It was a stretch, she had to admit, but no more than finding the Stanley blade Christopher had hidden. And it was Ford himself who had given her the key.

They met Ford in the main atrium of the hospital, Ford saying he wanted to be in Jen's vicinity after her appearance on TV.

'Come on,' he said. 'Spoke to a nurse I know, blagged a favour. We've got the use of a conference room to talk.'

Susie and Troughton followed him through a labyrinthine network of corridors, heels squealing on the industrially polished floors. And, as they walked, Susie felt a familiar thrill of revulsion tickle her skin. She had never liked hospitals, the smells, the charged atmosphere of inherent danger, like a pub just before a fight broke out. She supposed that, like everyone, health was more on her mind now, the world dramatically illustrating that killers could remain invisible if they wanted to. But at least she could drag one into the light now.

The conference room could have been modelled on a police station, or any public building constructed over the last twenty years. A series of desks had been lined up in a rectangle around the room to give the impression of one large space. Phones were dotted around the table at regular intervals and, on the far wall, a large TV monitor sat idle.

Ford didn't so much take a seat as collapse into it, nervous exhaustion and impatience radiating off him in waves. He sat back, blew a long breath up at the ceiling, rubbed his eyes, then looked back to Troughton. 'John, we just passed a vending machine. Get some coffees, will you? I have the feeling we're going to need them.'

Troughton nodded, dropped his laptop and notes on the table, then left the room. Susie took a seat a couple of spaces away from Ford, who had taken to studying his hands as though the answer to some question he had was written on them in very small text. She thought about saying something, wondered what that could be. Was still trying to decide when Troughton re-entered the room, back first, three cups of something that smelt vaguely like coffee held in a triangle in both hands.

Susie nodded her thanks as he passed her a cup, moved on to Ford and then took a seat. His gaze rested on Susie, eyes glittering. He had helped put the story together as he drove. He knew what was coming.

'So,' Ford said, nose wrinkling in disgust as he sniffed his coffee. 'What was so important that it couldn't wait until the morning briefing, Drummond? I know you young things are full of pep and enthusiasm, but I'm the one who's got to sign off the overtime sheets on this case, and this might just kill me.'

Susie gave a tight smile, acknowledging the joke. He had made them complicit in an investigation that broke just about every rule of policing, yet he was complaining about overtime? Hardly. 'Yes, sir. Sorry. It's just that Troughton and I were doing some late work, and we found something that might explain what's been happening and, specifically, what DCI Morgan's role in all of this was.'

Ford stiffened in his seat, eyes hardening, as though she had hit an old bruise and he was trying to mask the pain it caused him. In a way, she thought, she had.

'Go on,' he said.

'Well, sir, it's something you said. We looked into Martin Christopher, found a link between him and Tim Montgomery. Which got me thinking about how Morgan fitted into all of this. It was something you said, about him being a bad copper. One who would do what he thought was necessary to get a result. And then there was that message on the wall – *This is not murder. This is justice.* I couldn't get past that. Justice for whom?'

Ford grunted, his eyes flashing a warning to both Troughton and Susie.

'I wanted to understand the link between Montgomery and Morgan. Why would a policeman, even one like Morgan, cover up for a child abuser? Why not follow up Cameron Donald's widow's statement and nail Montgomery to the wall? Be a hell of a collar, a senior civil servant done for child abuse? He would have been a legend in the police.'

'So?' Ford said.

Despite herself, Susie felt a wave of frustration. It was so obvious when you looked at it, so easy. Martin Christopher had been telling them all along. They had seen the message, but not understood it.

This is justice.

'The problem was, sir, Morgan already was a legend. You told us he worked in Glasgow, at the old Pitt Street station, took on some of the worst gangsters on the west coast. So why would a police officer like that end up taking statements for Operation Calderwood, and why would he cover up for a paedophile?'

Ford sighed, rubbed his forehead. She was losing him. Time to play the trump card. She nodded to Troughton, who fired up his laptop and started to hit keys.

'We looked at Morgan's record, sir,' she said, nodding to Troughton. 'It seems that, after a drugs raid on a football team social club, Morgan became very interested in other avenues of investigation. The letters took a while to find, but he lobbied the chief constable at the time to be transferred to Galashiels, which was where he heard the allegations against Montgomery. And from there, he practically demanded a transfer to Operation Calderwood.'

Susie could see the first vague glimmer of understanding in Ford's eyes. And something else. Something she hadn't expected to see.

Hope.

She nodded to Troughton, who slid the laptop over to Ford. 'That's a report from last year, sir,' she said, pointing to the screen. 'The BBC carried out an investigation of historic child abuse at football clubs around Scotland. Coaches taking advantage of their positions to prey on children in their care. It was covered up at the time, only came to light in the last couple of years. But if you look at the victim statements, you'll notice a couple of things. The abuse took place about six months before Cameron Donald was attacked, and the club . . .'

'Heart of Strathclyde,' Ford whispered. 'Same club as Morgan raided. You think it's connected?'

'Too much of a coincidence to be anything but,' Susie said. 'It's a leap, but try this. Morgan raids the club looking for drugs, finds something that hints at the abuse that's going on. Starts following it. We know from those reports,' she nodded to the laptop, 'that it was happening. He hears about the Montgomery allegations, in an area he just happened to ask for a transfer to. Nah, he must have planned it.'

'But why?' Ford asked, exhaustion creeping into his voice again now. 'Why go to all that trouble only to let Montgomery go free. Unless . . .'

Susie nodded, bit down on the sudden smile she felt play on her lips. Finally. 'Exactly, sir. You said it yourself. About Morgan being a bad copper. One who would do what he thought was necessary to get a result. So what if he was on to something, something big, and Montgomery was only a means to an end? We know that Montgomery had intimate knowledge of Tracy Westerly's death, he taunted Martin Christopher with that. And we know Dessie Banks isn't averse to dealing in filth. So what if Morgan was blackmailing Montgomery, but not in the way we think? Not for personal gain. What if he was using him to go after other abusers? People like Tracy's killer, John Peterson?'

'OK,' Ford said slowly, rocking back in his chair and looking up at the ceiling again. Susie could almost hear the gears in his mind turning. 'Morgan was capable of it, using one villain as a chess piece to get another, or twist a case the way he wanted it to go. But what about the message - *This is not murder. This is justice.* How does that fit in? And why was Jen MacKenzie,' he tilted his chin upwards, as though they could see her on one of the floors above, 'targeted?'

Susie sighed. 'That's where I get a little hazy, sir. It fits so far. We need to—'

She was cut off by an impatient rap at the door to the conference room, which was quickly followed by the appearance of a uniformed officer.

'What?' Ford snapped, his voice so hard that both Susie and Troughton jumped in their seats.

'S-sir,' the officer said, her face paling as her eyes darted between Troughton and Susie, a silent scream for help. 'Sorry to bother you, but a man's just turned up, demanding to see Ms MacKenzie. Big lad, looks like he's just had a bar fight with the Incredible Hulk. Says his name's Connor Fraser. Asked to speak to you as well.'

Susie spoke before Ford could. 'I'll talk to him, sir,' she said. 'I think a word with Mr Fraser would be very useful for everyone concerned.'

CHAPTER 57

'My God, Connor, what the hell happened to your face?'

Connor winced, offered a smile he hoped was casual and didn't look as false as it felt on his lips. 'Ah, nothing,' he said, as he approached the bed, taking Jen's outstretched hand. 'I just thought you made your bruises look so good I'd get some myself.'

She swatted his arm, tutted as he leaned in to kiss her forehead. 'Fine, don't tell me,' she said, her tone leaving him in no doubt she would find out soon enough. 'But I take it they're part of the reason you wanted to see me? Marie's not impressed.'

Connor nodded, the image of Jen's formidable nurse-cum-bodyguard flashing through his mind. Her eyes had danced across his face when he arrived at the ward, a quick, cool appraisal of his injuries. She had muttered her acceptance that he needed to see Jen, finished the conversation with 'Come and see me when you're done. I'll set that nose for you.'

Connor wasn't sure if this was intended as a kindness or a threat.

'Come on, then, what's going on?' Jen asked, jarring him from his thoughts.

He eased himself into the chair next to her bed, ribs moaning a dull protest. 'I just needed to talk to you, see you,' he said. It was half the truth at least. After the perverted horror Duncan MacKenzie had shown him, Connor had wanted nothing more than to scoop Jen into his arms, let her warmth soothe whatever part of him had been frozen by what he had seen. But that was a luxury he couldn't afford. Not now. Not when he was so close to the truth.

A truth he wasn't sure he wanted to see.

'The thing is, Jen,' he said, 'I really need to find Paulie. He's disappeared, and I wondered if you could think of anywhere he might have gone. I think he's in danger, and I need to get to him, now. I spoke to your dad,' he swallowed, blinking back another flash of that video, the sound of small heels drumming frantically on a stone floor, 'and he can't think of anywhere. Was wondering if you could.'

Jen stared at him, brow furrowing in concentration. Connor stared back, trying to look beyond the bruises and the injuries, trying to see what he had not seen before, half hoping he wouldn't.

'I really don't know,' she said. 'I mean, Dad and Paulie are practically joined at the hip. They've always been close, especially after, well, after Mum died.' She nodded towards the bedside table and the photo there: Jen, her mum and dad, Paulie. 'I always thought Paulie was a bit of a pain in the arse, to be honest. You know I hated it when he followed me to work and back – Dad's way of keeping me safe. But still.'

'There's nowhere you could think he would go?' Connor asked again, her words echoing in his mind even as he turned and picked up the picture, ran a finger over the oh-so familiar frame as his mind drifted back . . .

'Not really. He's got that place out at Sauchenhall, looks like a farm, and he's always around the yard or at Dad's place, but other than that, I can't really think. If Dad can't help you, not sure I can.'

You already have, Connor thought, something cold twisting in his guts. 'About that,' he said, trying a different tack. 'You said Paulie was always around when you were growing up?'

'Yeah,' Jen said, confusion on her face. 'He, Dad and Mum knew each other from when they were kids, grew up together. Used to call themselves the Three Musketeers, if you can believe that. All got a bit funny when Paulie got married, but that didn't last. The woman, can't remember her name, ran off with another guy. Can't really blame her. I mean, Paulie's not exactly God's gift. But he was always there for us, especially Dad, after Mum died.'

Connor put the picture down, squeezed Jen's hand. 'What was that like?' he asked, the memory of his own mum sparking an ache deeper and more melancholic than the one radiating from his ribs.

'Hard,' Jen said simply, returning his gaze. 'Typical Scots, we both tried to be brave. Dad for me, me for him. But it was harder for Dad, I think, because I reminded him of Mum so much. But Paulie was there, every step of the way. There were nights I could hear the two of them in Dad's study. Talking long into the night. About Mum. About taking on the world, about what they were going to do for Mum. But, of course . . .' The first tears slid down her cheeks.

Connor leaned forward, kissed her forehead. 'I'm sorry,' he whispered.

She shook her head, as though banishing the thoughts. 'It's fine,' she said. 'Took a lot of years, but I'm OK with it now. I mean, of course I miss her, but at least I had her for that long. Huh.' She laughed. 'Dad always used to say that. "At least I had her."'

Connor gave her hand another squeeze, then let it go as he stood, swallowing a cough of pain as he did so. 'I should go, let you get some rest,' he said, seeing the tiredness roll over her eyes like a fast-moving cloud.

'Sorry I couldn't really help,' she said, smiling weakly up at him. 'But find him, Connor, please. He's an arse but, well, he's Paulie, you know? He's not all bad.'

Connor pulled another fake smile, this one feeling almost natural on his lips. 'Don't worry, Jen,' he said, eyes drifting to the picture again. 'I'll find him. Promise.'

He stepped out of the room, saw Simon walking towards him, pace urgent with concern. 'Been quiet around here?' he asked, before his friend could articulate his worry.

Simon laughed. 'Round here? Fuck, man, you seen the state of yourself? Looks like you've been having all the fun. What the hell happened to you?'

'Good question.'

Connor and Simon turned, saw DS Susie Drummond standing behind them, a half-smile dimpling her cheeks. 'I heard you wanted to see the boss. Got a minute or two for me instead?'

Connor smiled, this one genuine. 'Of course, Susie,' he said. 'But give me a minute or two, will you? I've got to find a nurse who wants to break my nose again.'

CHAPTER 58

Marie's promise to set Connor's broken nose had, it turned out, been both a kindness and a threat. He had found her after seeing Susie Drummond, using the time to order his thoughts, test what he thought he now knew from different angles. But it didn't work. No matter how many different ways he looked at it, no matter how many times he tried to convince himself he was wrong, that it was just the fatalist in him looking for another piece of bad news, he turned back to the same conclusion. A conclusion based on picture frames, interior décor, crystal glasses, and something Paulie had said just before he had attacked Connor: 'She always was headstrong, got what she wanted, and fuck the consequences.'

When he found Marie, she had hauled him around into the nurses' station, ordered him into a chair. He had sat, a child taking his seat in class, feeling vaguely bewildered as to how this small, compact woman completely dominated the space. He wondered what she would do if she was cursed with the memories he had acquired that night, found he didn't want to know.

She made a swift, thorough examination of his face and the rapidly blossoming bruises around his neck, the latex gloves she was wearing doing nothing to dampen the heat radiating from her hands.

'No concussion,' she said, after dazzling him with a pen torch, 'but you've probably not got much of a brain to rattle, anyway.'

'Can't argue with that,' Connor muttered. It was true. Anyone with half a brain would have seen the answer a lot quicker than he had.

He was jolted from his thoughts by an explosion of pain as Marie attended to his nose. Tears sprang into his eyes as she manipulated the bones back into position, the world flaring brilliant white as the agony lanced through his skull.

She applied tape to the nose, leaned back to study her handiwork. 'Not bad,' she said. 'You'll never be an oil painting, but it's the best I can do. You really should see a doctor properly.'

'No time now,' Connor said, moving to rise from his seat.

Marie's hand on his arm was soft but insistent. She looked into his eyes, the bravado and gruff façade gone, leaving only the person who was driven to help those who were hurt. It made her look younger, Connor thought. And immeasurably sadder.

'I don't know what type of trouble you're into, son,' she said at last, 'but that wee girl in there has been through hell, and the last thing she needs is more misery, OK? So try to keep it away from her.'

'I'll do my best,' Connor said, wondering how much of his promise was a lie.

He walked back to Jen's room slowly, using the time to send a text message. Found Susie Drummond standing there, Simon lounging against the door jamb. He looked relaxed, casual. But Connor knew there was no power on earth that would get Simon to let anyone he considered a threat into Jen's room. The thought calmed him.

Susie led him to a conference room a couple of floors down, where Ford and his detective sergeant, Troughton, were waiting. Connor could almost taste the atmosphere when he walked into the room; shrill excitement and spent adrenalin. He knew that the three police officers had found something.

'Looks like you've been in the wars, Fraser,' Ford said, nodding towards Connor's face. 'Who did you piss off this time?'

'Mutual acquaintance,' Connor said, easing himself into a seat. 'Which is, funnily enough, what I wanted to talk to you about. Have you made any progress in relation to Martin Christopher?'

Ford gave a short laugh, shook his head slightly. 'How many times have I had to tell you, Fraser,' he said, 'you're assisting the police with our enquiries, not the other way round? So how about you start telling us what happened to your face, and what you know about Paulie King?'

Connor shrugged. There was no point in trying to hide anything at this stage, and he needed to know what the police knew if he was going to finally understand everything that was going on. It was like two people trying to do the same jigsaw puzzle – no one would see the complete picture unless everyone shared. But there was one piece he didn't want to share, wasn't sure he could. The video of the child. He wasn't ready to speak about that yet. To do so would make it real again. And if that happened, if Connor stared at that horror for too long, he would lose the ability to act, to do what needed to be done.

He took a breath, ignored the pain in his sides. Told Ford and the other two officers what had happened that night, about Paulie's alleged plan to track Banks's deliveries, find out where he was going and who he was delivering to. How Paulie had, ultimately, betrayed him, that he was somehow working with Martin Christopher. Connor saw something spark in Ford's eyes at that, felt Susie and Troughton's gazes sharpen on him.

'What?' Connor said. 'That means something. What have you got?'

Ford glanced at Susie, who nodded. Interesting, Connor thought. Ford's pragmatism and ability to ignore standard procedure was obviously catching.

'We believe Martin Christopher killed Timothy Montgomery because he had knowledge of the death of his stepdaughter, Tracy. We also believe Montgomery was being used by a former police officer in an investigation into wider child abuse across Scotland.'

Connor swallowed, felt his throat click as the air in the room seemed to thin. Closed his eyes for a moment, pushed back the image of the boy in the video bouncing off the wall. Later. He could deal with that later.

Somehow.

'So, what are we saying?' Connor said, feeling his way through the idea as he spoke. 'That Christopher knew Montgomery was involved in his stepdaughter's death, and was being helped by Paulie, the man who killed Tracy's killer? That a police officer was using this to investigate a wider . . .'

He trailed off. The thought hit him harder than Paulie's headbutt, fireworks ricocheting through his brain as it all fell into place.

'Connor, what?' Susie stepped forward, concern etching itself into her face.

'The message.' Connor said, biting on his lip. '*This is not murder. This is justice.* And Banks smuggling porn. Jesus Christ. That's it, isn't it?'

'What?' Ford said, his tone telling Connor that he had seen the answer too, but wanted Connor to be the first to say it. Why was that?

'Look at the big picture,' Connor said, smiling despite himself. 'What have we got? A child abuser who knows intimate details of a girl's death is murdered very publicly, with a message scrawled on a wall. Then a known associate of Dessie Banks, who we know is dealing in images of abuse and God knows what else, is killed, with the same message. Meanwhile, MacKenzie gets a threatening note, demanding he kill Paulie.'

'Yeah, OK, we know that,' Susie said, concern giving way to frustration. 'So what?'

'*This is not murder. This is justice,*' Connor said. 'It's a message all right. A message to whoever was dealing in this filth along with Tim Montgomery. You said it yourself. Your rogue policeman - I'm assuming that's your former guvnor, Dennis Morgan, by the way - was investigating abuse "all over Scotland". So what if there's a bigger network out there, a network Martin Christopher found out about from Montgomery, a network he's sending a message to?'

'Jesus,' Ford whispered. 'You think Paulie was telling you the truth, don't you? That he was tracking Banks's delivery, that he was going to use that against him?'

'Yeah,' Connor said, the revelation almost a relief. 'He said it himself. He was going to deal with Banks, old school. And what better way to do that than by setting an avenging angel in the shape of Martin Christopher on him? The man has killed twice. What do you think he'll do to Banks?'

'Kill him,' Susie said bluntly. 'But wait. If Paulie and Martin

Christopher were working together, why the hell did he demand MacKenzie kill Paulie, and why did your girlfriend get run over?'

Connor swallowed, the image of the video rising in his mind again. The time and date stamp on it. MacKenzie's words, how Peterson had killed the boy after Paulie was already meant to have ended him.

Why do you think Paulie lied about that, Connor, and why did the poor wee shite in the video have to die for that lie?

Then Jen, whispering in his ear: *At least I had her.*

'Justice,' Connor said. 'A twisted justice.' He reached into his pocket, produced a small zip drive, a present from Duncan MacKenzie. Slid it across the desk to Troughton. 'I got that from Duncan MacKenzie. It'll let you track the truck with Banks's driver, just like Paulie and Christopher are. I suggest you find them. Now. Otherwise, a lot of people are going to end up looking a lot worse than I do tonight.'

Ford nodded agreement, and Troughton got to work, Drummond moving to stand over him. Connor kept his face impassive as he felt his phone buzz in his pocket, knew that, if it was a reply to the message he had sent, it would either absolve him or damn him.

CHAPTER 59

Duncan MacKenzie swirled his whisky slowly, watching as the crystal caught the light from the chandelier and sent it dancing across the room. He knew drinking was a mistake, that he should be sober, sharp. He shouldn't even be here. He should be at the hospital, with Jen, keeping vigil on his injured daughter. After all, wasn't that what loving fathers were meant to do?

He drained his glass, held it up. Hannah had loved these glasses when they had bought them, at the same time as they had moved into this house. MacKenzie had balked at the price. After all, a glass was a glass. As long as it was clean, what did he care? But Hannah had insisted. Given some of his own demands over the years, it was the least he could do.

'They're elegant,' she had told him, in the tone he knew only too well meant *just nod and get on with it*, 'and after all your hard work, you deserve the finer things in life.'

The company that had made the glasses had gone bust a few years ago, meaning that they weren't only elegant, they were now collectable. Rare. Irreplaceable.

Like so many other things.

He sighed, eyes sliding to the laptop on the table, the memories of that video flashing through his mind. Fraser's revulsion and horror had been understandable – it was the same reaction Duncan had experienced. Just for totally different reasons.

The world lurched suddenly, as if the whisky had finally caught up with him. Duncan closed his eyes, tightened his grip on the glass as thoughts and memories flashed through his mind.

Timing is everything . . . My question is, how much time do you think Paulie has left?

So why do you think Paulie lied about that, Connor, and why did the poor wee shite in the video have to die for that lie?

They're elegant.

Tell me, Duncan, who decorated this place?

He was on his feet before he knew it, chair crashing to the floor as he half staggered back. With a cry, he threw the glass, the sound of it shattering driving shards of realisation into his mind, forcing him to see what he had been unwilling to look at for so long. He whirled, grabbed the picture on the table, placed where Hannah had insisted; him, Paulie, Hannah, Jen and Paulie's former wife, Jane. Jane, who had run off with another man, a man Paulie had paid to take her away from him.

The phone was in his hand before he realised it, finger hovering over the keypad. He was, strangely, reminded of the day Hannah was diagnosed with cancer, sitting in the consultant's office just before they got the results, their future teetering on a knife edge between joy and despair.

They're elegant.

He dialled the number, didn't have to wait long for a reply. Got talking while he still could, before sense overcame the whisky and love overcame hate.

'It's Duncan MacKenzie. I'm guessing you boys are in the shite right now, that your boss is missing and you're out looking for him? Aye. Doesnae matter how I know. Question is, do you want to know where to find him and Paulie or not?'

A pause, then excited, wary chatter down the line. Duncan barely heard it.

'Aye, aye, fine,' he said, eyes sliding to the wall and the dent where the whisky glass had hit it. 'Whatever. I'll tell you everything you need to know. I just have one favour to ask in return.'

CHAPTER 60

Connor had finished his meeting with Troughton, Susie Drummond and Ford with a promise: that he would stay out of their way as they followed the lorry that Paulie was tracking, and that he would hand any information he had on Paulie's whereabouts over to them as soon as he had it.

Ah well, one promise out of two wasn't bad going.

He headed back to Jen's room, found Simon still on guard duty.

'You OK if I keep the car a bit longer?' he asked.

'Depends,' Simon replied, a smile on his lips, something brighter than mischief dancing in his eyes. 'You gonna drive off and have all the fun again? Looks like you've already had a skinful of shits and giggles tonight.'

A flash of the boy in the video, the sound of his choking sobs. Connor closed his eyes, took a deep breath. Felt Simon's hand on his shoulder.

'You all right, Connor?'

Connor placed his hand on Simon's. Squeezed. 'Yeah, I'll get there. Just been a hell of a night.'

'Want to tell me about it?' Simon asked.

So Connor did. In low, hushed tones, he told Simon about his clash with Paulie, the video Duncan MacKenzie had shown him. The link between Martin Christopher, Tim Montgomery and a wider child abuse ring that spread, cancer-like, across Scotland. As he spoke,

Simon's face grew pale, his expression tight and unreadable, a clear sky suddenly blackened by an approaching storm. Connor's friend was gone. The man standing in front of him now was a police officer. A police officer being told crimes had been committed.

A police officer who wanted to make those responsible pay.

'Right, let's get some more bodies here, then we go make this right,' Simon said, his Belfast accent thicker now, almost guttural.

Connor shook his head, smiled. Typical Simon. He would walk into fire for a friend if he needed to. 'No, Simon, not this time,' he said. 'If I'm right about all of this, then Jen isn't in any real danger. Not now. But I need you here, in case . . .'

'In case what, man? Come on, Connor. From what you've told me, there's some bad shit going down. This place is virtually a fortress, what with the goon patrol in the grounds and downstairs, and the uniform your pal Ford has spared. I'm not needed here. So what gives? Why are you so fucking determined to go Lone Ranger on this one?'

Connor took a breath. Started talking again. Told Simon of his suspicions, of crystal glasses and tasteful décor, of picture frames that he had seen in three separate locations. Three locations with one singular link between them. And then he drew out his phone, showed him the message he had just received from Robbie at Sentinel. The wrong answer to the right question. 'I have to do this alone, man. Please.'

Connor could see the war between the desire to protect his friend and the need to honour his wishes wage itself in Simon's eyes as he studied Connor's face. Then, after a moment, the smile returned, sun breaking the clouds, and he clapped Connor's shoulder again. 'Go,' he said. 'Give these bastards hell. There are a few wee treats in the car's boot. I took the spare wheel out, put a lock safe in the well instead. Code is six four nine three. Thought it would be easy for you to remember.'

Connor smiled. Nodded. It had been the code for his locker at Musgrave police station in Belfast. 'Thank you,' he said.

Simon shrugged off the thanks. 'Just go, do what you need to do. But do me a favour, will you?'

'What's that?' Connor asked.

'Don't miss. No quarter given, Connor. You get those sick fucks. For Jen. And me.'

CHAPTER 61

They traced the lorry to a garage on a nondescript industrial estate in Bonnybridge, a small village south-west of Stirling, which had gained a reputation a few years back for a rash of UFO sightings. The situation had become so serious that the then-Provost of Falkirk had written to three prime ministers, demanding the issue be investigated. The demand, like so many others sent south, had gone unanswered, and the stories persisted, occasionally resurfacing in a tabloid newspaper or on a TV documentary.

Standing in that garage, Ford had a sudden urge to run out into the night and scream at the sky, see if any passing alien would do him a favour and abduct him. After all, anything would be better than this.

The lorry sat almost diagonally across the garage, the cab at a near right angle to the trailer, making it look like an animal that had had its neck snapped by a predator. The double doors to the trailer had been thrown open, the contents, mostly electrical equipment, such as TVs, washing-machines and fridges, strewn across the floor of the garage. The vehicle had been gutted, the seats slashed open, the small living area behind the driver's seat ransacked, door panels and facings ripped free.

But what was worse was the human wreckage that had been left behind. Three bodies – one sitting propped up against the front wheel of the cab, a dark bib of blood from his slashed throat glistening in the harsh fluorescent lights overhead. Ford thought the man had brownish-blond hair, but it was hard to tell with the amount of greyish-pink brain matter, and hellishly white bone that was now streaked through it, as it leaked from a splintered wound to the top of the man's head.

The second body was lying amid the items thrown from the trailer, face down, legs splayed out at odd angles behind him, one white trainer sitting close by, obviously torn from the foot by the force of a blow. He could almost have looked as if he was sleeping – but Ford knew that no one slept with their chin twisted around almost to touch their back. A blackish-green band of bruising tattooed the exposed flesh like the devil's own necktie.

But it was the third victim that was the worst, the one that made Ford want to run screaming into the night. He had seen the reaction of Drummond and Troughton, knew they felt it too. He watched as they fought with their natural impulse to run, their faces pale, jaws clenched tight. Felt a wave of guilt as he did so. What right did he have to inflict this kind of life on them? They were good police officers – he had seen that in their work. But he knew the cost that kind of talent for the job could extract. He was paying it himself in a strained marriage, a heart that had grown a callus of cynicism, and a certainty that he would never enjoy another peaceful night's sleep in his life.

He took a deep breath, stepped forward, unwilling to get too close to the body and contaminate the scene.

And what a scene it was.

The man had been pulverised. It was the only way Ford could describe it. Whatever had been used to cave in the head of the man propped up against the lorry, it had been used to full effect on this man. He lay at the foot of a fire door at the back of the garage, broken body contorted into such unnatural angles that it made Ford's eyes hurt to look at him. Bone peeked through his jeans at the knees and along the shins, as though bombs had detonated in his legs. His hands, which lay at his sides, palms up, were nothing more than smears of meat on the harsh concrete floor, the fingers ruptured like sausages, spilling blood and bone. Forcing himself to look up, Ford found himself transfixed by the almost hypnotic brutality of what had been done to the man's face. It was as though his entire head had been a papier-mâché bust that someone had taken in their hands and squeezed. The bones that held the features in place had been shattered, the cheeks, nose and lips sloughing down the face, like melting candle wax, leaving eyes that looked as though they were weeping blood. The mouth, what was left of it, hung loosely, lolling off the man's chest, clearly held on to the face by skin alone, the jaw having been destroyed.

Ford thought briefly of Terry Glenn's mutilated body in Edinburgh, sightless eyes looking up at the sky, his tongue ripped out and left in his hand.

He had died easily compared to this man.

'What the hell happened here?' Drummond whispered.

'Old school . . . Isn't that what Fraser said King had in mind?' Troughton replied, his voice dull and sounding suddenly very old.

'Any IDs on the bodies?' Ford asked, unable to take his eyes from the body that lay like a discarded mannequin in front of him.

'Not sure yet, sir,' Drummond said. 'SOCOs are en route, so we've not had anyone make a full examination yet, other than the doc to confirm the obvious, that these guys are dead. But we can make a fairly good guess. There are two cars parked out the back. One of them is registered to a taxi firm owned by Dessie Banks, the other . . .'

Ford turned, finally able to wrest his gaze from the horror in front of him. 'Go on.'

'The other is registered to Banks himself, sir. Jaguar XJR, private plate. So it's a good guess that he was here. Question is, where is he now?'

CHAPTER 62

Simon's Renault bounced and rattled along the single-track road, the potholes, scree and rapidly thickening snow making progress torturous. Connor sympathised - the car had been designed for performance, something to throw around B-roads or scream around a track. Now he was requiring it to be a four-by-four. It was like asking a blind man to pin the tail on the donkey. Possible – but highly improbable.

The place hadn't been hard to find, once Connor had known what to ask Robbie, one of his agents at Sentinel, to look for. The title deeds were there, along with the planning permission and even, fortunately, the architect's drawings of the property, which gave him a detailed floorplan of his destination. It was, Connor was forced to admit, perfect. A converted farmhouse, nestled in the rural countryside north of Stirling. Situated up the steep hill Connor was now approaching, its location would provide total seclusion, and the added bonus of a 360-degree view to see if any unwelcome visitors or prying eyes were planning on paying an unannounced visit.

Connor chewed his lip, glanced at his phone, which was mounted on the car's dashboard. It didn't have satnav as Simon hated the technology, dismissing it as 'an affront to proper driving'. Connor could have handled a little effrontery at that moment.

The map on his phone told him he was coming to a junction, and a sharp left turn that would take him up the hill to the farmhouse. He pulled the car into the layby, considered, even as the burbling of the Renault's twin exhaust made the decision for him. He got out of the car, glad he had taken the time to head home and change into warm clothing before coming here. Moved round to the boot and opened it, the lock safe set into the spare tyre well, just as Simon had promised. He keyed in the number, heard the lock spring clear with a dull *thunk*, then swung the door open. Used the light from his phone to illuminate the 'treats' Simon had left for him.

'Jesus,' Connor whispered, even as he felt a smile play on his lips. He reached into the safe, selected what he needed. Then he closed the boot, locked the car and got walking.

It took him ten minutes to make the climb, his progress slowed by staying off the road and in the uneven, rutted ground behind the trees. The soft glow of lights from the steading was unwavering in the falling snow, a beacon guiding him on. It was a standard house-and-barn configuration, a two-storey stone-faced main house with a large garage to the side of it, which would give the building an L-shape if seen from the air. Connor found a tree just off the road leading up to the driveway, ducked behind and fished a pair of mini-binoculars from his pocket. He could see enough to tell him there was one large floodlight on the eave of the main garage, angled to illuminate the courtyard in front of the house. Connor swore under his breath. No doubt it was motion-activated. And the last thing he wanted to do was telegraph his arrival.

He swept his binoculars across the rest of the building, looking for some avenue of approach. Missed it on his first pass, almost missed it on his second. The driveway that led to the courtyard meandered towards the house then swept right, the road splitting off as it led to the garage and then on towards the courtyard. Where the road split, there was a mound of stone, atop which sat what looked like a sundial sketched out by the snow. The plinth, Connor guessed, about four feet high and two feet wide. Not great, but if he could get across the grounds and in behind it, it might mask him from the floodlight, give him a chance at the element of surprise.

Maybe.

He glanced at his watch. No time for indecision. If he was

right, and the existence of this place told him he was, then Martin Christopher was living on borrowed time. Assuming, that was, he was still breathing.

Taking a deep breath of the cold night air, Connor moved forward.

Slowly, eyes flicking to the house every few steps, he crept towards the sundial. The near-perfect silence of the night seemed to scream at him, the only sounds the occasional cry of an owl, or the creak of trees as they shrugged off the latest blast of snow-filled wind. He felt as though his senses were straining out in front of him, searching, probing for any sign that he had been seen.

So far, so good.

He got to the sundial, ducked beneath it. The courtyard remained in near darkness, only light spilling from the upstairs of the house illuminating it softly. Connor popped his head up, took in the lie of the land. The garage barn was almost straight in front of him, the front door to the house about twenty feet to his right. To the right of the front door a massive bay window looked down on the driveway and the lawns leading back to the house. But between the door and the window was a sliver of darkness, a lightless window barely visible in the gloom. A bathroom, Connor remembered from the architect's plans. Which gave him an idea.

He crept forward, staying low, hardly daring to breathe. Managed to loop round, out of the range of the floodlight, and get to the sliver of shadow between the door and the bay window. He didn't need the frosted glass in the window to tell him it was a small toilet off the main hall: the plans had been right.

He considered for a moment, Simon's words echoing in his ears. *Don't miss. No quarter given.* He slid his gun from the pancake holster on his back, the sound of the safety clicking off impossibly loud. Then he reached into his pocket and found another of Simon's gifts. Took a deep breath, pulled the pin and threw.

The flashbang detonated as it hit the ground in front of the garage, the floodlight flaring into life, the falling snow and rising smoke seeming to dance in the glare. Connor heard a barked curse from inside the house, followed by the sound of heavy footsteps. Shrank back into the darkness as the front door opened slowly, a gun emerging followed by a huge forearm and a slab-like arm that Connor knew could choke a man out in seconds.

Don't miss.

The owner of the gun stepped forward, head swivelling as he took in the scene. Connor waited until he was a half-step in front of him then moved forward, training his gun on the stubble-shaved head. 'Evening, Paulie,' he said. 'Put the gun down, slowly, like a good boy. Then invite me in for a drink. It's fucking freezing out here, and I think it's well past time we had a proper talk, don't you?'

CHAPTER 63

It hadn't taken long to identify the bodies found at the garage; the SOCOs found wallets and licences on each of them. Not that Ford was surprised: what had happened at that garage had been no simple robbery.

Two of the three men were nothing to write home about: Kerr MacAskill and Scotty Franks were known associates of Dessie Banks; low-level thugs with long and uninspiring records that told of stints in prison for possession, assault and theft. But it was the identity of the third man, the man whom the killer seemed determined to disassemble, that really caught Ford's attention.

Troughton's jaw had dropped open when Henry Tait's file appeared on his screen. Ford would have found the scene almost comical if he hadn't been so tired, the taste of stale coffee doing nothing to mask the sting of bile at the back of his throat.

'Fucking hell,' Troughton had whispered, before remembering where he was. He blushed, eyes darting between Ford and Susie Drummond, who was pacing around Ford's small office like an animal looking for easy prey.

'It's fine.' Ford sighed. 'Go on, Troughton, what have you got?'

Troughton glanced back at the screen, as if he was confirming that what he had just read was true. Then, slowly, he started to tell Ford and Susie about Henry Tait. As he spoke, Ford could see the weary satisfaction in Susie's eyes, acknowledgement that she had been right all along. Ford wished he could share that feeling.

Like the other two men, Henry Tait was a known associate of Dessie Banks. But, unlike the other two men, there was nothing low-level about Tait. He seemed to have risen quickly from his humble beginnings in the south-west of Glasgow to become one of the city's most feared criminals. He was linked to bank robberies, drug deals, prostitution – if there was money to be made and it was on the wrong side of the law, chances were that Henry Tait was involved. The problem, as was so often the case, was corroborating evidence. Any time Tait's name was mentioned in relation to a crime, evidence and witnesses suddenly seemed to vanish.

Ford thought of Dennis Morgan when Troughton mentioned this, could see in the young officer's eyes that he was thinking it too.

The cat-and-mouse game between Tait and the police had gone on for years, with the drugs squad and major crimes unit reporting that, despite strong suggestions Tait was now effectively Banks's ambassador on the west coast and ran his criminal empire for him, there was still a lack of evidence. It was almost as if he knew when he was being watched, and when the police were closing in.

Until he'd made one mistake.

It was billed as the Battle for Hearts and Minds – a Premiereship match between Edinburgh's Heart of Midlothian and Glasgow's Heart of Strathclyde. But with the bad blood between the teams, and the match being critical to both clubs' title challenges that season, the press and the fans quickly gave the clash a more appropriate nickname – the Heart Attack.

The trouble had started before a ball had even been kicked, Strathclyde fans spilling out of Haymarket station in Edinburgh and swarming into the nearest pubs. Despite a heavy police presence, it wasn't long until the first fight broke out, in a pub called The Angle in an area of Edinburgh called Dalry, not far from Hearts' Tynecastle Stadium. According to the report Troughton read from, the fight started when drinkers in the pub started jostling for position to get to the bar, and the door staff for the day collectively decided it was time for a tea break. It wasn't long before glasses were flying, along with fists and feet, and the bar descended into a brawl that wouldn't have looked out of place in an old-style Western.

By the time officers arrived, several people were hurt, some seriously. And the casualty who needed the most medical attention was a young man called Michael Walker. The police had found two men stamping on him as he cowered in a ball tight against the bar, hauled them off. The arresting officers had no idea whom they were arresting, or the shitstorm they had just unleashed.

Henry Tait and Terry Glenn stayed silent when they were booked into the custody suite at Dalry police station. They asked for their lawyers only when they were searched. Both men were found to have class-A drugs on their persons, along with knives that would give Crocodile Dundee a case of blade envy. But the real discovery, the one that ensured the two PCs who arrested Glenn and Tait didn't buy a round in a pub for six months, was the pocket drive found on Henry Tait. Ford could imagine the reaction of the officers who had opened that drive: revulsion, disgust, fury, and a sudden urge to switch off video cameras and have a quiet chat with Tait in the cells.

The drive was packed with images of child abuse. Troughton had read the list of what had been found, his cold, efficient delivery making the depraved sound almost routine. Tait said nothing, merely repeated his demand for his lawyer. Ultimately he was jailed for five years, having been charged with being in possession of indecent images of children. But that wasn't what interested Ford. No, what interested him were the pictures linked to the arrest report, the pictures of Tait's pocket drive that the images were found on.

It was an old flash drive – the type with a swinging metal arm that folded over to protect the port that connected to the computer. As with so many of that type of drive, it was branded with a logo, obviously given away as a promotional item.

A promotional item for Heart of Strathclyde.

Ford read the rest of the report, detailing how the club had strenuously denied any links to the images or Henry Tait. A trawl of the records found that Tait was a season-ticket holder at the club and a member of the social club, which it was assumed was where he had got the drive.

But, Ford thought, had he got the images there as well? Was that what Morgan had found when he had raided the social club, what had led him to Tim Montgomery and a wider abuse ring? And if there was such a ring, which connected Montgomery to Glenn, why had both men been killed in such a brutal and public manner? Was Fraser right? Was Christopher acting as an avenging angel, letting the abusers know he was coming for them?

Ford didn't know what was worse. The fact that there was a murderous vigilante on the loose, who had killed five men and disappeared with the most feared criminal in Edinburgh, or that, secretly, he wished the man well.

CHAPTER 64

The hallway Connor followed Paulie down was almost identical to the one he had found in Paulie's own home – same décor, same tasteful prints and heavy picture frames, same carefully neutral colours on the wall, contrasting the rich wood flooring. He had expected it, but the effect was still disorienting. The only difference was one of scale: where Paulie's home had obviously been designed for a single person, the dimensions of this house screamed family.

A family that never was.

Paulie turned right at a door at the end of the hall, Connor following closely. He knew from the plans he had seen that Paulie was leading him into a large living-dining room area, the kitchen set off it. Braced himself for whatever horrors awaited within.

Nothing. The room was perfectly normal. Apart from being fastidiously clean, it could have been a living room in any executive-style home where money wasn't an issue and furniture was bought for aesthetic appeal rather than budget. But the very neatness of the place gave it a sterility Connor found disturbing. This was not a place of refuge. This was a place of memorial.

Paulie stood in front of a large sandstone fireplace, turned to Connor. The slash from the picture frame Connor had cut him with was angry and puckered, red-black against the anaemic pallor of Paulie's skin. He had always given off an aura of strength, his sheer size transmitting a non-verbal threat to anyone in his path. But the man in front of Connor now looked old, shrunken, almost defeated. As though he was a boxer facing the last fight of his career, knowing he was going to lose.

'What the fuck you doing here, Fraser?' Paulie asked, small eyes glittering as they flitted across the injuries on Connor's face. 'You want me to finish the job I started on you back at my place? Want you to know that wasn't personal. Just couldn't have you getting in the way of what had to happen tonight, what's still going to happen.'

Connor studied Paulie's eyes, saw nothing but resolve there. No fear of the gun he had pointed at him, no doubt, not even anger. Just a steady, unwavering resolve, like a sprinter on the starting blocks, focused on nothing but the finish line.

'Whose blood is that on your hands, Paulie?' he asked.

Paulie looked down, almost as if he had forgotten he had hands at the end of his arms. He turned them slowly, huge, misshapen paws, studying the streaks of blood that radiated from his fingers up to his wrists. Connor felt the wounds to his neck shiver as he watched, the memory of those fingers closing around it flashing across his mind.

'Unfinished business,' Paulie said, more to himself than to Connor. 'Been a long time coming.'

'Aye,' Connor said. 'Since 1997 by my guess, September the fourteenth, if I'm right.' He shuddered, pushing back the thought of the boy in the storeroom. 'The night you didn't kill John Peterson like you told Morgan and MacKenzie you did. I think I understand why you lied, so I guess my real question is, is that Dessie Banks's blood, Martin Christopher's, or both?'

Paulie looked up from his hands, a dead, empty smile on his face. It was a smile that somehow reminded Connor of his own mother, and the way she would look at him in those last days before the cancer claimed her.

'Come on, Paulie. No more shit. Tell me who's here. I know you gave Christopher the tracker, know you probably helped him grab Dessie Banks. I'm guessing you've got one or both of them here somewhere. So where are they? And why the fuck would you help Christopher after what he did to Jen?'

Paulie's eyes hardened, his expression telling Connor he was trying to decide if he was faster than the bullets in Connor's gun. He obviously concluded he wasn't.

'You want that drink?' Paulie asked, after a moment, turning from the fireplace and heading for a drinks cabinet in the corner of the room. He reached it, picked up a glass, gestured towards Connor. 'No funny business this time, promise. Not here.'

'I'll pass,' Connor said, as Paulie poured himself a whisky, drained it.

'Your loss.'

'Paulie, I—'

'Gimme a fucking minute, OK?' Paulie snapped, the heat from the whisky jumping into his voice and flaring in his eyes. 'Fine, you're here. Kind of expected you would be, if I'm honest. You always were a stubborn wee shite. So you know, great. Well done you. But don't think for one minute I'm working with Christopher, OK? Not now. He'll fucking pay for what he did to Jen. But before he does, I have to pay my own debt to him, right? So give me a bloody minute.'

Connor flexed his grip on the gun, lowered it slightly. 'You mean the debt you owe him for not killing Peterson when you said you did?'

Paulie looked at Connor, jaw tensing as his knuckles whitened on his glass. Then he relaxed, as though he was finally able to set aside a weight he had been carrying for years. A weight he had carried alone. 'Aye, something like it,' he said. 'But there's more to it than that, Fraser. It's not all black and white, good guys and bad guys, you know. It's messier than that.'

'I suppose it is,' Connor said. 'As messy as seeing your boss's wife behind his back.'

Paulie recoiled as if slapped. He opened his mouth, closed it, as though he had lost the power to form the words that were caught in his throat.

'She really did have an eye,' Connor said, looking around the room. 'That's what put me on to it, Paulie, the décor. I'm sorry, but your place was just too tasteful, too perfect to be your work. Like those glasses. The same glasses I saw at your place, and Duncan MacKenzie's. The picture frames too. Very tasteful, very expensive. At your place, Duncan's, and in Jen's flat when we picked up some things for her at the hospital. That's when I really started thinking about it, not sure why. But I asked Duncan about that, and he told me Hannah had decorated their house. She did your place too, didn't she? And, of course, she did this place. Designed it as well. Client name on the architect drawings was Hannah King Taylor. Bit sloppy, that. What if Duncan had found out? But, then, what was it you said? "When Hannah wanted something, it was her way or no way. And fuck the consequences"? Tell me, Paulie, what would the consequences be of fucking your oldest friend's wife?'

'It wasnae fucking like that!' Paulie roared, spittle flying from his lips as his eyes glittered with the threat of tears. He took a step forward, eyes flicking again to Connor's gun. Stopped. 'It was more than that - *she* was more than that. Fuck's sake, we knew each other our whole lives, Hannah, me and Duncan, the three fucking musketeers, since we were bairns.' He paused, took a breath, a silent pleading for understanding in his eyes. 'I mean, all right, there was the odd drunken fumble when we were teenagers before she got serious with Duncan, but she was more than that to me, Connor, and more than a friend. You know how rare that is? She knew me, I knew her. Living with someone like Duncan, fuck, living with someone like me, isn't easy. I was there for her, that's all. This place,' he looked around, 'I built this place for her. And Jen. So that if things ever got really, really bad, they had a place to go and be safe.'

Connor stayed silent, remembering what Jen had said: *Paulie was there, every step of the way. There were nights I could hear the two of them, in Dad's study. Talking long into the night. About Mum. About taking on the world, about what they were going to do for Mum.*

He could see it now: two men grieving for the woman they both loved. Whether Paulie was driven by loyalty to MacKenzie, or a desire to protect Jen from whatever Hannah had feared in MacKenzie when they were married, Connor didn't know.

'OK,' he said at last. 'But the thought that you two were an item gave me what I needed to look at the land register, see if either you or Hannah had another place off the books. Registering this under your name and her maiden name was a bit daft. Not hard for MacKenzie to find.'

'If it ever came to that, I would have dealt with it,' Paulie said flatly. 'So you found the place, found out about me and Hannah. Whoopdie-fucking-do. Now what?'

'Now you tell me whose blood is on your hands, and what the fuck is going on.'

CHAPTER 65

After another drink, Paulie walked past Connor, keeping a wide berth but otherwise ignoring the fact he was holding a gun. 'Come on then,' he said, his tone almost casual. 'Best way is to show you.'

He walked back up the hall, stopping at a door in the eave of the staircase. Connor paused, casting his mind back to the house plans. Not a place he wanted to go, especially after he had told Paulie he knew his greatest secrets.

Paulie seemed to read the trepidation in Connor's eyes. 'It's fine. I'll go first. You can keep that cannon aimed right between my shoulders. I'm hardly likely to try and run back up the stairs at you, am I?'

Connor said nothing. Paulie merely shrugged, turned, opened the door and walked through. 'Suit yourself,' he muttered.

Reluctantly, Connor followed him. The door led to a staircase that Connor knew descended into what the building plans referred to as a wine cellar/storage area. Arriving at the bottom, Connor had a simpler description for the room in front of him.

Torture chamber.

It was an empty, windowless space, bland concrete walls illuminated by naked bulbs that hung from the exposed rafters of the ceiling. The glare from the lights was inescapable, exposing the scene in front of Connor with horrific clarity.

What looked like a cadaver in a designer suit sat in the centre of the room, tied to a simple wooden chair at the wrists and ankles.

Connor recognised the man as Dessie Banks: his face was clear to see even beneath the blood that clung to his sallow skin, like a sheen of sweat. His face was a mess of cuts, over the forehead, eyes, around the nose and cheeks. Connor spotted the implement used on a small table next to the chair – a bloodstained scalpel sat next to a power drill. Seeing the blood on the tip of the drill made Connor's mouth suddenly dry.

At Banks's feet, lying in a pool of slowly widening blood, was another man. His face was turned away, but Connor could see enough of the salt-and-pepper hair to guess it was Martin Christopher. He had been hog-tied: cable ties looped around his arms, which had been pulled behind his back, and his feet, which had been yanked back to touch his hands. Connor studied both men, wasn't sure if he felt relief or disappointment when he saw both of them were still breathing.

'What's that for?' he asked, gesturing to the corner of the room.

Paulie looked up, studied the video camera and tripod as though he had never seen them before. Smiled. 'Justice,' he said at last. 'That's the debt I owe Christopher. I've done that now. Just one more thing to do, then I'll deal with him for what he did to Jen. How is she, by the way? I asked the boss, but that was almost a day ago now.'

Connor stopped, the sudden, almost casual change of subject throwing him. He was about to speak when a light started flashing on the wall. 'What's that?' he said, staring at the light, knowing it could be nothing good.

'Trouble,' Paulie said, already moving. 'Come on.'

Paulie led Connor back up the stairs and into a small study across from the cellar door. He tapped the keyboard of a laptop sitting on a desk in the centre of the room, swore as it flared into life. 'I take it you walked in, kept off the road and close to the tree line?' he asked.

'Yeah, why?' Connor said.

Paulie grunted. 'That's why you didn't trigger the motion alarm on the driveway, but those arseholes did.' He gestured to the screen and the grainy footage of two SUVs driving up towards the house, snow spurting from their tyres, like spray from a wave.

'Banks's men,' Connor guessed. The SUVs were the same make and model as the one Banks's goons had turned up in at Paulie's house, same as the one used by Mo when he had tailed him. 'No doubt come to get their boss.'

'Maybe,' Paulie said. 'Might as soon kill the bastard as try to get him back, though. Amount of shit he spilled in that basement, lot of people will want to make sure he keeps his mouth shut. Permanently.'

"That's what the video camera was for?' Connor said. 'You tortured him? For information?'

'Not me,' Paulie said, turning away from the monitor. 'Anyway, that doesnae matter now. Those bastards are coming, and not for tea. What I want to know is, how did they find me? You been telling tales, Fraser?'

Connor held Paulie's suspicious gaze, shook his head in denial even as the idea of how these men had found this place crossed his mind. 'How do you want to play this?' he asked. 'I can call Ford. He can have officers here ASAP. All we'd have to do is hold out until they get here. You could end all this, Paulie, the right way.'

Paulie laughed, a warm, genuine belly laugh that made Connor's skin crawl. No matter whom he claimed to love or try to protect, this was the real Paulie. The Paulie who had caught the scent of violence in the air and was salivating at the prospect.

'Aye, it'll be the right way, right enough. Those bastards aren't getting Banks, or that tape. Believe me, there's enough there to put a lot of important people away for a lot of years. After everything, I'm not letting these sick fucks get away with that. Not one more child suffers. So I'm going to stop these men. The only question is, Fraser, are you going to help me or not? Tick tock. They're almost here.'

Connor glanced at the screen, then back to Paulie. Heard Simon in his mind. *Don't miss. No quarter given.* Thought of the video MacKenzie had shown him, the boy's terrified whimper, Peterson closing in.

'How do you want to play it?' he asked.

CHAPTER 66

There was nothing subtle about their approach: two cars, straight up the driveway at speed. The floodlight flared into life as they slid to a halt in the snow, doors opening. Nine men got out of the two vehicles, each armed in one way or another. Watching them on the monitor in Paulie's study, Connor wasn't surprised to see that Mo Templeton, the thug whose nose he had broken, was among them. He reached up, touched his own nose. In better circumstances, he would have appreciated the irony.

The harsh racking of a shotgun pulled Connor from his thoughts. Paulie was turning away from a cupboard, weapon in hand. He looked calm, at peace, the worries Connor had seen etched into his face earlier gone, replaced by the Paulie of old; more force of nature than man, menace radiating from his pores as naturally as some people sweated. Connor was at once comforted and terrified.

'Front door's deadbolted, steel-lined. Won't be making the same mistake I made with you,' Paulie said, as he stared at the wall, almost as if he could see Banks's men through it. 'Should hold them back for a bit, give us time to—'

He was cut off by his phone ringing. Paulie fished it out of his pocket, the handset looking like a child's toy in his massive paw. Smiled at the screen, then hit answer.

'Evening, Mo,' he said, voice cheerful and relaxed, almost as if he was hearing from an old friend. Maybe, Connor thought, he was.

'Hold on a minute, will you?'

He laid the phone on his desk, thumbed the speaker button. 'Sorry, Mo. Nice night for it. What brings you out here? And how did you find me anyway?'

'Cut the shite, Paulie,' Mo replied, his voice flat, nasal, thanks to his broken nose. 'We both know why I'm here. So just send the boss out and we'll call it a night. It's too cold for this crap, and you're not going to want us coming in to get out of the cold.'

'Ah, sorry,' Paulie said. 'I've got a strict door policy here. No kiddie fiddlers or fucksticks. So why don't you just turn around and piss off, save everyone a lot of trouble?'

Mo's laugh was made a cruel, painful thing by a sudden rush of static down the line as the wind picked up outside. 'You might want to rethink that, Paulie. Aye, you really do want to think about that again.'

'Oh, aye, and why is that?' Paulie asked, muscles in his forearms tensing as he tightened his grip on the shotgun.

His phone beeped as a message arrived.

'I've got six men there, right now,' Mo said. 'One of them just sent me that picture. So send Mr Banks out now, or I swear the next picture you get won't be so pretty.'

Connor got to the phone before Paulie, fingers numb as cold certainty rolled through his gut. Opened the message, felt the world give a sickening lurch.

The picture was of Forth Valley Hospital, where Jen and Simon were. It looked like the hospital was in a snow globe, lights glowing in the night. To Connor it seemed fragile, vulnerable. Unprotected.

He had his phone out almost instantly, whirling away from Paulie, willing the call to be answered.

'Connor, you OK? You—'

'Simon, listen,' his voice was low, urgent. No emotion. One professional relaying vital information to another. 'You've got trouble coming. Bad trouble. I'm told six hostiles, but fuck knows, could be more. They're going to try and get to Jen. I know you've got police there, and MacKenzie's men, but I need to know, can you handle it?'

'Fucking right,' came Simon's reply. 'I kept a few toys from the car just in case. No one's going to get to Jen, I promise you.'

'Good enough,' Connor said, then ended the call. He turned back to Paulie, saw the confused hesitation on his face. Nodded. Took a breath.

'Mo, Connor Fraser. Small world, isn't it? Listen, just talked it over with Paulie and we decided it would be best all round if you just go fuck yourself. Oh, and if any of your boys lays a finger on Jen, then I will personally break every bone in your body, understood?'

The phone beeped as the call ended.

'That went well,' Paulie said.

CHAPTER 67

Simon pocketed his phone, looked down the corridor. Jen's nurse, the formidable Marie, had insisted he clear the ward, along with the police, so he was standing outside it. He ran calculations in his head quickly. One uniform downstairs. Visual deterrent, not much use if the shit really hit the fan. Same with MacKenzie's men. He had counted four when he had taken a casual stroll down to the main atrium for coffee earlier. They were the same as any of the thousand thugs he had encountered in Belfast: big, intimidating men who got the job done with a snarl and the threat of violence. They could probably handle themselves, at least in the short term, but even with the hospital quiet at this time of night, Simon didn't want civilians in the line of fire.

The thought made him reach for the gun at his back. Not his service weapon, he'd left that in Belfast, but a lethal little automatic pistol that, conveniently, had lost its serial number somewhere along the way. He also had a small extendable baton in his pocket, an aerosol can of pepper spray, and a lockblade strapped to his ankle. He smiled despite himself – knowing Connor Fraser could make a man paranoid. But he knew Connor, knew what it had meant for him to call for help in the first place, and the trust he had placed in Simon by asking him to protect Jen.

But, still, the question remained, what was the best way to do that? He was in an open building, with multiple entrances and exits.

Lethal weapons were only one cupboard or drawer away. Scalpels and syringes could be used to harm as well as heal. He also didn't know how many men he was facing. Connor had said six, but how accurate was that? He had no real way of knowing, though he thought it unlikely that whoever was coming for Jen would try to storm the building *en masse* - a show of firepower like that would trigger an immediate call to the police, who would respond with brutal, immediate force.

So, a small team then, focused on a single goal. Get to Jen. Which left him with a simple choice. Wait for them to come for him, or take a more proactive approach, neutralise the threat before it ever got that far?

He looked back to the ward, made a decision. Took a step forward. Fuck it. He had never been a patient man. Why start now?

CHAPTER 68

Paulie had obviously made some off-plan modifications to the architect's designs for the house. Either that, or steel-lined, steel-framed deadbolting doors were more popular than Connor had realised.

They made their way back out into the corridor, Paulie locking the cellar door and sealing the door to the living room.

'They'll try the window when they get bored of battering the front door,' Paulie explained. 'The living-room door is made of the same stuff, though. They'll get in eventually, but the door will slow them down a bit, give us some time.'

'Time for what?' Connor asked, vaguely wondering what type of danger Paulie was trying to protect Hannah and Jen from when he had modified the house. What was it Jen said? *At least I had her. Huh. Dad said that too.*

Paulie gave him a you-know-better stare and a knowing smile. 'These wankers threatened Jen,' he said, gesturing to the front door with the shotgun. 'So I am going to fuck them up. Then I'm going to use what Banks told Christopher just now to burn his house down, with as many of his sick bastard pals inside as I can get.'

'So that's what this is all about,' Connor said, the last pieces of the puzzle falling into place in his mind. 'Christopher wanted to get to everyone in the porn ring who was involved in the murder of his step-daughter, Tracy. You served him up Banks to, what, get the names of everyone else involved? Given Montgomery was pretty high up in the

Scottish Government, I'm guessing there are some interesting names on that list. Some embarrassing ones? But I still don't get why you would help him, Paulie, after what he did to Jen.'

The humour evaporated from Paulie's face, which seemed to harden and grow dark. When he spoke, his voice was a low rumble, like the first sound of thunder in the distance, warning of worse to come.

'That wasn't meant to happen, wasn't part of the deal,' he said. 'When I figured out what Banks was doing, what he was using our drivers and trucks to transport, I promised Christopher I would help him, but I didn't know he was going to target Jen. Should have seen it, though. After all, it was Duncan's trucks Banks was using to move that poison around the country.'

A sudden dull thud reverberated down the hall, as though the house was clearing its throat. Connor heard swearing coming from the other side of the front door, followed by a cry of 'Hit it again!'

He ignored it, turned back to Paulie. He was on the verge of answers, and nothing, not even Mo and his gang of thugs, would stop him getting them, finally understanding why Jen had been hurt and his unborn child murdered.

'So you knew Christopher?' Connor said. 'How? And why the hell did you get in touch with him when you found out what Banks was doing?'

Paulie shook his head, his scalp gleaming in the lights of the hallway. 'You've got it wrong, Fraser. I didn't contact Christopher. He contacted me. Montgomery, the guy he killed in that swimming-pool, made some remark about Tracy Westerly, and Christopher ran with it. Got in with the guy, pumped him for information. Became his friend by telling him he had fantasised about killing Tracy himself - after all, the whiny bitch was only his stepdaughter. Sick fucker swallowed it, hook, line and sinker. Welcomed Christopher like a long-lost brother. Took him in. Showed him everything. Including,' Paulie coughed, his voice wavering now, 'including other videos of kids. Videos that showed what happened to Tracy.'

The thought hit Connor like a punch, rocking him back on his heels, Paulie's words echoing in his mind. *Fantasised about killing*

Tracy himself. Thought again of the boy in the storage room, the small, fractured whimpers. Then Ford: *None of the Calderwood investigation victims were sexually assaulted.*

'Snuff videos,' Connor said flatly, feeling vomit roil in the back of his throat. 'That's what Banks was dealing in, what Montgomery was after. Snuff videos. Kids being killed. He started with abuse with Cameron Donald, what, found that wasn't enough and refined his perversion. Which was what Morgan was on to, wasn't it?'

Paulie nodded slowly, some pain deeper than sadness in his eyes. 'Aye,' he rumbled.

Another explosion at the front door, more commotion outside. It reverberated in Connor's head, shook another revelation loose. 'Jesus,' he whispered, flashing back to the picture of John Peterson they had found at Gina Westerly's house. 'You didn't kill Peterson at all, did you?' he said at last, forcing his mind to slow down, think it through as he spoke. 'Morgan did. He tortured him for information on the abusers, didn't he? But, then, why did you take the blame for it? And why give Christopher that photograph of Peterson's body in the first place?'

Paulie glanced up the hallway, as though he had just remembered something. Walked up it to the door leading to the cellar, checked it was secure. 'The poor bastard down there deserved some peace, Fraser. He had lost his kid, knew she suffered a horrible, agonising death. So I tried to give him peace by giving him the picture, and telling him that Peterson suffered before he died. It was almost true. I'm sure Morgan made that bastard scream before he finished him. All I did was lie about who killed him.'

'To protect Morgan and his investigation,' Connor said. 'Imagine if it got out that a policeman investigating an abuse ring was a killer. It would discredit any arrests he made, anything he did. But if you did it, then Morgan could keep going. Except I never saw any arrests, never saw anything about a high-placed ring of abusers being exposed. So what happened?'

'*This is not murder. This is justice,*' Paulie replied. 'Remember about fifteen years ago the High Court judge who was found dead in his car down at Leith Docks in Edinburgh, heart attack caused by his hooker girlfriend sucking him off a little too enthusiastically? Morgan. And that TV presenter who allegedly got pished and drove his car off the M8? Same again. Look back at the news over the last twenty-odd years or so, any big-name deaths in mysterious or strange circumstances. Chances are your pal Morgan had something to do with it. I have no idea how far up the chain he got before he was turned into a vegetable, but from what Banks said, he had a few more stops to make along the way.'

Another slam at the door, this one more urgent. 'But why Jen?' Connor asked. 'From what you said, Christopher knew you were trying to help him. So why target Jen after he killed Montgomery? And why use your car?'

Paulie sneered at that, almost as if, amid all the chaos, using one of his cars to hurt Jen had been the real affront. 'Because he blamed Duncan and me for the loss of his kid, Fraser. He was lashing out.'

'Tracy,' Connor said.

'No,' Paulie replied. 'His other kid, Moira. When Tracy died, her mum, Gina, went to pieces. Tried to find answers at the bottom of a bottle. She surfaced occasionally, but always sank again. She got pregnant, but even that couldn't keep her from Mr Smirnoff. So she drank, and the baby was stillborn, and Christopher couldn't take it.'

Connor opened his mouth, closed it. Saw Jen lying in her bed, face set, a pain greater than that inflicted by her physical injuries in her eyes. *I was pregnant.* 'But why after all this time?' he whispered, his voice sounding small. Defeated.

Paulie reared to his full height – an angry, vengeful god about to punish the faithless and the sinful. 'You saw that video of the wee boy getting killed, Fraser,' he said. 'That video was made after I said I'd killed Peterson. If I'd done what I said I would do, and delivered him to Morgan as we'd initially agreed, then that wee boy would still have been alive. Christopher blamed me for that, rightly so. Man wasn't in his right mind, so he lashed out, and Jen paid the price, which is exactly what I told Hannah she would never do.'

Connor felt the final piece of the puzzle slot into place. 'You were here,' he said. 'That Sunday night, when you said you grabbed Peterson and killed him, you were here. He was free to kill that wee boy, then you grabbed him and delivered him to Morgan the next night.'

Paulie's face twitched – a boy in front of his dad, trying to explain why the football had suddenly turned up in a shower of glass in the living room. 'They'd had a bad argument, her and Duncan,' he said. 'She was fucking terrified. Duncan liked the drink a bit too much when this business was starting off, and he had a temper. He never hit Hannah, I would have fucking killed him if he had, but he scared the living shite out of her. Which is why she was here. To get away, let him cool off. She called me, asked me to meet her and I . . .' His voice trailed off, his eyes haunted by what-ifs and could-have-beens.

Another crashing bang screamed through the house, this time from behind them. Paulie looked up, eyes clearing as he did. 'Ah, good,' he said, his previous smile returning. 'They've finally decided to try the living-room window. Shall we say hello to our house guests? I believe you made Mo a promise. Be a shame to let the man down.'

Connor found it hard to argue.

CHAPTER 69

After telling Jen's nurse, Marie, just enough to ensure she called his mobile at the first sign of trouble and did him one simple favour, Simon got moving. He wanted to get to the main atrium at the entrance of the hospital, either meet the goons coming for Jen there or, preferably, outside the front doors. He might have been in a hospital, but Simon wanted to keep the casualty count to a minimum. Say around six.

The main entrance to the building reminded Simon of a library or a shopping centre more than it did a hospital. It was a large, high-ceilinged space, bright colours designed to make the most of the light that would be let in by the large windows that dominated the front wall. At this time of night, though, the entrance was quiet, almost deserted. A few staff were dotted around, huddled over coffees as they spoke quietly, trying not to disturb the few visitors who milled around, keeping silent vigil for whichever loved one was in one of the wards.

Simon spotted the police officer Ford had arranged to be on the grounds hovering near to the now-closed sandwich shop, as though his presence would somehow force the roller gate to open and the shop to spring into life. He was young, by the look of it, tall and rangy, with slicked-back dark hair and colourful tattoos that snaked down one thin arm. Simon was just thinking how useless the kid would be if and when trouble hit when he unexpectedly proved himself invaluable.

Three men entered the hospital, flanking a wheelchair carrying a fourth man, whose left leg was in a plaster. They were doing an almost passable job of looking casual, but when they spotted the police officer, their reaction was almost comically ingrained: a faltering pace, wary glances exchanged as they took in this new variable. They regained their composure quickly, headed for the building directory on the wall next to the entrance.

Simon took in the space, calculating variables as he looked between where the men were and the lifts at the other side of the atrium, double doors next to them, leading to stairs.

A quick, muttered discussion and the group got moving again, the wheelchair squealing softly on the floor. Simon studied them as they walked past him, the scrubs, clipboard and pen he had borrowed from Marie rendering him invisible to them: just another hospital worker on the night shift. They were all dressed in jeans and T-shirts, obviously no strangers to the gym, their hair ranging from shaven to almost mullet-esque. Except the man in the wheelchair. Simon smiled. Connor had told him he'd broken the leg of a thug with a mop of red hair. It must have been this man, though Simon was impressed by the guile of the group to use him as camouflage.

He fell in behind them keeping a discreet distance. Glanced across at the police officer, who was still focused on the sandwich shop. Sighed internally. Complacency like that could get you killed in this job.

The group came to a halt at the lift, one of them leaning forward and jabbing the call button. Simon stepped forward, felt a sudden stab of adrenalin as his breath shortened. Thought of his promise to Connor. No one was getting to Jen tonight.

'Evening, boys,' he said, the three standing men wheeling round at the sound of his voice. 'Sorry to tell you, but you missed visiting hours. So you'll have to come back and see Jen MacKenzie some other time. And when you do, catch yerselves on and bring the girl some flowers, will you?'

He saw shock ripple through the men, didn't give it time to harden into rage or decision, He jabbed the clipboard into the neck of the first, whose hands flew for his throat as his knees buckled. Then he spun left, stabbing his pen into the ribs of the second, following up with a quick, snapping uppercut that rattled up his arm as teeth splintered under his knuckles. He kept moving, caught sight of the man in the wheelchair fumbling in his coat out of the corner of his eye.

Time to wrap this up.

He kicked the gasping, choking man on his knees once in the head, sending him crashing back into the wheelchair, buying himself a few more seconds. Heard, dimly, the clatter of feet on hard floor, guessed it was the cop finally waking up and getting in on the act. Ignored it. Studied the last man standing.

He was shorter than Simon, maybe five ten, and wide with it. He had the build of a bare-knuckle boxer, and the face to prove the credentials. His nose was a huge, misshapen smear of flesh across his face, which was pitted with scars, the biggest of which ran from his left ear up to his left eye, which glittered coldly. He said nothing, just bared his teeth in a snarl and charged. Simon stepped forward, into the path of the man's run, then ducked down and lashed his leg out as he spun, sweeping the man's feet from under him. The sound of his head crashing into the floor echoed around the hospital before it was drowned by a shout of 'Police, stop. NOW!' as the young officer arrived.

Simon turned to the man in the wheelchair, pounced. Got to him as he pushed his now-unconscious comrade from his lap, tightened his hand on the fist in the man's pocket, which Simon could feel was holding something small and heavy and lethal. 'You shouldn't play with guns, son,' he said. 'My pal Connor already tried to teach you that lesson, I think, but here, let me give you a quick refresher.' With that, Simon twisted, brought his elbow crashing down on the plastered leg. Felt something shift and grind as the bone beneath the plaster shattered anew, the man in the wheelchair howling in pain.

He grabbed the gun from the man's pocket, stepped back and turned to the police officer, whose eyes suddenly grew very wide as his skin turned very pale.

'I - I—'

'Get on your Airwave, son,' Simon said, as he unloaded the gun and pocketed the bullets. 'Call DCI Malcolm Ford. Tell him we're having a bit of trouble, but Connor Fraser's pal is dealing with it. I'm just going to have a wee word with Gimpy here about where his other mates are. Then I think I'll need to step outside for a wee bit of air.'

CHAPTER 70

They took up positions at either side of the living-room door, Connor turned slightly to look back up the hallway to the front door, just in case Mo and his men decided to try to mount a two-pronged attack. Connor could hear the sound of breaking glass and furniture from behind the living-room door, saw pain digging into Paulie's expression. He felt an unexpected wave of sympathy for the man - what must it be like to listen to the house the love of his life had designed for him being destroyed? One more dream shattered, one more memory tainted.

'You ready?' Paulie hissed.

Connor tightened his grip on his gun, nodded. The plan was simple. Open the door, let whoever was in there either come to them or waste whatever ammunition they had firing into the empty doorway. Either way, it would let Paulie and Connor know what they were facing.

'Right,' Paulie whispered, his tone brisk, business-like, as though he was a labourer about to start another day of work.

He grabbed the door handle, pressed the button set into it. Connor heard a heavy *thunk* as the deadbolt cleared. Paulie pushed the handle down, then swung the door open and ducked back behind the frame, pressing himself against the wall.

There was a moment of perfect silence, and Connor could almost feel the men in the living room exchanging confused glances. Then the moment was shattered by the deafening roar of gunfire. Connor ducked, flattening himself against the wall as bullets strafed up the hallway, walls exploding in plumes of dust as they smacked into them. A bitter smell of burning filled the air as Connor looked across to Paulie. He was crouched down like Connor, but his face was calm, serene, like a man sheltering under a tree, waiting for the rain to pass.

A shout from the room, Connor recognising the voice as Mo's.

'Quit it!' he roared to his men. The gunfire ceased, and a ringing noise rushed into Connor's ears. He closed his eyes. Tried to do the maths. Nine men, probably all armed. How many rounds would that be? More than enough to kill him and Paulie a dozen times over. He thought of Jen. Wasn't going to happen. No one else was going to die tonight.

'Paulie? Paulie, you out there?' Mo called. 'Come on, man, this is fucking stupid. Just give us Banks and we can go on our way. It's either that or my boys have some fun with Jen MacKenzie. You've seen the videos, Paulie, you know how rough they can get. You really want that for her?'

Connor felt himself twitch, the urge to charge into the room and grab Mo by the neck almost overpowering. He looked over, saw the same thought flash across Paulie's face before taking root in the pulsing vein in his neck.

'Paulie, no!' he hissed, pulling a small, round object from his pocket. He gave it a second, saw Paulie's eyes widen in surprise, then understanding. Connor pulled the pin, held up three fingers of his left hand.

Three . . .

Paulie smiled.

Two . . .

Connor took a deep breath.

One . . .

Jen . . .

He slid around the wall, lobbed the flashbang grenade into the living room then retreated. Heard startled cries then saw light stab from the room as the grenade detonated with a deafening boom. Pointed to his chest, then got moving, surging into the room.

The men were weaving around it, as though they were at the end of a night out, pawing at their ears, which Connor could see were oozing blood. He moved quickly, economically, targeting jaws as he knocked the dazed men down. He felt Paulie enter the room behind him, didn't bother turning round. The man hated him, but he was no killer, he knew that now.

He found Mo at the back of the room. He had obviously tried to get away from the blast, was further away from the detonation site. Connor slid his gun into its holster, tapped Mo on the back of the head just hard enough to put him on the floor, then crouched down, following him. Grabbed a handful of Mo's shirt and dragged his head off the floor. 'Remember when I told you what I would do if Jen was hurt?' he hissed.

Mo made a noise halfway between a cough and a moan as his eyes opened and he focused on Connor.

'Man of my word,' Connor said. He laid Mo back down, almost gently. Then he lifted his arm, grabbed the wrist and, with one swift, hard twist, broke it. Clarity stabbed into Mo's eyes, cords in his neck bulging as he started to scream. Connor clamped a hand on his mouth, stifling the cry. Fought back the urge to grab his nose between his fingers and choke the man to death. But no. Like Paulie, he was no killer.

'I'm going to take my hand away in a moment,' he said, voice soft, reassuring, 'and when I do, you're going to tell me who sent you here tonight, and why. I think I already know, but you're going to confirm it for me. And if you lie, I'm going to break your other wrist. Then I'm going to let Paulie have some quality time with you. Understood?'

Mo whimpered on the floor, nodded his understanding even as a shadow fell on him. Connor felt electricity arc down his back even as he heard Paulie's heavy breathing. He turned, half expecting to see the shotgun pointed in his face. But it hung loosely by Paulie's side, like a toy he had forgotten he was holding.

'Before you talk to him, I need a wee favour,' Paulie said.

CHAPTER 71

Simon had given up smoking years ago, mostly due to Connor's almost evangelical preaching about the dangers of lung cancer and the other health risks. It hadn't really bothered him: he could quell the desire for a cigarette with a stick of gum or a glass of wine if it really got bad.

But standing in the car park outside the hospital, the wind whipping snow into his face, he would have cheerfully killed for one draw on a cigarette.

Finding the other thugs hadn't been hard. The red-haired goon in the wheelchair had proven to be a very talkative chap, especially when Simon had decided to be helpful and try to reset his plaster for him. It turned out whoever had spoken to Connor was telling the truth: there had been six men sent for Jen, the four who had entered the hospital and another two who waited in the car park. Simon could have found the car without the description from Mr Wheelchair: it stuck out like a sore thumb in the nearly deserted car park. A huge, blacked-out SUV in a land of hatchbacks and saloons.

Simon had considered being subtle, decided he was too tired from his previous exertions. He wandered casually up to the car, making a line for another vehicle parked beyond it. Stopped when he got to the driver's side window, caved it in with the butt of Mr Wheelchair's gun. Reached through with one fluid motion and smashed the driver's head on the steering wheel, then trained the gun on the passenger.

He got out of the car without complaint, Simon tracking him with the gun as he walked around the front of the car to him. When they were standing in front of each other, Simon lashed out with the pistol, dropping the man to the snow-covered ground. Then he leaned back into the car and grabbed the keys. Took the zip ties he had kept from his own car out of his pocket and tied the men up, before heading back to the hospital. He could hear sirens in the distance now, presumably Ford responding to his officer's call. There would be an armed response unit with him, standard procedure when a firearm is drawn at a hospital. And that was when it hit him. The craving for a cigarette. The desire to stand in the snow and smoke as he waited for the cavalry to arrive and the explanations to begin. Instead, he grabbed his phone and dialled Connor, was mildly surprised when he answered.

'You OK, man?' he asked.

'Yeah, yeah, fine,' Connor said, his voice cold, almost distracted. 'You dealt with things there?'

'Aye, no bother,' Simon said. 'Amateur hour, really. Just waiting for Ford and his men to arrive for mop-up duty.'

'Good,' Connor said, relief warming his voice now before he fell into a silence that Simon knew all too well. He ground his fingers into his eyes, swallowed the exhaustion he felt. Remembered an old line his dad used to say when faced with a long shift on the beat: *Miles to go, son, miles to go..*

'What do you need, big lad?' he asked.

So Connor told him.

CHAPTER 72

The price Connor demanded for his favour to Paulie was simple: two lives and one call to the police. Surprisingly, Paulie agreed to let Martin Christopher and Dessie Banks live. Unsurprisingly, he wasn't happy at calling the police in. But he agreed, he and Connor both knowing that the police were going to be involved at some point, and it might as well be on their terms.

So Connor had called Ford, who had arrived at the house just as the first morning light began to stain the sky. The weather was easing, alternating between rain and snow, as though the new day couldn't decide what shade of gloom it was going to wear yet. Connor was waiting outside for Ford when he arrived, partly because he wanted to get away from Mo and his thugs, who were now trussed up on the floor of the living room, obscene Christmas gifts waiting to be collected by the police, and partly because he wanted to get some clean air into his lungs, feel the cold pinch of the morning on his skin. He had watched the video confession Christopher had tortured out of Dessie Banks before calling Ford, wondered what type of man it made him that watching the gangster whimper and beg and plead gave him an almost perverse feeling of satisfaction.

For what he had done, he deserved far worse.

Ford's car slid to a halt in front of the house. As requested, he had come alone, though Connor could see he wasn't happy about it. He almost felt like telling him not to worry, the house would soon be the focus of every police officer in Scotland, one way or another.

'You want to tell me what the hell is going on?' Ford asked, as he slammed his door shut and marched forward. 'You call me here, alone, on the promise of delivering Martin Christopher and more, while your pal goes Terminator and flattens six of Dessie Banks's men at the hospital. Where is McCartney anyway? I want a word with him. He was meant to stay at the hospital till I got there, but he's vanished.'

Connor bit back a smile and the urge to look down the road Ford had just driven up. Simon had arrived twenty minutes previously, in a black SUV with a smashed-in driver's side window. Connor was about to ask his friend what had happened, thought better of it. They had been on the clock, and time was short. So they got down to business, Simon doing Paulie's favour, then taking all the weapons Connor and Paulie had used with him back to his own car, which Connor had left in the layby at the foot of the hill.

'Don't know, sir,' Connor lied, with a shrug. 'But I can tell you why Simon acted like he did. He was protecting Jen. She was threatened earlier this evening, by the men you'll find tied up in the house. They wanted to use her as leverage, against Paulie and me, to get us to release Dessie Banks.'

Ford's eyes darted towards the house. 'You've got Banks in there?' he said. 'He was snatched earlier tonight, a warehouse in Bonnybridge. We found the truck Paulie and Christopher were tracking. Three more men dead, Connor.'

Connor nodded, processing the information. Paulie had told him about Christopher's raid on the warehouse. He had set it up to get Banks, had gone to town when he recognised the three men with Banks from various videos he had found in the possession of Tim Montgomery. The way Paulie described it, the punishment had been swift, brutal, almost poetic. The man whose hand he had destroyed had a predilection for touching children in the most barbaric ways, so Christopher had taken those hands away. It was, Connor thought, justice.

'So, we going to stand here freezing all morning, or are you going to tell me what the hell happened here?'

'Sorry, yes, sir,' Connor said, snapping his focus back to Ford. 'Paulie's inside, says he's happy to talk to you without a lawyer. As you know, I was looking for him in connection with what happened to Jen, and I managed to trace him to this place, where I found he had Banks and Martin Christopher. We were just discussing contacting you when Mo Templeton and several of Banks's men turned up, heavily armed. I helped Paulie subdue the men, while Simon dealt with the threat to Jen. Then we called you.'

Ford sneered, as if he could smell the bullshit on Connor's breath as he spoke. 'And how long have you been practising that little statement?' he asked.

Connor smiled. 'Only statement I'm going to give, boss,' he said. 'And, besides, after you see what's in that house, my statement is going to be the last thing on your mind.'

'What the hell is that supposed to mean?'

'I'll let Paulie tell you.'

He led Ford down the hallway towards the living room, the policeman stopping occasionally, throwing pointed glances at Connor as he studied the bullet holes in the walls. Connor said nothing, just headed for the living room where Paulie sat on the couch, Mo and his men strewn around him like throw rugs. He rose when Connor and Ford walked into the room, a fresh glass of whisky glinting in the light.

'What the fuck?' Ford whispered, as he surveyed the room. Connor could only imagine what he was thinking – nine hardened thugs on the floor, tied at the feet and hands and gagged, enough guns to stage a small coup in Edinburgh stacked neatly in the corner of the room.

'Had some uninvited guests,' Paulie said. 'Dealt with them, the old-fashioned way.'

Connor could see anger flash across Ford's eyes. And something else, something he hadn't expected, but fully understood. Jealousy. Ford had always been a pragmatic police officer, and Connor got the feeling that just beating the shit out of the criminals he faced and leaving them tied up on the floor appealed to him on some level.

'Will one of you please just tell me what the hell is going on?' Ford said, his eyes flitting hungrily to the glass Paulie held.

Paulie glanced at Connor, and he nodded encouragement. They had agreed that, after calling Ford, Paulie would take the lead, tell him what he knew.

So he did. Slowly, calmly, Paulie told Ford everything. About how his old boss, DI Dennis Morgan, had tortured and killed John Peterson for information on a paedophile ring that involved Dessie Banks, Tim Montgomery and Terry Glenn. About how he had found out about Banks using MacKenzie Haulage's trucks to transport videos and other materials that were too brutal to be sent online, even via the dark web, to a select list of clients. A list of clients that included civil servants, lawyers, politicians and even some of Ford's superiors. Connor watched the policeman's face darken, knew he wouldn't truly believe what Paulie was telling him until he had proof. And he would get it. It was downstairs, waiting for him. Martin Christopher, Dessie Banks, his taped confession and the videos Christopher had taken from Tim Montgomery, including the nameless boy Connor had watched John Peterson kill.

Connor took a deep, steadying breath. He trusted Ford, knew he would do the right thing. But it wasn't just Ford he had to worry about. The names Banks had provided were a virtual who's who of some of the most powerful public figures in Scotland. Men and women who would go to any lengths to keep their perversions quiet. Connor wondered about that. Morgan had decided killing these people was easier and more direct than trying to bring them to traditional justice, but then he had stopped. Why? Had he run out of names, or had they somehow got to him, bought his silence, as they had no doubt done with so many other people?

Ultimately, Connor thought, it didn't matter. He had an insurance policy against that: Paulie's favour. A favour Simon should be fulfilling even as Paulie spoke.

CHAPTER 73

Simon opened the door as gently as he could, crept into the flat. Donna was standing in the doorway, a cardigan wrapped tightly around her. She put a finger to her lips, gestured towards a closed door with a rainbow sticker on it spelling 'Andrew'. Simon nodded, followed her down the hall to the living room. When he saw the pot of coffee sitting on the coffee table alongside two mugs, he had the sudden, almost overpowering urge to take her in his arms and kiss her.

'Grab a seat,' she said, as she eased the door shut. 'Then you can tell me why I'm sitting here talking to you, when it seems all the excitement is out at the hospital where Jen is. I take it she's OK, or I doubt you'd be here.'

'Aye, true enough,' Simon said, watching as Donna filled the mugs and passed one to him. 'Look, I appreciate you seeing me this early in the morning, and Connor is sorry he can't be here himself. But he's got other matters to attend to. And, believe me, what happened at the hospital is small beans compared to what I'm about to tell you.'

'What happened at the hospital,' Donna repeated. 'So you were there? Simon, what the hell is going on? Connor calls me, tells me you're on the way, that you need to talk to me about something he didn't want to get into over the phone. Then I check the wires, see there's been some kind of disturbance at the hospital. I should be there, Simon, reporting on that. It is my job after all.'

'Your job . . .' Simon considered the word, and the significance it was about to take on '. . . is the news. What happened at the hospital tonight was nothing, just a wee to-do with a couple of hard men who thought they could use Jen to get to Connor. Amateur hour. I'm here about real news, a story that could change your life. But, first, I have a question. How serious about your job are you?'

Donna rocked back on the couch, face creasing into a frown. Something in that expression made Simon want to kiss her all over again.

'I'm a reporter,' she said finally. 'I report the news. I've given up a hell of a lot to get to this point, to be able to do this job. But why the question? Does Connor doubt my commitment or something? Because if he does . . .'

Simon raised a hand, wanting to cool Donna's anger before it could catch light. He reached into his pocket and produced a zip drive, laid it on the table between them. 'I got that from Connor earlier tonight. It's a confession by Dessie Banks about his involvement in supplying material and kids to a network of child abusers across Scotland. That's why Tim Montgomery and Terry Glenn were killed. They were part of it.'

Donna's eyes darted between Simon and the zip drive. 'Jesus Christ,' she whispered, reaching forward for the drive.

Simon placed his hand on hers. Her fingers were cool beneath his, strong. Her head darted up, eyes full of questions. 'What . . .?'

'Before you watch that, you need to understand something. It's why Connor wanted me to come to see you personally. To explain. This is dynamite stuff, Donna. I've watched the tape myself. I'm no boffin when it comes to Scottish politics and the like, but even I recognised a couple of names Banks gave up, including one area commander for the police. This is big, Donna, and if you report this, you're going to be inviting a shitstorm into your life. Connor and I will do everything we can to protect you and Andrew, but he wanted you to understand what this could mean, and what these people could do to you.'

Donna leaned back, leaving the drive on the table. She looked across to the living-room door, and Simon didn't need to be a detective to know she was thinking about her son. He had meant what he said, had already agreed with Connor that he would stay for as long as it took to help, but he was prepared for her to say no and send him on his way. Secretly, he almost hoped that she would.

Almost.

She stood, paced around the room, ran a hand through her hair, as though soothing the thoughts in her mind. 'It's that big?' she asked him.

'Aye,' he replied. He'd seen abuse covered up before - hell, the Catholic Church could have written a book on protecting paedophiles and keeping their secrets - but in the digital age, when allegations and innuendo were only a click or a tweet away, it was harder to make problems disappear. Once your name was linked to an allegation, the stench of it never went away. And that was what he and Connor were counting on. That the story, when it broke, would reach a critical mass, the questions and the allegations snowballing until they crushed everyone associated with the story.

All they needed was someone to break the story. Someone to make it news.

She leaned over again, took the zip drive. Studied it. Looked to Simon, then back to the door. 'Better get my laptop then,' she said. 'Then we can see what we're dealing with. Get yourself another coffee, Simon. This might take a wee while.'

'Yes, ma'am,' Simon said, with a smile.

CHAPTER 74

Connor waited for Ford to call in his back-up, then made his excuses. He could see that Ford wasn't happy about him leaving the scene, but there wasn't much the policeman could do. Given everything Paulie had told him, arresting Connor for helping a man defend his home from armed intruders, albeit a home that had two bound and beaten men in the basement, was probably the last thing on his mind. So Connor left, taking the SUV Simon had arrived in. After the cramped, angry and noisy Renault, it was a revelation, and he could almost feel the leather upholstery soothe his aching muscles. He wound what was left of the driver's side window down, letting damp morning air rush into the cabin. It would help keep him awake as he drove.

It took him twenty minutes to reach his destination, though it felt to Connor like an eternity as he wrestled with what he was about to do. He knew it would be easier just to turn around, either head home or to catch up with Simon and Donna, knew also that he couldn't do that. He felt partly responsible for what had happened at Paulie's home, Mo had confirmed that much to him, and after everything he had seen and been told since Jen had been run over, Connor was in no mood to dance around difficult decisions or problems any more. What was it Simon had told him? Don't miss? No quarter given?

It was a philosophy Connor could live with.

He pulled up in front of the house, wasn't surprised to see lights burning from the windows. Wondered briefly if he had made a mistake in giving his gun to Simon, then realised he preferred things this way. After all, some jobs needed the personal touch.

He walked up the path to the front door, made no effort to disguise his approach. Felt a faint jangle of unease as he saw the door was open, kept moving anyway into the house where he played a hunch, and headed for the study. Duncan MacKenzie sat barricaded behind his desk, the mad king at his throne. His eyes were bloodshot and, given the empty glass beside his left hand, Connor wasn't sure if the redness was from exhaustion or alcohol.

'Fraser,' he said, his voice crisp and neutral, the words not dulled by drink, 'you keep some hellish hours. It's OK, though, I'm just about to head off to see Jen. I understand there was a wee bit of drama at the hospital earlier. She's fine, though.' His tone sharpened the statement into an accusation. Connor didn't care.

'I know she's fine. I made sure of it,' he said, his tone matching MacKenzie's. 'What I'm not sure of, Duncan, is whether you were hoping Mo and his men would kill Paulie and me or just fuck us up when you set them on us earlier. Tell me, how long did you know about Hannah and Paulie? Jen told me something you used to say, *At least I had her for that long.* Odd, I thought, until I remembered you're a heartless cunt who treats everyone like property, even the kids you helped Peterson abuse for your sick mates' pleasure.'

MacKenzie surged to his feet, teeth bared. 'How fucking dare you?' he hissed. 'I would never be a party to that filth, never allow them to do what they did to that poor wee boy. That was a fucking obscenity! I never . . .'

Connor held up a hand. 'Aye, it's all fun and games until you're forced to watch what you've unleashed, isn't it? The one thing I couldn't figure out was why Jen was targeted in all of this, especially after you, Morgan and Paulie took care of John Peterson for what he did to Tracy Westerly. It made no sense. Unless Martin Christopher found out that you were part of it, that you knew exactly what Banks was dealing in. Something Paulie said got me thinking. *I didn't know he was going to target Jen. Should have seen it, though. After all, it was Duncan's trucks Banks was using to move that poison around the country.* Tell me, Duncan, who gave John Peterson his job with your company in the first place? Oh, and what did happen to your men when it all kicked off at the hospital? Funny none of them stepped in to protect the boss's daughter. Wonder who told them to stand down.'

MacKenzie's eyes blackened, the eyes of a snake about to strike its prey. 'Be very, very careful about what you say next, Fraser,' he whispered, his voice as dead as his eyes. Connor's own vision darkened at the edges, tightening so all he could see was MacKenzie's face. He felt his hands itch, as though they wanted to spring forward on their own, grab MacKenzie by the neck. Squeeze. But not yet. Not yet.

'I wondered how you knew where to send Mo and his boys,' he said slowly. 'Then I remembered something Jen said. That you, Paulie and her mum had always been close, that things only got a bit funny when Paulie's wife ran off with another man. Is that when you found out about him and Hannah? The time they were spending together? What did you do, Duncan? Blackmail her to stay with you, to be yours? What did you threaten? Paulie's life? Hers? Jen's?'

'Paulie fucking paid to have his wife taken off his hands!' Duncan exploded, as though this was a truth he had waited decades to share. 'I could never understand that. Jane was fucking around with another man, and Paulie gives him money to take her away and start a new life? Sure, he beat the living shit out of the snivelling little rat first, but then he set them up together? Made no bloody sense, until I had Paulie followed and he was seen with Hannah, putting their wee love nest together. So, yes, I talked to her and she told me the whole story. About how Paulie was the only one to understand what this life we had built was like for her, how she needed someone to talk to when my moods got, ah, black. But we worked it out and she stayed with me. Right until the end. She was mine. Mine. I loved her, Fraser. She was the mother of my child. Do you have any idea what that means?'

I was pregnant, Connor heard Jen whisper.

'That's not love,' he said finally. 'Men like you don't understand what love really is. I thought Paulie was a monster. He's not, not really. He's just a simple man with a taste for violence. But he's loyal. He was loyal to Hannah, loyal to Jen, even . . .' Connor laughed at the bitter irony '. . . even loyal to you. Jen told me how he was there for you after Hannah died. Wonder if he would have been if he'd known the truth, known you were a sadistic fuck who manipulated everyone and everything around him.'

MacKenzie was moving almost before Connor could react. He swiped the glass across the table and it crashed into Connor's hip as he turned away from it, trying to protect his crotch. He staggered back, MacKenzie using the time to get around the table and lunge at him.

'Dead man,' he hissed, as he jabbed at Connor's ribs. Connor gasped, pain exploding from his sides as MacKenzie's blows reawakened the agony Paulie had planted in his bones with his boots the previous night. He brought his elbows in tight to his sides, trying to protect himself as he backed off. Dodged a swinging hook MacKenzie aimed at his nose, obviously trying to take advantage of his injury. Thought briefly of Jen, of what she would think if she saw the man she loved locked in a fight with her father. Wondered if her thoughts would be any different if she knew who and what Duncan MacKenzie really was.

I was pregnant.

The thought was sudden, electrifying, overpowering. Everything Connor had been feeling - his fear for Jen, his grief over the loss of a child he had never even seen, the revulsion and bitter impotence he had felt watching the nameless boy being murdered - exploded within him. He roared, stopped stepping back, dropped his defence. He had taken enough pain. It was time to dish some out.

MacKenzie aimed another blow at Connor's face, this time a straight jab. Connor stepped into the swing and slightly to the left, scything his forearm up to catch MacKenzie's. He cried out as Connor's blow landed, staggered to the side, carried by inertia. Connor spun round, helped him on his way with an elbow to the temple. Stepped back, grabbed MacKenzie's neck and added his own weight to his fall, smashing him into the desk. He staggered back, blood exploding from his nose and mouth in a dark red torrent. Connor adjusted his grip, got a handful of hair, dragged MacKenzie back so he was prone, knees bent, back arched: a tortoise on its back, unable to right itself. He flailed his arms uselessly, trying to swat Connor away, his swearing punctuated by blood and spit, which flecked Connor's face as he leaned forward. He wrestled back the urge to crush MacKenzie's windpipe, settled instead for another elbow strike to the man's chest. Air exploded out of him in a barking cough and he tried to lean forward. Connor didn't let him, instead dragging him further back, then stamping down on his left ankle. MacKenzie's mouth turned into a blood-smeared rictus of agony as his Achilles tendon ruptured.

Connor let him drop, backed off. Pushed away the wave of self-revulsion he felt. He had always been good at inflicting pain on others, either intentionally or by accident, but finally he had found a man truly worthy of his rage. A man who had lied and manipulated. A man who had turned a blind eye to the suffering of children in order to satisfy his own desire for power. MacKenzie's name hadn't come up in Banks's confession, but Connor wondered what would happen when he asked Robbie to cross-check MacKenzie Haulage and Duncan MacKenzie with some of the other names he had mentioned.

A job for another day.

He crouched on his knees, MacKenzie rolling on the floor, moaning as he tried to reach for his ruined ankle.

'Here's the deal,' Connor whispered. 'This stays between us. All of it. For now. Jen doesn't need this - she's got enough to deal with. But a day will come when she's healed, Duncan. And on that day, I promise you, I will come for you. After I've told Paulie every fucking rotten thing you did. In the meantime, I'd keep my head down if I were you. See, my friend Donna is about to turn the heat up on all of your perverted little chums, and I don't think you're going to be very popular when that happens. I might not hurt you, but I'm not going to cry any tears if someone else does. Don't worry, though. If that does happen, I'll be there for Jen.'

He stood, looked down at MacKenzie. Despite everything he had just said, he had a sudden, almost overpowering urge to cave the man's head in with his foot.

'You're fucking dead, Fraser!' MacKenzie hissed, the blood smeared across his face giving him a clown's empty leer. 'You hear me, dead!'

'Aye,' Connor said, as he headed for the door. 'Feel free to fucking try.'

CHAPTER 75

Connor stopped off at the hospital to check on Jen. She was fine, having slept through the night, unaware of the chaos and violence erupting all around her. He met Marie on his way out of the ward, wondered if the woman ever slept or took a break. Left the hospital shaking his head and laughing at her message.

That Simon was already in the flat, on the sofa, feet up, was no surprise to Connor: the man was as adept at picking locks and disabling alarms as he was. What was a surprise was that he was sitting watching the TV with Tom curled contentedly on his chest, purring loudly.

Despite everything that had happened, Connor had only one question. 'How the hell did you manage that?' he said, gesturing to the sleeping cat.

'This?' Simon said, running a hand down the sleek tortoiseshell fur. 'Ack, met her when I came in through the back garden. She's a grand wee girl. Asked her in for a drink and a bite to eat, you know what it's like.'

Connor laughed. Despite the pain it sparked in his ribs, it felt good. Normal. Human. 'How did you get on?' he asked, taking a seat opposite Simon.

'See for yourself,' Simon replied, pointing the remote at the TV and turning the sound up slightly. Donna was on the screen, squinting into the camera against the wind and rain that ripped through the hospital car park. The caption below her was the familiar yellow and black Breaking News flash, followed by: 'Child abuse claims investigated'.

'. . . and while the police are yet to make an official statement, I understand at least fifteen people have been named in relation to allegations of a child abuse network that has been running across central Scotland for decades. The allegations echo the recently uncovered abuse of children at football clubs across Scotland that dates back to the early nineties . . .'

'Tell you this,' Simon said, 'that wee girl does not piss about. Moment she decided to take on the story, she was like a general. Organising care for her wee boy, getting her cameraman sorted out, telling her editors what the story was going to be, phoning lawyers. Aye, quite an impressive sight.'

'Careful, Simon,' Connor said. 'You've already got two women in your life. Last thing you need is a third.'

'Two?' Simon said.

Connor gestured to the cat on his chest. 'Tom for one. And then there's Marie. She wants her scrubs back, by the way.'

'Oh, shite, I forgot about that,' Simon said, with a laugh. 'Ack, I'll—'

He was interrupted by Connor's phone ringing in his pocket. He frowned, fished it out, saw wary attention spring into Simon's face. 'Robbie, what's up?'

'Morning, boss,' Robbie Lindsay said, his voice excruciatingly eager after the night Connor had just endured. 'Sorry to call so early, especially when you're on leave, but Mr Argyll wanted me to flag this up to you ASAP.'

Mr Argyll. As in Gordon Argyll. One of Sentinel's directors. 'Go on,' Connor said.

'Seems we've been contacted by a Brian Clarke, QC. Based in Edinburgh, Stockbridge. Says he wants a complete security review. Home and office. Asked for you by name.'

Aye, Connor thought, remembering Banks's confession. I'll bet he did. 'You got his number, Robbie, I'll give him a call. We can't take the job, but I'll give him a buzz, tell him personally.'

'Oh,' Robbie said, confusion in his voice. 'Why not, boss?'

Connor looked up at the TV, Donna still making her report. 'You'll find out soon enough, Robbie,' he said. 'Soon enough.'

CHAPTER 76

Three weeks later

Connor stood in the nearly deserted street, his breath turning to mist and drifting up into a sky that promised nothing but cold and misery to those unfortunate souls who had left shelter to walk the streets.

He looked down at the bouquet that had been left on the pavement in front of him, then hunched down to study it more closely. It was nothing special, just a random selection of flowers in red and orange and yellow, defiantly bright and cheerful in the face of a day sharp enough to wound. The wrapping told Connor they had been bought from a supermarket, probably the one he had passed on the way there. He felt a stirring of melancholy as he realised his gran would know the name of every flower in the arrangement, wondered what she would think if she knew what the flowers that made up this anonymous memorial really meant.

Of course he would never tell her, but Connor did know. He had made it his business to find out. It hadn't taken long. He had checked disappearances of children for two years both before and after Tracy Westerly had been killed, beginning in the Central Belt then widening out to Glasgow and Edinburgh, sticking to the main haulage routes. There was a depressingly high number of reports, but Donna had helped him go through them. He hadn't been able to bring himself to show her the tape, but he gave her as accurate a description of the boy John Peterson had killed as he could. They found him two days later, in a report from the *Western Chronicle* dated 9 August 1997. It told of how thirteen-year-old Thomas Elliott Wilson had been on his way into Glasgow city centre from his home in Knightswood to meet friends. He was last seen on James Watt Street, near what would become Scottish Government offices on the Broomielaw next to the Clyde, when he had disappeared. His parents had appealed for information and a major search was launched, but he was never seen again. Reading the report, and seeing the smiling face of the boy he had watched being murdered by a monster, Connor had felt something blacken and die inside him. For some reason, he had been compelled to visit the place Thomas had last been seen alive, the smiling boy in the photograph, the next time he was in Glasgow. And that was when he found the makeshift shrine.

Connor didn't know what had happened to Thomas's body after Peterson had killed him, wasn't sure he wanted to. But somehow, the riot of colour in the bleak numbness of that winter day cheered him, soothed him. Someone remembered Thomas, cared enough to leave flowers for him, even after all this time, even after all expectation of the boy returning had been lost. Life conquering death. Hope conquering fear.

Donna's initial report had proven explosive. Politicians, police officers and lawyers, including Brian Clarke QC, had been caught up in the abuse scandal. Persistent questions were being asked, the issue even managing to knock talk of another independence referendum off the front pages. And while no arrests had been made yet, Connor knew that Ford, Troughton and Susie Drummond were working flat out to make sure that changed. He had spoken to Ford the day the story broke, and it was like talking to a different man. Gone was the embittered, beleaguered police officer he had become used to, replaced by a man driven to deliver justice, real, lasting justice, for those who had been reduced to mere playthings for the perverted.

Connor wondered how much of this new-found zeal was due to Ford's need to atone for the sins of his former boss, Dennis Morgan. Ultimately, it didn't matter. Ford had everything he needed, including Paulie's full cooperation in return for significantly reduced charges, and he would not stop. Neither would Troughton nor Drummond. Connor had been impressed by both officers, wondered when he would run into them again. It was, he thought, almost inevitable, especially now Simon was taking an extended break in Stirling. He had stayed to help out in case Donna was threatened for breaking the abuse-ring story, but Connor could tell from the way his friend spoke that he was thinking of a longer stay. With the way things were in Belfast, with the Good Friday Agreement looking shakier than it had in years and a resurgence in sectarian violence, Connor could understand Simon's thinking – he just wasn't sure he could offer him a quieter, less eventful life in Scotland.

He took in one more breath, the pain in his ribs still there but less pronounced, like an old scar aching in the cold. Stood and turned to take in the street one last time, then got moving. He was heading for the spinal injuries unit in the west of the city. Jen was there, having physiotherapy, getting stronger. She was facing a long, slow recovery, but Connor would be there for her, make sure she got whatever she needed. And they had a date to keep, a goal to work for. Connor's gran had said she wanted to meet Jen as soon as she was well enough. And one thing Connor never did was disappoint his gran.

If Duncan MacKenzie made good on his threat, so be it. If he came himself, or sent his thugs, he would find Connor waiting.

And on that day, no quarter would be given.

ACKNOWLEDGEMENTS

No Quarter Given goes to some very dark places, and when you do that as a writer, you need light to balance you out. So my thanks go to my family and friends, in particular Ed James, Derek Farrell and Douglas Skelton, for providing the laughs and the listening ears when I needed them.

Special thanks to crime blogger Louise Fairbairn, @Scarletrix, for the early read and helpful comments, and to the keeper of the Sacred Red Folder (writers, superstitious? Naaah . . .), Alasdair Sim. Of course, there's a whole host of other folk who attended the scene of the crime whom I need to thank for their advice and support, but I don't have the space to list them all here, and I'm likely to miss someone out anyway. But you all know who you are.

And, of course, the biggest thanks go to everyone who has ever picked up one of my books. Writing books is all I ever wanted to do, and I know how lucky I am to be doing it.